THE OMEGA PROJECT

A SEAN WYATT THRILLER

ERNEST DEMPSEY

138 PUBLISHING

PROLOGUE

The cold of early fall bit at the man's skin, what little remained exposed to the elements. It wasn't the sharp, stinging cold of winter. This had a different feel to it, milder in some way.

The air smelled of dry leaves and campfires. The man knew the source was the hearth of Grinder's Tavern. He'd stayed there before on his travels through this part of southern Tennessee and knew Mrs. Grinder would likely be cooking some kind of stew right about now.

On cue, he caught a whiff of onions and beef. The smell filled his nostrils and went straight to his stomach, causing a deep rumble.

He hadn't eaten all day, save for a biscuit he'd had for breakfast and a piece of dried meat for lunch. His plan had always been to travel light and fast, then eat a big dinner.

He couldn't see the lights of the tavern, but he knew it was coming around the bend.

He tugged on the lengthy collar of his jacket to ward off the final few minutes of chill. A light breeze rustled through the treetops and flicked leaves from their branches. The colorful flurries danced through the air as they fell around the man, seated atop his horse.

While he would have liked to enjoy the display illuminated by the light of a half-moon, he knew the sooner he arrived at Grinder's, the better.

The Natchez Trace was a dangerous patch of road, patrolled by bandits and the occasional natives. The bandits were the worse of the two—though there were stretches that ran through some of the more aggressive tribes' land.

Something other than the wind rustled in the forest to his right. The man pulled one of his pistols and swung it around, aiming it into the pitch-dark thicket of oak, maple, and poplar trees. The branches above loomed like skeleton fingers against the pale glow in the sky and the twinkling stars.

The noise to his right grew louder. The horse snorted and shifted its feet. The man in the saddle kept his focus. He wasn't new to this sort of thing and didn't spook easily. In fact, the sense of fear sent adrenaline coursing through his veins, and for the first time in three years he felt alive.

His breath pulsed out of his nose and mouth in short bursts of misty clouds. His eyes remained focused on the dark as the sound grew closer. Someone was coming, and they were being clumsy about it. A drunk from Grinder's, perhaps, lost in the woods?

The sound swelled, feet clomping through leaves and sticks, fur brushing against the bark of tree trunks. The man's trigger finger tensed, and he cocked back the hammer. If he missed, he had three more, plus a rifle and a tomahawk.

Suddenly, the intruder's eyes flashed white amid a long, pointy face covered in light brown fur.

"Just a deer," the man said. He sighed, almost disappointed, as the animal emerged from the forest. Its antlers branched out in several directions, showing the buck's age.

The man bit his lip, took another look around to survey the area, and stuffed the pistol back in the folds of his coat.

"Easy, boy," he said, rubbing his hand on the horse's neck, "I'm sure we'll find some kind of adventure."

Three years. Three long years since he'd come back to a hero's welcome. There'd been parades, fanfare, and every luxury he could have ever imagined. Luxury, however, wasn't something Meriwether Lewis desired.

The Corps of Discovery mission to map a large section of the Louisiana Purchase and—hopefully—discover a northwest passage to the Pacific Ocean had been an immense success. Though they never found the legendary river system that could connect the eastern part of the continent to the west, they did make it to the Pacific Ocean at the mouth of the Columbia River. Captain Lewis and his friend Second Lt. William Clark had explored farther than any American up to that point and were lauded as celebrities.

Those days seemed like ancient history now.

The adventures they had encountered along the way were something right out of legend. They'd met natives of almost every kind. His friend Sacagawea had been instrumental in the success of the mission. She'd made it possible to safely communicate with the various tribes they had met along the way and helped them navigate difficult terrain that was unfamiliar to Lewis and the rest of the Corps.

He needed a drink.

The matters pressing on him had taken his anxiety to new heights. When he was out in the wilderness with Clark and the Corps, he didn't have to worry about stupid financial matters or politics. His new life forced those things on him, squeezing him like a vise.

Politics. He hated the thought of it.

He was one of the larger landowners of the Louisiana Territory and had been made governor, a position he loathed. President Jefferson had also been on his back about the journals he'd kept during the mission. Three years later, Lewis still hadn't delivered his entire report to his friend, and for good reason; Jefferson was no longer in office.

Lewis did his best to skate around the subject, come up with excuses as to why his full report had yet to be given to the president, but time was up. He couldn't run from the truth any longer.

The horse's hooves clopped along the dirt road. The monotonous sound was almost peaceful, and Lewis found himself dozing off numerous times only to be awakened as he nearly lost his balance and fell off his steed.

He shook his head side to side to stay awake, knowing the safety and warmth of Grinder's Tavern were just around the bend.

Instinctively, he reached down and touched the satchel at his side. His journals were in there, detailing every aspect of the Corps of Discovery's journey, including one particular piece he knew would be a shock to former president Jefferson.

Lewis hadn't told anyone about what he found that fateful night. He trusted his team implicitly, especially his friend William Clark. There were one or two they'd picked up along the way that he didn't trust, but they weren't the reason he'd kept his discovery a secret. What he found would have profound implications, not only on history but on the young nation as people began to migrate west. Indeed, the security of the United States could be at risk.

After they'd established a base camp at Fort Clatsop with temporary structures such as tents, construction on the permanent fort began. While he assisted in as many ways as possible, Lewis stole away in the early hours of the night to work on his own project, something he couldn't tell anyone else about, at least not yet. He'd have to communicate directly with Thomas Jefferson first before telling anyone else about what he saw.

He burned the candle at both ends, working during the days to survey the surrounding countryside, building living quarters for the winter, and then taking care of burying his secret after the sun went down.

Those nights were long. He'd suffered from sleep deprivation on more than one instance, but he'd had no choice.

Clark had expressed concern over his condition. Lewis knew he must have looked rough, and there were times when he caught himself having a conversation with no one—except himself.

His focus on the task at hand, on covering up what he'd seen, was intense. It took nearly three weeks, but he was satisfied that he'd done the best he could. Once the president was apprised of the situation, a more suitable solution could be organized and carried out.

Lewis sighed as he saw a dim light coming from the cracks in the windows of the tavern up ahead. A bonfire raged outside, pouring a thick pillar of smoke into the air amid a flurry of bright orange sparks. The chimney on the end of the house tried to rival the bonfire's output, but only allowed a faint trickle of smoke to churn out of its top.

The plan was to stay the night at Grinder's then wake up early and continue on the trail toward Virginia, and then to Washington where he would meet with Thomas Jefferson and finally give him everything, even the secret he'd discovered near the mouth of the Columbia.

The mere thought of it sent a shiver down his spine. On top of all that was the fact that Jefferson was no longer the president. While Lewis still referred to the man with that title, James Madison was now in control and technically the person who should receive the journals. Lewis knew Madison, but not intimately, and he wanted to make sure the documents were delivered to someone he could trust. That meant Thomas Jefferson. The former president could then do what he saw fit with the information, deliver it to Madison, or perhaps someone else if necessary. At this point, Lewis just wanted to be the delivery boy and be done with it. The whole thing had weighed on him long enough.

He snapped his head around to shake off the chill and flicked the reins to hurry his horse along the last hundred yards to the clearing and the promise of a warm bed, good food, and a long night's sleep.

Lewis thought he heard another sound in the forest, a second deer, perhaps. Whatever it was, he didn't hear it again, but his nerves remained on edge until he reached the clearing and could hear the sounds of voices inside the building.

He hopped down from his saddle and looped the reins around a hitching post in front of the log cabin. Blood pumped through his legs, sending a tingling sensation coursing over his body. He reached down toward his toes and stretched to get the circulation back to normal and then stood up straight again, securing the satchel at his side.

He removed the rifle from the holster attached to his saddle and propped it over his shoulder as he walked toward the entrance.

Lewis pressed against the door and it creaked open with a loud, grinding squeak that would have frightened any animal courageous enough to wander too close to the inn.

Inside, there was a counter to the left in front of a fireplace. As suspected, a large iron cauldron hung over a smoldering pile of orange coals, steam wafting up from the top. The smells he'd noted outside were much stronger in here. Simmering beef, onions, pepper, and other vegetables caused his stomach to grumble again.

There was one patron sitting at the bar with a tankard in one hand, probably filled with warm ale of some kind.

Lewis saw Mrs. Grinder standing behind the counter and offered a smile. "Good evening, madam. I trust you're doing well."

She offered him a welcoming smile, albeit with a hint of nervousness to it. "Meriwether Lewis," she said in a warm, faint Southern accent. People in the Southeastern United States had begun developing an accent of their own that was a sort of mix between English and Irish. The sound was pleasant; at least Lewis thought so. He enjoyed visiting this area and wished he could do so more often. Tennessee or, Tanasi as the natives had called it, offered much in the way of outdoor adventure and natural beauty. "It's so good to see you again." She put out her arms as if to hug him but didn't come around the bar to do so. "What can I get you?"

"I'll have an ale and some of that fine stew I see cooking back there." He took off his pack and set it next to a chair at a little square table off to the side of the room. There was a window close by, though the shutters were closed. He thought it odd but didn't make mention of it. There was no need to have the windows shut. It was a lovely night out, and there were no signs of bad weather on the horizon. Perhaps the Grinders were just trying to make the place feel cozy so any travelers that stopped in might be inclined to stay.

"You have my usual room?" Lewis asked.

Mrs. Grinder nodded as she finished filling a tankard with red ale. She brought the frothy drink over to him and set it on the table. "Sure do. It's clean and ready if you'd like it."

She sounded hopeful. Perhaps business hadn't been good lately. Their little outpost was sort of in the middle of nowhere, which could be a good or bad thing. A place like this could be a godsend to a weary and desperate person on a long journey. Then again, how many of those came through this part of the region? The Natchez Trace was infamous for theft, rape, and murder. The bandits hiding out in its woods and in the surrounding hills were notorious for their ruthlessness. Lewis could handle them—as long as their numbers weren't too many. He'd once taken on four bandits by himself, leaving two dead and the other two maimed for life. It was a story he'd never shared with anyone, but he figured the two remaining bandits would take care of that for him.

It never hurt to have a little legend about you circulating around when traveling treacherous roads.

"Where you headed, Captain Lewis?" Mrs. Grinder asked as she returned to the fireplace and picked up a bowl. She grabbed a long wooden spoon and dipped it into the iron pot, scooping out a hefty portion of stew.

"Washington," he said. His right hand slipped down to the satchel again, fingers rubbing over the worn leather. "I have to meet with President Jefferson."

She grinned at him and placed a spoon in the bowl of steaming food. "You know he's not the president anymore, right? Or has being out in the wilderness knocked you out of your senses?"

He chuckled as she set the bowl down on the table in front of him. He rifled through a coin purse and produced enough money to cover the meal, the room, and a little extra. Lewis had always been generous when it came to his accommodations and the people providing them. Maybe it was due to the fact he didn't care about money or material possessions. That was one of the most stressful facets of being a landowner and a governor. He felt more at home in a small cabin or in a tent out in the forest. Civilian life, it seemed, was better suited for someone else.

Clark had seemed to adapt to it fairly well, but not Lewis.

"I wish that were the case," he said. "Unfortunately, I've been imprisoned behind a desk these last three years. There's been almost no time for adventure, save for when I come through these parts."

"You sure have a load of courage to be traveling the Trace at night, that's for sure."

"Courage or foolishness," the patron at the bar said, his voice full of gravel. He was an older man with a graying beard that stretched down to the top of his chest. His wiry hair poked out from under a leather cap. A trapper's coat hung on the chair back behind him. Lewis couldn't make out the stranger's face, but something about the voice was oddly familiar in a distant sort of way.

Lewis took no offense. "Maybe both." He clutched the handle of his mug and took a long sip of the ale. He was pleasantly surprised to find it cooler than expected. In the summer, beers tended to be a little on the warm side: fine for getting drunk but not great for the overall tasting and drinking experience. In the fall and winter, beers and ales were much cooler and far more pleasing to the palate.

He drained nearly half the tankard before setting it down.

Drinking had become the norm for Lewis. Some of his peers were concerned he'd developed a bit of a problem. The truth was he did have a problem. Drinking was the only thing that kept his mind off it. His anxiety had been higher than ever in his life, as far as he could recall. It had started after returning home from the expedition, the moment he realized he was no longer going to be an outdoorsman or a soldier. He would be a puppet for propaganda.

That was half of it. The other half came from the knowledge laid bare in the documents at his side. What would Jefferson say? What would he do? Would he take the information to Madison? If so, what would happen after that? Maybe it was nothing. Maybe the secret he'd discovered on the West Coast was no big deal, something that could be brushed aside. Deep down, he knew that wasn't the case.

He scooped up a spoonful of the stew, blew it off to cool, and then shoveled it into his mouth. Lewis took a second to enjoy the salty and savory flavors. He chewed a piece of beef and then swallowed before splashing another dose of ale down his throat. Then he repeated the process, making quick work of the hearty stew.

Lewis hadn't realized how hungry he truly was until the food was set in front of him.

Mrs. Grinder was cleaning a mug and looked up to see him finish the meal. "Hungry, were ya?"

"Yes, madam. I suppose I was."

"Would you like another bowl? On the house?"

"You never gave me anything on the house," the trapper grumbled.

"And you never paid the way Captain Lewis does, you ingrate."

He muttered something under his breath and then took another swig from his mug.

Lewis laughed at the exchange. Then he hefted his tankard and finished off the ale.

"Thank you, madam," he said and stood. "I appreciate the hospitality. I'm exhausted, though, and need some rest."

"Should I show you to your room?"

He smiled weakly. "No, thank you. I'm fine, and besides, you're busy."

The inn wasn't large. It consisted of one floor with the kitchen and bar in the main area, then some smaller guest rooms at the other end of the building. Lewis had always stayed in the same room and didn't know what the others looked like, though he figured they were identical. Mr. and Mrs. Grinder occupied one of the rooms; that much he knew.

"Have a good night, Captain Lewis."

"Thank you. You as well." He turned and walked toward the door on the left, though he couldn't help but notice a strange tone in her voice at her last comment. It sounded almost...menacing. He had to be delirious. That's all it was: overactive imagination coming from a lack of sleep and being on the road for far too long. Nothing a good night in a comfortable bed wouldn't cure.

Lewis opened the door, stepped into the bedroom, and closed it behind him.

1

Sean held on for dear life. He felt his fingertips slipping, the lines of his fingerprints losing their grip against the rough limestone wall. He twitched his digits and shifted them up again to hold the thin edge just above his head. There was no chance he was going to look down. He knew what that would do.

Ever since childhood, Sean had been cursed with a fear of heights. Tall buildings, high mountain peaks or roads, and pretty much everything in between were all things he tried to avoid. This particular scenario was doubly bad. They were on a rock wall in the midst of the Prentice Cooper State Forest near Chattanooga, Tennessee. The mountain offered incredible views of the surrounding peaks and the rolling foothills leading down to the valley below where the Tennessee River snaked its way through the gorge. Being up on the mountain made the cliff face feel even higher.

He hung from the ledge with white knuckles, his body pressing as close to the wall as he could. The rope tied to his harness was nearly taut, only giving a small amount of slack to the lead climber fifteen feet above him.

Sean tilted his head back and looked up at Tommy. "I don't

understand why I have to do this with you!" Sean shouted. "And why am I in the lead here? You're the expert."

Tommy leaned back, holding onto the rock face with one hand, letting the other dangle down by the powder bag on his hip. "I told you. If this thing is as big as I think it is, I can't carry it down by myself."

"Yeah, I know, but..." Sean felt his fingers slipping again and pushed up to the next narrow ledge, driving with his toes and legs until he felt his fingers catch on the flat surface above. It was only a half inch deep, but it might as well have been a jug handle—a rock climber's dream.

A cool breeze blew over the mountain. It sent a cold chill over Sean, bristling the exposed hairs on his neck and tickling the drops of sweat on his skin.

Sean didn't think his heart could pound any faster, but as he clung to the rock he realized he was wrong as the muscle pumping blood through his body ratcheted up the pace once more.

He pressed his cheek against the cold surface and wished he didn't have to move another inch. His gut stayed tight in a knot.

It wasn't the best of days for a climb. Not that there was ever a good day for that activity as far as Sean was concerned. The only thrill sport he partook of was riding his motorcycles, and that wasn't because he was looking to get his jollies by doing something danger-ous. He'd been a rider since childhood. It was in his blood. And as any motorcyclist would tell you: once it's in your blood, you can't get it out.

His modest collection of cafe racers, sport bikes, and a single Harley Davidson Sportster '48 composed his single vice, the one extravagant thing he allowed himself in life. He'd never been a car guy, per se. Sean had no interest in buying a Ferrari or a Maserati. That wasn't his style. Not that there was anything wrong with those cars. It just wasn't him.

He'd always believed that traveling in a car was like being in a glass box. To truly experience the world, to be in it, you had to be on two wheels, maybe three if you were on one of those Can-Am

Spyders. Outside a vehicle's cabin, you could feel the wind, the elements, and the road passing under your feet.

Now, he was feeling the elements but not in a way he appreciated. It was bitterly cold, much cooler than normal for this time of December in the South. Over the years, as the earth continued to warm as it had for thousands of years, the winters seemed to start later and later. Fall, too, had been affected for as long as he could remember, the leaves waiting longer and longer to turn from lush green to brilliant oranges, reds, and yellows.

Today, however, was as cold as he could recall at such an early point in the season. Or late, as it were. Technically, winter was still a few weeks away. Sean couldn't help but feel as if the thick gray clouds overhead were just waiting for the right moment to dump a foot of snow on the area.

In reality, the temperature was only in the lower forties, not nearly cold enough for snow. Then again, they were at a higher elevation here, so perhaps they might see a flurry.

He shuddered at the thought. The last thing they needed was the surface to become slippery.

"Couldn't this have waited?" Sean yelled up at his friend. "You know, until one of the warmer months? I'm thinking, maybe, June. We come back in June and find this thing."

Tommy chuckled and clipped a carabiner into a hex he'd jammed into a crevice that ran horizontally across the rock. He looked down at his friend, allowing himself to lean back on the rope to test the anchor he'd just placed. It held firm, not even a wiggle.

Unlike Sean, Tommy had no problem with high places. He'd enjoyed rock climbing when he was in college but had lost interest when he took on the overwhelming task of founding and running the International Archaeological Agency, an organization specializing in the recovery and transport of priceless artifacts. On occasion, they were even tasked with finding said artifacts.

Things had been slow lately, especially during the last few weeks. There hadn't been much need for their services, and so Tommy set about working on solving a few local mysteries.

One such mystery was based on local oral traditions. The stories claimed that there were several gold bars hidden on a cliff overlooking the Tennessee River. Apparently, the gold had been placed there by Confederate soldiers who were on the run near the end of the Civil War.

Tommy initially thought the story was a hoax, or simply a piece of the fabric of local lore that had been perpetuated over time. As he tracked various clues left in history, though, he found himself considering the tale might actually have some validity to it.

He pulled out a piece of paper from his back pocket. The sheet flapped in the wind, but his fingers held firm. He was looking over his notes and the sketches he'd created to mimic the rock face. His eyes traced the line he'd drawn of the exact path they'd need to take across the stone.

"We're almost there!" Tommy shouted down.

The clue on the paper said that the treasure could be found in the mouth of a ghost overlooking the mighty river. The details had been heavier than that, which had led Tommy and Sean to this spot. Tommy didn't need all those now. He'd done his homework, his due diligence. Now they were here, only minutes from the town the two of them had grown up in and where they still both kept weekend homes.

Sean's was a small condo down on the South Side, while Tommy's larger bungalow was situated in the trendy North Shore area of town.

He knew about ghosts and their place in nineteenth-century culture, especially in regard to Civil War treasure hordes. These apparitions had little to do with actual spirits. They were symbols, nothing more.

In the waning days of the conflict between brothers, many rebels feared they would be persecuted for seceding and treated as criminals. These thoughts weren't necessarily unfounded. Stories about houses and farms being burned and salted, women raped, and husbands murdered, ran rampant through the ranks of the wilting Confederacy. General Sherman's march to the sea had produced a thousand such horror stories. It was little wonder why rebels ran for their lives, many heading west to Texas and even Mexico to escape the North's brand of justice.

Desperate and on the run, soldiers had taken whatever fortunes they'd discovered or stolen and hid them in places they figured were safe, hoping to return someday and start new lives.

Most never made it back for one reason or another, which provided treasure hunters more fodder than they could have ever imagined in the subsequent one hundred and fifty-plus years.

Tommy wasn't looking for the gold because of its financial value. Once found, he would donate it to a local museum or university. Southern Adventist University had a unique collection of biblical artifacts from the Middle East, but they'd discussed including more local historical items in a new wing—were a donor willing to throw a few extra dollars their way to build it.

Tommy hadn't balked at the idea. He thought it would be cool to have a new section of the archaeology department at SAU featuring regional and local historical artifacts. Perhaps this find would be the first exhibit put on display.

He stuffed the paper back in his pocket and looked down at Sean, who was still clinging to the rock for dear life.

Sean must have felt his friend's gaze and risked a look up. "I can't do this!" Sean shouted.

Tommy shook his head. "You know, you've been way higher than this before. There was that monastery in Bhutan. Remember that? That place was way worse. Besides, you're only, like, twelve feet off the ground."

Sean frowned at the comment and risked a look down. He immediately wished he hadn't. The world spun below him, and he felt gravity tugging back on him. His fingers slipped as he desperately reached out to get even a fingernail's hold on the ledge.

It was too late. Sean could feel the empty vacuum of air beneath him, nothing to stop him from plummeting to the ground below. His friend had teased him, told him he was only twelve feet up. In truth, he was nearly forty feet up, certainly high enough to be killed by the fall. At least it would be a quick death. That was the last thing Sean thought before an abrupt tug on his harness snapped him out of his panic. The rope went taut, sprang down, then up, and then he felt himself being drawn back to the rock face.

He swung toward it and was grateful to feel his palms slap against the cold surface.

Sean scrambled and found a narrow ledge he'd used before, clutching it with all his might. Then he slid his toes onto a landing and steadied his position.

He looked up at his friend with rage in his eyes. "Not! Funny! Tommy!"

Tommy laughed and shook his head. "See? You're fine. I told you the harness would hold. This isn't my first time lead-climbing, buddy."

"I hate you."

"Now, that's not a nice thing to say to someone you're tethered to on a rock wall way up on a mountain."

Sean swallowed. Anger and embarrassment, fueled with adrenaline, pushed him forward. He reached up and grabbed a handhold, moved his right foot to the next ledge, and climbed. He said nothing as he kept going, his fears pushed aside by determination. The sooner he could get up to where Tommy was, the sooner he could kill his friend and get down off this forsaken place.

The thought sent a grim smile creasing across his face. He quickly dispelled the notion, but the grin remained.

He scurried up the wall like a spider monkey. His long, slender frame was actually perfect for this kind of activity, though he would never do it for the fun of it.

"That's more like it," Tommy said, now only ten feet above Sean. "You're doing great."

Sean ignored the encouragement, fully intent on grabbing one of his friend's ankles and jerking him off his ivory perch.

"Take it easy, though. Don't go too fast." Tommy suddenly looked concerned. "Sean?"

"You better move because if I get to you I'm throwing you off this blasted rock."

For a second, Tommy thought his friend was joking. Then after seeing the look in Sean's eyes, he wasn't so sure. "Buddy? Take it easy. We're almost there."

Tommy turned and faced the mountain again and resumed his ascent. He traversed to the left, using the horizontal crack as a path toward the ghost, or what he figured would be the ghost.

Soldiers in the nineteenth century, and in particular during the Civil War, had a habit of attaching their hidden treasures to emblems they either carved into trees or rocks, or that were naturally occurring formations that looked like things they would recognize later on.

Tommy was certain this was the case regarding this particular hidden trove. Sean reached the crack and watched as his friend placed a cam into a vertical wedge in the rock face. He clipped the rope in and tugged hard on it to make sure it would hold.

"I can't believe you trust these things," Sean said, his anger forgotten and replaced once more by a persistent fear.

"It's simple science. Friction, you know?"

"I guess."

Sean grabbed a hold over his left shoulder and shifted his left foot in that direction, closing the gap between him and his friend.

"I'm really close," Tommy said. He craned his neck back and gazed up.

Five feet overhead, he could see the unmistakable shape of a primitive ghost chiseled into the rock face. Its rounded top and jagged bottom edge reminded Tommy of the ghosts from the Pac-Man arcade game he'd enjoyed so much as a child. Perhaps the programmers had taken the antiquated design and made it their own when constructing the game's framework.

He heard the sound of voices from up above, at the top of the cliff, probably another thirty feet up.

Sean heard them, too. It wasn't uncommon for high school or college kids to come hiking out here on the weekends. It was a popular spot for mountain-biking, though most of the better slopes for downhill rides were along the tops of other mountains or down along the hillsides into the valley.

Prentice Cooper was also a semipopular rock-climbing location, with a multitude of climbs varying in difficulty that could provide hours of challenges for the novice to the seasoned expert.

Today, however, there were no other climbers, at least not in this spot, probably because it was much too cold for most people. Frigid fingers made holding on to anything far more difficult than normal. Especially when it was your bodyweight you were trying to keep from falling.

The voices overhead sounded young. There were some laughs amid the chatter, which eased Sean's overactive imagination.

He was always on alert, most of the time. It was his default setting. Through the years, he'd worked on taking time out to relax, making sure that he wasn't always high-strung and perpetually paranoid as a result of his previous life as a government agent.

That life had made him the way he was: alert, focused, and always ready for action at the drop of a hat.

Going to work for his friend in the IAA had been a move, he thought, that would gradually allow the rust to seep in and eventually coat his sharp edges. That notion couldn't have been more wrong. He'd found himself in nearly as many life-or-death experiences as he had working for the covert government agency known as Axis. That didn't mean he liked it.

It had been months since anything harrowing had happened, and he was beginning to feel the strings of relaxation tugging on him again.

He heard another squeal and a laugh up above, and reassured himself that no one knew why he and Tommy were there or what they were up to. They'd only told the kids, Tara and Alex, before leaving IAA headquarters in Atlanta. Sean had also mentioned it to Adriana, but she was busy handling some family business back in Madrid. Her father, Diego, was apparently still in hiding. From whom, Sean had never gotten a clear answer.

He snapped his mind back to the moment and shuffled his hands to the left, following the path his friend had taken a few minutes before. He'd forgotten about how high up he was—for the moment—

and was moving with the deftness of an experienced climber. He traversed the crack and reached the next one that ran vertically toward the summit of the rock.

Tommy was already moving again, and Sean could see the figure of the ghost etched roughly into the wall's façade.

Sean heard more laughter above and shook it off. He wanted to get whatever was here and then climb down as fast and as safely as possible.

Tommy reached the right side of the ghost's figure and held on to a jagged point that jutted out from the mountain. It was a dream handhold and made balancing on the thin ledge at his feet much easier as he investigated the strange engraving in the rock.

"You see anything?" Sean shouted up to his friend.

"Not yet. Hold on."

Tommy leaned out away from the wall and tilted his neck sideways so he could see into the mouth of the ghost. Whoever had carved the figure into the stone had done so around a natural gap in the surface. The cavity was about two feet wide and at least a foot high, making it the perfect home for local bats, or perhaps a few of the indigenous spiders.

For a fleeting second, Sean hoped one of those creatures actually *was* hiding out in the crevice. It would, no doubt, scare the crap out of his friend and send him sprawling. Only problem was that Sean was connected via the same rope. So, he quickly dispensed with his mischievous thought.

Tommy reached up and flipped on his headlamp. He tilted his neck again and shone the light into the dark hole. Then he stuck his left hand in, stretching his right arm as far as possible, and felt around in the recess.

His search lasted less than ten seconds before he pulled the arm out. He looked down at Sean and shook his head.

"It's empty."

Sean started to say something disparaging about it being a wild-goose chase, a waste of time, and that the thing had probably been empty for a hundred years. But all of that was cut short before he could even take the breath to say it.

A young woman's voice cut through the chilly mountain air. The sound was horrific, a panicked shriek for help.

Sean and Tommy both snapped their heads to the right, toward the source of the noise. There, on the face of the rock, they saw what the commotion was all about.

Dangling from the top ledge, a young woman—probably in her early twenties—was hanging by her fingertips. Eighty feet from certain death.

2

CHATTANOOGA

Tommy glanced down at Sean for an idea as to what they should do, but Sean was already in motion.

His hands rapidly overlapped as he traversed the horizontal crack. His feet shimmied across a ledge, the hardened toes of his Sportiva climbing shoes being put to the test as to whether or not they could hold the edge.

Tommy didn't have to ask what his friend was doing. He already knew. Thinking wasn't something Sean did in situations like this. Action was his thing. Hesitation caused problems. In this case, it could result in the death of this girl.

Sean reached the point where their previous path had veered right and found himself facing an L-shaped ledge that jutted out from the main wall. It was a point where the limestone had likely fallen away hundreds or thousands of years ago, leaving a secondary wall that ran perpendicular to the primary one.

There were weathered bolts drilled into the stone near the seam between walls. The patina on the metal fixtures told Sean they'd been put there long ago, most likely before planting such things was outlawed by the local forestry service. Trees, too, had been protected as part of a broad-sweeping mission to slow down the damage to public land they perceived rock climbers were causing.

Sean found a crack in the stone to his right and jammed his hand into it. He felt the rock grind on his skin, but it didn't hurt much. Hand jams were a common maneuver for rock climbers, and while he didn't partake in the activity often, he'd learned a few things back in high school while climbing with Tommy and a few other friends.

"Hold on!" Sean shouted up to the girl. She was only a dozen feet away now, just above his right shoulder, and still screaming amid sobs.

Her friends were little to no help, none willing to lean over far enough to grab the poor girl by the wrists and help her up. One of the boys was on his knees, telling her to grab his hand.

She was probably fortunate she hadn't listened, instead choosing to trust her grip on the rock edge under her fingers. That grip, however, would soon falter if she didn't have something under her feet.

Sean let go with his left hand, put most of his weight on the hand jammed into the crack, and then swung over to the secondary wall while jerking himself up toward another edge above the crack. His left hand smacked the rim, and he squeezed it then walked his way up until his feet were where his right hand was and pulled it out, replacing it with the toe of his shoe.

He must have looked like a deranged monkey pulling off the move, but it worked and now he was only ten feet from the girl and directly below her.

"Don't let go of the edge!" he shouted up to her.

"What?" she asked, then realized there was someone below. She didn't look down for fear of losing her balance.

"Just hold on. And for the love of all things, don't listen to what that boy is saying. Just hold the rock. Okay?"

"Oh...okay." She didn't sound reassured, but she did as instructed.

"I'm coming up, but you're going to need to stop kicking your legs. Understand?" He didn't wait for her to respond. "There's a ledge just above your ankles. It's not much, but you can put your toes on it and relieve a little strain on your forearms."

She was wearing a hoodie, but Sean could imagine the veins in her forearms popping up on the skin as the muscles beneath struggled to maintain their grip on the rock that was, at the moment, preserving her life.

To Sean's left, Tommy was unhooking one of the cams from a carabiner and quickly fastening it to his belt, next to the other unused devices. Once it was on the loop, he descended to the horizontal crack and made his way across the rock toward Sean's position.

Sean climbed higher, forgetting all about his phobia as he focused all his energy on the girl hanging above.

"Right there," Sean said. "Just a little higher and you'll have it. See?"

Her left toe touched the edge that jutted out from the cliff's edge. Then her right foot joined the other.

"I...I got it!" she shouted with no small amount of relief in her voice.

"That's great," Sean said. "Keep holding on tight, okay? Don't let up."

He knew what could happen, even with his modest amount of climbing experience. Climbers had the tendency to relax when they found a good place for their feet. It was a natural reaction and one that he'd been guilty of on a few occasions, including about twenty minutes ago when he'd begun his ascent.

"Okay," she said, her voice returning to the unsteady waver that it had before.

"I'm nearly there," Sean said. "Just below your feet."

"What are you going to do?"

It was a good question, and if he'd been honest she might have freaked out. Truth was, he didn't know right off the bat. He'd seen trouble and reacted, moving to it as his instincts demanded, without regard to personal safety.

He was close now, only a foot or so below the girl's feet. The soles of her Converse All-Stars were easy to make out, and he realized that this girl was way out of her element. Those weren't the kinds of shoes to wear out on a hike, especially in this weather.

"I'm just beneath you now," Sean informed her as he stabilized his grip on a ledge under her feet. "I'm going to put my hands on either side of your shoes. Do me a favor and don't try to move them. Okay?"

"O-okay," she said with a stammer, and there was no sense of surety in her voice. The girl was terrified, as Sean knew he would be too in her shoes. He'd been just as scared only minutes before, and he was connected to a rope that would catch him if he were to fall.

He let go with his left hand and stretched out his arm. The fingers brushed against the lip and clenched it hard. Sean's muscles were starting to strain. He'd been on the rock for what seemed like an hour, though it had probably been less than twenty minutes. That didn't matter. Ten minutes on a climb was a long time to someone who hadn't done it in years. Twenty felt like a marathon.

His chest rose and fell with every deep breath, feeding air to his lungs so his racing heart could keep pumping.

He ignored the burning in his legs and raised his left knee. He stuck his shoe onto the next ledge and pushed, driving his right hand up to the lip where the girl's right foot was still shaking. Her shoes weren't made for this kind of thing, and the soles bent awkwardly up as she fought to keep them from slipping off.

That fight would be lost soon if he didn't do something.

Sean noticed Tommy below him. It was a glance out of the corner of his eye, nothing more. Sean still had no intention of looking down to the ground. At the moment, he was okay, but doing something like that would surely send his fears cascading over him again and he'd likely falter or do something careless. Either way, the girl would probably end up dead, and that wasn't something he wanted on his mind.

All the people he'd killed in the past were one thing. They were bad people with evil intent. They'd made their choices, and he'd done what he could to stop them.

This girl, however, was—as far as he knew—innocent. Saving her was the only thing that mattered at that moment.

"My hands are right next to your feet," he said. "I'm going to come up to where you are now. Okay?"

"How...how are you going to do that?"

He wasn't sure, either, but it was the only thing he could think of. "Just stay still."

He saw her feet slipping and knew she didn't have much longer.

"I...I don't think I can hold it."

There was sheer terror in her tone now. It was the fear only a person in their prime could feel, the knowing that their life was about to be cut abysmally short, that they'd never do or see all the things they wanted. He'd heard that tone before when a friend died as a result of injuries in a car accident. He was in the hospital and fading fast, and there was nothing the doctors could do.

Sean had heard it in the field, as well, when one of his partners had been killed in the line of duty. He was only twenty-seven and had his whole life in front of him.

In an instant, a bullet had taken away all those dreams of travel, seeing the sights of the world, experiences that other cultures could bring, visions of family vacations, children, and marriage, all of it. Every single goal and vision had been ripped away by an assassin's bullet.

He wasn't about to let that happen to this poor girl. Sean spotted a crag to the left of the girl's hip. It wasn't much; maybe just a few millimeters deep. It was something, though, and all he had.

He took a deep breath and pushed up with his right leg once more while stretching out his left hand. He felt the toe of his shoe slip, and, for a second, fear surged through him.

Sean leaned forward as his fingers scratched the surface of the rock and caught on the minuscule lip next to the girl's side. He was surprised to find it was slightly wider than he expected and he was able to get three fingers dug in to it to stabilize his momentum. He kept lifting his right foot until it was even with the girl's and then planted the tip of the shoe on the ledge. He quickly brought up his left foot and stuck it next to hers, then pressed in on her back with his chest.

"It's okay," he said. "Just hold on a little longer. We'll get you out of this."

He could feel her breathing heavily. There were sobs mixed in with the panting.

"What's your name?" Sean asked. He knew that in these kinds of situations, getting the person to talk was key. It helped take their mind off the direness of their situation.

"M-Molly," she stuttered.

"Okay, Molly. My name is Sean, and the guy down below us—don't look—is Tommy. We're going to help you. Just keep a hold on the rock for another few seconds."

Sean had no idea how he was going to get the girl down. She was probably five feet, six inches tall, half a foot shorter than him, and likely forty to fifty pounds lighter.

He checked the harness around his waist. There was no way he could get that off and slip it on to her, not given the current situation.

He could try to give her a boost to the guy above, who Sean had surmised was the boyfriend. That was no good, either. He'd likely lose his grip and she would tumble down over his back.

"Sean!" Tommy shouted from below.

Sean risked a glance down at his friend, focusing his vision on Tommy and not the deadly drop beneath.

Tommy had unhooked his rope, immediately plunging himself, as well as Sean, into danger. The two were connected, but now Tommy's rope was no longer tied to his harness. That meant that if he fell, he was a dead man. And if Sean fell, same result.

Tommy held the rope in one hand with the knot tied on the end. He held on to the ledge with his other hand and started twirling the rope like a lasso. "Incoming!" he yelled.

Sean reached out his hand to catch the rope. Tommy flung it up, but Sean missed it, nearly losing his balance in the process. His left hand gripped the lip tighter to compensate, but the rope's knot wrapped around his ankle and came to rest.

He swallowed and looked down at the knot hanging loosely on the top of his shoe. The slightest move and it would fall. He didn't know if they had another chance. The girl's feet were slipping with greater frequency. Sean took a breath and lifted his right knee toward his hand as he lowered his hand toward his knee. It was a delicate move, one that could have sent him and the girl tumbling to their death.

His balance held and he grasped the knot, clutching it tight with his fingers and thumb. He looped the rope under the girl's armpits, around her waist, and back up under her armpits again.

"You," he said to the boys and the other girl still above. "Take this rope and pull. Get away from the edge so you don't come over. If the three of you pull, it should be easy. Got it?"

They nodded.

Sean tugged on the rope until he had a good chunk of it in hand and then tossed it up and over the ledge. The boyfriend grabbed it and backtracked to the other two, handing each of them a piece. The second girl was crying but took control of her emotions enough to pitch in.

The three pulled on the rope until it went taut.

"Okay, Molly. They're going to pull. Just do your best pull-up, all right? Just like in gym class."

"I can't do a pull-up," she whimpered.

"That's okay. I'm going to push. They're pulling. It'll be easy. Ready?"

"Not really."

"Too bad."

"Pull," Sean ordered.

The other three tugged on the rope. Molly's knuckles whitened as she gave every ounce of strength left in her arms and back. Her feet scampered up the wall as the three kept backing up, dragging her up and over the lip until she was safely on top.

Sean felt relief wash over him as he saw the girl crawl away from the ledge. He swallowed hard. The lump in his throat scratched its way down his esophagus. He hadn't even realized how thirsty he'd become due to the stress. Now it was hitting him.

"Hey, Sean?" Tommy shouted from down below.

Sean glanced over his shoulder and immediately felt a rush of fear come over him again. He held on tight to the rock's lip.

"Yeah, Schultzie?"

"You think you could get that rope back from them? I don't feel like free-climbing back down to the bottom."

Sean forced a grin onto his face. "Now look who's afraid of heights."

3

ELLIJAY, GEORGIA

Former president John Dawkins sat in the humble dining room of his log cabin. It was situated in the Blue Ridge Mountains of Georgia, far away from the hustle and bustle of Atlanta, but close enough to a few towns that any conveniences he required were easily obtained.

There was a grocery store about fifteen minutes away by car, electricity was reliable and cheap, and he had decent cable service for the one flatscreen television hanging over the fireplace, though he hardly used it.

This place was his getaway from the pressures of life and all the steaming sewage that seemed to permeate American politics and culture these days.

He was glad to be out of the game and had retired to his primary home back in Nashville. His log cabin was for long weekends or the occasional vacation, a time to enjoy some local fishing, or simply to take in the fall colors.

Most of the leaves had already fallen from the branches, leaving the skeletal brown silhouettes across the forests dotted intermittently with a random coniferous tree such as a spruce, fir, or pine.

Emily had just left to run to the supermarket for some groceries while he stayed around and enjoyed a cold Oktoberfest lager, one of the last he'd have for the year. It was annoying to him that some of his favorite brews were only available seasonally, but that was the nature of marketing, he supposed. Or maybe the breweries actually cared about tradition. Either way, he fully intended to savor this one, knowing there wouldn't be more for another ten months.

The fire crackled in the hearth. Sparks shot up into the chimney's flume as the tongues of flame spewed warm swaths of heat.

His Secret Service detail was outside the cabin, as they always were. He'd invite the men inside out of the cold, but he knew better. They were as resilient and tough as they were stubborn to their duty. Loyal to a fault, Dawkins had been surrounded by most of these guys since before winning his first presidential election.

There'd been a few changes. One of the older agents had retired last year. Another had taken a different position with the government. Other than that, however, his rotation of guards had stayed largely the same through the years, and Dawkins was happy to call them friends, though he thought of them more as family.

He took another sip of the lager, letting the bottle dangle in his fingers as he stared into the flames. It was getting late in the afternoon, and soon dark would be on them. He didn't like how the sun went down so early in the late fall and winter, but he tried to make the best of it, usually with a good drink and, now, even better company.

Emily Starks was the director of Axis, an ultra secret agency that worked under the umbrella of the United States government. Getting her to take any time off seemed like a chore, and she often bemoaned the fact that she had too much work to do to simply run off to the mountains with a former president.

He usually laughed at her, calling her a workaholic more times than he could remember.

She'd protest during the drive up, as she had on this occasion, but by the time she stepped into the cabin, all her troubles and responsibilities would seem forgotten. She would melt into his arms while on the sofa and stay there, resting her head on his chest for hours before even stirring.

He loved that woman, more than he had loved anyone in a long time. He'd been in a position that required him to be strong all the time, 24/7. She brought out the vulnerable side of him, exposed who he really was as a person, and could—if needed—be strong enough for the both of them. Emily made it possible for John Dawkins to be human again.

Fate had brought the two together, an unlikely but beautiful sequence of events that had put them squarely in each other's space. She'd worked for him as director of his most ultra-secret agency. She reported only to him and that intimacy had led them to an understanding of each other that very few other Americans could comprehend.

As director of Axis, she had reported solely to him during his terms in office. As time went by, the two developed a strong foundation of trust. It didn't take long before Emily and President Dawkins grew close in a more personal way.

Very few outside the Oval Office ever truly knew who Emily Starks was. Anonymity was crucial in her line of work. The less the public knew, the safer they'd all be. Her tasks were often ones that were carried out in the dark of night, deep in the shadows where no eyes dared wander.

Dawkins could tell she was ready to slow down. She'd been at the helm of Axis for nearly a decade, and it wasn't difficult to see that her job was taking its toll. Most of the directors had come and gone within five years of taking the gig. The burnout rate was understandably high.

Dawkins was accustomed to having to make difficult decisions. On any given day, the president of the United States would be yoked with the unenviable task of deciding who had to die somewhere in the world. It might be an unwitting janitor working in a weapons factory in Afghanistan today, a group of terrorists in a training facility tomorrow.

Each choice he made would have a lasting effect on the world, but

more importantly, on a very personal level with someone he'd
never met.

Bombing a weapons factory was an easy decision. Doing it when
you knew there were innocent lives that would be lost? That was
something entirely different.

Dawkins took a sip of his beer as if that would wash away the
thoughts—the guilt, the lingering doubts—that hung in his mind.
He'd done his job the best he could. And he always believed that he
did it better than the other guy might have. That was up for debate,
but not his debate. He'd let scholars, historians, and talking heads
figure it out. They never had to decide whether to push the button or
not, whether to drop the ax or sheathe it for another day. It was all
well and good until you had to actually make an earth-shattering
decision.

Those types never would be in the position to do that.

He prayed every day that he'd done what was right, what was just,
and that he was forgiven for what sins he'd committed. Dawkins
found himself growing more spiritual as he aged. Even though he
still hadn't hit sixty years old, he was already in constant contemplation about the end of his life, what happened after, and if he'd been a
good enough person.

He was thankful for grace in that respect. His faith taught him not
to worry about being good enough. That was impossible. Broken
vessels couldn't mend themselves, a pastor had once said to him.
They can only be remade by the potter.

Dawkins grunted at the thought and took another swig, then set
the bottle down on the end table.

A sound outside the cabin roused him from his thoughts. It was
low, a thump of some kind. He figured it was probably an acorn or
some other kind of tree nut that fell and struck the porch.

He dismissed it and went back to thinking about his time with
Emily.

She'd been an incredibly beautiful addition to his life, and he
loved her deeply. They were planning on getting married in the
spring. The wedding would be small. Only a select group of people

would be invited, including their mutual friends Sean Wyatt and Tommy Schultz.

Those two had recently gone through the nuptials and were, as far as he could tell, happily married. They'd apparently found women who were as crazy and adventurous as they were, which certainly made for some interesting dinner conversation around the holidays.

The fire crackled and popped again, louder this time. A stinging pain burned from a single point on Dawkins's neck, as if a bee or wasp had planted its sharp weapon into his skin and started pumping venom into his bloodstream.

He reached up and swatted at his neck, expecting to see some kind of insect tossed to the ground so he could step on it. It had been colder than usual in this part of the mountains, and he was surprised there would be any insects out of hibernation. Now was the time when they began receding back to their nests to wait out the cold season. There had been a few mosquitoes a couple of weeks back, but that was at his Nashville home near the lake.

He saw nothing fly off his neck and realized that whatever was embedded there was in deeper than he thought.

Dawkins pushed his palms into the armrests and tried to stand, but a sudden wave of dizziness washed over him. The room spun, and his body felt twice as heavy as normal. He slumped back down in the chair and picked at the spot on his neck. His fingernails brushed against something small and feathery, with a metallic cup attached where the soft bristles tickled his fingertips. He pinched the object and removed it, held it up to the light, and realized what it was.

A tranquilizer dart.

His vision blurred and he forced himself to blink rapidly, though he soon realized it was an exercise in futility. Through the haze, he could see dark figures outside the window, silhouetted by the light of the moon through the treetops beyond. He thought he made out the outline of a gun, but his sight continued to deteriorate.

The sound of the front door creaking open snapped him out of his fog, but only for a second. He saw three figures enter the room, each wearing ski masks and black tactical gear, including Kevlar vests.

The men strode across the hardwood floor and stopped; the one in front loomed over Dawkins like a terrifying scarecrow.

Dawkins was armed, as was normal for him. He carried a SIG Sauer 9mm on his right hip and, being out in the woods, he felt like it was a good idea since there'd been a few cougars and black bears spotted in the area in recent weeks.

Black bears didn't usually bother people, but he'd rather be safe than sorry, especially if he was out for a walk and had asked the Secret Service guys to hang back.

The agents! The thought smashed into his mind and weighed on his chest like a fifty-pound sack of sand. Were his bodyguards dead? Guilt racked him again, but he felt his consciousness yielding to the drugs that were quickly making their way through his blood and into his brain.

He couldn't think, couldn't even form the words he wanted to yell at the men. He desperately wished he could draw his firearm and dispatch these three, ending them in a blizzard of gunfire that they would never see coming, never suspect from a retired politician.

But the muscles in his arms were useless. They felt like Jell-O, trembling under their own weight. He couldn't even manage to twitch his fingers, and his eyelids were dragging across his eyeballs in slow, methodical blinks.

Dawkins could feel it. He was about to black out, and there was nothing he could do to fight it. The drugs were making quick work of him, tugging his mind into the darkness where it would reside until he woke—if he was awoken at all.

Of course he would wake up. If these men wanted him dead, they would have killed him already. Then again, who went after a former president? They were never targets, horses that could no longer race and weren't bred for plowing fields. Retired politicians typically only had three options: go into the corporate or media worlds, write books, or fade into obscurity.

His eyelids continued to grow heavier.

The figure standing before him shook his head back and forth.

Dawkins couldn't see the person's face, but the whites of his eyes glowed in the cabin's light. The skin was covered in a black paint, camouflaged for the evening mission that would lead them here to Dawkins's cabin.

Why, though? Why would they want him? And who were they?

The answers he hoped for didn't come. Instead, he surrendered to the overwhelming fatigue and fell asleep, slumping over on the couch.

The leader of the assault team touched his finger to the president's neck, then looked at the others and nodded.

"Let's get him out of here."

4

CHATTANOOGA

The reporters arrived on the scene within minutes of the first responders. Sean always thought it was strange how news crews could somehow get to a scene nearly as fast as people with sirens, flashing lights, and radios. He knew how it worked, at least from a technical aspect. They were like bloodhounds, always sniffing the right channels—often literally—to find the next story. Often, first responders would even tip off reporters to big local stories.

Sean had tried to slink away, blending into the forest until he and Tommy could get to their vehicle, but that wasn't going to happen.

The girl whose life they'd saved brought up the two heroes immediately.

Sean imagined the live feed on the televisions in most of the homes in the area. They were likely running a banner along the bottom that said something about two guys from the IAA saving the girl's life.

He wasn't sure how they would have worded it, but he'd witnessed enough breaking news stories that he could come up with a pretty close idea. While Sean enjoyed the anonymity of his life and career with Tommy's organization, there were certainly times when

that was flushed down the toilet. During those brief moments, Se
did his best to shove his friend out in front of the cameras and let him
do the talking.

There were, after all, still people out in the world who wanted
Sean dead for one reason or another.

He'd taken precautions, done everything he could to wash his
hands of the blood he'd shed over the years that he'd worked for the
government. Still, there were some loose ends—demons that could
resurface at any time and make a play for his life.

Sean didn't know where the attack would come from, but having
his face plastered all over the news wasn't a good way to keep a low
profile. Tommy was the IAA brand. He was the one usually put front
and center, but the girl they'd saved had wanted to publicly thank
both of them.

At least for now, Sean looked different than he had all those years
ago. While at Axis, he'd usually sported a simple disguise: hair color
change here, facial hair difference there, put on weight, lose weight,
that sort of thing. Now, his scruffy, dirty blond hair would make it
hard for his enemies to recognize him—unless they'd kept track
of him.

"These two men saved my life." Sean heard the girl say, and knew,
with those magical words, that the camera would switch over to
them.

The reporter shifted his feet and turned to Tommy, who was
closer. "Chris Caldwell reporting. We're here live with Tommy
Schultz, founder of the International Archaeological Agency in
Atlanta, hometown Chattanooga boy, and now local hero. Tommy,
tell me, what were you and your friend here doing up on that rock?"

Tommy smiled at the camera the way only he knew how. He was a
natural, just like a football coach giving a brief synopsis at halftime.
"Well, we were actually here looking for artifacts."

"Artifacts?" Caldwell shoved the microphone a little closer to
Tommy's face.

"That's right, Chris. We had a lead that there was a Confederate
treasure hidden up here on the cliff, in the cliff actually."

"Treasure? That sounds pretty fantastic. How did you hear about that?"

"Well, I'm not at liberty to reveal my sources, but let's just say they were either wrong about the treasure, or it's been so long since it was hidden that it's likely been removed, probably many years ago."

"Is this what you normally do, treasure hunting?"

Tommy chuckled. "No, Chris. This was something my friend here and I wanted to do for the fun of it. Things have been a little slow lately, and we thought it would be fun to do something like this."

"Well, you didn't come away completely empty-handed. It was lucky that you two were on the scene to save Molly's life."

"That's true." Tommy motioned to Sean. "My buddy here heard the screams and reacted. I have to be honest, I've never seen him move like that before, especially in a high place like this."

The reporter stepped closer to Sean. "Chris Caldwell here with Eyewitness News. I'm speaking to Sean Wyatt from the International Archaeological Agency. Sean, what were you thinking when you made the decision to attempt to save Molly?"

"Thinking?"

"That's right?" Caldwell shoved the mic closer to Sean's head.

"I wasn't thinking. I...I just heard the scream and reacted. It's what...it's just an instinct, I guess, something deeply rooted in me. When I hear someone in trouble, I run that direction. I don't know why." He lied. He knew exactly why, but the public didn't need to know.

"We've seen the video taken by one of the observers with a cell phone. What you did was absolutely heroic. I'm sure Molly's parents will be extremely grateful that she's safe, thanks to you two."

Sean hiked his shoulders and dug his hands into his pockets. He didn't like being on camera and wanted the interview to end, but it seemed to be dragging on forever.

"Tommy, do you two have any idea where that treasure might have gone?"

Back to this old thing.

"No, Chris, but I assure you, treasure hunting isn't really our thing. We specialize in recovery, security, and occasionally manage organized dig sites, but we're not treasure hunters."

"Well, there you have it," Caldwell said as he turned back to face the camera. "Two hometown heroes in the right place at the right time, and with the right stuff. From all of us here in the Tennessee Valley, thank you, Sean and Tommy, for saving this young woman's life."

The light on the camera cut out, and the reporter lowered his microphone. "How was that?" Caldwell asked.

The cameraman was checking something on the back of his device and without looking away gave a thumbs-up.

He turned to Sean and Tommy. "Thanks, guys. Great stuff."

"Happy to," Tommy said.

It was the truth. He was always looking to get a little extra publicity for his organization. The IAA wasn't exactly a charity operation, though it was essentially a nonprofit. They weren't trying to make tons of money from it like an ordinary corporation. The main purpose was to preserve as much history as possible.

Caldwell's eyes fell over Tommy's shoulder, and a grave expression crossed his face. "Looks like you two have a few more questions to answer."

The reporter slunk away as two men in black suits and ties approached. Their matching aviator sunglasses gripped the skulls that sat atop muscular, veiny necks. The men were stout and had broad shoulders. One was black, the other white, both clearly high-end security guys and both with shaved heads.

There was an older man behind them. He wore gray slacks and a white button-up shirt. From the looks of it, he'd just gotten home from the office and was about to undress when he got the call to come up to Prentice Cooper. Who he was, though, Sean and Tommy didn't know.

"Gentlemen," the guy said, "I owe the both of you an extraordinary debt."

Sean and Tommy shared a curious glance.

The man stepped between the two bodyguards and extended a

hand. His skin was marked with sunspots, as was his forehead. His gray, wispy hair danced in the breeze. Skin hung loose from his chin, and he had deep bags under his eyes. Still, the guy gave the impression he was only in his mid-sixties, not old by most standards.

"Name's Maynard, Maynard McIntyre. Molly is my daughter."

Sean and Tommy looked at one another again, this time with a dash of recognition in their eyes.

"Mr. McIntyre, it's a pleasure to meet you," Tommy said, taking the man's hand first and shaking it firmly.

Sean repeated the gesture when his friend was finished. "Nice to meet you, sir."

"The pleasure is all mine, I assure you." He looked over his shoulder at his daughter standing by the edge of the forest with her friends. When he returned his gaze to the two men, there was a distant sadness in his expression, perhaps even a hint of disappointment. "Molly...she doesn't always make good decisions. That's my fault as her father. I'm afraid I spoiled her from a very early age."

"That's an easy thing to do as a dad," Sean said. "Fathers love to spoil their little girls."

"You have kids, Sean?" There was a hint of hope in the man's voice.

"No, sir. I don't. But I have friends that do, and I studied parenting extensively while in the psych program at Tennessee. It's a common theme, from my external perspective."

The man nodded and grinned. "I suppose it is. Daddies just want their little girls to love them. I guess if that's a crime, I'm guilty as charged." He chuckled.

Sean and Tommy shared a short laugh to be polite.

"Anyway, I just wanted to thank you two. If you hadn't been here, my little girl might be..." His voice trailed off, and he cupped a hand over his mouth. Tears welled in his eyes.

Sean and Tommy stood silent for a moment, letting the guy work through his emotions, his thoughts, his fears that his daughter could have died that day.

"I want to thank you properly," he said when he'd finally reeled in a semblance of composure. "I'd like to take the two of you out to dinner, to the finest restaurant in the city."

Sean smirked. "That sounds great, Mr. McIntyre—"

"Please. Call me Maynard."

"Okay, Maynard. That really does sound amazing, but we have to get back to Atlanta this evening. We're about to start on another project, and there are some logistical things I have to work out."

"That's true," Tommy said, though the truth was that the project could wait. They weren't scheduled to begin operations for another two weeks. A dig site in the Congo was being set up around what was believed to be an ancient civilization, far more advanced than any ever discovered in that region.

As yet, there wasn't anything for the IAA to extract and secure, but that could change at any time. The director of the project had requested Tommy be on standby, and so that's what they'd done, hanging out and waiting until they got the call. Of course, that call could also never come if the site turned out to be a dry well.

Maynard looked crestfallen, but only for a few fleeting seconds. "No worries," he said, immediately cheering up. "The next time you two are in town, I'd love to treat you to a good steak dinner. And if you're ever out west, let me know. I have property in Montana, Colorado, and Oregon. You're always welcome to use one of my cabins, or if you'd like to go out there for a fishing trip on one of the rivers, just let me know. My home is your home."

"Thank you, sir, but that's not necessary," Tommy said.

Maynard held up a hand and dramatically shook his head back and forth. "Nope. I'm sorry. I won't take no for an answer. And if the two of you don't reach out to me in the coming months, I'll track you down, kidnap the both of you, and make you go out there for some trout fishing with me." He had a mischievous look in his eyes that told the two friends that maybe he'd done that very thing before.

Sean grinned and nodded. "Sold. I do love doing some trout fishing. Most addictive thing in the world if you ask me."

"Perfect!" Maynard exclaimed. He reached into his pocket and fished out a business card. "Whenever you're ready, just call. I'll make sure to take care of the arrangements."

"Thank you," Tommy said.

The older man shook his head. "No, thank you. You saved my little girl's life. Anything I can do to repay that, I will. For the rest of my life, I am in your debt."

Maynard turned and started back toward his daughter. The two guards nodded at Sean and Tommy and then followed their employer back up the slight slope to the edge of the woods.

Sean waited until they were out of earshot before he spoke. When he did, it was barely a whisper. "*The* Maynard McIntyre?" he asked.

"Unless you know of another one."

The story of the McIntyre fortune was something of a local legend. The McIntyre family had started a small restaurant chain on Cherry Street during the Great Depression. It had been a gamble, especially during tough economic times, but by providing people with a cheap, clean place to eat, it had become an instant success—despite the lack of disposable income floating around at the time.

Their restaurant became two, then four, and before long the little burger places were all over the Southeast and pulling in millions during a time when very few people were making money.

Maynard was the son of the founder, Marshall McIntyre. Apparently, having some alliteration in their names was something of a family tradition.

"I thought his hands felt soft," Sean said, not intending any insult. "Guy has worked in corner offices his entire life."

Tommy nodded. "That and manicures, most likely." He arched one eyebrow, but Sean didn't see.

"You sound jealous," Sean quipped. "Want to make an appointment at the spa before we head back?"

Tommy shook his head and then lowered it. "You're an idiot."

"I can make it a couples massage if you like."

"Okay—and we're done here."

Tommy started up the hill toward the trail leading back to the parking area. Sean stayed put for a couple of seconds longer. "They can do the whole hot stone thing on your spine. Or, ooooh, maybe we can do the thing where they walk on your back. I've never had that before." His voice climbed as Tommy got farther away.

The cameraman looked at him with a curious expression as he stuffed the expensive equipment back into his camera bag.

"He can get so testy sometimes," Sean said with a wry grin.

The cameraman snorted and went back to packing.

Sean turned around one last time and gazed out at the valley below where the river slithered through the gorge. A burst of cold air rushed up the slope and splashed over his face. It tickled his ears, and he tugged down on his beanie to keep them warm. Destin sure would be nice right about now.

He could feel the warm sand of the beach, hear the gentle gulf waves calling him, but a trip to the Emerald Coast would have to wait.

His phone started to vibrate in his pocket, shaking him back to the moment. Sean reached into his pocket, pulled out the device, and pressed the green button on the screen.

He pressed it to his ear, already knowing from the caller ID who was on the other end of the line. "How was the honeymoon?" he asked.

Alex laughed, the sound filling Sean's ear. "It was great. Fiji is a beautiful spot. If we didn't love you guys so much, we probably would have just stayed."

"I can relate," Sean said, peering out over the mountains across the way. "What's up?"

Alex and Tara were Tommy's lab techs. They'd proved invaluable over the years in many capacities, including watching over HQ while Sean and Tommy were out gallivanting around the planet. They were also crack researchers and a tremendous resource for information gathering, capable of pulling up, or tracking down, facts swiftly when the guys found themselves in a pinch. For years, Sean and Tommy thought something romantic was going on between the two. That fact had finally come out, and a few months ago the two had married.

Sean didn't really have any interest in working with his wife, not in a professional sense. He and Adriana got along great. They had a wonderful life together, traveled pretty much whenever they wanted, and enjoyed each other's company. Working together, Sean thought, might strain that. He couldn't imagine the stress that could come from being employed together with her in the same confined work-space. Even the closest couples needed time apart, and for most, leaving the house and going to work provided that.

"We got something here. In the mail," Alex clarified. "It's kind of strange."

"What is it?"

"You'll have to see it for yourself. I'm not really sure."

That was odd. "You can't tell me anything about it?"

"I didn't open the box. It's addressed to you, specifically, Sean. I don't open other people's mail."

Sean frowned at the revelation. Not at the fact Alex or Tara hadn't opened his mail; he could understand that. But he never got mail delivered to HQ.

"Does it say who it's from?"

"No," Alex answered. "It just says, 'A. Colleague.' The return address is in Saint Louis, Missouri."

Someone wanted to remain anonymous. Who would be sending him a box and addressing it to IAA?

He figured that was a question that had to wait until he was back in Atlanta. He took one last look out over the mountains and then turned to the trail. "We'll be back down tonight," Sean said. "I'll take a look at it then."

5

BARING, WASHINGTON

Andrew Boyd sat in the living room as he watched the television reports coming out of southeastern Tennessee. Dark wooden beams braced the ceiling overhead, contrasted by the white paint between them. A fire crackled in the fireplace. Boyd steepled his fingers together on his lap as he listened to the interview.

Upon seeing Sean Wyatt and Tommy Schultz on the evening news, he wondered where they were now and if the incident would keep them in Chattanooga or if they would return to Atlanta that night. Not that it mattered. Things were already in motion.

In another time and another place, perhaps Andrew and Sean could have gotten along, even come to be friends. Not in this life, though, and not this time.

Andrew spread his hands out to either side, stretching his arms across the back of the tan fabric of the sofa cushions. He breathed evenly, forcing down the anger rising from his belly. That fire could be put to better uses.

Phase one of his plan had already begun. He could feel a tingle of excitement swelling inside him. It was a thrill much like he'd felt on his first date with a girl, or on Christmas Eve when he was a young boy. The stakes now were much greater.

Andrew had spent the majority of his life in luxury. He'd been raised by wealthy parents in Saint Louis but had moved to Seattle where he felt more at home in the vibrant, thriving city on the coast.

He had two homes there: one condo downtown in the Lower Queen Anne district and a second outside the city in the forest leading into the eastern mountains. The condo was fashionable, professionally decorated and adorned with all the modern amenities a person could want. Its views swept over the majestic downtown skyline and out over Elliot Bay to the west. It was for sale now, a fact that gnawed at him on a daily basis. He hated letting it go, but that was where he was at the moment.

His parents had suffered greatly in the last two years. Their enterprises collapsed before their eyes. Everything they'd worked to build, their entire family business, had fallen apart. Most of their homes had been repossessed. They declared bankruptcy to avoid certain creditors, but by then, winning that battle was barely a consolation prize, a scrap for them to chew on.

Andrew's father had taken his own life, choosing to walk out into the woods behind their cabin in Arkansas with a pistol and a single bullet.

Andrew's mother was so shaken that she never recovered. One month later, she joined her husband by way of a handful of prescription pills.

Neither of them had ever been particularly close to Andrew, not since his decision to enter the military. When he tried to recall happier times, perhaps birthdays or Christmases, all he could recall were friends and relatives getting more attention than him.

That didn't change the fact that Andrew blamed Sean Wyatt for his troubles. He even believed that what happened in the army had been the catalyst for the downfall of his family business.

Now Andrew was trying to sell his once-posh condo in Seattle to make enough money to fund his plan, a scheme for revenge that involved some formidable challenges.

The cabin in the woods, contemporary in design like so many he'd seen in Scandinavia, was large at four thousand square feet and featured mostly views of the surrounding forest, save for a few peeks at the mountains to the east in the Okanogan-Wenatchee National Forest.

It was here, in this cabin, that he watched the news reports out of Southern Tennessee. Normally, local news broadcasts from that region wouldn't be seen in the Pacific Northwest, but apparently when two celebrities of the academic community did something heroic it made national news.

Andrew shook his head in disgust as the reporter and then the news anchors figuratively kissed Sean's and Tommy's rears over the dramatic rescue of the young girl.

In a way, the incident was somehow poetic.

Sean had been on Andrew's mind for a long time now, his plot for revenge stewing, simmering in the cauldron. He'd been planning on launching the second phase of his operation within the next twenty-four hours, but this—this was too perfect.

The anchor touched his ear, and then a serious expression flooded his face.

"And now, breaking news out of North Georgia, mere miles south across the border from where today's heroics took place. We have just received word that former president John Dawkins has gone missing. Federal investigators are on the scene working with local law enforcement, but as of this moment they have no leads as to where the former president could have gone or what may have happened to him."

Andrew grinned at the censored information. He knew they had more. The Secret Service agents guarding the president were dead. But the news didn't dare report that. News executives didn't like a panicking public any more than did those in the ruling class. For now, they were content to let the public think perhaps Dawkins had wandered off, perhaps a victim of early onset dementia.

That was far from the truth.

While much of the nation worried or, as had become the modern norm, pretended to care, the president was safe. For now.

Andrew had connections, and he had money, though only a fraction of what he had before. Most importantly, he had influence.

Over the years, Dawkins had made enemies in Washington. While he'd been one of the most beloved presidents in recent memory, if not history, that came with a price. It was, after all, impossible to please everyone. When you move a rock here, you disturb the dirt there.

The people who disliked Dawkins were glad to see him out of office, although they feared his successor would be just as bad for business, if not worse. He'd pushed through bills that would help the environment and, with the majority of Congress on his side, the laws were easily created.

Getting the information needed to track down Dawkins and kidnap him had required promises; promises Andrew believed he could keep. His family was one of the wealthiest in their region, and one of the most influential. Their money ran deep from the Industrial Revolution. While Andrew Carnegie had forged his steel empire, the Boyds were content to ride his coattails, supplying Carnegie's factories with equipment, raw materials, and often land for new foundries. Carnegie's name became one of the most famous in the modern period and he was once known as one of the three wealthiest people in the world.

Andrew's ancestors were content to keep their names out of public view, but their fortune was made in the same industry as Carnegie's. The Boyds, however, were more discreet about their spending. They squirreled away their money, reinvested in dozens of other ventures. Eventually, their portfolio ran into the billions, featuring land, businesses, and other assets.

He'd grown up spoiled. While Andrew wouldn't admit to that, there was still something missing in his life, at least early on. Even with all the money, family, power, and influence, he'd resorted to thrill-seeking to fill the gap.

It wasn't uncommon for him to go skydiving, base jumping, and swimming with sharks on a given weekend. He'd tried to fill the void with women, too, funding extravagant charters to the Caribbean, or to other exotic places around the world, often taking a dozen guests at a time.

His friends, of course, loved every second of it. But Andrew had felt empty, unfulfilled with his life of debauchery.

Drugs hadn't appealed to him despite several friends encouraging him to try a smorgasbord of illegal and dangerous delights.

Oddly, he'd found his place in the military.

His parents hadn't approved of his decision, but when he was twenty-one years old, he went to his local recruiting office and signed up. His father had been angry, his mother disappointed.

"Someone else can do that," she'd said.

"You have a life here," his father had said. "A good life where you're free to do whatever you want."

Andrew didn't care. There'd been no sense of purpose for the first twenty years of his life. It had been a hollow existence.

He'd caught grief when he went to basic training. Some of the new recruits apparently knew who he was, billionaire playboy Andrew Boyd. They called him the prince or "your highness," but he kept his nose down and pushed ahead. After he kicked a few butts in the process, the men around him started to show hints of respect. Maybe this rich boy wasn't the sissy they all thought he was.

He rose through the ranks with an uncommon rapidity and, after a heroic display of leadership in a firefight in Iraq, he received an unusual call.

Special Operations wanted him, so he had joined the 160th, known to many as the Night Stalkers. Their more formal title was the 160th Special Operations Aviation Regiment.

He'd forged a strong bond with a few of his fellow soldiers and promised them that when their time was up in the military, they would always have a job working private security for him.

At first, he hadn't been certain how some of the guys would take it, but the offer was too generous to pass up.

Now he had five highly trained, extremely talented spec ops

soldiers working for him. He'd been waiting, planning, and timing things behind the scenes. All the while, he had watched Sean Wyatt.

The thought of the man's name sent a surge of anger through Andrew.

He remembered the events like they'd happened a few hours ago.

His team was in Iraq, investigating a possible connection to bioweapons that the Iranians were supposedly smuggling across the border to insurgents. He'd cornered a man they suspected—with good reason—of being the primary contact with the insurgency.

Andrew and his team captured the guy and his family, tied them up in their home, and proceeded to interrogate him in front of his wife and two small children—a boy and a girl both under the age of seven. When he wouldn't talk, they began torturing the man's wife.

Andrew enjoyed that part. To him, those people weren't human. They were something else, caught between animals and people in the evolutionary chain. He actually enjoyed hearing the woman's screams, the begging of the husband, the sobs of the children as they watched blood oozing from their mother's toes where the nails had been ripped out.

And still the man wouldn't talk.

Andrew had come to the conclusion that they would have to use even stronger leverage to get what they wanted. One of his men, a hulking lumberjack of a guy named Ted, hadn't hesitated. He pressed the barrel of his sidearm against the boy's head and tensed his finger.

Amid the screaming, the begging, and the tears, Andrew was about to give the order to spray the kid's skull across the room when the door burst open.

Sean Wyatt and another guy appeared in the entrance.

Andrew's men had spun and pointed their weapons toward the doorway, but upon seeing an American had lowered their guns.

Sean had not. He pointed his pistol straight at Andrew, knowing precisely who was running the show.

The conversation had been brief, questions about what Andrew was doing, how immoral it was, and how he would have to face an inquiry about the whole scenario. The standoff, however, was much longer.

Andrew's men had re-aimed their weapons at Wyatt and were ready to take him down, though Wyatt had been clear that he would get his shot off first and take out Andrew before any of his men could flinch.

None of them knew who Sean Wyatt was before that day. Now there was no forgetting him.

Andrew had returned home in disgrace. Thanks to his connections and essentially bottomless pockets, he'd been able to influence the outcome of the court martial to the point where he was honorably discharged. His career in the military, however, was done.

It was the only thing that had ever given him a sense of purpose, some semblance of meaning in his life. Sean Wyatt had ripped that away from him, storming in with his self-righteous bravado.

Andrew had done all he could over the years to track down Wyatt. His original plan had been simply to kill the man while he slept, or perhaps wake him up to a muzzle in his face just before it flashed and fired a bullet through his brain.

That was too easy, though, Andrew thought. Wyatt had tried to tear away the brotherhood Andrew had forged, the life that he'd made for himself away from the mansion and the billionaire lifestyle. Andrew was doing good in the world. He was a leader.

Now all he had left was his money and his influence.

His parents had stopped speaking to him, although that was more because he'd joined the army against their wishes and less about what happened while he was enlisted. He wondered if they'd even heard about the court martial. Part of him didn't care.

His focus was elsewhere. It was time for Sean Wyatt to lose everything he held dear.

6

ATLANTA, GEORGIA

S ean and Tommy had returned to Atlanta the day before, hours after their harrowing experience with the girl on the cliff. They'd gone to their homes—Sean to his place near Buckhead, Tommy to his house in Virginia Highlands—and enjoyed a quiet night with their wives.

Tommy's wife, June Holiday, had taken a position with Emily Starks, heading up a new unit within Axis.

Adriana had resumed her life of investigation into lost art from World War II but was content, it seemed, to plant her roots in Atlanta —at least for now.

The next morning, Sean woke up early to head over to the IAA building. His curiosity had kept him up most of the night, and he wanted to see what this strange parcel was and why he'd received it.

Not surprisingly, he found Tara and Alex there in the lab before he arrived. The two practically lived there, perpetually wrapped up in the work they loved so much. They studied and analyzed ancient artifacts, checked their authenticity, and even had the technology to date items just as precisely as some of the top research facilities in the world.

Sean stood in the underground laboratory, arms crossed as he looked down at the package. It was the only thing on the desk, the surface cleared off to accommodate the box. He couldn't decide whether he wanted to open it, especially considering the mysterious and suspicious return address.

"Maybe it's a secret admirer," Tara offered. She sat in a rolling chair a few feet away from the workstation, eyeing the box for what must have been the hundredth time in the last ten minutes.

"I doubt that," Sean said. "And I hope not. I've never seen Adriana jealous, but I have a feeling that would be a very bad thing to behold."

Tara and Alex laughed.

Beyond that, they had other capabilities and talents that had proved useful through the years. One such talent was with computers and cutting-edge technologies.

"All the scans check out," Alex said, staring at the box. "There's nothing harmful in there like snakes or something explosive."

Sean turned his head, eyebrows knitting together into a scowl. "Snakes or explosives?"

"Yeah," Alex said, head bobbing. "You know, dangerous stuff."

"Two very different ends of the spectrum," Sean said with a sigh and turned back to the package. "Fine. Screw it."

He picked up a knife and sliced through the tape on both ends and then across the top. He set the blade back in its place and pried open the flaps. There were foam packing peanuts inside to protect the contents.

Sean sifted through the packing and discovered something smooth and hard in the center of the box. He brushed away some more of the foam and leaned over the package. The other two crowded around and looked in with him.

Inside was a shiny wooden box. It was two colors, one a darker brown finish, the other a light tan. There was an emblem on the top, made from the lighter-colored wood and set into the darker. The object was turned on its side, with a thin rectangular block sticking out of each side.

"What is that?" Alex asked, his face scrunching into a befuddled frown.

Sean blinked for a moment and then put both hands into the box and lifted the strange object. "We'll come back to that," he said. Sean set the object on the table next to the cardboard container and inspected each side. One side featured a series of mountains with sharp-angled peaks and slopes. Another side featured a cliff next to an ocean. Coniferous trees dotted the edge near the drop-off.

Sean spun the box around and looked at the third side. It showed a river winding through rolling hills with the sun on the far horizon. The final side displayed a ship. The boat was old, something from the early ages of exploration. Sean recognized the style as a Japanese vessel. It featured a single, tall mast in the center with thin sails much like the paper curtains that could be found in Japanese homes or wrapped around lanterns. The boat's draft was shallow, and the living quarters for the sailors were fixed to the aft section like a small cabin atop the back deck.

"Why would someone send you this?" Tara asked. "Seems like a strange gift."

"It's not a gift," Sean said, leaning closer to the object. "It's a Japanese puzzle box."

"A puzzle box?" Alex asked.

"Yes. See all these lines? Those are seams. It takes a skilled craftsman to make one of these and have everything fit together so perfectly. Run your finger along the surface. You won't feel any breaks in the wood; that's how minuscule they are."

Alex did as told and rubbed one side of the box. "You're right. I can't feel any of the seams."

Sean nodded. "Whoever made this particular box was extremely talented...and very careful. They wanted it to be perfect."

"It looks old," Tara added.

"Indeed. Very old." Sean inspected the object's surface all the way around for a second time and then stood up straight. "This one...it's several hundred years old at the very least."

The eyes of the other two went wide with surprise, admiration, and a touch of concern.

"Perhaps we should put this in a safe place then?" Tara asked.

Sean wasn't ready for that just yet. He tilted the box and heard something move inside.

"There's something in there," Alex stated the obvious.

"Whoever sent this wanted me to open it, I guess." Sean set the box down on the table and stuffed his hand back into the packing foam.

"Aren't you going to open it?" Tara asked.

"In a second," Sean answered. "I want to make sure there's nothing else in here."

His hand rifled through the foam peanuts until his fingers brushed across something smooth on the bottom. It wasn't the cardboard. He found an edge and pulled the item out.

It was a sheet of paper; a photocopy, to be precise. The writing on it was faded almost to the point of being illegible. Sean held it up to get a closer look and found that the letter had been written in elegant cursive, much like it would have been done prior to the twentieth century. Based on the fading, he estimated the writing to be at least one hundred and fifty years old, but it was difficult to tell since it was a copy of the original.

His eyes quickly darted to the bottom of the page, skipping over the contents that filled the paper.

The name at the bottom was one he'd seen before, the autograph as familiar to him as his own. He knew immediately that this letter was more than one hundred and fifty years old. It had been written by one of the Founding Fathers of the United States.

"What is that?" Tara asked.

Sean swallowed and stared blankly at the page, contemplating what he was holding. "It's..." he faltered. "It's a copy of a letter written by James Madison, former president of the United States, the father of the Constitution."

You could have heard a feather drop in the room.

The kids said nothing for a long moment, until Alex broke the quiet.

"Where...um, where is the original?"

"I don't know. Maybe whatever's in this box can answer that."

"What are you guys looking at?" Tommy asked as he entered the lab. He wore a goofy smile, a Fleetwood Mac T-shirt, and jeans with frayed pockets.

The look mimicked Sean's, though he was wearing a gray Spider-Man shirt.

"Something I got in the mail," Sean said without looking away from the paper. He gently set it down next to the package and picked up the wooden box again.

"Ooooh, is that a Japanese puzzle box?"

"Sure is." Sean held it up and then pushed on one end. One of the pieces slid free. He stuck his finger in and dragged the next in the opposite direction. He took his time, careful not to damage the relic as he removed each piece until they could see inside.

Everyone huddled around, each holding their breath to learn what mysterious secret the puzzle box contained.

The group frowned collectively. Every single one of them was expecting to find something ancient—a jewel, perhaps, maybe a ring or a necklace—but not what was resting in the bottom of the box.

"That's odd," Alex commented. "Right?"

"Yeah," Sean said with a bewildered sigh.

Inside the antique container was a modern device, something they all used on an almost daily basis.

The thumb drive was silver with a black plastic tip on one end. There were no identifying marks, not even a brand name.

Sean picked up the box, turned it over, and let the flash drive fall out into his palm. He pinched it between a finger and thumb and held it up to the light as if that would give him a better idea of who sent it or what it contained.

"What do you think's on there?" Tara asked, cocking her head to the side to further inspect the device.

"There's only one way to find out."

"Yeah, but that thing could have a virus," Tommy said. "We plug it in our computers, and the entire system goes down."

Sean had already thought of that, too. The last thing they needed was their entire operation shut down or hacked because they had been careless.

"Who did you say sent that?"

"A cryptic name," Sean answered. "A. Colleague."

"Right. And the address is likely a fake as well."

"Mm-hmm."

Alex raised his hand like a schoolboy trying to answer one of the teacher's questions. "We do have a few old computers in here that we don't use much anymore. We keep them around mostly for parts or to run simple tests." He pointed to a corner in the back of the room where three monitors were propped up on a workstation next to three PC towers. The units had keyboards and a mouse beside each one. The computers were definitely old, at least four or five years as far as Sean could tell. In an industry where technology aged within hours of being released, those computers might as well have been from the Stone Age. Still, if they were offline, using one of those would be the perfect way to safely check out what was on the thumb drive.

The four made their way through the maze of artifacts, robots, wires, beakers, and all the other gadgets that were haphazardly arranged on the tables and display cases on the lab floor.

Alex arrived at the workstation first and pressed a button on top of one of the PCs. Red lights came to life on the front in a V shape.

"It's an old gaming PC," Alex defended as he noted the speculative looks on Sean's and Tommy's faces.

The screen bloomed to life and displayed the word Lenovo for a moment. Then it went black and the image changed to a flaming background with a torch on the right.

Sean reached over and plugged the thumb drive into one of the USB ports. Tara took the initiative and slid into the chair, cupped the mouse with one hand, and waited for the new drive to appear on the desktop.

When the white folder appeared, she double-clicked it, and a new box appeared on the screen. There was only one item in the folder, a movie file.

"It's not connected to the network, right?" Tommy double-checked.

"No," Alex said. "We keep these offline at all times, specifically for running stuff like this."

"Okay," Tommy said with a nod. "Play it."

Tara clicked the video. There was a momentary lag, and then a new black box appeared on the screen. She clicked the white arrow in the center of it and waited.

The timer on the bottom left of the box started ticking forward: one second, two, three. At the seven-second mark, every person at the desk wondered if there was something wrong.

Then a light clicked on. It was coming from the corner to the right, behind the camera so that it shone at an angle on the subject. In the middle of the screen was a person sitting at a wooden table, tied to a matching chair. It looked to be a man, though who it was, how old they were, and any other meaningful details were impossible to discern due to the black pillowcase over his head.

"Hello, Sean," a voice said. It was a man's, but it was running through a modulator so there was no chance of recognizing the speaker.

Tommy cast a sidelong glance at his friend. Alex did, too. Tara and Sean kept their eyes locked on the screen.

"You probably wouldn't remember me, but just in case you do I hope you don't mind me changing the sound of my voice for now."

Sean's eyes narrowed. He didn't like this, not one bit. A bad feeling crept into his gut and sat there like a meal of too much fried chicken.

"Since you're watching this, it means you were able to figure out how to open the puzzle box. I hope you liked it. I think it's...appropriate for what you're about to do. Oh, and please, do check the bottom of the box. None of this will make any sense if you didn't get the letter out of there."

Sean glanced over at the sheet of laminated paper but said nothing.

Tommy's eyes wandered to the letter as well, wondering where this person was going with his little video.

"So, here we are, Sean. Together again. Again, you might not remember me, but I remember you. Oh yes, I remember you very well."

"I take it you don't remember this guy," Tommy whispered.

Sean said nothing but shook his head.

"You ruined my life, Sean. And now, it's time for a little payback."

"Ruined his life?" Tommy snorted. "That doesn't exactly narrow it down, does it? I mean, that could be any of a million people. Not a short list."

"I get it, Schultzie," Sean said, finally tired of his friend's ribbing.

"Loooong wait," Tommy added for good measure.

The man on the video spoke again. Sean almost felt grateful.

"I'm going to give you a chance, though, Sean. It's a chance you never gave me before you destroyed everything I had and everything I'd worked for. Do you see the man sitting at the table? Do you?" The voice was taunting, made more so by the distorted sound the modulator applied. "This man is a friend of yours. Not only a friend of yours, but he's very special to someone close to you."

Sean really didn't like where this was going now. Had this sicko kidnapped his father? Or had they taken Tommy's dad? Sean felt the knot in his stomach turn over.

"Getting to him wasn't easy. Then again, we are professionals."

First clue. He said the word *we*. He also said they were professionals. That meant probably former military. Sean kept his thoughts to himself for the moment, taking in every detail he could.

"I'm going to give you the chance to free your friend here, Sean. All you have to do is a few simple things. I'm sure you and your buddy will be able to handle it. After all, it's kind of what you guys do, right, figuring out clues to ancient treasures and all that?"

Sean got the overwhelming feeling that whoever this guy was, he could see them, as if it wasn't a recording but a live feed. He knew that wasn't the case, of course, but there was something about this man that hit close to home. Sean strained to detect any sort of familiarity in the tone that slipped through the modulator, but it was a vain effort.

"You see, Sean, you took everything away from me, everything I cared about. And now it's time for you to give it all back. I figure a few hundred million in treasure will do the trick, and I have just the treasure for you to find for me."

The sickening feeling in Sean's belly got worse. He reached into his pocket and looked at the screen. Adriana. Where was Adriana? She'd been kidnapped before, a mistake by the man who'd done it. He was dead now, pieces of him floating in the ocean somewhere, or long ago consumed by sea life. Sean didn't want to think about it. He couldn't lose her. Not again.

The nauseating thoughts quickly faded as he remembered he'd just received a text from her in the last hour. This package had been sent the day before. That meant she was safe. Then who was behind the hood, tied to the chair?

"You boys are historians," the narrator continued, "you looooove history." He smacked his hands together, mocking the viewers. Tommy and Sean glanced at each other quizzically then looked back at the screen. "Well, have I got a mystery for you. But first, I'd like to show you your prize, should you be successful."

A dark figure appeared behind the man in the chair. The newcomer's face was covered by a mask. He gave away no identifying features; his skin was covered from head to toe, even wearing gloves for this little ruse.

When the guy stepped forward and yanked the hood off the captive's head, the entire lab was plunged into a deep silence. The only sound was a short gasp of horror that escaped Tara's lips.

"You paying attention now, Sean?" the distorted voice asked.

He stared at the face on the screen, the face of a friend, someone he trusted and cared about.

It was the former president of the United States, John Dawkins.

7

ATLANTA

S ean wanted to punch the monitor, to throw it across the room and, in the most fanciful dream, dive into the scene and kill every one of the people responsible.

"That's right," the voice said. "Your good buddy the former president."

Dawkins had a cloth stretched across his mouth, forcing apart his lips. His teeth bit into it, but he couldn't make a sound. The gag was doing its job despite the president's struggling.

"Now, as I was saying, you're going to find something for me, Sean. You and your friend Tommy. But what is it you're to find?" He raised his voice dramatically, which sounded even goofier through the modulator. "That is the question! What indeed?"

"This guy's insane," Tommy remarked.

Sean nodded but kept his gaze locked on the screen.

"The Corps of Discovery," the man said, "which I'm sure the two of you know well, was formed to search the newly purchased Louisiana Territory. To map it and to learn exactly what the country had bought from France. As you are aware, Lewis and Clark were also trying to find the fabled Northwest Passage, a water route to the

Pacific Ocean that could make for faster travel between the two halves of the continent."

Sean rolled his eyes at the obvious statement though his jaw remained firmly set.

"When they reached the Pacific, they set up camp there for a while before returning across the country. However, Capt. Meriwether Lewis didn't turn in his report for years. While he delivered some of his documents to Jefferson, much of his report was missing. Why? Why didn't he tell his boss, the president, about everything he'd found?"

It was a good question, one that Sean had actually never considered before despite knowing the story of the Corps of Discovery's journey west.

"No? Nothing? Well, I have an answer. I believe that Lewis found something, something of immense power. If it had been an ordinary treasure, he and his men might have taken it back to the east, at least some samples of it. He would have happily reported it to his employer. Or...let's for a moment say he was a dishonest person. If he'd saved some of the treasure for himself, he wouldn't have been nearly broke when he died. So, that all comes back to the conclusion that what he found must have scared him. It frightened him so much, he didn't even tell his closest friend about it. Clark appears to have never encountered anything unusual and turned in his reports as expected."

This guy sure was long-winded for a kidnapper. Sean wondered when he was going to get to the point.

"So, here's the game, Sean," the man said.

"About time," Sean quipped angrily.

Tommy snorted.

"You will find what Lewis discovered on the West Coast. When you do, you will deliver it to me. If you fail, your friend Mr. President here will die. And I promise, it will be a painful, agonizing death. He will take a very long time to expire; I swear that to you."

Sean's eyes narrowed.

"Inside the box, you will find a letter. It was written by James Madison."

The four didn't need that confirmation. They'd already seen who had written it.

"This letter was written to his successor—James Monroe, but he also wrote it for every president that would come after him until one was elected in an era with both the technology and the know-how to deal with whatever it is Lewis had discovered on his adventure. Madison knew that, at the time, he and the government weren't equipped for it. That knowledge could only have come from details in the Lewis report. And this is where you come in, Sean."

There was a sneer in the ripples of the modulated tone. "You will read the letter and decode it. You will then track down whatever it is Lewis found out west and bring it to me. Only when you have it will you contact me." A phone number flashed across the screen. Sean immediately committed it to memory.

"Call this number before you have Lewis's secret, and I will kill the man you see in the chair. You have one week to find and deliver whatever it is Lewis discovered. Don't fail me...or your friend here dies."

Dawkins didn't struggle. He didn't moan or cry. He sat there, resolute in his chair as a proud former leader of the free world. He wouldn't be bullied or used as a pawn in some sicko's game.

Sean admired his courage. He wasn't surprised, though, having known Dawkins for nearly a decade. Still, a burning rage roared inside him. This maniac had taken one of his friends and was using him for leverage.

"Oh, and Sean? I almost forgot."

Sean's thoughts snapped back to the screen and the voice coming through the speaker.

"There's one more itty-bitty little wrinkle to this whole scenario. I'm not going to tell you what it is because, quite frankly, that would ruin the fun. It's probably best for you to just find out on your own, which should happen any minute now. Just know that you won't be able to do things the way you normally do. But like I said, you took everything from me. Now it's time I do the same to you. Good luck, Sean."

The screen went black, and the sound vanished.

For over a minute, no one said a word. Tara glanced down at the flash drive, wondering if it might burn up like some kind of *Mission Impossible* delivery system. It didn't, though, and the screen flashed back to its desktop like it would have any other time.

There were no ill effects that a virus would have certainly caused, at least not that they could see right away. So, that begged the question: What was this guy talking about regarding the wrinkle?

"What do you think he wants?" Tommy asked, finally cutting through the silence.

Sean's head twisted back and forth. "I don't know. I guess we have to read the letter to find out." His eyes wandered down to the laminated sheet on the table.

He didn't admit it, but a big part of him suddenly didn't want to read what the former president had to say. He knew that wasn't an option. This freak on the other side of the camera was playing the hardest ball there was to play. He'd kidnapped a former president and was threatening to kill the man if Sean didn't cooperate.

He picked up the paper and started poring over it, skimming through the formalities to get right to the meat of whatever it was Madison needed to pass on to future generations of leaders.

Tommy and Alex leaned in close. Tara stood from her chair and looked down at the sheet.

Every eye was fixed to the copy of the old page.

Sean sighed as he finished reading. He turned it over when he was sure everyone had finished and checked the back. There was nothing on it.

He shook his head. "Any ideas?"

"It's confusing to say the least," Tommy confessed. "What's that about the power to control the sea supposed to mean? I hope we're not looking for something like Poseidon's trident. We've already had one of those we had to deal with."

"I don't know," Sean said. "We'll have to sit down and piece it together."

"The box," Tara said. "Do you guys think the box is a clue?"

The men's eyes flashed to her and then down to the puzzle box. Sean picked it up again and analyzed the designs on the sides. "Could be," he admitted. "These pictures are certainly interesting. And why would he send us a puzzle box like this if it didn't have something to do with the case?"

"It must," Tommy said. He turned and paced to the other side of the lab and back. "If he sent that video in the box, that must mean there is something about that container that has to do with what Lewis found."

"You'd think," Alex said. "Otherwise it sure is a strangely dramatic way to send a message."

"Right."

"The clues are there," Sean interrupted. "It's all there. We just have to figure it out." He pointed at the third paragraph. "Right here; this is where the riddle begins."

Sean's phone started buzzing in his pocket. He frowned and fished it out, glanced at the screen, then answered.

"Hey, Em," he answered in a somber tone as he pressed the device next to his ear. He figured he was about to be the bearer of bad news.

She and Dawkins had become close, so close that they'd thrown inhibitions to the wind and were in a full-on relationship. She was still working for Axis, but it was anyone's guess how long that would last. Emily Starks was only in her mid-forties, hardly ready for retirement by most career standards. Her job, however, was different than most. Sean knew she'd saved up enough money to retire years ago, but she was good at what she did and couldn't force herself to walk away, not yet.

Sean knew Dawkins was nudging her in that direction. There were beaches for them to lie on, cities for them to visit, mountains to hike. He was ready to enjoy some nonpolitical travel. The only thing holding him back was her. He didn't view it that way, though, and Sean knew that. Dawkins was supportive, encouraging Emily to work for Axis as long as she wanted. Still, Sean knew the man's desires. Sooner or later, she would have to call it quits: either the relationship or her career.

"Sean," she said in an urgent voice, "where are you?"

"I'm in Atlanta. Why? You okay?"

"Shut up and listen. I don't have long. For all I know, this phone is tapped."

"Tapped?" Sean couldn't have been more confused. Emily's agency operated above most others, answering to one office only. If she was being investigated for something, there was certainly trouble afoot. He turned away and took a few steps in the other direction, leaving Tommy and the others staring at him with concern. "What do you mean tapped?" he hissed.

"I said to shut up." There was an intensity to her voice he'd never heard before in all their years working together and being friends. Sean's lips pinched together tight enough to crush a rock to dust.

"Someone took John."

Sean hesitated. He felt himself standing on a tightrope a thousand feet above a rocky gorge. He didn't know if he should tell her he knew or not. If he said he did, she'd wonder how. Then again, he couldn't lie to her. It was against his nature to lie to anyone, especially a friend.

"I know," Sean said. He spoke quickly before she could say anything else. "Someone sent me a package. In it was a thumb drive with a video file on it. We just watched the file. John is okay, for now."

"Sean," there was despondence in her voice, "the Feds...they're saying you did this. They want you to turn yourself in."

The words didn't register at first. The statement was so outlandish he almost laughed, but he held back, knowing Emily wasn't the type to joke about such things.

"What do you mean they're blaming me?"

"There was evidence at the scene of the crime," she said. "We were out of town at John's cabin. I went out for groceries. When I came back, he was gone."

"And you called the authorities."

"Yes. They arrived...faster than I would have expected, especially way out here. Pretty much every kind of cop you could think of, which immediately raised some red flags for me." She lowered her voice. Sean could tell she was trying to speak as quickly as possible to keep anyone from hearing. "Look, I know you didn't do this."

"No. And I was with Tommy in Chattanooga yesterday. I have an alibi."

"Won't matter," Emily said. "This is coming from somewhere... somewhere high up. I don't know how or where—or who is involved."

He detected a hint of fear in her voice. Emily wasn't one given to outbursts of emotion very often. For a long time, he'd wondered if she even had feelings. That was until he got to know her.

Emily was a complex woman, with many layers. Sean had once referred to her as an onion, saying you have to peel away the layers to get to the core of who she really was.

But he wasn't surprised to hear the fear and concern in her voice. She loved Dawkins. That much was clear.

"Why do you think they're blaming me for this?" Sean asked, changing the subject to get her mind away from thinking the worst.

"I don't know. All I know is that one of them claimed he found something. The guy had a shaved head. He was one of the suits."

"Can't you override them?"

"Doesn't work like that, Sean. Most of them don't even know about Axis or what we do. That's one of the downsides of answering to one person. We essentially serve a monarchy."

"So, tell the president. She'll help you."

"She's out of the country on a political trip."

"Yeah, but you have a direct line to her."

He was right, and she knew it. That didn't mean she should just up and call the president of the United States on a whim.

"I'll definitely reach out to her, but I had to call you and warn you. Sean, these guys, they're dirty. I can feel it. You know what I'm talking about, that sense you get from certain people."

"They're legit Feds?"

"Yeah, I think so."

Think so? She should know, but he wasn't going there right now. She was in the most fragile place he'd ever seen her. Honestly, it was a stupid question for him to ask anyway.

"Then they're dirty, or someone they're working for is setting me up."

"You said there was a video of John?"

He knew where this was going. "He's fine, Em. I swear. They had him tied up, but I saw him. He was breathing and looked pissed."

She offered a feeble chuckle. "I bet he is."

"I don't know how they got around his security, but whoever did this must be pro. Amateurs couldn't take out Secret Service like that. I promise you: I will find John, and I will bring him back. Okay?"

"I know you will. In the meantime, I have to go, and so do you. The first place they'll check is your house in Atlanta. I'm pretty sure they already went there. The next spot will be IAA. You need to get out of Atlanta as quickly as possible."

Sean sighed. A million thoughts ran through his head. There was a place he knew he could go, but it would be difficult to reach. It was all the way on the other side of the country. However, the good news was that it was right along the path Lewis and Clark had taken on their Corps of Discovery mission across the continent. If he could get out there and get set up off the grid, maybe he could figure out this riddle James Madison had written about so many years ago.

It was a long shot, but there were few options. She was right. If the Feds were pinning him for the abduction of the former president, they'd be here any minute.

"Okay, hang up, Em. I know how to reach you if I need to. Meanwhile, you work on figuring out who is behind this. I'll work on finding John."

"I'm so sorry, Sean."

"Don't be. It's not your fault. And I'm sorry, too."

She ended the call, and he held the phone down to check the screen.

He stuffed the device back into his pocket and looked up at the other three in the room.

Tommy stepped close. "So...what is going on?"

"Well, you guys already know that Dawkins was abducted. Turns out the Feds are blaming it on me, which means they'll be here any minute."

Tommy's brow folded with worried wrinkles.

"What do you mean they're blaming it on you? You've been with me the last few days."

"I don't think that's going to matter," Sean said. "We're dealing with someone, apparently, with pretty deep connections."

"Wait a minute," Tara said. "The Feds are coming here? Shouldn't you get going?"

Sean nodded. "Yes. But not without a copy of that letter."

Alex picked it up and ran over to a printer/copier in the corner. He placed it down on the glass surface, closed the top, and pressed the copy button. The machine warmed up for ten seconds and then spat out the duplicate sheet on the tray attached to the end.

He returned with both sheets and gave Sean the still-warm copy.

"Thanks."

Alex nodded.

"You can't actually be considering solving this right now?" Tommy asked, incredulous. "You need to go hide somewhere and lie low. Let us handle figuring out whatever this psychopath wants. We can handle it."

"I know you can, but I have to help in any way I can."

"What are you going to do?"

"I'm going to the cabin."

"The cabin?" Tommy asked, but he knew exactly where Sean was thinking of going. "That's a long way. And you won't be able to fly."

"I know. I've made that drive before. Heck, I've driven to Seattle before. I can make it."

Tommy sighed. "So, you're dropping off the grid."

Sean nodded. "I'll get rid of my phone when I leave the building. I have a burner I can use. When I get to the cabin, I'll call you."

Tommy's worry was written in the long, drawn lines that etched his cheeks from the corners of his eyes to the ridge of his jaw. "I don't like this."

Sean put his hand on his friend's shoulder. "Me either, buddy. We'll sort it out."

"There's nothing Emily can do?"

Sean shook his head and reinforced what she'd said on the phone. "Doesn't work that way, pal. Don't worry. It's going to be fine. We just have to do our thing. Okay? You work from here. I'll work from out there. Besides, if we're looking for something along the trail Lewis and Clark took, that puts me right in their path."

Tommy took in a deep breath and sighed. "Okay, fine. Go. But be careful." He didn't have to say that. And he didn't have to ask if Sean needed anything. "Take the new 4Runner," Tommy said. "Get your bug-out bag and go."

Sean nodded. "Thanks. I'll be in touch soon." He turned and rushed out of the lab, bursting through the side door and into the hall.

Tommy watched his friend sprint to the end of the corridor and disappear through the door leading to their underground garage. The second the door slammed behind him, Tommy's phone started ringing. He glanced at the screen. It was the receptionist upstairs.

He let out a long exhale through his nostrils and answered. He already knew what the call was for.

"Yeah?" he said, pushing the device to his ear.

"Mr. Schultz, I'm sorry to bother you, but there are some officers asking to see you and Sean."

Tommy glanced over at the kids. Both Tara and Alex looked forlorn.

"I'll be right up."

8

ATLANTA

Adriana tiptoed into the big kitchen and went straight to the coffee pot. The aroma of fresh-brewed coffee spilled out of the kitchen and filled the entire house. The toasty warm scent had awakened her before the alarm on her phone went off, something she much preferred to the invasive and often surprisingly loud noises the device offered.

She reached into the cupboard, took a white mug with the words Rosemary Beach on it in teal, and set it on the counter next to the hot coffee carafe. She took the pot by the handle, poured the dark contents into the cup, and then placed the glass back in its holder. She made quick work of adding a half cup of milk from the fridge and then stirred it, turning the steaming dark liquid to a creamy brown.

Coffee ready and prepped, Adriana made her way around the kitchen island to the counter side where three black stools sat neatly arranged at an angle. She passed on the stools, opting for a chair at the table where she could see the small television mounted in the corner between two sets of windows looking out into the backyard.

Birds were chirping noisily, feasting on a pile of seeds Sean had put out on the platform feeder behind the center window of the breakfast nook. There was no snow outside, but she knew it was cold. The forecast had called for mid-thirties as a high, much colder than the area was accustomed to at this time of year. The weather, it seemed, was revolting against the whole global warming phenomenon.

Adriana reached across the table and drew the remote closer to her. She pressed the power button, and within a second the television's screen blossomed to life. It was on ESPN, probably because Sean enjoyed watching the morning shows on *SportsCenter* before heading into the office at the IAA building. The last time he'd watched it in that room had to be more than a week ago. He'd left this morning before Adriana woke up. Sean was good about making sure she was taken care of, and the best way he could possibly take care of her was to prep and brew the coffee for her on his way out the door.

He'd set the brew time late enough that she could get some rest, though he'd briefly woken her with a peck on the cheek and a gentle "I love you" as he left the bedroom.

Adriana sipped the delicious brew and changed the channel to see what was going on in the world. She didn't trust the media, another of the many things she and Sean had in common. They both believed that, most often, the mass media was there to promote fear and divisiveness, serving the self-interests of the highest bidders.

Still, she thought there was some merit to keeping up with what was going on around them. Adriana wasn't going to put her head in the sand just because she had a mistrust of the press.

The second the channel changed, she caught something on the ticker at the bottom of the screen that immediately sent a chill through her body.

Her eyes shot up to the anchor and the headline in the top corner. It matched the Breaking News tag at the bottom. Both said the same thing, the message the clean-cut mid-forties man on the screen was conveying.

"President Dawkins abducted."

Adriana unconsciously set the coffee down and watched with rapt attention as the anchor went over the details surrounding the abrupt and confusing kidnapping of former president John Dawkins.

"Reports are flooding in regarding a video the kidnappers sent in just hours after the abduction. We do need to warn you that this video is disturbing in nature. Please look away or change the channel for a moment if that sort of thing bothers you in any way."

The anchor's warning did nothing for Adriana. She leaned closer, picking up the mug and stealing another long sip from it.

The screen changed to a scene at a table with Dawkins tied to a chair, his mouth taped shut. A voice came through the recording, claiming to be Sean Wyatt. The man's voice was altered, making it unrecognizable. Adriana knew right away that it wasn't Sean, not just because of the voice distortion but because of the scene. John Dawkins was a trusted friend, and kidnapping in general wasn't even on the map for Sean, be it the president or anyone else. The rest of the public, however, might not be clever enough to realize that.

The scene in the basement with the president transitioned back to the anchor. A new red digital box hovered over his shoulder, showing a picture of Sean with his name underneath it. Next to it was a word Adriana never believed she'd see associated with Sean.

Wanted.

"Sean Wyatt, once a trusted friend of the president, has abducted him and is holding him for what appears to be a ransom, though Wyatt has not asked for anything specific yet. He claims that another video will come out in one week. In the meantime, a nationwide manhunt is underway to try to apprehend Wyatt and rescue the president."

The anchor went on to say that the authorities believed Sean was armed and extremely dangerous.

Adriana shook her head. She didn't understand. Her mind raced. Confusion warred with anger; all while she tried to put the pieces together to comprehend what was going on.

Sean hadn't been gone more than an hour or so. He would be at the IAA building downtown right now. She had to warn him. Adriana picked up her phone and called his number, but there was no answer.

That wasn't highly unusual. Most of the time their digital communication was by way of text messages rather than a phone call. His job often put him in places where cell service was hit or miss. Then there was the other fact that he sometimes simply didn't feel the device vibrating because he was working, on the move, or occasionally in some kind of altercation.

Adriana stood from her chair and hurried back to the bedroom upstairs. Time was her enemy, and she knew it with an overwhelming sixth sense that permeated her mind and body.

As she reached the bedroom door, she felt her phone vibrate and, for the briefest of moments, thought it might be Sean sending her a text. She pulled the device out of her pocket and glanced at it. The number was one she didn't recognize. It was an Atlanta area code, but other than that the digits on her screen were unfamiliar.

The screen unlocked, and she quickly read the text message. It was easy to read, but difficult to understand. It only said, "Get out."

Adriana frowned. There were no names attached to the message. No clues as to who might have sent the warning. While she'd already gotten the distinct impression that leaving the house was the best possible option at the moment, this cryptic note only reinforced it.

Her fingers flew across the keys on the screen as she typed out the words: "Who is this?"

Then Adriana set the device down and dressed as fast as she could, throwing on a pair of jeans, a long-sleeve Pearl Jam T-shirt, and a pair of black boots. She was nearly done, slipping into an overcoat, when she realized what she'd done.

She reached over the bed and picked up her phone once more. She tapped out a quick message to Sean and then snapped her head to the right, looking between the long, grayish-blue drapes and out the window. She caught a glimpse of something through the open window overlooking the property.

Sean's home—now her home as well—was built at the top of a knoll in the Buckhead area of Atlanta. It was one of the few properties that had multiple acres, which meant they weren't too close to the neighbors. Sean and Adriana both appreciated many of the amenities the flourishing city provided, but they also enjoyed their peace and quiet. This house was a rarity in that it allowed for both.

At the moment, she was even more grateful for the positioning of the home because the movement she detected at the main gate was from several police cars.

A chill shot through her. She counted four squad cars, none with lights on. A single, undeniable fact washed out all other thoughts in her head. They were here to arrest Sean or, at best, take her in for questioning. There were other scenarios that could have been possible, even likely. She knew Sean didn't do what the media said he did. That was the undeniable truth. Sean was being set up, but by whom? Why would someone kidnap the former president and pin it on Sean?

Her mind raced. If she stayed, they would take her in for questioning. She knew what she had to do.

Adriana shoved her phone in her pocket, forgetting about Sean for the moment. A bell dinged downstairs. The cops were ringing the bell down at the gate. That was a good sign. They were at least being courteous. That would change when there was no response. They'd break through somehow and charge up the hill. Either the cops were there for her, Sean, or both. Either way, Adriana had no intention of being here when they came.

She'd spent the majority of her life on the run, hiding and changing her identity more times than she remembered. Deep down, she'd always been Adriana. Her father, Diego, had been sure to remind her of that during her training with the great ninja masters. He'd reinforced it later on in life when she was at university under an alias. The cops, more than likely, wouldn't know who she really was. The design was for her protection as well as for her father's. There were too many dangerous people out there who wanted the two of them dead, and if they ever discovered where they were—who they truly were—that would be the end.

Only trusted friends got to know the real Adriana, and that circle was extremely tight.

She rumbled down the stairs and turned the corner toward the kitchen, risking another short glance out the window as she ran by. The cops were still down at the gate, but there was no doubt their patience was growing thin. Another ding on the bell signaled their second attempt. After the third, she figured they would say screw it and open the gate on their own, one way or another.

Adriana zipped by the laundry room and stopped at the door leading downstairs to the basement. She flung it open and jumped into the stairwell, taking the steps two at a time until she reached the bottom. She pushed through the door into the lower level and stepped into the garage. Sean's motorcycle collection lined the wall to the right. The row contained several older bikes and a couple of new ones, but she knew his favorites were the vintage ones: the Triumph Bonneville, the 1978 Suzuki cafe bike he'd rebuilt, and a few others from that era.

It was too cold to make her escape on one of those. Adriana loved riding, but even she had her limitations. She scooped a set of keys off the key ring next to the door and ran toward Sean's new car, a black Audi S5 with matte black wheels and dark-tinted windows. She could have taken her own vehicle, but it was parked out in the front of the house. In retrospect, it was probably for the best that she was going to take Sean's ride. It was faster than her SUV, and this little escape could call for some extra speed.

She skidded to a halt and opened the door. As she climbed in, her sense of smell was overwhelmed by the scent of black leather. It was stitched with white threads through the seams. The leather and stitching wrapped around the seat frame, enveloping her in the luxurious fabric. She pressed the ignition button, and the motor revved to life. The digital console behind the steering wheel bloomed and displayed the speedometer, tachometer, and mileage. She reached up and pressed the button on the garage door opener and watched as the gate slowly inched its way toward the ceiling. Every second felt like a year, and Adriana expected to see feet and legs revealed as the door climbed higher.

There were, thankfully, no policemen waiting outside. That wouldn't be true much longer.

She threw the car into drive and stepped on the gas as the garage door reached a height that allowed her safe passage.

The vehicle lurched forward, and she steered it out and around toward the secret entrance in the back. They didn't use it very often, only when the need arose. And right now, it had arisen.

She was careful not to drive too fast, wary that the tires might squeal and alert the encroaching authorities to her getaway. When she was two hundred feet from the hidden back gate, she pressed another button on a separate garage door opener.

The fence wrapping around Sean's property was wrought iron, most of it covered in dense ivy. Some of the ivy had wisteria intertwined with it. One section of the fence, however, was fake. The vines and leaves were made to look like the rest of the plants, but they were plastic, designed to keep up appearances.

That section of the fence started moving the second Adriana pressed the button. The gate slid sideways, overlapping behind another section on well-hidden tracks. The driveway came to an end on a patch of grass that merged with the street beyond. Adriana carefully slowed the vehicle as it crossed the grass, rolled over the curb, and onto the road. She glanced both ways, but there were no cops to be seen. They'd put all their forces at the front of the property, at the main gate. They obviously didn't know about this way in and out.

Adriana was thankful for that. She'd taken a gamble, and apparently, it was paying off. She wasn't out of the woods yet, though, and getting away from Atlanta was going to be tricky. The city had gotten so big over the years that it seemed there were people everywhere.

There were, however, some subtle differences about Atlanta that made it easier to hide in than many other large cities.

Outside of downtown, Atlanta and its bedroom communities such as Chamblee, Dunwoody, Buckhead, and others were designed to keep the area looking more natural despite the presence of millions of people.

That meant many homes weren't tightly packed together. There were large lots, rolling forests everywhere, as well as back roads she could take to disappear. The topography could play to her advantage. Of course, that also depended heavily on the traffic.

The population of Atlanta had exploded over the last few decades, and a lack of decent public transportation had resulted in more cars on the roads. There were only a few hours in the day that you wouldn't encounter heavy traffic somewhere in the city.

Fortunately for Adriana—she hoped—this was one of those times.

She steered the car down the quiet residential street, peering out the windshield, looking for any sign of trouble. She also checked the rearview mirror every five or ten seconds to make sure she wasn't being followed by someone else, someone who wasn't with the authorities.

The car swooped through the rolling hills. Barren old oak trees dotted the huge lawns in front of lavish mansions, leaves long gone for the winter. The morning sun poked rays through the scraggly canopy above, sending darts of sunlight through Adriana's windows. Her eyes flinched at every beam. That didn't keep her from constantly checking her surroundings. At every turn, she expected to find a roadblock or checkpoint. As she continued out of the city, though, the way remained clear.

After fifteen minutes that felt more like a thousand, she found the interstate and merged into the moderate traffic going north. She knew the interstate would be free of roadblocks. Car chases happened, but it was exceedingly rare for the authorities to block off entire sections of interstates. And Interstate 75 was even less likely to play host to something like that. Being one of the most traveled roads in America, it was an essential thoroughfare between Michigan and South Florida and all points in between.

The only problem she might have would be stopping for gas. Cops would have received information on all the vehicles registered under Sean's name. That meant they'd be on the lookout for the car she was driving.

Luckily, she wouldn't be in it long. Adriana had a plan. She just had to make it a little farther north.

9

CARTERSVILLE, GEORGIA

Adriana arrived at the exit for Cartersville, a small town about thirty minutes north of Atlanta. She'd been there before to visit the Etowah Indian Mounds, a state park and historical landmark where many huge earthen mounds dotted the area.

It had once been an important place to the Cherokee Nation, a place of worship, trade, and government. Sean had spent a good amount of time there with Tommy. Many people didn't realize that underneath the earthen structures, immense pyramids had been constructed by the natives. While the Cherokee certainly occupied the area, including the fifty-four-acre property, they hadn't arrived until the nineteenth century. Most historians placed the construction of the temples and other buildings around the time of the Early Mississippian era, or 1000 AD.

There were some, however, who believed it to be even older. Sean was one of those people.

But Adriana wasn't there to visit the mounds. She merged onto the exit and turned right instead of left, driving away from the little city and toward the outskirts of town that rimmed dense forests and foothills leading toward the Blue Ridge Mountains.

She'd turned off her phone, knowing that every tower it pinged could lead the authorities straight to her. The entire drive north had been one filled with an overwhelming sense of concern bordering on paranoia, but she'd stayed focused. It was part of her nature now. It had been since she was a child, after her first year of training with the master.

Ninjas never let fear get the best of them. Instead, they used it, harnessed it, let it drive them to their goal with an unrelenting force. It fueled her and—more often than not—had saved her life.

She'd wanted to call ahead and give a heads-up that she was on the way, but Adriana knew that was too risky. Whoever was on the investigation—she imagined federal agents along with local and regional law enforcement—would trace the call. She could use her burner phone and had considered doing so but decided against that, too. While the cops wouldn't know about that particular device—no records, registration, or paper trail—she was fairly confident the people on the other end of the line would be monitored for calls from Sean or any of his associates. That list included his wife.

After passing some gas stations and fast food restaurants, the signs of civilization dwindled, and soon Adriana was surrounded by never-ending forests of pine, oak, maple, and poplar. With the leaves gone from most, she could see between the rows of tree trunks and spotted a few deer loitering near the edge of the road. There was a buck and two does, along with a younger fawn. The animals perked up at the sound of the passing car and then immediately darted away from the road, bounding into the woods to find safety.

Adriana allowed herself a moment to admire the beauty of nature and the fearful white-tailed deer before returning her focus to the road ahead and behind.

It took another fifteen minutes after leaving the interstate before she reached the long gravel driveway she'd visited on several occasions in the past.

There was a mailbox next to the driveway. The receptacle was surrounded by mountain stone, a common tactic for homeowners who both appreciated a more rustic design and also wanted to protect their mailboxes from mischievous vandals with baseball bats.

Adriana turned into the driveway and felt a hint of calm touch her senses as the sound of gravel crunching under her tires filled the sedan's cabin.

She drove slowly along the winding path, leaving any view of the road behind. Within twenty seconds she was deep into the forest. She steered the car around a bend in the road, and the outline of the cabin appeared between stands of trees. The vehicle emerged from the cover of the woods and rolled into the clearing that surrounded the modest home.

A thin trail of smoke trickled out of the chimney, a signal that at least one of the cabin's occupants was home.

That was a good sign. Adriana had hoped someone would be there. The last thing she wanted to do was have to break into a friend's house and steal a car, but she also knew they would understand if it came to that.

She pulled up close to the cabin, put the car in park, and turned off the engine with the press of a button.

Adriana stepped out of the sedan and was greeted by a cold blanket of wintry air. The smell of smoke drifted into her nostrils. She enjoyed the smell of campfire smoke or, in this case, smoke from the hearth within the cabin. It was a comforting scent, one that always caused her to relive some of the more enjoyable moments from her childhood when her mother and father would take her camping.

For the briefest of moments, Adriana was overcome by a sense of peace and comfort, even serenity. When she'd woken up this morning, everything was fine in her life. Now it was all turned upside down, and the only thing that had offered a sense of calm in the storm was the smell of campfire smoke. Funny how the little things in life are the most important.

Adriana walked toward the steps leading up to the wraparound porch. When she set her foot on the lowest step, the front door opened, and she was greeted by a familiar, welcoming face.

"Adriana? What are you doing out here?" Helen McElroy stood in the doorway with her arms folded against the cold of winter. Her face was tight, though she wore a smile. Her green eyes and pale, freckled skin were framed by auburn hair that dropped down around her ears to her shoulders.

Adriana skipped up the steps and reached the woman within seconds. "Mind if I come in? I'll tell you what's going on."

"Sure, honey. Come on in. I was just making some coffee."

Helen stood to the side so Adriana could pass and then stepped in to close the door, taking one wary look back out onto the driveway, perhaps a habit that had formed long ago.

She closed the door and motioned for Adriana to have a seat on the leather couch near the fire. "Get yourself warmed up, girl. You want some coffee?" Helen went to the kitchen to her right while Adriana found a seat on the sofa to the left.

The cabin was cozy, and the fire in the hearth was doing more than enough to keep it toasty warm. A quilt hung over the back of the sofa. The colors of the fabric mostly featured green, red, and white, all tributes to the upcoming Christmas holiday. The exposed logs that made up the walls gave the cabin a rugged feel, as did the smell of the fire and even the coffee in the kitchen. There was a lingering scent of sausage in the air, too, probably from a breakfast Helen had eaten not long before Adriana arrived.

"Where's Joe?" Adriana asked, striking up a little friendly conversation before she got into the nuts and bolts of why she had inexplicably shown up on Helen's doorstep unannounced.

"Oh, he's gone into town for some things. Groceries, mostly. They're saying we may get some snow tomorrow night, so we just want to make sure we have enough to get through the weekend. Although we don't usually get much snow here. Personally, I think he just wanted to get out of the house."

Adriana chuckled.

Helen walked around the counter separating the kitchen from the living room and sat down in one of the leather club chairs, a steaming cup of coffee held carefully in her right hand.

"So, hon, what brings you here? I woulda cleaned up a little if I'd known we were going to have company."

Adriana waved a dismissive hand and shook her head. "That is never necessary with me. You know that. And I'm terribly sorry to show up uninvited."

"You're always invited, sugar." Helen's sweet Southern accent melted any reservations Adriana might have still been clinging to.

"Thank you for that."

"Sure thing. So, what's going on?"

Adriana swallowed. She rubbed her palms on her knees and then began telling the story. She told Helen about how she'd managed to escape the house in Buckhead, how the cops had shown up, and what was being said about Sean in the news, she assumed, across the country.

Helen listened intently, taking intermittent sips of coffee now and then during the story. When Adriana was done, the calm look on the woman's face hadn't changed much.

"I don't watch the news much," Helen confessed. "So, I didn't know any of that was going on. Now it makes me think I should watch more often."

"Truthfully, I don't, either," Adriana admitted. "But I do check it now and then."

"It's a good thing you did, honey. You might be in an interrogation room right now. Do they think you had something to do with all this?"

"Probably," Adriana said.

"That is...if it's a legitimate investigation."

Adriana had had the same cynical thought, that everything going on with this entire kidnapping and subsequent manhunt was all just some kind of manufactured conspiracy to cover up something else, something much bigger. If that was the case, who was pulling the strings?

"I wondered about that," Adriana said.

Helen gave a slow nod. "You were right to. You and I both know

Sean wouldn't do something like this. He and Dawkins go way back. Dawkins trusts Sean completely."

"Some would say that was the president's mistake that led to what happened."

"Yeah, but that can't be it. Have you heard from Sean?"

Adriana shook her head. "No. I don't expect to, either. He's probably on the run."

"You don't think they caught him?"

"No. Not according to the reports. There's a nationwide search going on for him, which means he's still on the move. Where to I have no idea."

"Curious," Helen said. She thought about the dilemma for a few seconds. "If Sean didn't take the president, then who did? That's what you need to find out. If you can track down the people who really did take him, then maybe you can stop all this."

"That's the plan, but..." She hesitated.

"But what?"

"I need a vehicle. The one I drove here is Sean's, and the cops will be looking for it. I don't want to put you out, but I'm desperate and don't really have any other play here."

"Not a problem," Helen said. "We can hide Sean's car in the shop out back, and you can take my truck."

Her easy answer wasn't unexpected, but it was still generous nonetheless.

"Are you sure?" Adriana's tone was humble. "I don't want to be a pain."

"It's no pain at all, honey. You take whatever you need. You have a gun on you?"

Adriana shook her head. She wanted to slap her forehead with her hand. In her rush to get out of the house, she'd forgotten to grab one of her firearms, though she was fairly certain there might be one in Sean's vehicle.

"That would be great. I hope I don't need it, though, especially considering the circumstances."

Helen understood what she meant. Sean was being pursued by

government agents, cops, and who knew who else. Getting into a gunfight with any of them would not only be a bad idea; there was no way that could end well. There was, however, the possibility that the authorities weren't the only ones pursuing Sean, and in that case Adriana knew she might need a little firepower.

"A gun would be good. Maybe a hunting knife, too."

"You got it, sister. Let's get you fixed up."

Helen stood with coffee in hand and walked over to the coatrack near the door. She set down the mug on the corner of the dining table and grabbed one of the coats, stuck her arms through it, zipped it, and resumed drinking her morning beverage.

"You...could finish your coffee," Adriana offered. "I wasn't followed."

Helen squinted. "I figured you weren't followed, sugar. You're good like that. I don't mind taking the cup with me. Come on. I'll show you to the collection."

Adriana raised one eyebrow. *Collection?*

Helen saw the question in her guest's eye and flashed a sly grin. Then she motioned for Adriana to follow her and led the way past the kitchen and down the hall to a door in the back of the cabin. It opened up onto the other end of the wraparound porch. Behind the cabin were a couple of buildings. One was an old barn. The red paint had faded through the years, and the tin roof looked like it was in need of repairs decades ago. Huge, rusty holes punctured the metal roof; some were the size of a basketball. Others were smaller, maybe the diameter of a quarter. Adriana didn't see or hear any animals inside, but it looked like there was fresh straw flowing out of the side of the barn where a slot opened to feed horses.

Helen seemed like she might be a horse person. She was outdoorsy, adventurous, and had an appreciation for the old ways. She was also one that liked to be prepared, as was Joe, her husband.

The pair now worked for the IAA doing much the same kind of work that Sean and Tommy did: retrieving artifacts, hunting down missing relics, and occasionally getting into trouble.

Helen had been a government asset for many years, which—like

Sean—provided her with a wealth of talents that proved useful in the field. It was a secret her longtime husband hadn't even known about until one fateful night when a group of henchmen attacked their cabin.

Then Joe found out everything about his wife and her past.

Joe, or "Mac" as everyone called him, was no slouch when it came to survival skills or fighting his way out of a tough situation, but Helen was the real deal. Adriana couldn't help but wonder what the woman meant when she'd said "collection."

They walked across a crushed gravel path that cut through the green fescue in the backyard and veered to the right toward the second of the two buildings. The shop was a long garage with four bay doors on the front and a gray metal door on the left end closest to the path leading to the cabin. The building was painted white and featured the same tin roof as the barn, though it was in impeccable shape, the polar opposite of its sibling. There were no holes, no signs of oxidation anywhere. Maybe, Adriana figured, they were letting the barn stay like that for historic appeal?

Helen reached the door to the shop, withdrew a key from one of her pockets, inserted it, and opened the door. It swung open with a loud creak, the hinges protesting their rude awakening. Fluorescent lights flickered on automatically in the ceiling above, running all the way to the other end of the shop in two rows.

Two vehicles were parked inside. One was a Nissan Titan pickup, the other a GMC Yukon Denali. Both vehicles were black with dark window tinting.

Helen turned to her friend as she closed the door behind them. "You can have either one of those," she said.

"Thank you," Adriana said.

Helen motioned to the back corner at the opposite end of the long room. There was a corner with a black rail made from metal tubes. "Guns are over there."

"Over where?" Adriana looked but didn't see any weapons. The back wall was lined with shelves and racks full of tools and reference materials for working on various mechanical things. There were no guns.

"Follow me," Helen said, her tone laced with mischief.

The two women strode across the garage to the back wall and then pivoted, making their way along the gap between the parked trucks and the cinder blocks. The smell of rubber and oil filled the air, scents Adriana remembered from her dad's garage so many years ago. She fought off the memories, willing the thoughts from childhood to exile in the back of her mind. She had to stay focused.

They reached the railing, and Adriana saw it was shaped like the letter L. She also realized what Helen was talking about when she said the guns were over here. The rails wrapped around a somewhat hidden staircase. The metal-grated steps went down into a basement that might have otherwise gone unnoticed to someone not curious enough to check.

Helen grabbed the rail on the corner and whipped around to the stairs. Her feet moved rapidly as she deftly descended the steps.

Adriana followed, and when they reached the bottom they were greeted by another metal door. This one was newer. It was painted gray but looked to be fire rated, able to withstand high temperatures to keep safe whatever was on the other side.

An entry access panel was just to the right. Helen pressed in a five-digit code and stepped back. The keypad beeped, a green light flashed, and a heavy click came from within the doorframe a second before the door swung open automatically.

"Impressive," Adriana said, "although I half expected you to have a retinal scanner or a fingerprint reader."

Helen tugged on the door to open it faster. Lights blinked on in the room beyond. "We thought about it," Helen said. "But then if someone wanted to get in they could just cut out an eye or remove a thumb. Keypad information can't be cut out."

It was a macabre point, but one Adriana understood, especially considering the careful nature with which Helen approached so many things in life. The woman was prepared, but Adriana didn't know exactly how well prepared until she stepped into the next room.

The poured concrete walls were lined with gun racks, each filled with almost every assortment of weapon known to mankind. There were shotguns, pistols, katanas, grenades—both the smoke and explosive varieties—and a wide assortment of rifles and submachine guns.

Adriana's eyes were wide, like a child who'd just stepped into a candy store for the first time. A table in the center of the room had a vise block on it and parts for at least ten more weapons arranged neatly across the surface.

"Do you make these?" Adriana asked, her voice mirroring the wonder in her expression.

"Some of them," Helen said. "Joe and I find it somewhat calming. It also satisfies that need to make stuff."

Adriana nodded. "Sean enjoys the same thing, but not to this extent. Remind me not to let him see this place. He'll want one of his own."

"He might already have one that you don't know about," Helen said, her voice climbing to reflect the mischievousness of her statement.

"True. That's certainly possible." Adriana didn't act like it would bother her if Sean did have something like that back home. For now, it didn't matter anyway. She needed to get moving and had taken longer here than she planned.

Helen walked purposefully over to a rack on the left and picked up a black gear bag from the counter under a column of AK-47s. There were four AR-10s next to those.

"Let's get you all set up," Helen said in a cheery voice, as if she was putting together a bag of toys from a theme park gift shop. "Then you can get a move on. Based on what you told me, you need to get going soon. Where do you think you'll go?"

Adriana's head turned from side to side. "I don't know, but I need to figure out what's going on. Maybe then I can get the truth out there and clear Sean's name."

"What about him? Do you have any idea where he might have gone?"

Adriana shook her head. "No. And right now there's no way to find out. I'll have to do what I can from here, at least for now."

Helen nodded. "Let's get you set up, then."

10

BARING, WASHINGTON

John Dawkins sat on the thin cot in the corner of the basement. There were two fluorescent lights fixed into the drop-down ceiling. The floor was bare concrete and cold to the touch. Fortunately, he had socks and shoes on, but they were the same ones he'd worn since the day he was abducted. His clothes felt dingy and grimy. They were soiled in spots from dirt or grease or some other substance he'd been forced to lie in or sit in during his abduction and subsequent imprisonment. The tiny room smelled of dry dirt, which was a strange blessing in a way. He'd rather it be dry down here than damp. That would make things more difficult, especially if his captivity turned out to be prolonged in any way. The fact that it was perpetually chilly down here didn't help, but it could have been worse.

The men who'd taken him had provided little in the way of food, water, and accommodations. The cot was an old military surplus variety, made from green canvas and aluminum rods. The thing creaked every time he rolled over in the night, rousing him from his tenuous slumber. It wouldn't have made a difference if the cot was the quietest one ever made. Dawkins barely slept, though the night before he'd finally found some semblance of rest, at least for three or four hours.

Sheer exhaustion had taken him then, snatching him in its claws and pulling him down into dreamy darkness until a sound at the door had roused him.

It was one of the guards bringing him the meager breakfast of oatmeal and toast he'd had every morning since arriving.

The slop wasn't much in the way of taste, but it was better than nothing, and the humble meals had helped keep Dawkins alive.

He looked around the room for what must have been the thousandth time. The basement was, for all intents and purposes, in the bottom of a home, though he couldn't be sure. It looked like some unfinished basements he'd seen before when shopping for a house. The frames for most of the rooms were still exposed. The electrical wiring had been done, connected to outlets and switches along the walls in multiple locations, but only the room where Dawkins was being held had drywall covering the studs, headers, and runners. There was a barred door and matching wall fixed into the entrance to his cell. It reminded him of old spaghetti western jail cells used by movie companies in the 1960s.

Of course, he'd fiddled with the lock a couple of times, even jiggled the door when no one was around. There were no guards down here with him, but there was also no other way out except up the stairs. There were no windows, just a few vents in the wall, but those were too small for him to fit through; although Dawkins had most certainly considered that option.

He sighed as he reflected on his situation. He wasn't so concerned for himself and his personal safety, but he knew that somewhere out there, Emily was worried sick and would be doing everything in her formidable power to find out where he was and who had done this.

He'd been on a jet for nearly five hours. That could put him in a number of different locations, though he was able to eliminate several of those thanks to his perceptive senses.

The bitter cold that hit his skin when he was taken from the plane told him he was farther north than he had been, but there was a certain element of humidity to the air that eliminated the Rocky Mountains as a possibility. Then there was the scent of coniferous trees when he was removed from the vehicle after a drive of over an hour. He'd been moved to a forest somewhere, and because of the heavy smell of fir, pine, and spruce, he figured he'd been taken somewhere in the Pacific Northwest. He ruled out Canada because that would just make things complicated for the kidnappers. That meant Dawkins was likely in one of only three or four places.

He could be somewhere in Oregon, Washington, or possibly Northern California, though he doubted the latter due to the drive time after their flight.

None of that helped, of course. Knowing where he was only solved a minor part of the former president's problem.

The door at the base of the stairs clicked and then swung open. A man appeared in the doorway with another standing behind him. Dawkins recognized the one in the lead. He was in charge of this operation, the guy calling the shots, but Dawkins had the distinct impression that this man was taking orders from someone else.

"Wait out here," the younger man said. The guard closed the door to the stairs behind him as he shrugged the submachine gun tighter onto his shoulder.

The leader stepped deeper into the basement and meandered over to a wooden chair he'd placed there on an earlier visit. He sat down, crossed one leg over the other, and folded his hands in his lap, lacing the fingers together tightly.

"What?" Dawkins asked, still sitting on the edge of the cot. His voice was as cold as the temperature outside and harder than the concrete floor.

"I just thought I'd pay our little VIP a visit."

"Appears you don't know how to treat an important guest."

"Well, maybe you're not *that* important."

Dawkins forced a chuckle and nodded absently, returning his gaze to the floor.

"But you're important to my employer, and that's what matters. Personally, I couldn't care less about you. If my boss told me to turn you loose right now, I would have zero issue doing that."

"Then why don't you?" Dawkins asked, though he already knew the reason.

"You know why, Mr. President. You've seen my face."

"And signed my death sentence."

"That's right, but it's not my sentence."

"You already alluded to that."

The younger man shrugged. "Seeing how you're never going to get out of this alive, I may as well introduce myself. My name is Andrew Boyd."

"I don't care." Salt filled Dawkins's voice.

"I know." Boyd took a long breath. "Of course, you probably wonder what I'm getting out of all this. If I don't care, why am I holding you here? It's simple, really."

"I actually wasn't wondering anything about you."

"That's okay. I'll tell you anyway. You see, my employer wants something very powerful, something that you would never have let him have."

That was a strange thing to say. Dawkins didn't know what that meant, but he also didn't have time to ask.

"Me, on the other hand, I'm just after good old-fashioned revenge."

"Oh really?" Dawkins didn't hide the sarcasm in his voice.

"Yes, indeed. And it's interesting that you are the link to bring me what I want and get my generous employer what he wants."

"Which is?"

"Honestly, I don't have a clue what that old guy wants. I don't even think he knows what it is. That's why he's using Sean to find it. You're just the carrot in front of the mule to get him to do his job."

Dawkins thought hard, then it hit him. "You want revenge on Sean?"

"Bingo," Boyd raised one finger and pretended to fire a gun with the thumb hammer dropping to mock-shoot his captive.

"What did Sean ever—"

"Ever do to me? Great question. See, I was in the military, Mr. President. I served our nation, your nation, selflessly and with pride.

Then your friend Sean Wyatt took that all away from me one day. Thought I was doing things unethically. I was court-martialed, thrown out of the military I'd served so honorably. All because of him."

"I'm sorry to hear that."

"Save it."

"Thank you for your service," the president goaded.

"I said save it."

"Obviously, you must have done something pretty wrong for Sean to come after you. He doesn't take out good guys."

Boyd shot out of his chair, fury flaming in his eyes.

"Sean Wyatt is no angel, Mr. President, and when I'm done with him, no one will remember his name. He's falling right into our trap. And when he does, I'm going to let you watch him die. Just thought I'd let you know."

Boyd stalked to the door, flung it open, and disappeared up the stairs.

"That was a bratty thing to do," he muttered under his breath. The little cuss sure enjoyed hearing the sound of his own voice. Dawkins wondered if Boyd was just trying to get a rise out of him. Maybe the whole monologue about getting revenge on Sean was somehow cathartic for the guy.

He'd considered threatening Boyd, but Dawkins knew that wouldn't work. And it wouldn't prove anything. If you were dumb enough to kidnap a former president, you had most likely run through most of the scenarios and understood the imminent danger in doing so.

His thoughts gravitated back to Emily. He hoped she was okay. While Dawkins knew that the entirety of the government's resources had been focused on finding him, he knew the chance for a favorable outcome was bleak at best.

Dawkins exhaled and looked down at the floor again. He'd set his expectations low for how all this would turn out, but now it seemed like things were only getting worse. He just hoped Emily wouldn't be devastated.

11

ST. LOUIS, MISSOURI

Sean drove all day and into the night until he reached Saint Louis. It was one o'clock in the morning when he stopped at a tiny motel just on the western side of the city. He had no intention of staying on the eastern side of the river. It was renowned across the country for its high crime, which meant there would likely be a lot of law enforcement over there, as well. The last thing he needed was to be hanging around a bunch of cops. While he doubted they'd received any sort of APB yet on what was surely being called a fugitive situation, it wouldn't be long before his name and image will be in the hands of every officer on the force.

He'd been careful on his drive up through North Georgia, Tennessee, Kentucky, and southern Illinois. The farther away from Atlanta he drove, the better he felt in some ways and the worse he felt in others.

On the north side of Atlanta, just out of the city, he'd tossed his phone out the truck's window as he crossed Lake Allatoona. The biting cold ripped through his skin for the few seconds he'd had the window open. It was unseasonably chilly in the south, and he was happy to get the window back up as fast as possible. Later on that night, as he drove through Paducah and then Illinois, he'd forced himself to lower the window a few times just to stay awake. The cold air sent a shock through his body every time and woke him up, only to be ravaged by fatigue twenty minutes later.

By midnight, he was ready to stop somewhere and get some rest, but he wanted to clear Saint Louis first. His plan was to drive through Kansas City the next morning and go all the way to Rapid City, South Dakota, by the next night. He'd considered going a little farther and trying to reach Sturgis, but it would depend on how the drive went. Many of the Midwestern states and the mountain states beyond were already getting pounded by snow. That would make travel slow.

He'd made the drive before, cutting up through South Dakota, Wyoming, and then Montana all the way through Idaho, but that was in the summer when there wasn't a trace of snow on the ground. Now there would be tons of it. Some of the roads would likely be closed, and he would probably have to figure out some alternate routes to reach his destination.

The cabin was located between Columbia Falls, Montana, and the Canadian border, though the road didn't provide access to the country to the north. It went right up to it and then came to a stop, at least that's the way it was the last time Sean was there.

The place was completely off the grid. He'd paid for the property without using any banks, any lenders, and without much of the paperwork that came along with mortgages. A friend had helped him with the build during one long summer. They'd paid for the materials in cash and built it with their own hands. In doing so, Sean had installed a few additional features that would have caused a normal contractor to raise an eyebrow. The solar panels he'd installed in the clearing near the cabin provided power year-round, save for when he had to clear off the snow or when the days were cloudy, which wasn't too often. For those times, he'd invested in a new kind of technology that used large heat sinks to provide thermoelectric power.

Of course, he could always use candles for light if he needed to. Sean was accustomed to roughing it. He'd been in Third World countries with little more than the clothes on his back and a canteen. There'd been hard nights in Central and South America. He'd been hot and sweaty, barely able to sleep during those missions. Driving through the cold of Illinois and Missouri, he contemplated those hot nights with a fondness he'd never had before.

Sean opened the door to his motel room and stepped inside, poking his head out one last time to make sure no one was watching or that he'd been followed. Then he closed the door and set his pack on the chair near the window.

The room was unimpressive. The single queen bed in the middle featured a light green comforter with white sheets. The brown wallpaper with white stripes was peeling in a few places. As Sean looked down at the bottom of the door, he could see light coming in through the opening between the threshold and the door's edge. He almost didn't want to see the bathroom, but he needed a quick shower.

He walked through the diminutive bedroom area and stopped at the sink. The bathroom was to his left, the shower, tub, and toilet separated from the wash basin by a narrow door hung flimsily on its hinges. He wondered if it would fall off and if he'd be responsible for the damages, but he shook off the thought and stepped into the bathroom, electing not to close the door just in case. Besides, there was no need for privacy since he was alone.

Sean had stopped at a twenty-four-hour drug store a few minutes before arriving at the motel. He'd avoided the news on his satellite radio, instead choosing to have a blissfully ignorant trip across country, but knew the net would probably be expanding. Cops and federal agents all over the nation would be looking for him. That meant he'd need to change his appearance.

As luck would have it, he'd started growing his beard the week before in preparation for winter. It was also something he did in the depths of hockey season as had been his tradition since college.

He set down the bag from the drug store on top of the toilet's water closet and pulled out the hair dye he'd purchased. He stared at the box with disdain and shook his head.

Sean thought—for what felt like the millionth time in the last decade—he'd left this cloak-and-dagger life behind. He sighed and set the container down on the edge of the tub, took off his shirt and pants, and then picked it up again. He squeezed some of the liquid into his left hand, put the tube back down again, and then started massaging the dye into his hair.

He walked back into the sink area and looked over at the door. His senses were on full alert. They had been since the call he'd received from Emily.

Sean knew that at any moment there could be a knock at the door followed by the bang of a battering ram. No sense in worrying about it. He looked to his past and his studies in psychology to alleviate the anxiety. Worrying, he told himself, never fixed anything. It simply occupied the mind with one more thing when it could have been used to solve problems or come up with more efficient, helpful thoughts.

Worry, he figured, was humanity's default setting.

He let the dye soak another few minutes and then turned on the shower, let it warm up to a reasonable temperature, and stepped in.

Once he'd washed the dye out of his hair and gone through the rest of his usual routine, he turned off the water and got out, dried off, and put on a T-shirt and jeans.

Sean preferred to sleep in his boxers and T-shirt, but in this instance, he was going to have to sleep fully clothed. Should the need arise, he'd have to be ready to hit the road in seconds.

He grabbed his Springfield XD .40-cal from the tactical bag on the chair and rechecked the magazine.

His eyes were getting droopy, pulled by the dense core of the earth as he grew more and more tired. Falling asleep wouldn't be a problem. Staying asleep might be.

He walked over to the bed, set the pistol on the nightstand, and crawled under the covers.

Sean didn't open his eyes again until five o'clock local time. He'd slept like the dead for the last three hours or so, but something had roused him. Through the crack in the drapes, he could see it was still pitch dark outside. He sat up and scanned the room, lit by the pale glow of the moon shining through the window.

It was empty, save for the cheap furnishings and television on the dresser. He'd heard something, though; he was sure of it.

Then the sound came again. It was a click, like someone was messing with the door, trying to unlock it.

His right hand moved to the pistol on the nightstand. Sean knew if it was a cop or a Fed that he couldn't kill them. That would put him straight into a max security prison and, most likely, on death row. If it even got that far. Clearly, someone wanted him dead or arrested. He thought back to the voice of the man on the video and the things he'd said.

The guy claimed Sean had taken everything from him. For the entire length of the drive between Atlanta and Saint Louis, Sean had pondered that very issue. He couldn't narrow down the list of candidates enough to come to a definitive conclusion. He'd made so many enemies over the years, it could be any of two or three dozen people, maybe more, who wanted his head.

This guy, however, was different. Sean could apparently find something he wanted, a treasure or relic, perhaps. But he was willing to sacrifice losing any chance at that by framing Sean for the abduction of former president John Dawkins, which meant whatever secret Sean had to find to save Dawkins was superfluous.

Did that mean if Sean failed the kidnapper would release Dawkins?

Sean doubted it. If the former president had seen the faces of his captors, even heard their real voices, it was probably going to be curtains for Dawkins. Sean knew that was likely going to be the case even if he delivered the artifact, or whatever it was he had to find. There was only one reason to try to find whatever it was they wanted. If he could locate this mystery and deliver the goods, perhaps he could find a way to free his friend. That was a long way off, though, and he was already down one day.

The sound at the door startled him from his dreamlike thoughts, and he swung his legs around the edge of the bed and planted his feet on the floor. In the blink of an eye, Sean whipped around the bed and stood against the door, right shoulder nearly touching it, with his weapon held up close to his face. If anyone tried to come through, he'd be ready.

Another sound came from the door's exterior, this time sounding more like a scratching noise, like claws on metal.

Sean frowned and shuffled a few inches away. He glanced down at the bottom of the door and noted the shadow outlined by the light beyond through the narrow gap. That wasn't a human shadow. He was sure of it.

So, what was it?

He gripped his pistol with his right hand and then unlatched the door chain and unlocked the deadbolt. Still ready for an attack by an intruder, he grabbed the doorknob, twisted it, and yanked it open, leveling his weapon at the same time in case he had to blast someone in the chest.

There was nothing there.

His eyes and weapon dropped simultaneously to the ground where he found, to his surprise, the source of the shadow he'd seen a minute before, as well as the sound at the door. A raccoon looked up at him with surprise in its eyes. The creature chirped and then scurried away into the darkness at the end of the building before disappearing around the corner.

Sean shook his head and took a few deep breaths to calm his nerves.

He closed the door after stepping back into the room and shook off the cold. It was freezing out there, and he knew that the journey ahead was only going to get more treacherous. He looked over at the bed and sighed. No chance he was going to fall asleep again, not after the raccoon incident.

The good news was he'd get an early start, one he probably needed anyway. The bad news was he was still tired.

He was about to collect his things and head out to the car when another thought occurred to him. All this time, he had been so intent on getting out of town and trying to evade police that he forgot to analyze the Madison letter.

He exhaled through his nose and stepped over to his bag, pulled it out of the secondary compartment, and plopped back into bed. He flipped the switch on the lamp next to him—half expecting it to not work—and rested his head against the headboard while holding the letter in both hands over his lap.

The yellowish light cast an eerie glow onto the paper as he began reading.

Captain Lewis forged a path across this great nation, a mirrored birth to the intrepid and strong. Not far from where life began, a mere hundred paces from the northwestern corner, the serpent guards the gateway to the secret the late captain stowed away.

Sean paused and considered the paragraph. Nothing jumped out at him in the cryptic text save for the part about the secret the captain hid.

Mirrored birth? Hundred paces from a corner? A serpent? He let out a long exhale through his nose and ran both hands through his now dark brown hair.

Sean went on to the next paragraph.

Where disappointment dwelt in the hearts of the men, a second piece leads the way to what he feared. Find it near the serpent's head, beneath a stone misplaced long ago, and you will be one step from what took the fabled city of Plato.

Without the clue from the first location, he couldn't possibly know where to look for the next. Or could he? That part remained unclear.

The last portion of that paragraph, however, gave Sean chills that shot from the top of his head, down through his arms and legs, all the way to his toes. The fabled city of Plato? Surely, that couldn't be right. Could it? Was James Madison actually talking about—dare Sean think it—Atlantis?

There'd been countless oral traditions handed down through generations regarding the mythical Greek city that had vanished so long ago, supposedly under the surface of the ocean. In modern times, a flood of books, movies, and television shows had been dedicated to dissecting whether the fabled city had ever truly existed. Now Sean was reading a letter from an American president, a man regarded as intelligent in almost every way, yet here he was making a reference to a place often considered apocryphal by most historians.

Was there another city Plato mentioned that was more mysterious than Atlantis? If there was, Sean couldn't think of it, at least not one nearly as prominent as the Atlantis story.

He read the next paragraph, which also appeared to be part of the mysterious riddle.

At last, our journey ends, across the river to the southwest of the final camp, the secret is buried there within a dark chamber, put there long ago by an ancient people.

The power hidden there must only be used in the most desperate of times, for the destruction it brings is immeasurable and it cannot be controlled, for the ocean is something that can only be unleashed, not tamed. I pray those times never come. If they do, it could be the end of all things, including our young nation.

This is the reason for our precaution, our vigilance against such mystical and relentless threats. The ring of three has been spread across the land, and only one with wits, courage, and a humble heart should take the challenge. For if you complete this journey, death awaits for many.

The last paragraph was intriguing. There was absolutely no way to know where it was talking about, which meant Sean would have to stick to his original plan. Sort of.

He'd planned on heading out to Montana, both to do his research and to lie low, but now he wasn't so sure.

This first paragraph suggested a detour, but what was the exact location it was specifying?

"A mirrored birth," Sean muttered. "What does that mean? A mirrored birth?" He pulled out his burner phone and opened the Google app. He typed in the words and waited a few seconds for the results. When the page finally populated, he discovered a multitude of medical descriptions, products, and discussions, but nothing he thought would help him.

He clicked over to page two of the search results, something he almost never did, but found nothing useful there, either.

"What in the world is a mirrored birth?" he whispered.

He wished Tommy was there with him. Not to mention Adriana. He'd had to relay through Tommy what was going on. Sean knew his friend would let his wife know what happened, but that did little to comfort him. She was an oak for him, someone he could lean on when things got tough. Tommy was, too, but they weren't here at the moment. He was on his own. Sean also knew that it was still too early in the morning for a phone call.

He figured he could call them in an hour or so. He was on central time at the moment, so the east coast was an hour ahead. Yes, he could call in an hour, while he was on the road. And the sooner he got going, the better.

But where?

That problem lingered. He could take off toward Kansas City. By the time he was past Columbia, he could call Tommy and the others to see what they thought. West was certainly the right direction, for now.

12

Sean stared at the road ahead. The horizon was still dark in the distance, barely hinting at dawn, with a dim illumination from the sun rising to his back in the east. Sean glanced into the rearview mirror and noted the brightening sky behind him, though the sun still hadn't come into view. The cloudy sky ahead, too, would blot it out.

He'd checked the forecast on one of his weather apps, and it looked like there was only a 25 percent chance of precipitation. Odds were it was going to rain, but that could change on a whim out here.

Weather in Missouri was unpredictable at best, and the closer he got to the Kansas border, that unreliability only increased. Cold air blew down into the prairies and plains from the Rocky Mountains, chilling the air to the east for hundreds, if not thousands, of miles.

He glanced at the clock as he passed the signs marking the exit for the University of Missouri. Close enough.

He picked up his phone and tapped Call on the number he'd entered before leaving the motel earlier that morning.

The device began ringing and he hooked his headphones into his ears, choosing not to use the SUV's system. He recalled a case from a few years ago where someone was located using that very method. He imagined they had even better means of tracking people now.

"Hello?" Tommy answered in a groggy voice that signaled he'd just woken up.

"It's me."

"Hey S—" He caught himself and stopped. "Hey, buddy. How are you?"

"Still alive and still on the road," Sean said. "I needed to talk to you about the clue from Madison's letter."

"Which one? Seems like there are three."

"The first one. Doesn't look like we can work on the other two until we know the location of the first."

"Yeah, we came to the same conclusion. Seems like Madison or Lewis or whoever...left something for us to find that will fill us in on the next spot."

Sean laughed.

"What?" Tommy wondered, his voice growing steadier as he continued waking up.

"Nothing. Just the way you said it. That's all."

"Said what?"

"That they left it for us to find, as in no one else was supposed to locate it."

Tommy chuckled. "Oh, right. Yeah, anyway, it's an interesting riddle, to say the least. One of the tougher ones we've encountered. And there doesn't seem to be a code or cipher involved."

"It's starting to sound like you don't have any ideas as to where it could lead."

"Well..." Tommy paused for a second, which concern spiraling through Sean's head. "I mean, we don't have an exact location, per se."

"So, you got nothing."

"Not nothing. It's just that we're not 100 percent. Do you have some thoughts on it?"

"I did a few searches on the mirrored birth thing but came up with zilch. Most of it was medical stuff or products for new moms."

"Yeah, we got the same. Alex had a thought, though. Might be worth considering."

"I'm all ears at this point."

"He said that maybe the first paragraph has a dual meaning. So, Madison mentioned the great nation and then the birth thing. That leads you to think that he's talking about the birth of the nation. You know, the Louisiana Purchase more than doubled our size or whatever and essentially got the whole Manifest Destiny thing rolling."

"I thought the same. Continue."

Tommy yawned.

Sean imagined him stretching his arms up high over his head.

"Yeah, well, what if it's not just that. While our country is strong and intrepid, as the riddle suggests, the word *mirrored* gives the impression that it's referring to two births, not just the birth of the country."

"Right, but what other birth would it be talking about?"

He guided the SUV into the left lane and passed an 18-wheeler that was rumbling slowly along on the right. When he was by the truck, he merged back over and glanced into his rearview mirror. It was still early, and there weren't many vehicles on the road, mostly truckers who were eager to get their loads to their destinations on time. Very few travelers were out at this time, and the few that were, likely had the ski slopes beyond Denver in their sights.

"Well, it's interesting. See, Sacagawea gave birth just before the Corps of Discovery mission began their westward journey."

"Yes, that's true. She was not only a brave and amazing woman, willing to endure the hardships and all the challenges the wilderness could throw at her, but she did it with an infant."

"Right. So, her child, Jean-Baptiste Toussaint, was born in North Dakota at Fort Mandan, the place where they started heading west."

A chill shot through Sean's body. His heartbeat picked up, and his breathing quickened. "That's it," he said.

"Well, we're working on a few other possibilities, but yeah, that might be a good place to start."

"Yeah. Yeah, do that," Sean said. "But I think you got it. Why didn't I think of that before?"

"Because...you're on the run?"

"Yeah, tell me about it."

A silent pause came over the phone for a moment. Tommy wasn't dumb enough to ask his friend where he was. If his phone had been tapped, they would zero in on Sean's location. That could still happen, but calling from a burner phone gave him a fighting chance.

"How...how did..." His voice cut off, catching in his throat.

"She took it fine. She knows where you'll be."

"You told her not to come out there, right?"

"Yeah, but you know her."

Sean's lips cracked, and he nodded. "Yes, I do."

"We're going to figure this out, buddy," Tommy said, trying to encourage his friend.

"How'd it go with the people that came to see you?" It was a question that had been on Sean's mind since he left Atlanta. The Feds that stormed the building, so to speak, could have done something nefarious to his friends, especially if those agents were less legitimate than they represented. The fact he was talking to Tommy at this very moment meant that nothing bad had happened. Sean didn't voice his relief, but he definitely felt it.

"They had all the right credentials, said all the right things. They're legit," Tommy said. "From the way they spoke, it sounds like they really believe you did it."

"That means there's someone higher up the chain of command pulling the strings."

"But who? Who would you have ticked off in the government that would go to such lengths?"

Sean didn't have the answer for that question. He'd been considering it, though, and had a few ideas. During his time in the government, he'd been careful not to step on any toes. Even so, that happened from time to time whether he wanted to or not. With a juggernaut as large as the American government, it was impossible not to tick someone off every now and then, no matter how careful you were. Sean had likely made a few enemies, but none that jumped right out at the moment.

Then there was the other possibility.

He had no evidence to support his other theory, but the fact that he couldn't recall upsetting someone high up in the rankings made him think there was at least a little validity to it.

"I may not have upset anyone high up," Sean said. "It's possible that whoever is behind all this is simply using the guy in the video to get what he wants. Then there's a win-win for them. The puppet master gets his. The guy who hates me gets what he's after."

"And they all lived happily ever after," Tommy finished.

"Right. Except us and our friend President Dawkins." He turned on his blinker and weaved around a minivan with six stickers on the back displaying their family unit: the husband, wife, two kids, and a cat and dog. "Did President McCarthy say anything about the situation?"

"She did. She said the nation is praying for John and doing everything they can to find him and bring the perpetrators to justice. I'm sure they've increased security around her and the other former presidents to make certain this doesn't happen again."

Sean knew it wasn't necessary to increase McCarthy's security detail. She'd have plenty anyway. For the other former presidents, though, it was probably a good idea. They were almost never a target for something like this, but they had their own security people on hand all the time just in case. A few upgrades here and there wouldn't hurt. Sean knew, though, that John was the only president that would be targeted. He wasn't friends with the other former leaders, and the man from the video had been very clear that the entire purpose of this ruse was to get back at Sean. Now it seemed there was more than one person involved, potentially a very powerful person.

"I gotta hang up," Sean said. "Will check in when I arrive."

"How much longer you think it will take?"

"Not sure. Depends on the weather. If I find anything there, I'll let you know."

"Okay, buddy. Be careful."

"Thanks, Mom. I mean Schultzie."

"Hilarious."

Sean ended the call, then took a deep breath and sighed. What in the world was going on?

He gripped the steering wheel and focused on the long stretch of road ahead. Next stop, Kansas City. Then on to North Dakota to see if Meriwether Lewis had left anything there that could help him with his mission.

His life and the life of his friend John Dawkins hung in the balance.

13

CHATTANOOGA

A driana waited patiently as the phone rang once, twice, three times. For a moment, she wondered if the man on the other end would pick up. It was fifty-fifty whether that would happen or not. He'd lived in the world of intelligence and espionage for a long time. That lifetime of experience made him paranoid, cautious, and meticulous.

She sat in her car along a backcountry road in southeastern Tennessee. She'd spotted the gravel driveway that was chained off at the entrance to an empty pasture. There was a for sale sign there, so she knew that no one would be coming around anytime soon—unless there was a buyer out visiting properties in the cold.

She'd spent the night in a cheap hotel, using cash to pay for the room and using one of her false identities to make sure the transaction couldn't be traced in any possible way.

Before going to bed the night before, she'd stopped by a drug store and picked up some essentials, one of which was hair coloring. She'd gone with a bright, almost platinum-blonde shade. She hoped Sean wouldn't mind the temporary change as much as she did, but then again, it didn't matter. She had to do whatever it took to survive.

Now that her face was about to be, in all probability, splashed across the media, she'd need to have a new look.

It wasn't the first time Adriana had gone through an identity change. She'd done it numerous times in the past whenever she needed to avoid unwanted attention.

The phone rang one more time before something clicked in the speaker.

"Hello, Hija." The man issued the greeting she'd heard nearly every time she called. It was endearing, gentle, welcoming. Whenever she heard him say that, Adriana found every worry in her heart seemed to melt away.

"Hello, Daddy," she said.

"It's been a while."

"It hasn't been that long, Papa. You were at the wedding."

"True, but for a father, even a few minutes is a long time to go without hearing from his little girl."

She cracked a smile. Diego Villa was a smooth talker, but he was never insincere. He truly was a romantic, in every conceivable way. That passion carried over to the love he held so deeply for his daughter. She was everything to him, and he never let her think otherwise.

He'd been forced to go into hiding long ago. Assisting the United States government had its perks, but it also made enemies, the kinds of enemies that didn't play by the rules. If they found him, they would execute him in a way that would be horrifically painful.

Fortunately, he had enough money from their family business back in Spain, and also the wealth he'd accumulated working for the United States. He'd never been on the books with the Americans, not officially, but they were the ones buttering his bread, and the butter they used was very expensive.

He'd been in hiding in Ecuador for many years now and had set up a comfortable life there, albeit an incognito one. Diego, however, wasn't a man of luxurious tastes. He was able to live modestly without drawing attention to himself with lavish things or extravagant spending.

That fact alone had probably saved his life.

He'd risked making the journey to the States when Adriana married Sean earlier in the year. He was one of only a handful of people who even knew about the wedding since they'd chosen to elope. That and the fact neither Sean nor Adriana had many friends were the major contributors to their decision to have a small wedding.

Diego didn't care if it put him on the map of the cartels, of terrorists, or of anyone else. Nothing could keep him from his daughter's wedding day.

"To what do I owe this...unexpected call, my darling?" His voice was smooth, the accent smoother than the flat side of a knife. She'd seen the sharp edge on more than one occasion growing up, but it was that edge that had made her sharper, as well.

"I need a favor."

She sat there for a moment and let the words sink in.

"A favor?" He let out a soft laugh. "That doesn't happen often, you asking me for help. Are you in some kind of trouble?"

"I assume you saw what is being said about Sean and the abduction of John Dawkins, the former president."

"I have."

"I need to know who did this, Papa. Sean didn't kidnap the president."

There was a long sigh on the other end of the line. Adriana pictured her father rubbing his temples with a thumb and index finger.

"That, my dear, will be difficult."

"You excel at difficult."

He laughed softly. "My sweet girl, even I have limitations."

Adriana felt her heart sink into her gut.

"But I may be able to help." He stopped to consider the problem. "I know a man. This man is very difficult to find."

"Difficult to find is right up my alley."

"I thought you might say that. I'm glad I raised a girl who is ready for a challenge."

She imagined him smiling with pride in some dark room in his little apartment, probably sitting in a worn leather chair in the corner.

"His name is Tyler Lawson. He works with the CIA."

Adriana noted the way he phrased the man's employment status. "You said works with. Not for?"

"You think I'm the only one who does side jobs for them?" There was mischief sprinkled in his voice.

She'd often wondered how many people were out there in the world, doing the same kinds of things her father had done for the Americans. That always brought up more questions, questions that probably didn't need to be answered. What other countries paid for those kinds of skills? And were any of the contractors working for both sides—playing the middle as it were? It would be easy for a person with information from one side to sell it to the other, especially if the paying party was behind the times. There were many Middle Eastern groups who were happy to pay for out-of-date information simply because they were unaware it wasn't current. Her father had told her about that once, and Adriana had wondered if he'd done it himself, but only for a second.

Diego was a good man, not given to the persistent temptations of material wealth. He would never betray his morals and his loyalties for something as trivial as money, or anything else for that matter.

If Tyler Lawson was a contractor like Diego, he'd be lying low; if he was smart. There were any number of foreign entities that were always hunting down intelligence contractors. And those were just the state actors. There could be dozens of other groups, such as terrorists, cartels, and organized crime syndicates on the hunt, as well.

"No, Father. I know you're not the only one. How do I find this Tyler Lawson?"

"Oh, you can find him...with some effort. He's one of the more brash contractors I've ever come across. Flaunts his money like a banner flapping over him at all times. My guess is he believes his false identities and highly paid security teams will keep him safe, but those things will only work for so long. All it takes is one good hound to figure out what he does, and his name and face will be plastered all over the dark web. Once that happens..." His voice trailed off.

Adriana could fill in the gap after that.

The dark web was a seething place of unholiness, the likes of which most mortals didn't dare investigate. There were things there that should never be seen, much less done. It was the darkest pit on the face of the earth, which made it the perfect location to find a hit man or hire a squad to take out a target.

If Tyler Lawson was careless, sooner or later his face would end up there right next to his address—a big payday for the first one to pull the trigger.

"I'm sending his details to you now," Diego said. "They'll appear in your inbox shortly."

The two of them shared an encrypted email service that allowed them to send direct messages back and forth. These messages and accounts were impossible to access by anyone else, using the most powerful technology available at the time, though now and then they would upgrade the security measures just to be extra safe. Diego once told her that it would take a dozen of the world's best AI-driven computers, along with a dozen of the best hackers, to even get close to cracking their software.

"Be careful when you find him," Diego warned. "You can use my name. He knows me. I'm pretty sure he trusts me, too, though that is difficult to do in my line of work. Tell him you are Diego's daughter, and he might let you in."

"And if he doesn't?"

There was a snicker in the earpiece. "Well then, you'll have to do what you do best."

14

ANNAPOLIS, MARYLAND

Admiral Forrest Winters sat behind his desk and watched the news on the flatscreen hanging in the corner near the door. The anchors had been talking about the disappearance of former president John Dawkins for the entire morning. Speculation was running rampant, and apparently, the authorities had no leads. Nor would they.

Winters had taken the greatest of care in orchestrating this campaign. He knew he'd have to be careful—after all, he had everything to lose.

He'd been in the navy most of his adult life, joining when he turned nineteen the summer after finishing high school. He'd gone back to college after his initial enlistment, earned a degree, and then returned to the service, rising through the officer ranks quickly—due in no small part to that college degree.

As the years went by, Winters grew to love the navy. When he'd first signed up, it was a matter of trying to avoid being deployed to Vietnam with the rest of the ground forces. Joining the navy had been his way of ensuring he'd be in what he believed to be the safest place during the conflict.

Now, it was his passion, his true love. He believed strongly in the

United States Navy and knew that it was much more than just boats, big guns, submarines, missiles, and planes. It was about the men and women who served both on land and sea and about the standards they upheld in the world, standards that had fallen off sharply over the years as the world plunged further into disarray.

Then there were the threats. They'd always been there, lurking in the shadows. First, it had been the communists. The Cold War was in full swing when Winters joined up. It churned and boiled until 1989 when communism began to collapse. When Russia was no longer a threat, at least not directly, the military's efforts turned to North Korea and China. Cuba was close by but not a real concern. Castro was broke, as was the tiny island nation. While they may have had access to weapons that could threaten the American mainland, Cuba was small enough to manage.

North Korea and China, however, were another story.

Winters wasn't stupid. He knew that, for all the chatter and all the huff and puff, China and the United States needed each other from an economics standpoint. One couldn't attack the other because doing so would destroy the economic infrastructure each nation had in place. It was a symbiotic, albeit begrudging relationship.

North Korea had only been a concern to him due to the radical nature of their "Dear Leader." For all the man's bravado and his blatant show of nuclear testing and outrageous threats against all of America's allies and even the United States itself, Dear Leader could barely feed his citizens, power his cities, and support his nation in any First World capacity, much less wage a nuclear war on someone.

Then the accident in their testing facility happened.

Deep within a mountain, one of North Korea's nuclear testing sites collapsed, killing hundreds of scientists in the process, forever buried under thousands of tons of rock.

Of course, Dear Leader tried to spin it as some kind of a success. The fact they'd been able to detonate a nuke was his main focus. The deaths of his people didn't matter. They had a weapon they could use, or so he thought. The delivery method was still decades away, and by then North Korea would be so much further behind the current tech that it wouldn't be much of a threat.

Winters had seen it all during his time.

He'd served through Operation Desert Storm, been stationed in the Persian Gulf, then again sent overseas during the Iraqi War and the ongoing conflict in Afghanistan. By the time he was put behind a desk and given more power than he ever imagined, the Russians were beginning to become a threat once more.

Their leader, stubborn and indignant to the point of being cocky, had pushed the bounds of peace that had hung tentatively in the balance for over twenty years. Some kind of conflict, it seemed, was inevitable.

Winters knew this all too well. The Russians were a proud people and their leader the proudest of all. Winters had spent time in Moscow and grown to love the citizens, but now those times were all but forgotten as the threats poured out of the Kremlin.

Admiral Winters knew that it was only a matter of time until Russia made its move.

It wouldn't come as a land assault, and most likely not from the air. They would come via the ocean and could attack both coasts if they wanted to. While the United States Navy was strong and equipped to handle that sort of thing to defend the nation, Winters also knew the cost of such an attack.

He'd only voiced it to a few of his peers during the last few months as intel continued to land on his desk. No one listened. Since the end of the Cold War, Russia had ceased to be a real threat, in many minds, and was only a peripheral annoyance.

Winters knew better. They were coming, and while it was probably going to be a stalemate, hundreds of thousands would die, maybe more.

Unless there was a way to stop it.

The top brass had become soft.

It wasn't his fellow military leaders that had lost their edge. It was the bureaucrats in Washington. They'd been overrun by a new breed of politician, the kind that thought everyone in the world was to be trusted, kind, and good. This new blanket message of tolerance wasn't inherently evil. There was nothing wrong with trying to see the good in people, but not at the expense of ignoring the bad.

Nuclear war would solve nothing. Winters was well aware of that fact. He'd gone through every thermonuclear war training available in the military, run through the scenarios, all with the same results. The world would effectively come to an end, the planet made uninhabitable by the wars of men.

Russia still had nukes. During the heavy disarmament effort in the 1990s, there were dozens of nuclear warheads that were unaccounted for. Some were still being seized. Others had vanished off the map. But Moscow still controlled the lion's share of the thousands of nuclear warheads still floating around the former Soviet Union.

Winters knew that a more powerful, non-nuclear option was going to be necessary to fend off the Russians should they try to attack United States soil. But that was only the beginning of his desires.

Such a weapon could make the United States the unquestioned, unchallengeable power across the world's oceans. Once that happened, there would be no more oppression, no more deaths of the innocent at the hands of warlords or tyrants. World leaders would fall in line knowing that if they didn't, the United States Navy would force their hand, bending their nations to submission.

Winters believed America was a point of light to the rest of the world. It was one of the last bastions, along with a few allies, of capitalism and the power of the individual to rise above life's challenges. That message would be carried further than ever—if he just had the weapon.

For the longest time, it had been nothing more than fanciful imaginings. A weapon that could grant someone power over the sea was something from a fairytale, a fictional notion beyond ludicrous.

As he'd grown older, however, Winters had taken up studying ancient myths. He learned about the religions and cultures from thousands of years ago, paying particular attention to those revolving around nautical traditions. He'd scoured religious texts, even searched the Bible relentlessly for a clue as to what might have caused the Great Flood, aside from the command of God. That search had proved fruitless, but he endeavored onward, powering through the challenges until he'd discovered something interesting.

Throughout all of his studies, reading, and research, one theme continued to be a powerful beacon to what he hoped might actually exist. There were gods of the sea in nearly every culture, even ones that were landlocked. Some of these deities possessed great weapons that could control the tides, the waves, the life itself in the oceans.

The most famous of all, perhaps, were the tridents of Neptune and Poseidon.

Both deities were well known throughout the world, even in modern times. Stories had been written, movies produced, and even a few followings created to pay tribute to the magical possibilities these gods presented to the world.

While Winters wasn't a very religious person—only attending church once every few months, at most—he did find that in life, wherever there was smoke, there was fire. Sure, it was cliché, but that's how he thought, how he worked, how he had to believe.

All of these ancient weapons and deities possessed powers. Whether the stories were true or not didn't matter. He'd learned that there was usually at least an ounce of truth behind every proverbial pound of fiction.

One such story that had always fascinated him was the fall of Atlantis. The academic community seemed divided on the topic. Was Atlantis a real place or simply some piece of a philosopher's imagination?

He didn't fancy himself a person given to foolish pursuits. On the other hand, Winters knew for a fact that there were sections of the government, secret branches, that worked specifically on discovering lost ancient technologies exactly like the one he was trying to find.

Most of those people didn't have the vision he had.

Winters understood all too well what it could mean to have something powerful enough to command the seas.

In the last six months, he'd slowed his search, reeling in some of the aggressive studying he'd done for so long. After coming up empty with every single prospective myth, legend, or rumor, he was growing tired of looking. Perhaps there really wasn't anything like the weapon he sought. All the stories he'd read were just figments of someone's imagination.

He'd resigned himself to that fact and merely continued his studies out of sheer interest and curiosity. He gave up on the pipe dream of some powerful relic or artifact that could command the oceans and resorted to looking to history purely for entertainment.

It was funny. Despite his age, he was always learning new things about life. Now nearly seventy, he'd long ago learned that it was typically when you were close to giving up that the solution you so desperately wanted fell in your lap.

He'd forgotten that rule, until it had happened again.

He was sifting through some stuff he'd found on the Lewis and Clark expedition and decided to do a little further digging. One thing led to another until he realized he was in a rabbit hole he'd never imagined. It began innocently enough with the discovery of Lewis's death. Winters had learned about Lewis and Clark when he was in grade school, some fifty-plus years ago. He was shocked to learn that historians were still in a debate over what really happened the night Capt. Meriwether Lewis died. No one seemed to know for sure if the man committed suicide or if he was murdered.

There was certainly evidence for both theories, but the events of the evening had caused a spark to ignite in the admiral's head. What if he was murdered? And if he was, why?

He was far from a specialist when it came to investigations. The most he'd ever had to do was root out contraband on his vessels. Winters knew, however, that with every crime, especially murder, there had to be some kind of motive.

If Meriwether Lewis was murdered, what possible reason could someone have had to carry it out?

The man was a hero, a legend at the young age of thirty-five. Winters suspected he would have been treated like the first astronauts to walk on the moon: with parades, fanfare, and feasting.

Yet there he had been, according to some accounts Winters had read, dying on the floor of some Podunk tavern in the middle of southern Tennessee.

Witness testimony was inconsistent, which made Winters's suspicions soar. His immediate thoughts were that someone had wanted Lewis's money, but despite being a governor and the owner of a considerable amount of land, Lewis supposedly didn't have a ton, much less a valuable stash on hand.

That meant it wasn't a robbery.

Then there was the rush job on his funeral that only added to the conspiracy forming in Winters's mind. More research relayed that John Grinder, the owner of the tavern and inn where Lewis perished, was brought before a grand jury under the charge of murder.

He wasn't convicted, though, and was allowed to return home.

All of this led Winters to the incredible, if not slightly far-fetched theory, that Meriwether Lewis had a secret, something he'd discovered along his journey. But what?

Still, Winters didn't think much of it other than believing Lewis had something to hide. He'd given up his search for a magical artifact that could make his navy invincible. The Lewis story was simply an object of fascination for him.

That is, until he found the letter.

Admiral Winters's clearance level allowed him access to certain archives 99 percent of the population couldn't see or weren't even aware existed.

The letter was written from Thomas Jefferson to President James Madison. In it was an encoded message from Meriwether Lewis regarding something he'd discovered on his journey west. What he'd found and where it was, precisely, were not detailed in the message. What was laid out was the fact that Lewis was absolutely terrified of it.

He only described it as "the anomaly," saying that it was something covered in strange markings that looked like they could be letters or words, but in a language unlike anything he'd ever seen before.

If it had been in one of the Native American languages, Lewis would have recognized it immediately. Or surely, he would have asked Sacagawea's opinion on the matter.

That led Winters to the next bizarre piece of the Lewis discovery. It seemed Captain Lewis didn't tell anyone else from his expedition. How he managed to keep such a secret, or any secret for that matter, was a mystery, but more important than the how was the why.

What would lead Lewis to keep something from one of his closest friends and the group he'd grown to love and trust over the course of their long journey? The answer was simple, at least to Winters. Meriwether Lewis had found something terrifying. It was the only solution that made sense. And if it frightened this hardened military man that had traversed the entire country and endured extreme hardships, that meant it was likely something very powerful.

Maybe Winters was making a huge jump to that conclusion. Perhaps he was getting senile. He shrugged off that thought. He was still young, still had his wits about him. Digging for an answer, maybe, but he wasn't crazy.

He pored over the clues in the letter, which led him to search for other documents relating to the Lewis and Clark expedition. It was then that he discovered the letter from James Madison. It had been hundreds of hours into his exploration of the Library of Congress before he found it, but when he did, it had changed everything.

Winters took photos of it, made copies, and secured them in his personal office in his home, locking them in a safe in case anyone considered rifling through his things when he was out.

As it turned out, a home invasion likely wouldn't have mattered. A burglar would have never been able to figure out the riddle buried in the paragraphs of the Madison letter. Winters had spent more hours than he could recount trying to unravel the coded message, but in the end, he'd failed to figure it out.

As luck would have it, he knew of someone who specialized in that sort of thing. He'd heard of the IAA through the news and social media channels. Tommy Schultz and his friend Sean Wyatt had a knack for taking apart riddles such as Madison's and had made quite a name for themselves through the years. Winters couldn't simply reach out to them about this one. He would need Schultz and Wyatt to work on this without them ever knowing who was behind it.

After all, were they to succeed, he couldn't have them knowing what it was he wanted to find and why he wanted it. For this mission, he'd have to use leverage. But where to get it?

Fortunately, Wyatt had made his fair share of enemies over the years, and one in particular stood out during Winters's investigation into the man.

Andrew Boyd had been kicked out of the United States military, his family plunged into ruin, and Boyd personally lost everything. All due to Sean Wyatt's testimony. Winters knew Boyd would do whatever it took to get back at Sean Wyatt. Gradually, the plan began to formulate in the admiral's mind. He could use Boyd to get to Wyatt, and Wyatt would figure out the riddle embedded in Madison's letter.

That was the plan anyway, but there had to be a way to get Wyatt's attention.

Winters could have gone after Wyatt's wife, Adriana, but she was difficult to locate. Schultz would have been a good option, but not for the overall plan.

Then there was Boyd. Winters knew that if he truly wanted to get Boyd on board, he'd have to dangle an extra carrot in front of him. Winters could sell Boyd on the idea of revenge, but he'd need to make extra certain that Boyd understood he was all in on the plan.

That's when he came up with the idea to kidnap the former president. Once the deed was done, Winters was happy to leak information to the Feds so they could begin their manhunt. The search for Wyatt had to be timed precisely; do it too soon and Wyatt wouldn't be able to find what he was looking for. Once Wyatt had the letter in his possession, Winters loosed the dogs.

He knew Boyd would be pleased at seeing everything come undone in Wyatt's life. Winters didn't care about any of that. They were all just cogs in his machine now, each serving a purpose no matter how small or how large.

Now things were set in motion.

Winters sat back in his chair and steepled his fingers, watching the television screen as the news outlet continued coverage of the bizarre disappearance of the former president.

Soon, Admiral Winters would find out whether or not there was truly something to the Madison letter. He didn't dare get his hopes up, at least not too high, but there was something deep down in his gut that told him this path was going to lead to what he'd been hoping for for so long.

15

ASHEVILLE, NORTH CAROLINA

Adriana closed the car door and stepped out into the cold. A few patches of melting snow dotted the ground along the driveway. More coated the treetops, especially high up on the mountain behind the mansion situated at the base of the slope.

Her father had been right about this Lawson character. The home was a palace. From the looks of it, it had to be over eight thousand square feet. The exterior was white brick with black shutters and a matching roof. The guard house at the base of the driveway mimicked the color scheme and was protected by brick walls and black wrought iron fencing.

The black, cast iron gate swung open from two points—if a visitor was, in fact, to be allowed inside. That, it seemed, was going to be the trick.

Two guards—one white and one black, both muscular—stepped out of the guard house, pulling down black trench coats tight over their shoulders to keep away the chill. They were wearing chrome aviators, either to give them a more imposing look or to keep out the sunlight. Since the sky was overcast, Adriana figured it was the psychological reason.

"Hello," she said in her best flirty voice. "I'm here to see Tyler."

She strode toward the gate with a saunter that accentuated her hips.

"Mr. Lawson doesn't accept visitors."

She pretended to look hurt as she neared the gate. "Oh, that's not true. He has visitors all the time. There are the parties he throws. Then there are the dates. Of course, I won't get into the guests he pays to show up."

Adriana had done her research. Tyler Lawson was a playboy in every sense of the word. He'd come into a good chunk of money during his time as a contractor. He'd used that cash to fund every possible vice he could think of, but the most ostentatious of all wasn't his affinity for expensive luxury cars. It was his taste for beautiful women.

She cringed at the thought but stayed focused on the task at hand —getting through this gate.

"Those are invite only," the white guard on the left said. "You weren't invited."

"And how do you know?"

He leaned his head back and then shook it. "Because we keep a list. And you're not on it."

"Fine," she said, sticking out her lower lip for the briefest of seconds. "Tell him that Diego's daughter is here to see him."

The two men glanced at each other, wondering what that meant.

"Sorry, Miss. You need to go. You're trespassing."

Adriana rolled her eyes. "Look, just walk back in there to your little shed, call your boss, and tell him Diego's daughter needs to see him. I'd prefer this didn't have to get ugly for the two of you."

"Is that a threat?" The black guard seemed to take offense to the comment.

"It would be better if the two of you didn't find out."

"Why don't you run along?" The white guard waved a hand as if shooing away a stray dog.

Adriana sighed. "Look, just make the call. If he says no, I'll leave, and no one has any problems. Okay?"

Both guards sighed, cast sidelong questioning glances at each other again, and then the white guy walked back to the shack and picked up a phone. She watched through the window as the man chatted briefly with someone on the other end. She also took a moment to do a little reconnaissance. The winding driveway bent left, right, and back again as it meandered up the hill to the mansion on top. It was lined with bushy hemlocks and Colorado blue spruce spaced evenly along the driveway. She noted Christmas lights hanging on some of the branches and wrapped around the tree trunks. Each of the guard shacks was adorned with lush green wreaths accented with red and gold bows. The same wreaths hung from the iron gate blocking the way up the hill. Apparently, Tyler Lawson was a fan of the holidays.

The man in the guard building hung up the phone and stepped back outside. He shook his head sharply as he approached. "Sorry, ma'am. Mr. Lawson isn't taking any visitors. And he was adamant about you specifically not being permitted on the premises. Now, please move along, or we'll be forced to call the police."

The guard neared the railing of the gate. Adriana let her feet shuffle subtly forward so that her chest was nearly touching the iron bars.

"You don't want us to call the police," the guard continued. His partner stood close behind him.

She could smell the cologne on the white guard's neck. Why a security guard would wear cologne of any kind while on the job was baffling. That simple fact told her that these two weren't as highly trained as they might believe. Then there was the next piece of evidence. A smart, or at least wary, security guy wouldn't put himself so close to harm. He was well within arm's reach, perhaps comforted by the gate between them. Maybe it was simply overconfidence. Either way, if she'd wanted to kill the man, he'd already be dead. This, however, wasn't a mission where lethal force would be necessary.

Adriana pouted and put on her best disappointed look. "Is there nothing I can do to get in to see him? It's really important."

The guard closest to her narrowed his eyes and then glanced up at one of the cameras. He returned his gaze to her, this time with malicious intent sparkling in his eyes.

She'd seen that look before from men. It was driven by pure, uncaring lust. She knew exactly what the guy was going to ask for next. Based on the stories surrounding Lawson's parties, these two were probably accustomed to getting what they wanted from ladies who desired entry.

They were scumbags, no better than the trolls guarding backstage areas at a rock concert.

Adriana had no intention of being some kind of groupie, but she'd set up the chess board and rigged it in her favor. Reaching into her jacket to take out her pulse pistol might have caused the two guards to react defensively. She was fast, but even if she moved quickly she could have probably only taken down one of them before the other drew his weapon and dropped her.

Now she had an opening as well as a captive audience.

"Oh," she said. "You want to...see something?"

The man before her nodded slowly. It was a creepy gesture that would have sent shivers through a lesser person's soul, but not Adriana. She was beautiful and had used that on the less intelligent, less moral individuals who'd stood in her way before.

She reached up and unzipped her coat slowly, teasing him for a moment as her hand passed her chest. The guard's head tipped up a little while he lowered his eyes, full of desire. The second guard stepped closer and licked his lips.

These two were particularly degenerate. At first glance, you would have thought them respectable, hardworking, and disciplined. All of that went out the window. They were animals, nothing more.

"I guess you'd like me to take something out for you, huh?" she asked in her flirtiest voice, her sultry Spanish accent only heightening the desired effect.

Both guards nodded.

"Yeah," the white guy said. "You do that."

He acted like he was the boss, the one in control. He had no idea he and his partner had fallen right into her trap.

Adriana reached into her coat. She felt the cool metal of the pulse pistol against her fingertips. The weapon was something new to her, and non-lethal. It would take the two down in seconds, sending a high-voltage shock through their bodies by way of tiny pellets that would stick to their bodies.

Adriana gripped the weapon and tilted her head to the right, passing a seductive smile through the bars of the gate. The men's anticipation heightened. Their hormones would certainly be raging at this point, taking away all sense of peril that would have normally driven them to a more cautious path.

She drew the pistol in the blink of an eye. The trigger gave way easily behind the pull of her finger. The barrel clicked as the first round passed through the muzzle, striking the white guard in the forehead. His body instantly began convulsing, and he dropped to the ground, writhing in the mush.

The second guard saw what had happened, but the fastest reaction he could muster was a shocked expression with eyes opening wide. The gun clicked again, and a round smacked the second guard in the neck. He, too, dropped to the ground, first on his knees and then over onto his side as he grappled to control his muscles. He twitched and squirmed, only able to get out a feeble screech for help that no one would hear.

Adriana looked right, then left, and then grabbed a hold of a parallel bar running across the top of the gate. She pulled herself up with ease, years of training and workouts coming to fruition in a moment of need. At the top, she deftly raised her right leg over the menacing spikes on the tip then set her left foot on the top bar, using it as a brace until she could vault the rest of her weight over. She flew across the sharp points with graceful ease and twisted her body in the process, grabbing the vertical bars to slow her fall as she dropped to the ground on the other side.

She landed in the snow next to the white guard. The pulsing round on his forehead had spent its juice, and now he was incapacitated, for the most part. She leaned down close and whispered in his ear while, at the same time, drawing a small pen from her jacket. "Thanks for letting me see your boss on such short notice."

She shoved the pen into his neck and pressed the button on the end. A tiny needle shot out and jabbed through his skin, injecting a solution into his bloodstream. For a second, there was terror in his eyes as he anticipated the coming darkness of death. It took less than ten seconds for him to pass out. He wasn't dead. Adriana had no intention of killing Lawson's men. She'd left all but one of her deadly weapons in the car, opting to carry a small sidearm in case it was absolutely necessary.

She turned to the black man on the ground. He watched, unmoving as she approached and produced a second pen from her coat's inner folds. He wanted to shake his head, wanted to beg for mercy, but he would have none save the peaceful rest of a few hours' sleep in the cold.

Served them right.

She smiled cynically at him and then jabbed the pen into his neck. Within seconds, his eyelids grew heavy, and his head rolled to the side. Adriana dropped the device next to the unconscious body and then stood up straight. She stared up the driveway at the mansion.

No doubt, there would be more guards ahead. She checked the pistol's magazine through the clear back of the grip, noting how many rounds she had left. She carried one additional mag on her belt. That should be more than enough. If Lawson had more guards than she had rounds, the guy was way more paranoid than she expected.

16

ASHEVILLE

Adriana's boots didn't make a sound as she walked down the wide hallway. She'd become an expert at stealth long ago. Walking on the edges of her boots made sure there was only so much contact with the floor.

She turned to the right, cutting into a massive kitchen with a steel stove and oven, a matching vent hanging overhead, and cream-colored cabinetry. The façades of the refrigerator and dishwasher matched those of the cabinets and pantry, as was common in many affluent Southern homes. A black chandelier hung from the ceiling over a walnut farmhouse table in the breakfast nook.

Through the archway at the other end of the room she could see a fire crackling in the fireplace. The sound of burning wood popped, sizzled, and snapped. The intoxicating smell of a winter fire trickled throughout the mansion and teased her senses.

A man was sitting in a huge leather chair to the right of the fireplace, a snifter of brandy in his right hand, elbow propped on the armrest. He was young, as Adriana's father suggested, though he didn't look a day over twenty-one.

His tanned skin indicated a life of tropical pleasures, or perhaps outdoor adventure. His blond hair was cropped short, bent slightly to the left in a kind of spiked style. He was wearing a beige knit sweater with a hoodie on the back. His chino pants were light brown and contrasted with his black shoes. He looked the picture of a college kid trying to be sophisticated but barely pulling it off.

"There you are," he said, raising his glass. "Please, come in, Adriana."

She raised her pulse pistol and lined up his neck with the forward sights. Her arms were fully extended, both hands on the weapon to keep it steady. She knew better than to ignore her surroundings and kept watch out of the corner of her eyes in case someone tried to flank her. She still had six rounds left in the second magazine after taking out a battalion of guards at the entrance and inside the foyer.

One had managed to get a punch in, but she'd twisted enough to make the blow a glancing one and then shoved the weapon under her armpit, firing the electrified round blindly behind her and into the man's chest.

Tyler Lawson raised his left hand slowly, making his surrender as obvious as possible. "Easy now. Don't shoot. You got me. Okay?"

He put on his best innocent face, like a child who'd stuck his hand in the cookie jar only to pull down the whole thing and shatter it on the floor.

Adriana stepped through the archway and into the living room. The space opened up with a tall cathedral ceiling that shot up to the pinnacle of the roof. The ceiling itself was made from pale wood planks and separated by dark wooden beams. The hardwood floor was dark, textured oak. If she had to guess, Adriana would have said it was reclaimed from somewhere.

Her head twisted to the left. She scanned the area in a second. The room stretched over to a study. The desk sat in the center of an octagonal space that was surrounded by tall bookshelves, each lined with hundreds of books. The shelves rose a full fifteen feet until the tops reached a point in the ceiling that angled to a single point. The conical roof was made from huge glass panels that allowed natural light to pour in during the day and perhaps some stargazing at night.

Adriana's eyes only lingered on the study for a couple of seconds before she returned her attention to Lawson.

He was still sitting as before, one hand in the air and the other clutching the snifter.

"Would you like a drink?"

Her eyelids narrowed. "Little early for brandy, isn't it?"

His head twitched an inch to the side, and he flashed a smug grin. "Or a few hours too late, depending on how your day is going."

"Your day is about to get a lot worse."

"Now, now. Don't be that way. I saw how you handled my guards." He raised the glass an inch or two and then took a short sip. He let out a satisfied sigh and returned his elbow to the armrest. "I had to make sure it was you, Diego's daughter. I haven't heard that name in a while. Surely you can understand my...suspicions."

She kept the weapon trained on his neck, just above the sternum where the throat met the chest. "I could have killed your men."

"I knew you wouldn't do that, not if you were Diego's daughter. Your father is a good man. I would expect his little girl would be no different."

Adriana felt her irritation melting, though her focus remained. "That's an awfully big gamble to take with the lives of people you trust, people who trust you."

He shrugged. "I suppose it might have been, but I like to think I know people. You may have killed in the past, but I didn't expect you to murder my guards."

"The next time I come here I might not have a choice."

He snickered, and shook his head. "We both know there won't be a next time. You're here for something. I'm guessing information since that's what I do. But you won't come to me again. That's how it works, and you know it."

Adriana knew what he meant. If she tried to come around again, Lawson wouldn't hesitate to order his men to kill her. It was a fact she could live with. Of course, Adriana also knew there were other ways to get past his security detail, and she was confident those methods could be exploited if necessary.

She hoped this was going to be her only visit, though, and decided to stop with the pleasantries.

"I need to know who took President Dawkins."

He looked into her eyes for a moment, sizing up the level of her sincerity. Then he started laughing. It was muted at first, short, then it erupted into a full bellow.

She stood there unflinching with the weapon still trained on him.

It was another minute before he cut the laughter. He rubbed his nose and shook his head. "You came here to find out who took the president? You could have saved some time by watching the news."

"We both know the media doesn't spread the truth."

He puckered his lips for a half second and nodded. "I guess we do."

"Sean didn't take Dawkins. I need to know who would do something like that."

Lawson listened and then nodded his head slowly, dramatically. "I see." He took another sip, this one longer, taking in the remaining contents of the snifter. He swished the warm liquid around in his mouth, savoring the flavors before swallowing. He let out a satisfied sigh and set the glass down on a round end table next to his seat, then stood.

He kept both hands out wide, palms facing the intruder. "Please," he said, "put that thing away. I assure you, I will do you no harm."

"Forgive me if I don't trust the guy who just tried to have his guards kill me."

"If I wanted you dead, you would be. Besides, your father sent you here. If he trusts me, maybe you should, too."

She considered his point, eyeing him suspiciously. Finally, she lowered her weapon. "Fine," she said. "But if you don't impress me, I might shoot you with this thing anyway, just for wasting my time."

"What do I get for you wasting mine?" He arched one eyebrow.

"Fair enough."

A smile cracked his lips. "Your father helped me once, several years ago when I was just getting into this game. I don't think I would have survived if it wasn't for him. So, today only, I'll help you out. No cost. But if you ever come back, the next one won't be free."

"Understood."

His smile broadened. "Perfect." He threw his hands up in the air with the exclamation. "Let's get to work, then."

He walked through the archway, leaving Adriana standing in the living room for a confusing moment before she turned and caught up with him.

"You're not trying to figure out who took Dawkins," Tyler said as they passed through the kitchen and turned right. There were stairs leading up to the second floor and another set leading down to a lower floor. He took the downward steps, letting his left hand run along the oak railing propped up by wrought iron.

Adriana ignored the paintings on the walls, despite them being full of bright colors and striking surrealistic imagery.

"What do you mean?" she asked, following him down the steps, just over his right shoulder.

"Someone is behind this. You know it. I know it. The only people who don't know it are the ones who trust the mainstream, those who believe everything the news outlets tell them."

She knew he was right. And while she did want to find the person who took Dawkins, she knew that the best way to kill a snake was to cut off the head.

"What you're looking for is someone who's never quite had everything they wanted, someone with considerable power and influence but not enough to be the top dog."

They reached the bottom of the stairs and were confronted with two doors and a hallway with a glass exterior wall looking out to the pool area beyond. A hot tub leaked steam through the seam of its cover.

The door directly opposite of the staircase was open. Inside was the back of a wide, black leather sofa. It was facing the front of the room. The lights were dim, and no sounds escaped.

"Makes sense," Adriana said.

"That's the theater room," he said, pointing into the lavishly decorated entertainment area. She could make out the design of Gothic architecture inside, complete with gargoyles positioned over stone archways that held sconces within their recessions. "Had it designed to look like the Bat Cave."

Adriana raised both eyebrows. *This guy's a comic book nerd.* She didn't judge. She'd read her share of comic books back when she was little and always thought Wonder Woman was amazing.

"There's another option, though," he said as he opened the door to the right. Tyler stepped in, and the lights automatically flickered on.

This room was smaller than the theater room. There were no windows, and the walls were painted white. Adriana's attention wasn't on the walls. It was on the array of computers that Tyler had set up in the room. There were at least a dozen 42-inch monitors stretching around the far wall, the wall to the right, and the closest one. Each screen displayed different information. Some were host to scrolling lines of code that rolled slowly toward the top of the screen before disappearing. Others contained images or video, and still more had multiple windows open showing the latest breaking news out of several countries.

There were three black desk chairs scattered around, one for each table. Blue cables ran from the many computer towers. They stretched along the top of the wall and into a metal plate fixed into the corner.

The setup wasn't entirely unlike the one her father had in Ecuador, though this one was more advanced. Everything was newer, probably more powerful, too. She could see through the clear side panel of one of the computers and noted two Nvidia Titan graphics cards, powerful and necessary when working with so much information.

The room had two big vents in the right-hand side wall, constantly blowing cool air into the space. There was a long tube that ran along the wall on the floor. It had smaller versions of itself stuck into ports built on the sides of the computer towers.

"Air cooling vents?" Adriana asked. "But it looks like you're running liquid-cooled computers. Pretty high end stuff."

"Have to have the vents for the pumps, plus it keeps the water cooler," Tyler said. "You should see the setup I have for the servers out back."

She wondered if he had his own servers on site. It made sense to do it that way. Anonymity and autonomy were pillars of what Tyler and her father did. Those pillars she knew all too well.

"Like I was saying," Tyler went on, "we're not just looking for the guy who took your friend. We need to figure out who in the hierarchy is missing out. Who is always looking for something bigger? Who wants more power than they already have? Or who feels like they've been slighted all along?"

"Or who might Dawkins have angered during his tenure?"

He jabbed a finger her way. "Now you're thinking. We need to dig deeper, get into the weeds, and see who would have had it in for Dawkins."

"That could take a while. We don't have that much time."

Tyler nodded.

"Lucky for you, my babies here might already have something. We just have to look and see."

She didn't know what to think about the man calling his computers his "babies," so she decided to say nothing. Like her father said, the guy was eccentric.

"Information is everywhere," he went on. "Most of the population just thinks of it being available on the internet. You and I, however, know that isn't true."

Adriana nodded absently. She understood a little about what her father did, but the real ins and outs of it were foreign to her. How all of it worked didn't concern her; this was an alien world and one that she didn't really care about as far as the details were concerned. Right now, she just needed to know who had set all these wheels in motion.

Tyler plopped into one of the chairs and rolled it close to the nearest keyboard. "When Dawkins was taken, I immediately started looking around. I was curious."

"Curious?"

"Yes. I didn't for one second believe that Sean Wyatt took the president. So, in my mind, that meant that he was being set up."

"That's a big leap to take for a total stranger. For all you know, Sean might have been totally capable of doing something like that." Playing devil's advocate felt strange to her in regard to her husband, but she had a reason behind it. Adriana wanted to know what this guy's game was, what his price would be, and why he was helping her.

"You see?" He raised a finger and pointed it at her. "That tells me I'm on the right track. If his own wife is willing to be objective about all this, that means something fishy is happening." He turned back to his computer.

His fingers flew across the keyboard faster than nearly anyone she'd ever seen. When he was done, he hit the enter key and the screen blinked, then the images changed.

The monitor filled with pictures of men, dozens of them. Some were mug shots taken by police departments from all over the world. Others were images of men on the street captured by surveillance cameras or perhaps private investigators.

"I collected a list of names that would have been impaired the most by Sean's operations back when he was working for Axis. And yes, I know all about Axis." He twisted his head and gave her a smirk, then returned to the screen. "This one just died two months ago, so he's out." Tyler clicked on one of the images and dragged it to the trash bin located on the bottom corner of the monitor. "This one, this one, and this one are still in jail." He held on to the command button and clicked the three pictures then put those in the trash bin.

One by one, he eliminated the rest of the faces until there were only three left.

"Who are they?" Adriana asked.

Tyler reached over his keyboard and tapped on the image of the man on the far left. "This one is Mawri al Bakra. He was a known arms dealer that Sean took down. His business brought in tens of millions, and when Sean intervened he lost everything."

"Where is he now?"

Tyler's fingers tapped on the keys again. A moment later, a list of locations appeared in a separate window over the man's face. "Looks like his last known whereabouts was Turkmenistan. Date says two days ago."

Adriana cradled one elbow in her opposite forearm, her jaw resting on a middle finger as she rubbed her chin with the index finger. "He wouldn't have the resources or the capability to get to Dawkins. And the man on the video spoke clear English, even if it was muddled by the voice modulator."

"Fair enough. He's gone." Tyler deleted that image, leaving only two. A white man, probably in his late thirties, and a Hispanic man with tattoos on his neck and forehead.

"Might be safe to say that we can eliminate Jorge Espinoza," Tyler said. "He was one of the top dogs in a Colombian cartel. No known whereabouts, but he went underground a long time ago. Our guys are still hunting for him as we speak."

Adriana knew what he meant by "our guys." Tyler was referring to the efforts of the American government to reel in drug trafficking. That started by cutting the head off the snake. Espinoza, apparently, was one of those heads.

"That leaves us with this little guy." Tyler pecked at the keys one more time, and a new window of information popped up above the image on the screen. "Andrew Boyd. He's an interesting one."

Tyler expanded the window. The information contained within it spread out, covering much of the monitor. He dragged the guy's picture to the top-left corner to make room for the extensive dossier.

"Andrew Boyd, former military. Seems he was court-martialed for an incident in the Middle East. Looks like Sean and his team busted into a house about the time Boyd was involved with an interrogation. According to the testimony, Boyd wanted to torture the family. Sean stopped him and had him arrested."

Adriana leaned closer. Her eyes moved rapidly back and forth as she read the man's background.

"He came from a wealthy family. Went into the military. Spec ops?"

"Looks that way. Sounds like a rich brat with a chip on his shoulder. Didn't want to do things Daddy's way, so he joined the army. Wanted to make a name for himself, get some respect."

"Or forge connections he could call on later in life."

"Perhaps. Either way, I'd say he might be your guy."

"Where is he now?"

Tyler leaned forward and scanned the information on the screen. He turned slightly and looked at more intel on the monitor to his right. His head shook quickly. "I have no idea."

"What do you mean, no idea? He couldn't have just disappeared."

"No, that's true. And it's also incorrect. There are still plenty of places on this planet for a person to hide if they don't want to be found. I'd say, based on Boyd's past, that he has both the know-how and the connections to make that happen."

Adriana sighed and ran fingers from both hands through her hair. She stopped on the back of her head, stretching her arms for a moment.

"Of course," Tyler said, "there is another possibility."

Adriana's hands dropped, and she looked at him.

"Boyd doesn't have the finances to pull this off. He could put together a team, sure, but even a group like that would have a tough time extracting a former president from his home."

"What are you saying?" she asked.

"I'm saying Boyd may only be half of the equation in all of this."

17

NORTH DAKOTA

Sean eased into a corner seat at the diner and plucked a laminated menu from the metal holder next to the window. He scanned over it, only taking a few seconds to decide what he wanted.

He'd driven throughout the entire day, cutting through north-western Missouri and then skirting between Iowa and Nebraska before continuing into South Dakota. By the time he'd reached Sioux Falls, he was ready for something to eat and a place to sleep for the night, but he decided to just stop for food, thinking a little nourishment could help him push on the next few hours until he reached Fargo. Whether or not he could make it to Bismarck was still in doubt. It was probably a safer plan to stop in Fargo and wake up early the next morning to drive the remaining hours to Bismarck and then up to Fort Mandan. Then again, he didn't have a ton of time. Sean was up against the clock, and he still hadn't reached the first of what he figured were at least three locations he'd have to visit before—if at all—learning the secret Meriwether Lewis took to his grave.

A woman in a blue shirt and a white apron approached. Her curly brown hair framed a round face. She wore glasses that looked like they could have been twenty years old or more. She, herself, appeared to be in her mid-fifties. There was a tiredness in her eyes, enhanced by the droopy dark circles surrounding them. The bags of skin hung low onto her cheekbones. Sean wondered how long she'd been doing this job, but he didn't ask. Instead, he tried to stay as unmemorable as possible.

"What can I get for ya, hon?" she asked as politely as she could, but it still came out sour, bordering on annoyed. Her voice was exactly like every person he'd ever met from that region, a sharpness to some of the vowels and a hint of nasal tones.

Sean didn't mind it. He'd known several people from North and South Dakota. Whenever he heard that accent, it warmed his heart.

"I'll have the turkey melt with a side of fries, please," he said and flashed her a quick smile. He didn't want to be too friendly, but this woman clearly needed cheering up.

"What to drink?" She was all business.

He didn't blame her. It was late at night, which meant she was either at the end of her shift or at the beginning of it. He didn't envy either situation. This diner was one of those twenty-four-hour places. At least in the middle of the night there wouldn't be too many people coming in, though the ones that did were likely a bit sketchy.

"I'll have a Coke, please."

"Pepsi okay?"

"Um..." Sean hesitated. Being from the South, his ordering a Pepsi would absolutely not be okay. A love of Coke was indoctrinated into Southern youth early, and they had but few options when it came to beverages. There was Coca-Cola, Dr. Pepper, and sweet tea. Everything else was off the table. "Got Dr. Pepper?"

"Sure." She wrote down his order, spun away, and walked behind the counter where a long horizontal window opened into the kitchen. A line cook was behind it with a cloud of steam churning around him, the sound and smell of sizzling burgers pervading the small diner.

Sean could smell the grilled onions on the flatiron stove; the peppers, too, gave off a hint of aroma and mingled with the scent of frying meat. Sean's stomach grumbled in response to the smells as he waited patiently for his food to be prepared.

The waitress returned with his Dr. Pepper and set it on the table. The straw protruded from the top edge of the glass, with the remaining tube of paper still attached to the top. He glanced at her name tag, something he'd done before, but he wanted to make sure he recalled her name correctly.

"Thank you, Mary," he said.

"Welcome." She spun around and returned to the counter behind the register.

Yep. She wasn't happy.

Sean removed the paper top from the straw and pulled the drink close. He eyed the other customers in the room as he took a long sip, but not long enough to make much of a dent in the contents. It was more to keep up appearances. Mary didn't strike him as the type of server that planned on bringing a bunch of refills his way.

There was an older gentleman at the counter. He looked like a trucker or a farmer, complete with the long-sleeve flannel shirt and a brown Carhartt coat draped over the back of the chair. The coat matched his light brown pants. The secret of the guy's occupation, Sean figured, was in his boots. They were clean, untouched by dirt, but definitely worn. That meant this guy was a worker but not in a field. Sure, he could have been something else, but Sean pegged him for a truck driver. The hour of night, too, might have given it away. Truck drivers frequented establishments like this, especially after dark since they were the primary travelers on the road, especially desolate roads like the one he'd just been on.

Sean had gone for twenty minutes before seeing another driver at one point. Plus, it was really cold outside. This time of the year was when travel had pretty much hit its low point. It would kick up hard again at Christmas and then disappear until late spring.

The other customer in the diner was a younger guy. He had on a red hoodie, brighter than the crimson vinyl of the booth seats, and faded blue jeans. He'd been on his phone when Sean walked in and barely noticed as he passed by. Sean knew the kid hadn't seen any distinctive features, but now they were facing each other. Fortunately, the guy's eyes remained locked on the device in his hands.

Sean pegged him as being nineteen or twenty years old, though he might have been younger. He could have passed for a high school or college student. If he was in high school, it was awfully late to be out at a diner on a school night.

Instinctively, Sean reached for his phone and pulled it out of his pocket. He glanced at the scores on the ESPN app and then shoved the device back into his pants. The Predators were winning, but that was about all that was happening in the world of sports on that night.

The line cook placed a plate up onto the steel metal divider. "Order up," he said in a booming tone.

Mary whirled around like she'd probably done a thousand times that week and grabbed the plate.

Sean watched as she strode around the corner of the bar and walked up to him. She slid the plate toward him, put the bill on the edge of the table, and put one hand on her hip.

"Need anything else?"

"No, ma'am. I'm good. Thank you."

She nodded and turned around to make her way back to the counter.

Sean pulled the plate a little closer and picked up one half of the sandwich. He took a big bite and savored the different flavors that filled his mouth. It was a crunchy, gooey, meaty, buttery combination that caused his saliva glands to go absolutely crazy.

He took another bite, set the sandwich down, and picked up the ketchup bottle to his left. He twisted it open and slathered a few puddles onto his plate, then replaced the lid and put the bottle back where he'd found it. As he picked up a French fry, he noticed a car drive up and park directly outside the front door, in one of the spots marked for disabled drivers.

The lights remained on for several seconds, nearly blinding Sean in the process. He winced at the annoyance, but then the driver switched them off. The guy got out of the car and, from the looks of it, didn't have a disability at all.

The passenger door opened, and another guy, shorter and a little thicker than the first, also climbed out and slammed his door shut.

It was hard to get a good look at them through the windows and into the dark parking lot, but when the men entered the diner, Sean immediately noted that they were probably a similar age to the guy in the red hoodie.

They, too, were wearing hoodies. The taller one's was a heather gray, while the squatter one's was blue. It didn't take a genius to figure out that these guys probably knew each other. The driver paused at the newspaper rack by the door and pretended to leaf through some of the copies from various sources. The other one helped himself to one of the round stools fixed into the floor at the bar.

Alarm bells went off in Sean's head, and he immediately stood and walked to an alcove to his right that housed the men's and women's restrooms. He was still chewing on the fry when he pushed through and let bathroom door ease shut behind him.

Sean knew better than to question his instincts. Some might have called him paranoid or strange to behave in such a way, but those inner warnings had saved him through the years.

Something was going on with those three young men. If he had to guess, Sean thought they were about to rob the place.

His actions hadn't been out of cowardice. That wasn't his style. Not to mention he doubted anyone had noticed. The customer at the counter hadn't seen him, and Mary was focused on the incoming patrons. The line cook had his head down, focused on the grill.

Sean took in his surroundings. There was a sink near the door, a trashcan right next to him. Then there was a urinal and two toilet stalls. Not much he could use in the way of weapons. He walked over to the first stall, opened the door, and checked it out. Nothing. Then he went to the second. He'd have loved to rip the assist bar off the wall, but it was bolted down tight.

He padded back over to the door and pressed his right ear to it. He wasn't surprised at what he heard. The voices of the three men were muted, but Sean could hear them clearly enough. They were shouting orders at the people inside the diner, which was—according to his best guess—Mary, the line cook, and the trucker at the counter. He hoped the latter wasn't going to do anything stupid.

Sean figured the other two would be passive enough. These guys were here to rob their boss, not them.

He'd seen this sort of thing happen a couple of times before. His previous line of work lent itself to some late nights at the Waffle House when he was in the South or at cafés and diners like this one when he was abroad or traveling in different parts of the United States.

Most of the time, the thieves were after whatever was in the till. He hoped it was that and nothing more. He also hoped they weren't armed. Sean could take down three yahoos with knives or blunt weapons, but guns? Even a moron could get lucky now and then with a gun.

Those fears were realized when he heard Mary yell, "Please, don't shoot me! Please!"

Sean knew that the guy in the red hoodie who'd been so locked in on his phone had to have seen him. It would only be a matter of time until Red Hoodie realized someone was unaccounted for. To Sean, this was a good thing.

Charging out of the bathroom door to take on three armed guys wasn't his idea of a good plan. His weapons were still out in the car. Normally, he'd have one on him, but for some reason he'd stowed everything in his gear bag for the trip. Oh, right: because if he was pulled over he didn't want a cop asking why he had a gun on him. Every state varied on their concealment laws, and even with the appropriate permits Sean would rather spend as little time with the authorities as possible.

"Where's the other guy?" one of the robbers asked.

It had to be Red Hoodie. The other two likely wouldn't have noticed him.

"What other guy?" another voice said.

"There was another guy. Over there in the corner."

Sean imagined the speaker pointing at his empty booth where his half-eaten sandwich and barely touched fries were still sitting next to the Dr. Pepper.

"He must have gone to the bathroom. Take care of it."

Sean guessed it was the stumpy fellow giving the orders. He knew that the first guy would be hurrying his way, which was exactly what Sean had hoped for. If he went out into the main dining area, he'd be outnumbered and outgunned. They'd take the money he had on him, which wasn't a huge deal in the big picture, but he couldn't risk them taking his car keys. All his guns, cash, and supplies for the trip were inside the SUV. Lose that and he was done. Sean didn't care about himself, though he did care more than in the past, probably due to his young marriage. The real concern was for his friend, John Dawkins. If he screwed up, any chance of saving Dawkins was gone. Were these idiots to steal his vehicle, he'd be stranded.

Sean listened as the clumsy thug rushed toward the bathroom. He could hear the guy's pants swishing, and his feet stomping on the tile as he moved. These guys couldn't have been bigger amateurs, but they were armed amateurs, so that meant they still had to be treated like a legitimate threat.

Sean pressed his shoulder against the wall near the entrance. The door swung open toward the sink, which meant Sean would be concealed for an extra second as the guy came through. A pro would sweep to the right first, making certain any immediate danger wasn't present in his direct line of sight. Then he'd come back around behind the door to make sure no one was there before clearing the stalls.

More than likely, that's not what this guy would do.

The door burst open with a heavy thud, a result of the thief barging into it with his shoulder and left palm. He charged forward, immediately thinking that anyone in the bathroom would be hiding in one of the stalls. The stumpy guy was the one that had been sent in. He was four inches shorter than Sean, at minimum, and might have been the same weight, if not a few pounds lighter. Sean instantly sized him up, knowing exactly what to do with him. The rest of the plan came into view within seconds.

The guy had made a fatal error in skipping the sink area to go straight to the toilets. It wasn't an illogical conclusion for someone to make that had never been in an urban tactical situation, or any sort of combat situation for that matter. Sean, however, was more than glad to see his assessment had been correct.

Sean moved quickly, padding silently across the floor.

He saw the gun dangling in the guy's hand. He was probably the type to twist the weapon sideways and fire it like so many gangster movies he'd surely seen. Sean never understood that. Holding a gun that way made accuracy much more difficult, but hey, it made them look cool—he supposed.

He swept in like a bird of prey; silent and lethal. The thief never heard a sound until Sean's arms were wrapped around his neck. The victim gurgled a feeble noise that was meant to be a scream, but only came out as a gasp. His arms flailed around like fish flopping on the deck of a boat. Sean knew what was coming next. The guy would try to fire his weapon. To mitigate that, Sean used his right hand to grab the robber's wrist. In a quick, sudden jerk, he twisted the man's arm back around behind his lower back, straining the wrist bone to the point of breaking it. He tried to scream, but again the strong forearm across his Adam's apple squeezed his windpipe shut. The gun fell to the floor with a clack.

Sean kept squeezing the man's throat, knowing that it wouldn't be much longer now. The guy's eyes bulged from their sockets, face reddening, then turning white, then blue. The flailing dissipated, and Sean felt the guy getting heavier. Within thirty seconds, he was out.

After lowering the body to the floor, Sean picked up the gun—a Smith & Wesson 9mm, and stuffed it in his belt. He hated doing that, and knowing that his holster was out in the car made it worse, but he didn't have a choice.

He pulled his shirt down over the grip of the gun and took a deep breath. Then he kicked the thief in the ribs just to make sure he wasn't waking up anytime soon, but not hard enough to do any lasting damage. The man didn't move.

Sean stepped to the door, put his hand on it, and pushed it open.

18

NORTH DAKOTA

Up until the moment he walked out of the bathroom and back into the diner, Sean Wyatt had kept a low profile. Since leaving Atlanta, he'd stayed out of public view and blended in with all the normal people in the world.

Now, as he strode past the three rows of booths on his way back to his seat, he knew he was drawing the stares of every person in the restaurant.

He didn't look over at them, instead keeping his eyes locked on the booth straight ahead and the plate of food on the table.

Sean eased into his seat, picked up his sandwich, and took a bite. His nerves were steel, and he kept his heart rate at a calm, steady pace. He chewed the bite in his mouth, shoved a couple of fries in, and continued eating while the rest of the people in the diner stared with wide-eyed disbelief.

Red Hoodie was holding a gun toward the trucker, but he quickly turned it toward Sean, which was exactly what he wanted, unbeknownst to the gunman.

"Hey!" Red Hoodie said, brandishing the weapon in Sean's direction.

Sean took a sip of his drink to wash down the food. His ruse was playing two roles. One, he was still hungry and needed to eat something. Sean had no intention of letting a good meal go to waste, especially since he hadn't eaten for most of the day. Second, he knew that simply strolling out of the bathroom as if nothing was wrong would throw off the remaining two gunmen.

Sean took two more big bites of the sandwich to finish it off. His cheeks swelled like a chipmunk's, full of nuts for the winter. Red Hoodie's bewilderment was only tamed by his irritation.

"Hey, I'm talking to you!" he shouted. "Where's Dan?"

Sean's eyebrows climbed up his forehead, and he swallowed hard. Then he put another cluster of fries in his mouth and drew a sip through the plastic straw. He watched as Red Hoodie turned to his lone remaining accomplice and ordered him to watch the trucker and Mary.

He stalked toward Sean, still aiming the gun at him. The guy was reckless, a total amateur. He could see it from the way Red Hoodie was holding the weapon, the way he walked, the way he sounded brave but was clearly trying to cover up deep, underlying cowardice. This punk didn't know what he was doing. Maybe he needed the money for drugs. That was usually the case. They'd knock off somewhere easy, passing over bigger scores for a less risky location that could provide the small amount of cash they needed for their next fix. Other places would have much more money in the till, but they'd also be armed or have cameras and alarms rigged.

Despite their smart selection for a robbery, these guys were still idiots. Sean knew that the second he realized the situation.

Now their leader—if he could be given that title—had his sights on Sean. In a weird sort of way, Sean almost felt sorry for the kid. He had no idea who he was messing with. Still, Sean didn't take anything for granted. He knew better. Caution, even against pathetic people like this, had to always be taken.

"Are you deaf or just stupid?" Red Hoodie asked as he stopped short of the booth and extended the gun toward Sean.

Sean didn't react, instead staring up at the guy as he picked up another couple of fries and shoved them into his mouth. Then he lifted the cup, took another sip from the straw, and swallowed.

"These fries are pretty good," he said. "You tried them before?"

"Are you dim? Where is Dan?"

Sean thought for a second, letting his eyes drift to the window as if trying to recall a long-forgotten friend's name. "Dan?" He shook his head. "I don't think I know him. I mean, I know some Dans from college, but I doubt they're the guy you're looking for."

"The other guy that came in here!" Red Hoodie shouted. The gun barrel wavered as he spoke, his mannerisms becoming more and more exaggerated. "What did you do to him?"

Sean frowned and scooped the last of the fries. He held them up like a maestro's baton and thought for a second. "Oh, the guy in the bathroom?"

"Yes, you idiot. Where is he?"

"I guess he's still in the bathroom." Sean said in a matter-of-fact tone and then held out the fries. "You should try these."

"Get up," Red Hoodie said and smacked the fries out of Sean's hand.

The food shot across the table and slid to the napkin holder, coming to a rest next to the silver container.

Sean looked at the fries with remorse. Then he looked back up at the robber. "Hey, I was going to eat those."

"Get up," Red Hoodie ordered.

"Why? Now I need more fries?"

"You really are a moron, aren't you? Get up, or I will splatter your brains on that wall."

"Okay, take it easy. I just think it's a waste of good food. And honestly, it's rude that you did that."

"Get up now, idiot."

The guy reached out and grabbed Sean by the shirt. Sean let him do it. He didn't resist, even though he knew he could have broken the kid's arm, taken the gun from him, and shot the third gunman. The deed would have been done in seconds. But he trusted his instincts, and there were innocent people in the room, people who didn't need to be put in harm's way. He also knew that killing these punks wasn't the answer. Were they trash? Sure, but Sean wasn't in the business of killing civilians, not unless they were trying to hurt him or one of his friends.

If he could avoid death in this scenario, that's what he was going to do. So far, everything was going according to plan.

He knew the group's leader would react the way he did. Sean didn't usually make blithe assumptions. He assessed a situation, analyzed it, and came to a conclusion. In this case, it took just seconds. It wasn't always that easy, but these guys weren't your typical threat.

Sean figured the leader would leave the third dude to watch the diner while he was ushered in to the bathroom. Turned out he figured correctly.

The punk squeezed Sean's sleeve and jerked him toward the bathroom. Normally, this kind of behavior would have been a fatal mistake, but Sean kept calm, knowing he didn't have to kill these numbskulls. That didn't mean he wasn't going to teach them a lesson.

The guy fell in line behind him as Sean marched, albeit reluctantly, toward the bathroom. "I don't know what happened to your friend," Sean lied. "Maybe he had some bad chicken or something."

"Shut up and get in there."

"Look, I don't want to die. Please, just take everything I have. It isn't much, a few dollars and—"

The younger man brandished his pistol, threatening to whip Sean in the back of the head with it if he didn't shut his mouth. Sean wasn't concerned, but he did as told, feigning fear for a few more seconds.

They reached the bathroom door and Sean put his fingers on it. He knew what waited on the other side. The unconscious body of this guy's partner would, he hoped, still be lying on the floor. It typically took more than a couple of minutes for someone to come back around from being knocked out that way; although everyone was different. It was entirely possible that the guy would be on his way out when they opened the door.

Sean made a mental note to bind the two together once they were both incapacitated.

He pushed through the door and found, unsurprisingly, that the other guy was still blacked out on the tile floor. His face was resting on the cold surface, and he hadn't moved in the minutes since Sean had left him.

"Dan?" Red Hoodie shouted. He stepped forward, unthinking. "What did you do to him?" He swore in the midst of the sentence.

Now they were just inside the bathroom door, and Red Hoodie had made his mistake. In his rush to see what had happened to his friend, he'd forgotten the threat that was standing right in front of him.

"Did you kill him?" Red Hoodie asked.

"No. I didn't kill him."

"Liar. You killed Dan!"

Sean's head went back and forth. "No, I honestly didn't. He'll be fine. I think he slipped on the wet floor and must have hit his head. I was already out there eating my sandwich and fries."

Red Hoodie raised his weapon, which was Sean's signal that the jig was up. He twisted to one side, shot up his right hand, and clapped his fingers over the barrel. Another quick twist, a jerk, and a downward pull snapped the bone in the man's wrist. Before he could react, the pistol was in Sean's hand.

The guy was about to yell out in pain, or maybe for help, but Sean chopped his larynx and he became mute. Just like his friend, Red Hoodie's face turned red, then pale, then blue. He grasped at his throat with his lone good hand and fell to his knees. Then he collapsed to his side and passed out. That could often be a killing blow and Sean hoped he wasn't dead, but didn't think he would be. There was no intent to kill anyone tonight. Perhaps he was being too gracious with these three brigands who seemed set on robbery and violence. It didn't matter now. Sean was here, and there was only one left for him to handle.

He stepped back out into the diner, stuffed the second pistol into his belt next to the first, and made his way back to his booth.

The tall, skinny guy at the counter looked over at him. "Where are they?" This dude sounded panicked, as well he should have been. Sean had just gone into the bathroom with one and now two of his partners and had been the only one to emerge each time.

Sean shrugged and eased into his booth again. His food was gone, for the most part, but he still had some good sips of Dr. Pepper left in his glass.

"Don't know," Sean said. "Maybe they're helping each other?"

The gunman scowled and then stalked across the diner, flashing a warning expression at the trucker.

"Tell me what you did with them, or so help me I will put a bullet right through the back of your skull. Do you hear me?"

"Loud and clear," Sean said. "Now, it's time for you to listen. I'm going to finish this drink. If, by the time I'm done, you're out of here and on the road, you win. If you stay and decide you wanna try to take me out, that's okay, too, but you're going to lose, and it will be very, very painful."

The skinny guy approached and stopped close to the table.

Sean looked up at him as he drew a long sip of the cola.

"If you did anything to them..." He raised the weapon, putting the muzzle just a little too close to Sean, right in his personal space, which was essentially a *do-not-enter* zone if you were his enemy.

Sean went from looking sluggish and aloof to a deadly snake that had been coiled in the grass. He twisted his body, snapped his hand out, and snatched the gun out of the man's hand. This guy reacted by trying to get it back, but Sean was quicker. He dropped the weapon into the seat while grabbing the guy's shirt collar and yanking him down. The man's momentum made it easy to tug him toward the table. With his other hand, Sean wrapped his fingers around the back of the guy's skull and jerked hard.

The man's nose was the first thing to hit the table. It folded with a sickening series of crunches, followed instantly by a waterfall of thick blood spewing from the nostrils. Sean pulled again. It was even easier now that the guy was dazed and in terrible pain. His arms floundered, hands trying to both grab at the bloody nose and trying to defend, but it was all futile.

His head smashed into the table again and again. Each time Sean brought his head down, the man lost more and more of his grip on reality until he finally blacked out. When Sean felt his body go limp, he knew the guy was done. He let go of the shirt and the man's neck and let him slump to the floor in a heap.

Sean stood up, eyed the thief with an almost nonchalant regard, and then scooped up the weapon. He walked over to the trucker and the waitress, who were both staring at him with mouths agape.

Sean stopped at the register and set the gun down next to the trucker. "Think you can handle this until the cops arrive?"

The trucker glanced down at the gun and then nodded absently. Sean drew the other two pistols from his belt and set them next to the first. "Mary, you and the cook back there can have these if you want." He nodded at the cook behind the dividing wall. He, too, was gazing at Sean like he was some kind of angelic being.

Mary was half on the brink of tears and half in amazement. Sean did not intend to stick around. He'd had his meal, and now it was time to go before the blue lights and sirens appeared on the horizon. He took out a few bills from his pocket, placed them on the counter, and then turned to the door.

"That should cover it, plus a tip, plus a little for the mess." He glanced back at the unconscious man on the floor. His face was covered in dark crimson. "Sorry about the blood. The other two are also out cold on your bathroom floor, but I doubt they'll need much cleanup. Just keep these guns on them until the cops arrive. When they get here, tell them you're going to lower your weapons and that you're just securing the area. You can explain everything from there."

Sean stalked toward the door. He put his hand on the handle to push it open when Mary stopped him.

"Hey," she said.

Sean turned around.

"What's your name?"

"I don't have one."

"What you mean you don't have one?"

"Tell them whatever you want. Just don't describe me to them, okay? I'd rather avoid any legal issues. And I certainly don't want the attention on television."

Her lips curled and her brow furrowed, but she nodded despite the confusion. "Okay, Mr. Smith. I understand."

Sean nodded, gave a flicker of a grin, and then walked out into the cold night.

He doubted she understood. Who could? As long as she wasn't going to run her yapper about him, he didn't care. Either way, the sooner he got out to Fort Mandan, the better.

19

ASHEVILLE

driana needed sleep. It was late at night. Technically, it was early morning. She and Tyler had been at it most of the day and all through the darkest hours of evening. The answer had yet to present itself.

To his credit, Tyler had been unrelenting in his search. For a playboy that had, apparently, earned at least some level of disdain from his contemporaries for his brash antics, the man was a bloodhound when it came to his line of work. Diego had been right to refer her to him. She even doubted if her father would have been able to produce any of the information they had on Boyd in such a short time.

Finding Boyd's partner, though, was proving to be far more difficult, and it was starting to seem as though the man might have been working alone all along.

Tyler wasn't about to give up yet, though, and he kept a fresh pot of coffee brewing all night to make sure he didn't give in to the constant nagging of exhaustion.

More than once, Adriana caught herself drifting off, her eyelids pulling down hard as sleep beckoned.

Tyler stood up and stretched his arms for the twentieth time. He kicked his legs out one after the other to get the blood flowing once more.

"I can't believe my father does this all the time," she said as she stood and stretched her legs again. She, too, needed to get her circulation back.

Tyler shrugged. "Yeah, it's not a glamorous life; that's for sure. Then again, that's why I live a life like this when I'm not working." He raised his hands as if to show off all the things around them that were, at the moment, hidden by the walls of his inner office. "Gotta have some fun, otherwise life might pass you by."

She knew how right he was. She'd immersed herself in chasing down lost art, taking down bad guys, and zipping all over the world with her various quests. Most of her years seemed to have been lost along the way. She thought back on all the places she'd been. While Adriana had been fortunate enough to experience leisurely travel a few times in her life, those times were too far apart.

The world offered so much in the way of culture and fun, but those things had been blurry images as she had zoomed by. She'd forced herself to take some time off every now and then—but always got pulled back into something chaotic or dangerous.

As superficial and materialistic as this guy appeared on the outside, maybe he had a point.

One of the monitors dinged, and the screen froze on an image. The picture was of two men. The one on the left was Andrew Boyd dressed in a polo and khakis. His head was cocked to the side. From the looks of it, he was listening to the other man speak.

"Who's the older guy?" Adriana asked.

A look of deep concern cascaded over Tyler's face. His skin turned pale, and he shook his head. "Um, well, that guy could be a problem."

"What do you mean?"

"Hold on."

Tyler leaned close to the keyboard and began typing again. The screen changed once more, now displaying seven more images of the guy from the first picture. The man was probably in his mid-sixties, possibly a shade older. In most of the images, he was donning a naval officer's uniform, firmly pressed and impeccably clean. Medals, bars, and other regalia adorned the man's clothing.

"Who is that?" Adriana asked.

"That," Tyler said emphatically, "is Fleet Adm. Forrest Winters."

"Who is he?"

Tyler clicked one of the images and enhanced it. The picture swelled to fill up most of that part of the screen. In the background, John Dawkins could be seen chatting with one of his cabinet members.

"He's one of the Joint Chiefs. His position is one of the highest in the land, and he commands the United States naval operations."

"So, he's important. What does that have to do with Andrew Boyd? And why were the two of them talking in that other picture?"

Tyler's eyebrows flitted upward for a second, and he rolled his shoulders. "No clue—to either of those questions—but it's certainly odd that a man who was court-martialed from the United States military is talking with one of the most powerful commanders in the nation."

"When was that photo of them taken?" Adriana crossed her arms and bit her lower lip. The exhaustion she'd felt before was rapidly dwindling, replaced by a burst of unexpected energy that demanded answers.

Her host examined the image and found the date stamp. "Looks like it was recent. This summer. July fifth."

"Interesting."

"Yeah," Tyler agreed. "Sounds like maybe our boy Andrew was up in Washington for the Fourth of July holiday weekend, possibly to do a little business with Admiral Winters."

There were still so many gaps in what she understood about this plot. Adriana was having trouble wrapping her mind around it all.

"Why, though? What could Winters want with Sean?"

Tyler furiously typed more commands into the computer and sat back. The two of them watched the screens in silence for the next five minutes until the machine beeped. A small window on the screen popped up with the words "No Search Results Found."

"Looks like the two of them don't have any connections," Tyler said. "Have you ever heard Sean mention Winters?"

Adriana shook her head. Her eyes were droopy. Dark circles had formed under them. Despite the sudden rush of energy, she was still worn out.

"Then it's a power play," Tyler said. There was a definitive measure of confidence in his tone.

"Power play?"

He nodded. "Yep. Boyd wants something. We both know that's your boy, Wyatt. Winters must want something, too. If we can figure out what that is, maybe we can see the big picture. Might even lead us to Dawkins."

Adriana knew they didn't have time for false leads and half-baked tactics. A misstep could cost them dearly. For her, it could cost her everything.

"What can you tell me about Winters?"

Tyler spun around in the chair and leaned back. He laced his fingers behind his head and stretched. "What do you want to know? I don't have to use my computers for all that. The guy is pretty well known in the military world. That includes my world, too."

"Think about it. If he's behind this—along with Boyd—and if he wants something, that would mean somewhere along his career he was kept out of a loop, perhaps pushed aside, or possibly not given something he wanted."

"Well, he never ran for office. Doesn't strike me as the political type. So, if it's power he wants, I don't believe that was the way he wanted to get it."

"But if he wants power of another kind..."

Tyler clicked his tongue for several seconds and then sat up. "Oh, wow. I can't believe I didn't think of this before."

"Think of what before?"

He turned back to the computer and opened a new window.

Google appeared, and he entered a short string of keywords. When he hit the Enter key, a new series of results appeared on the next page. He quickly clicked on one of the videos, and the screen changed again. After an informative fifteen-second ad, the admiral appeared on the video. He was in the same uniform he'd been wearing in the photos. In the footage, he stood behind a podium with an official Pentagon seal emblazoned on the front.

Adriana and Tyler listened intently as the admiral's voice boomed throughout the crowd. The venue was outdoors and near the water. Politicians and every kind of American aristocrat imaginable were in attendance, all sitting in white chairs like those you'd find at an upscale garden wedding. A waterway was positioned behind him. While it was difficult to tell which one it was, Adriana thought she recognized it.

"Chesapeake," Tyler said, as if reading her thoughts. "That's in Maryland."

The date on the video suggested the speech had been given last year.

The admiral spoke about how the current administration needed to be stronger in terms of foreign policy, that the military needed the president's full support, and that military spending should be increased.

Adriana didn't know a great deal about the murky soup that was American politics, but she did know that Dawkins had curtailed some of the military budget in hopes of finding more efficient ways to fund America's armed forces, while at the same time retaining their capabilities and prowess.

Admiral Winters, it seemed, disagreed with the policies.

He went on to talk about how the United States should be the unchecked, unquestioned power on the land, in the air, and in the sea. His rhetoric reminded both Tyler and Adriana of speeches they'd seen and heard before when studying about Hitler's early years, just before he came into power. Neither of them said it, but they were both thinking it.

"This man sounds dangerous," Adriana commented.

"He certainly does. If he had his way, he'd probably nuke every enemy we have. Shortly after this, there were rumors that Dawkins was going to have him removed from the Joint Chiefs."

"But he didn't."

"Nope. You know as well as I that's not how Dawkins does things."

Adriana was starting to see the motive. "Boyd wanted revenge against Sean."

"And Winters wanted to get back at Dawkins for clipping his…" He let the insinuation linger in the air, catching himself before he said something inappropriate. "You get the point."

She snorted. "Yes, I believe I do."

Tyler sat up a little straighter, the energy starting to return once more. "If Winters is the one behind this, he'll have considerable resources. He could fund an operation like this, and not only that—"

"He'd have connections," she interrupted.

"Bingo. A man like that would have access to information, information that could help a team of assassins or kidnappers get to a former president in his own home."

Adriana considered the theory. Something still didn't add up. She hadn't heard from Sean, which meant he was either still on the road, hiding somewhere, or he'd been caught. She doubted the last option was the case. If he'd been apprehended, the news outlets would be exploding with the breaking story. No, Sean was still out there, and knowing Sean like she did, he wasn't just hiding under a barn somewhere. He was looking for the people responsible for this, just like she was. Was it possible that he was tracking down Boyd and Winters, as well? Or was there another angle he was pursuing?

"Adriana?" Tyler interrupted her thoughts. "What are you thinking?"

She snapped back to the moment and looked down at him. "I'm going to go ask this Admiral Winters some questions."

He snorted a derisive laugh that ended as a long chuckle. Then he realized she wasn't kidding. "Wait a second. Are you serious? You're joking, right? Come on."

"What? What's the problem?"

He blurted out a laugh again. "You are serious. Wow. Yeah, okay. So, I realize you're not from here and all—"

"I have dual citizenship. I've been in America a while now." She crossed her arms and gave him a stern, reprimanding glare.

"Be that as it may, you clearly don't understand who or what you're dealing with here."

"I'm dealing with a soldier. It won't be the first time."

He shook his head back and forth in dramatic fashion, like a cocker spaniel waving its tail to get attention. "No, not even close."

"What do you mean?"

Tyler twisted around to fully face her. He scratched his head. "Well, for starters, this isn't just some ordinary sailor or infantryman you're dealing with here. This is a fleet admiral, the guy in charge of the entire United States Navy."

"Yes, we've been over that."

"You realize that's an immense amount of power, right?"

"Obviously." She discarded the urge to roll her eyes.

"Okay," he prolonged the word, "think of every powerful person in the world. Prime ministers, presidents, kings—they all have something in common."

She arched one eyebrow. "Other than the power thing?"

"Security, Adriana. They all have almost unbreakable security. Secret Service, Marines, federal law enforcement, and those are just the people. That doesn't take into account the systems and technology they have at their disposal."

A dark cloud descended into the room and filled her mind with doubt. Adriana hadn't considered that. He was right. Powerful people like Winters would have considerable forces around him, security teams, alarms on his house—possibly unlike anything she'd ever seen. He'd have an entourage around him at all times. Still, she'd fought off elite security forces before.

"I'll have to risk it," she said.

He sighed through his nose and shook his head. "You don't understand. This isn't like my guys, the ones you knocked out earlier."

Tyler's security guys had since roused from their electrically induced slumber and rushed to the house to make sure he was okay. He'd given them a stern warning and told them he was fine, to go back to their stations. The two guards from the gate had seen her inside his office and given her a scathing glare.

"You ever heard of the PSU?" he asked.

She thought for a moment, forehead wrinkling slightly. "No. Doesn't sound familiar."

"That's because no one thinks about them. The entire world knows about the Secret Service and what they do because the president is front and center in just about everything. You can't go two hours nowadays without tripping over some social media post about her, some breaking news headline, or a radio announcer saying something about her. But how many times in a month do you ever hear anything about the Joint Chiefs? When was the last time you even saw their faces on the television or on the internet?"

Her blank expression gave him the answer he already knew was coming.

"Exactly," he said. "You don't. Those guys are, in many ways, far more secretive than the president. And their security detail is as well. The PSU is short for Protective Services Unit. They're composed of some of the best of the best of the best soldiers in the world. Agents come from multiple branches of the military. The Army Criminal Investigation Command as well as its military police units from the 202nd and 701st are involved. Ever heard of NCIS?" He didn't wait for a response. "The Naval Criminal Investigative Service? They're involved as is the Air Force Office of Special Investigations. They even have some of the elite people from the National Guard and reserve units help out now and then. I'm telling you, this Winters guy is as untouchable as the president. He might even be tougher to get to."

"Good to know."

He couldn't believe what he was hearing. "You can't actually believe you're going to just walk into his home, sit down, and have a conversation with this guy, can you?"

"Maybe I won't walk, but yes."

"Adriana, did you not hear a word I just said? The PSU scouts out everything within a half mile of anywhere their charge is going. That includes churches, homes, and family reunions. If you get within that sphere of protection, they'll bring you in. And let's not forget the little fact that your husband is a fugitive wanted worldwide on suspicion of kidnapping a former president. The authorities are looking for you almost as much as they are for him. If I were you, I'd lie low for a while and try to think of another way to skin this one."

She considered his words for about three seconds and then turned for the door. "Thank you for your help," she said. "I'll be sure to tell my father his gratitude is in order."

Tyler stood up and stalked toward the door, hoping to block her from leaving. He planted one palm on the doorframe. "I can't let you do this."

"First, you're not letting me do anything. Second, I'd move that hand if I were you. Would be a lot harder to type with it broken."

He caught her drift and lowered the hand, but he remained partially in her way. "Look," he relented. "You're right. I can't stop you. And I know you're well trained." That much was true, though he didn't know to what extent. Only a handful of people in the world knew about her past, about her training with the last of the ninjas that walked the planet. "But if you're going to do this, you're going to need help."

She was staring out the door, intent on leaving, but she turned and stared into his eyes.

"At least let me tell you where he is and give you the layout of his house. I can maybe even scoop some of the patrol details. That might give you the slimmest of fighting chances."

The corner of her mouth rose slightly. "Thank you."

He shook his head and went back to the computer stations. His fingers, once more, flew across the keyboard. "Don't mention it. And when I say don't mention it, seriously, I mean mention it to no one."

She turned and crossed her arms, leaning against the doorframe. "Understood."

He nodded. "Okay then. You'll also need some gear."

"I have gear."

"Well, you'll need more if you want to make sure you don't kill good American soldiers while you're trying to get to this guy."

She thought about his comment for a second. "Fair enough."

"And you're going to need a plan."

20

A gent Matthew Petty sighed as he stared at his computer. The hotel room was sparse, hardly the four- or five-star deal he was accustomed to in his normal routine. But he wasn't in his normal routine anymore. He was in the middle of nowhere, trying to track down the man who'd taken the former president of the United States.

Petty ran a hand through his thick brown hair and rubbed the back of his skull for a few seconds. He'd been staring at the computer screen for the last hour trying to piece together all the information he'd gathered so far.

Sean Wyatt had disappeared, Petty believed, shortly after he'd arrived in Atlanta at the IAA headquarters. Unfortunately, there was nothing he could hold the employees there on. He'd questioned Tommy Schultz, his two assistants, even the guy working security in the lobby. None of them knew where Wyatt was. Petty and his team had scoured the security footage in the building; not that it mattered. Wyatt had been there, but he was long gone by now. He'd disappeared minutes before Petty had arrived, though he didn't know how Wyatt got away. With his resources and his skill set, though, Wyatt could be on the other side of the country, or most likely, out of the country.

His team was poring over footage from traffic cameras and every place they could find, but they'd come up empty so far. He'd even had a net put around the perimeter of Atlanta to catch Wyatt if he tried to get through, but it had come up with nothing.

There were simply too many roads to cover.

Wyatt wasn't stupid enough to take a plane. That could be easily tracked. And he certainly wouldn't have gone to Harts-field International Airport. Too many eyeballs and too many cameras there, even with all the chaos the airport's travelers could pose.

He knew Wyatt wouldn't go there.

So, the question became which direction he *would* go.

Southwest to Mexico? Maybe. It was certainly a possibility, though he doubted it. The Mexican border was easy enough to get through, but it was a long drive. Canada, too, was a possibility, but again, the lengthy drive through some major cities would make it difficult to go unnoticed. The Canadians, too, had fewer leaks in their border patrol. Petty considered Mexico a higher possibility, but there was also a third option.

Sean might have decided to hide out somewhere in the mountains.

Petty recalled the manhunt that had taken place when he was just getting going in the FBI. Eric Rudolph had been at the top of their most-wanted list for a long time. He'd been responsible for bombing abortion clinics and gay rallies across the Southeast. In 1996, he'd left an explosive at Centennial Olympic Park that ended up killing two people.

Rudolph disappeared off the map and remained hidden for years. The man became something of a local legend in some ways, despite the fact he was a murderer.

According to his testimony, there were several times when federal and local investigators were close to his location in the mountains. He'd been hiding in leaves, dirt, creeks, wherever he could find cover.

His woodsman and outdoors skills had proved invaluable in thwarting any attempt to locate him.

Eventually, he ran out of places to hide and was captured, but not after an incredible expense of both time and money.

Sean Wyatt could probably pull off a similar disappearing act, if not better.

Petty knew about some of Sean's past. Much of what he did for the government was off the record, beyond Petty's clearance level. Still, he could fill in the blanks. It wasn't the first time he'd seen stuff that was wiped from the record books regarding a former operative.

Sean had worked for Axis, a government entity that answered only to one office. Petty knew all too well he would get no answers from their mysterious director, Emily Starks. She essentially had no checks and balances, which made Petty dislike her all the more.

There were days, of course, when he wished he could work that way, without the committees, the meetings, the bureaucracy dictating his every move. Maybe he was even a little jealous, though he'd never admit that to anyone.

The fact was Sean was a trained killer, a maniac, someone that had made a name for himself after leaving Axis, turning from government asset to head of security for an archaeological agency.

Petty still wasn't sure what that meant or what it entailed, but he'd heard things. People had been killed, often abroad, sometimes here in the United States. Each and every time it was deemed in self-defense or swept under the rug. It was mind-boggling. How could someone have such immunity to laws, both foreign and domestic? He was virtually untouchable. The few times Wyatt had been arrested and put in jail, he was out within hours. No arraignment. No charges. Simply let go. How was that possible? Was he the pope undercover or something? Petty felt like he was taking crazy pills.

Now Wyatt had kidnapped a former president. It was finally time to reel this loose cannon in and teach him a lesson, permanently. There would be no immunity for this one, no safe place he could hide. Sooner or later, Petty would find him.

Wyatt's friend, Tommy Schultz, had tried to cover up. He'd said the usual things a colleague or friend would say. "Sean wouldn't do that. Why would he? He and Dawkins are close friends." All of those things were Grade-A typical cover-up speak, and Petty could see right through it.

He didn't need a motive right now. He just needed to find Wyatt and the president.

That was another component; innocent people don't run. If Wyatt had done nothing wrong, he should have stuck around, let due process run its course and proved himself innocent.

Petty rubbed his temples with his thumbs.

He'd taken a chance going into the IAA building. The place was a labyrinth, full of halls, basements, secret rooms, all sorts of places to hide. He'd gone there hoping to get answers and maybe get lucky. He'd done neither.

In fact, he had more questions now than before.

Wyatt was on the run, which meant he'd ditched the president somewhere. Or did it? Hard to say.

If Wyatt had been in Atlanta, though, that meant the president was probably close by unless Wyatt had come into town that day, leaving someone to watch Dawkins while he visited. But why visit?

None of it made any sense.

The part that confused Petty the most was the message he'd been sent.

He'd received a tip from an unknown number via text message. The note had simply said, "President Dawkins has just been abducted by Sean Wyatt."

When Petty tried to call the number, it went straight to a nonexistent voice mail. He wondered, initially, if it was a hoax of some kind. He'd blown it off at first, but then the news came through the grapevine. Then everything changed. Petty went to work, tracking down everything he could find about Wyatt.

They'd searched his home in Atlanta. Now he was on the outskirts of Chattanooga, Tennessee, at a cheap hotel on the way to Nashville.

He'd been to Chattanooga once a long time ago on a family vacation. They'd visited the touristy places like Rock City and Ruby Falls. He'd been impressed by the town's outdoorsy feel and the beautiful views from the mountains. The city even boasted the world's fastest internet service. It was known as Gig City for being the first to have gigabit fiber-optic networks. Petty had to admit, he wished his internet service was that fast back in Washington.

Still, he felt like he was in a backwater town. It wasn't hard to feel that way. He came from the city, a place where politics, art, culture, and modern amenities were common. Maybe if he got into the downtown area or some of the trendy sections of the city he'd find more of that here, but he didn't have time. He wasn't on a vacation. He was trying to solve what was going to be one of the biggest cases, if not the biggest case, of his career.

He stood up and walked across the room to the entertainment unit where a bottle of water sat on top. He looked at the courtesy card behind it and read what was printed on the surface: "Complimentary water."

It didn't matter if it was free or not. He was there on the government dime. He twisted the cap and took several chugs. After he was done, he set the bottle back down and sighed.

He needed a break. Not a vacation. Just a break in the case. Something had to give. Wyatt had taken a former president hostage, for crying out loud. That couldn't be easy to hide. Someone had to have seen something.

Petty's mind drifted back to the text he'd received from the anonymous number. He'd actually called that number when he was at the IAA building, just to see if a nearby phone rang. Maybe it was one of Schultz's assistants that sent him the text. The hunch had proved unfounded. There'd been no noise, not even a vibration. Petty knew it was a long shot anyway. Still, worth trying.

He'd tried pinging the number, too, but that had come up empty. Whoever had sent him the text was intent on remaining anonymous. It was likely a burner phone, or perhaps the person knew the FBI could trace back to it so they either took the battery out or dropped it in a river. Who knew? Either way, the informant—if that's what they were—was unreachable.

Petty opened the fridge in the bottom part of the entertainment unit and pulled out a bottle of beer. He twisted the top off and took a big gulp, then another. The toasty flavor of roasted grains filled his mouth for a moment before the light burn after he swallowed. He wiped his lips and looked around the dim room. The light blue walls, the dark brown carpet, even the fluffy white pillows pissed him off. The room was nice enough, he supposed, especially considering where he was. That's not what made him angry. He was sitting here with no leads. That was the cause of his rage. He was a caged cheetah, ready to run down its prey and feast on the carcass.

He sighed and walked back over to the bed, slumped down on it as he let the beer dangle between his knees for a second, and then swung them over on top of the comforter.

He took another sip of the beer and thought about turning on the television to see what was on. There had to be a hockey game or something.

As he reached for the remote on the nightstand, his phone started dancing atop the desk in the corner.

He shot off the bed and hurried over to it. Part of him hoped it was his anonymous tipper, but a look at the screen told him it was one of his colleagues, a man named Ryan Tanner.

Tanner was a young go-getter, much like Petty had been before hours of filing reports and filling out paperwork had burned him on the effective impact he'd hoped to have when joining up with the FBI.

Petty pressed the screen's green button and then put it to his ear. "This is Petty."

"Sir? I think we might have a lead."

21

NORTH DAKOTA

Sean stepped out of his SUV and took a look around the parking area. He was one of the first people there, though he wasn't sure if Fort Mandan was a place that was frequented by a gazillion tourists, or if it was one of the more obscure historical spots that dotted the map of the United States.

His breath puffed out through his lips as big clouds of fog were quickly swept away by the frigid North Dakota air. The cold hit him in an instant, stinging his face like darts flung at a hundred miles an hour, pricking the exposed patches of skin on his wrists and face.

Sean winced, gritted his teeth against the cold, and pulled his beanie down tight over his ears. Dry flakes of snow blew by him as a gust of wind picked up, and he turned his back to it to get a brief respite. He'd checked the forecast and been prepared, at least mentally, for the freezing temperatures, but being from the South still kept its grip on him. He'd traveled to cold places before, so it wasn't new, but it always hit him hard for the first few minutes.

He took another quick look around and shoved a Springfield 9mm into his pocket. As his fingers wrapped around the grip, there was the same familiar comfort he'd become accustomed to whenever he picked up the weapon, or his other favorite, his trusty .40-cal from the same maker. Sean wasn't sure whether or not that was a good thing, that holding a firearm could bring such a sense of peace, but he didn't let the thoughts linger too long. He had work to do, and he needed to do it quickly. There were people looking for him, and at the moment he didn't know who or where they were. He turned back into the breeze as it died down again and started toward the refurbished log fort.

Fort Mandan was a triangular design with a rounded point at the back end. The houses inside were abutted to the exterior wall and wrapped the entire way around the inner courtyard until reaching the front gate. The structure was anything but imposing, though Sean figured an enemy might well have feared the sight of the fort a few hundred years ago when a garrison of armed soldiers would have been stationed there.

The fort was positioned on private land, which seemed a little strange to Sean, but there were a couple of historic landmarks he'd seen like that.

He trudged forward across the lot, a thin layer of snow crunching under his feet with every step. The forecast was for more precipitation later that day. The last thing Sean needed was to get stuck out there in the middle of North Dakota in a blizzard. Time was running out and he could ill afford any holdups.

Sean marched to the open gate and paused. There was no need to go inside and have a look around. He wasn't here to learn about the history of the place or take part in their post-colonial celebration of culture. He'd seen the charade online, both before he left Atlanta and again that morning when he brushed up on the details about Fort Mandan. The owner hired people to dress in clothing from the early 1800s, and those actors—for the benefit of visitors—would portray an authentic look into the past at the way life may have been at the fort during the time of the Lewis and Clark expedition.

Sean was about to veer to the left and work his way around the outside of the fort toward the northwestern corner when a man's voice caught his attention. The last thing Sean wanted was to be noticed by anyone. He'd hoped that pulling off that anonymity would be easier out here, away from city populations.

"Sir, may I help you?" The man's voice cut through the cold and filled Sean's ears.

Sean twisted his head to look over his shoulder. A guy, probably in his early twenties, was standing just inside the gate out of the cold. He held an authentic musket in one hand, the barrel laid across his shoulder and jutting out into the air behind his head. His uniform was a replica from the early nineteenth century, just like everything else in and around the structure.

"No, I'm good, thank you," Sean answered in a gruff voice.

"Where ya goin'?" the pretend soldier asked. "There's not much to see around there. And it's cold out."

The man's North Dakota accent caused certain words to sound much different than where Sean was from. The o's especially were drawn out, something Sean had always found interesting.

"I know," Sean said. "I'm checking out the layout of the place." His lips were numb, as were his fingers. He fought off the urge to chatter his teeth as he spoke to the younger man. "Just doing a bit of research, you know? Getting the lay of the land?"

"Cold day for that sort of thing," the soldier said. "Sounds like something you shoulda done during the summer months. Much nicer that time of year."

"I bet," Sean replied. This guy was chatty, and that was the last thing Sean wanted to deal with right now. "Thanks for the advice."

"Whatcha researching?"

Sean turned his head away so the guy couldn't see him roll his eyes. Would he not shut up?

"I'm investigating the layout of the land around the fort, trying to get a better understanding of what it looked like here around the time of Lewis and Clark. Research project." He hoped his explanation would get the younger man off his back, but he saw the uniformed actor take a step forward and instantly knew that wasn't going to happen.

"Sounds interesting. You know, this is the place where Sacagawea had her baby."

"So I hear," Sean didn't try to hide the disdain in his voice. It was drizzled with a heavy layer of sarcasm.

The soldier, apparently, didn't pick up on the snideness.

"Yeah, pretty cool that something so important in our history happened here." The guy cocked his head to the right as if thinking about something. "Of course, it wasn't actually here, though."

Sean nodded, pretending to understand, but then he caught himself just before he started to walk away. "Wait. What did you just say?"

The uniformed guy looked surprised. "Which thing?"

"The part about it not being here. What did you mean by that?" Sean felt the cold dissipate as his heartbeat quickened. His body temperature climbed, and he forgot for a moment he was standing outside in the bitter, chilling air.

"Oh. Yeah, you didn't know that." The soldier turned to the fort and extended his arm. "That's just a replica. Owner built it a long time ago to sort of honor the Corps of Discovery expedition and everyone involved. Gives tourists a way to connect with the past, although during this time of year we don't get many visitors. Too cold for them, I guess."

Sean ignored the chatter. The guy was rambling again, and he didn't have time to waste on chitchat.

"So, this isn't the original footprint of the fort's foundation?"

The guy shook his head as if it should have been obvious. "Nah. They think most of that is under the river now over that way." He pointed over a slight rise to the north. It was framed by outcroppings of tall trees on either side.

"They think?"

"Yeah, you know, archaeologists, historians, all that. They believe it might have been over there by the river, but when the river was widened a long time ago, the original place where the fort might have been was flooded. If it was there, it's underwater now."

A sickening feeling coated Sean's throat and dropped into his gut. He couldn't breathe, couldn't swallow. He wasn't given to sudden outbreaks of emotion or panic. Sean believed there was always a solution. This, however, was concerning news. If the original Fort Mandan location was submerged, that could possibly mean that the clue he was looking for might also be underwater. He didn't need to be reminded of what it would take to conduct a dive in the Missouri River at this time of year.

The river not only possessed a strong current, but it would also be freezing. A diver would need a dry suit to get in during these colder months. Sean not only didn't have time to procure such equipment; he had no idea where he'd get it. His connections were limited, not to mention the fact he was trying to keep a low profile. The fewer people he met, the better.

"Which side of the river do the historians think the fort might be on? North side or south?" Sean asked the question, doing his best to stem the hopes lying under the surface of his tone. If it was on the south side, the clue would likely be underwater and be unreachable. If it was on the north, there might still be a chance.

"They're not really sure," the actor admitted. "I've heard both, but I think the consensus is that it's on the north side of the river."

Sean felt a wave of relief wash over him. His friend John Dawkins's life depended on that answer. It weighed on him like bags of sand on his shoulders. Hearing this guy's answer poked huge holes in those bags and let the sand trickle onto the ground, lightening his load.

"There's not much to see, though. I'm telling ya." The guard planted the butt of his musket onto the snowy ground. "There's no building or anything to see. Not even any mounds around it."

"That's okay," Sean said. "I'm really more interested in the area around the fort."

"What did you say you're studying again?"

Sean turned and started back toward his car. "I didn't," he said curtly. "But I'm working on a study that analyzes the impact of the climate change on this particular part of North Dakota since it has some historical significance. We're losing too much of our history to this global warming thing."

The actor nodded and opened his mouth. "So...you believe in all that?"

Sean chuckled. "Look, the Earth's been getting warmer for thousands of years. And we're not helping. That's all I know."

"True."

"Thanks for the help," Sean said as he walked away. "You should get back in there and stay warm." He pointed at the fort replica.

"Will do. And come back by again. Would love to know what you find."

"You bet," Sean said, using a regional term he'd picked up from hearing other conversations. He had no intention of returning to the fake fort. He had to get to the other side of the river and figure out where the northwestern corner of the original fort had been.

He slid into the seat of his SUV and closed the door, thankful to get out of the biting cold once more. The motor roared to life, and he felt the welcoming hot air pour out of the vents in the dashboard. He turned up the seat warmer to the highest setting, then pulled the phone out of his pocket. This was going to require a little additional research, and there wasn't enough time for him to simply do a quick internet search. He was going to need more firepower.

Tara answered the phone. "Hello?"

"Tara. It's me. I need your help."

22

NORTH DAKOTA

gent Petty sat in the corner booth, sipping on a cup of steaming coffee. His suit jacket was folded in the corner, and his tie was still loose. It was too early in the day to worry about his appearance; the professional look he was required to display all the time.

He honestly didn't care.

Petty had been in the FBI long enough to stop worrying about what people thought of him. At this point, he just wanted to do his job the best he could, and everything else could fall in place, or not, as far as he was concerned.

Two other agents were speaking to a guy in a trucker hat in the far corner. A cook was in the back frying burgers, eggs, bacon, and hash browns. The smell of sizzling meat and cooking potatoes filled the air, with a hint of onion and bell pepper thrown in for good measure. Three police cars were situated in the parking lot. One of them had an officer behind the wheel. From the looks of it, the guy was on his phone, probably on some kind of social media. The other two were inside sitting at the end of the bar while they sipped coffee and told jokes. One kept his hand on his belt next to the pistol in his holster.

Petty noted the guy's hand had stayed there nearly the entire time since he'd walked in over twenty minutes ago.

Agent Petty returned his gaze to the subject across from him at the table and stared into the woman's eyes, then let his gaze fall to her name tag. "Mary?" He said the name like it was a question, one that didn't need asking.

"That's me," she said. Her accent was purely local, sharp and nasally with the e's elongated.

"Would you mind telling me what happened?"

"I can't imagine why you need me to do that. Your friends over there were very thorough with their questions. Didn't they tell you?"

"They did," Petty said with a patient grin that was as fake as the cubic zirconia on her ring. "But I'd like to hear it straight from the horse's mouth."

He flashed a grin, fully aware he'd just insulted her. Just like with the suit, he didn't care.

She chewed on a piece of gum that had lost its flavor over an hour ago. Her lips twisted and circled in constant rhythm as she gnawed on the gum, her eyes peering at him as if assessing whether or not she should trust this guy.

"I'm a federal agent, Mary. Please don't withhold evidence from me. I'd hate to have to take you in. Seriously, I have better things to do. I know you didn't do anything wrong."

"I'm not withholding anything," she chirped. "Like I said, I told your cronies over there everything that happened. But I'll tell you, too, since you seem to be set on it."

"That's all I ask." He laced his fingers together on the table and leaned forward, ready to listen.

"I was working. Guy came in and ordered a turkey melt. Sat here in this booth."

Petty's eyes flashed from left to right as he noted the detail.

"Don't worry about dusting for prints, either," she added. "We've cleaned off the tables and seats."

Petty nodded. He didn't care. He had a pretty good idea as to who was here.

"Keep going," he urged. "And leave out what he ordered. I don't care about that."

"Your kind wants details. So, I'm giving you details." She rolled her eyes and glanced over at the counter. "Anyway, these three guys came in. One was already here. He'd had something to eat and was just hanging out. All three of them had hoodies on. Must be a gang thing or something."

Petty resisted the urge to argue that point. It wasn't important if she thought they were part of a gang or not.

"Go on."

"When the other two came in, the first one stood up. They had guns." This part of the story caused Mary to come unraveled a little. Her voice quivered, and she blinked rapidly.

"It's okay," Petty said, feigning sympathy. "Take as much time as you need." What he wanted to tell her was to hurry up and finish the story. Every second he wasted here was another second Sean Wyatt had to get farther away.

She shook her head. "That guy, the one sitting in this corner, he went to the bathroom."

"Went to the bathroom?"

Mary nodded. "I didn't see him leave, actually. I didn't realize he was gone until one of the men—the leader, I guess—said something about it."

"And then what happened?" Petty did his best to stay patient.

"The leader, he sent one of the other guys to the bathroom to find him."

Petty raised both eyebrows. His thumbs lifted as if to say, "Go on."

"The one in charge and another guy stayed with us out here while the shortest one went to the bathroom." She paused and took a drink of water from the glass in front of her. She swallowed it, glanced out the window, then turned her attention back to Petty. "He didn't come out of the bathroom."

"Who didn't?"

Mary rubbed her thighs with her palms. Petty imagined they were sweaty. She was clearly unnerved by everything that happened and had been detained there through much of the morning. No doubt her shift was already over long ago, and she needed some rest.

"No one came out at first. Then the guy from this booth...he appeared and came back to his table, started eating again like nothing was wrong."

"Was there anything wrong?"

"Uh, yeah. We were being robbed."

Petty rolled his eyes and sighed. "Other than that, obviously."

"Anyway, he just started eating again like everything was normal."

"Then what happened?" Petty was getting annoyed that he had to corral the story out of her.

"The leader, the one in the red hoodie, he came over here to the table and started threatening the stranger. Flashed his gun at him and whatnot. I think he said the other one's name was Dan. Kept asking where Dan was, what happened to him, that sort of thing. Then the guy in the red hoodie made the stranger get up and go to the bathroom with him. I thought for sure he was going to kill the guy."

"The stranger or the hoodie?"

"The hoodie was the one with the gun. As far as I could tell, the stranger was unarmed. They disappeared for a minute. Then the stranger came back out again."

"Alone?"

"Yes, alone."

"So, he took out the two goons and left them in the bathroom?"

"Yep. Then, he comes out here, sits at his table again. The last guy comes over, starts panicking, freaking out. You know? Gets all loud and angry. You could tell he was scared because of the way he kept chattering, making threats. Then he got too close."

"Too close?" Petty leaned in again. The grip on his own fingers tightening to the point his knuckles turned white.

"Yeah. Like this stranger was a snake, coiled and ready to strike. He snatched the guy's head and started bashing it against the table. Broke his nose, I think. There was a good bit of blood. The stranger beat his head against the table until the guy blacked out and fell on the floor."

"And when the threat was done, the stranger left?"

"He stood up, walked over like nothing had happened, paid in cash for his food, and left us the guns he'd taken from the robbers. Told us to hold them until the cops arrived."

"And that was it? The guy just disappeared?"

"Yep. He walked out and drove off."

"Did you happen to see what he was driving?"

Mary looked up at the ceiling for a moment, considering the question. She thought hard for a minute and then shook her head. "Not really. He'd parked off to the side of the building. When he left, it was still dark. I saw the taillights, but that was about it. And even then I didn't get a good look. Might have been a pickup truck, though. Looked like those kinds of lights."

"This man," Petty said, "what did he look like?"

Mary gave the same description she'd given the cops earlier. It did little to help him out. She described a man with brown hair, cut short. His face had sported a scraggly beard. None of that matched the description for Sean Wyatt, but that meant nothing. Petty knew that if Wyatt was on the run, he would have changed his appearance. Wyatt was likely a master of disguise, as cheesy as it sounded. The man had served the United States government on an endless string of covert missions. The clandestine nature of his operations would have required him to have a firm grasp on staying inconspicuous.

Such a job would have made enemies all over the world, and keeping his identity a secret was paramount. Petty had gone undercover enough times to understand the routine. He'd never been caught, not even close. Wyatt would possess the exact same skills. So, even though Mary the waitress described a man that looked almost nothing like Wyatt, Petty knew it was him. There wasn't a doubt in his mind.

"Can I go now?" Mary asked, snapping him away from his thoughts. "I'm really tired, and I've been here over ten hours."

"Sure, Mary. Go get some rest. Thanks for your time."

He felt no sympathy for her. He'd not slept much in the last two days, either. She slid out of the booth and started toward the door.

"Oh, Mary?" Petty said.

She stopped and turned around slowly, wary he was going to ask a new series of questions. "Did he do anything or say anything unusual before leaving?"

She shook her head. "No. He was just nice. You know, heroic."

She turned back toward the door and left, disappearing a moment later around the corner.

Petty stared down at the table. Great. Now this guy is going to be some kind of outlaw folk hero. Not if he could help it. He needed to get in front of this thing, but how? There was no telling where Wyatt might be or where he could turn up next. That was the bad news. There was, however, a glimmer of hope. Petty was on the right track. It came down to simply waiting for Wyatt to make a mistake. Then he could pounce.

23

NORTH DAKOTA

Sean walked down the gentle slope with a heightened sense of caution. He glanced back one time to check on his car, but the real reason was to make sure he wasn't being followed. He'd only seen a few other cars out on the main road, but that didn't mean someone wasn't watching. For all he knew, whoever was behind this may well have arrived before he had and taken up position.

That, of course, was doubtful. If the person or persons behind this entire conspiracy had the slightest clue about Fort Mandan and its relationship to the Madison letter, they'd have no need for Sean and his friends.

He'd called IAA headquarters and spoken to Tara and Alex. Apparently, Tommy wasn't immediately available, but the kids had been invaluable with their research and insights.

Sean had stayed on the phone as he found a road across the river. Based on the guidance from Tara and Alex, he was able to locate an old side road that was little more than two grooves cut into the earth. Part of him wondered if it was an old wagon trail, untouched and overgrown from the last hundred or so years.

A few strands of long grass poked out from the veil of snow

covering the ground. The ruts were shallow but certainly pronounced against the rest of the surface.

While he was on the phone with Tara and Alex, they'd done a quick survey of the area, using aerial photos and satellite images to get a better idea of any potential anomalies that might exist in the local geography.

At first, he thought they would probably find nothing, and he sat in his SUV for nearly an hour, hidden behind a thicket of trees while they conducted their search.

It turned out to be worth the wait when Alex called back and let him know that they were able to find something.

"It's probably nothing," he'd warned, "but it's more than anything else we could find in that area."

Sean had to take the chance. He was there, after all. What did he have to lose?

They'd spotted an edge or a line in the aerial map. It was subtle, possibly nothing more than the location of an old farm fence or maybe a retaining wall used to stem the flooding during rainy times of year. He'd come this far. Sean figured it was worth a shot.

He walked down the embankment toward the shore, noting on his phone the images that the kids at the lab had sent. According to the map, the northwest corner of the original fort's foundation was down near the shore, barely cutting out into the banks by a mere ten or so feet. That was, of course, assuming that it was the fort they were all looking at and not some other man-made feature cut into the natural geology.

Sean slowed his pace as he neared the shore, and when he got to the edge he came to a stop as he gazed down at the dark river flowing below his feet.

The Missouri River was an impressive stretch of water. The longest river in North America, it stretched over twenty-three hundred miles, emerging from western Montana and running all the way to Saint Louis where it joined with the Mississippi River. It was not an insignificant tributary.

Sean caught himself gazing at the massive confluence, longer than intended, and snapped his attention back to the map on his screen. According to what he was seeing, he was standing on the point of the corner. He had to force himself to look down and focus intensely on the ground before he noted the anomaly.

It was subtle, barely noticeable, but as he stared at the earth he realized the aberration. The indentation was only inches deep, if that, and barely more than a foot wide. It stretched in a straight line for several feet until it disappeared into the grassy hillside where it met the shore's drop-off. He looked to the left and noted that the same kind of line formed another potential wall, this one longer. It ran at an angle to the shore another twenty feet down from where he stood.

Sean blinked against the cold breeze and tightened his Oakleys against his face to keep the chilly air from causing tears to stream down his face. He'd always had that issue, ever since childhood. When the weather turned cold, the slightest wind would cause him to tear up, blurring his vision and causing people around to ask if he was okay.

He chuckled at the thought and continued analyzing the terrain. He spun around, arms flailing in his winter coat like a child on a snow day. Just up the hill, about one hundred yards away, was the edge of a small forest.

He'd noted the woods when making his way to the river, and figured it was a likely location for something to be hidden, if in fact he was in the right area. He had to be. Sean shook off the negative thoughts. They were unhelpful, and he'd learned a long time ago to ask if something was helping or hurting. If it was the latter, he'd learned to let it go and focus on the solution. That's how he'd done things for years. That line of thinking had saved his hide more than once.

"This has to be it," he said to himself.

Another shiver of cold shot through his body. The coat and winter pants certainly helped stay the freezing air, but it couldn't be entirely prevented. Sean looked back at the river, once more at the two faint lines in the ground, and then returned his gaze to the forest. That had to be it. He recounted the riddle out loud. "A hundred paces from the corner."

It was time to see if there really was something there or not, or if he was even in the right place. Only one way to find out.

He trudged up the hill, finding it much more treacherous than the walk down. On several occasions, his boots slipped on the slick snow, and he caught himself scrambling to maintain balance.

He'd left his pack in the SUV, electing to go it with only a sidearm and a hunting knife to protect himself. If he needed to return to the vehicle, it was a short walk away, just across an open meadow.

Sean pushed up the hill, his feet slipping every few steps until he reached the crest where the slope rounded off at the top. There, it was only another fifty feet of flat earth to reach the forest.

His eyes darted left and right. He thought he heard the sound of a car in the distance, but one never came into view. He was off the beaten path—that was for sure—and the nearest road was several hundred yards away. The bad news was that, until he reached the cover of the woods, he was out in the open. The good news was he'd hear or see someone coming from almost a literal mile away.

Sean kept his eyes peeled, scanning the horizon in every direction until he reached the forest. Upon passing the first few rows of trees, he found himself overwhelmed with a sense of safety. The thick tree trunks surrounded him, a safety net against both the cold and any curious eyes that might be watching.

He was fairly certain he'd have seen someone observing his movement, but there was always the possibility. He'd been out in the open before, watching targets while camouflaged and they'd never been the wiser. The same thing could very well happen to him.

Sean shrugged off the paranoia. His immediate concern was finding the clue.

He walked dead ahead, doing his best to maintain a straight course from the corner of what he hoped was the old foundation of the original Fort Mandan. He pulled out the phone once more and glanced at the notes he'd made. The paper was still in his pocket. The copy of the original Madison letter was protected by laminate, but that didn't mean he shouldn't have a backup. Sean had transferred every piece of crucial information from the letter to his phone in case he ran into trouble at some point. Of course, if he did, anyone with half a brain would take both the note and his phone, so maybe the digital copy was more for his own peace of mind. He'd saved it to a Dropbox folder, though, which was password protected and also meant he could access it from essentially any computer or mobile device anywhere in the world.

Sean heard a sound to his right, and he pulled out his weapon, aiming it in that direction. He crouched to one knee and listened. The breeze was gentler here in the forest, the trunks partially blocking out the wind. Outside the woods, the wind had been a constant whistle in his ears. Here, it was barely a breath brushing against his eardrums.

His breath came out of his mouth in cloudy bursts, visible for a moment and gone the next. Even his breathing was a constant reminder of how cold it was.

He didn't see anything unusual in the woods and lowered his weapon. This time, however, he didn't return it to the holster. Better to be ready in case of an attack.

Sean turned back to his original path and was about to walk ahead when something caught his eye. There was a tree right in front of him, only a couple dozen feet away. The trunk was wide and thick, obviously older than many of the smaller, skeletal trees that occupied the woods. It was an oak, likely several hundred years old. Sean had seen trees like that before. There was one such oak on the campus of a local university he frequented that had been dated back to around the Middle Ages. He wondered how that was possible. That tree had likely gone through quite a history, and he often considered what it would say if it could speak. Such thoughts were silly and unproductive, but they came to his mind nonetheless during moments of quiet reflection or fanciful daydreams.

He locked his gaze on the tree as he approached, his feet moving unconsciously beneath him, carrying him toward the strange sight. In the two hundred-plus years that had passed since Meriwether Lewis had walked in this area, things had changed. Trees had grown. Settlers had established homesteads, farms, and even small towns. And the natural world had changed as well.

Sean stopped at the tree and stared at the surface of the bark. A long line curved back and forth from about six feet high down to around his ankles. The engraved design had healed over time, the bark growing back to cover up the wound that had been cut into it. That didn't change the fact that it was easy to see, especially considering the clue Sean carried on his phone. The way was marked by a serpent. It couldn't have been more obvious, even though now it didn't look much like a snake at all. The only discerning feature was the curve to the creature, but Sean knew that had to be it. Based on the scarring of the bark, it had to be close to two hundred years old, at a minimum.

He'd spent nine years of his life working for the founder of a massive snack cake empire. When Sean was in college, his boss had asked him to do some surgery on a giant oak that stood in the yard directly in front of the house. Sean had never done anything like that before but did his best to research how an arborist would handle it. He believed he'd done a good job, and more than a decade after leaving the place, he went back to see how the tree was doing. He was happy to find it alive and well, and the places he'd cut were growing back, much like what had happened to this trunk.

He wasn't an expert, but he knew a little, and Sean's rapid calculation told him this was the spot. He glanced around once more and then knelt down in the snow at the base of the trunk.

Sean started scraping away the hard snow, but he soon realized that would be an endeavor in futility. He panted for breath; once more dense clouds burst from between his lips and out of his nostrils.

He was frustrated but not defeated. This was the right place, but how would he dig up whatever was hidden here?

He stood and looked around for a big branch he could use to cut into the frozen earth, but he saw nothing that would do the job. Even if he had a shovel, the ground was as hard as stone. He put his hands on his hips for a moment then walked around the tree, tracing a line with one gloved finger across the bark. When he was on the other side, Sean found the solution to his problem. At the base of the tree was a hollow cut out of the trunk near the ground. It may have occurred naturally, or perhaps it had been the doing of Captain Lewis, but either way it presented Sean with the possibility that maybe he wouldn't have to dig several feet into solid ground with his bare hands.

He crouched down again and craned his neck to get a better view into the shallow darkness. The cavity wasn't deep, less than a foot into the trunk that was at least twice that thick if not more. The edges of the hole were scarred much like the serpent on the other side, which caused Sean to consider perhaps it had been cut on purpose. It didn't matter at this point. He had to find out what was there, if anything.

Doubt crawled into his mind and caused a burning sensation to seep into his gut. He knew that a couple of hundred years had passed, and in that time people had surely come through this forest constantly. It would take little more than a curious child wandering through the woods to come upon this tree and have a look inside the hole. That didn't matter, though, he had to check.

He got down on his hands and knees, the cold earth sending a freezing sting through his skin and joints. He tilted his head and switched on the flashlight on his phone, holding it into the dark recess. There was nothing on the ground or on the curved walls of the inner part of the tree. He noticed no signs of disease or insect infestation, either, which was surprising. Then he saw something that didn't belong, an object that dangled from a hook drilled into the interior wall of the trunk.

A metal box, rusted and corroded from time was hanging there by a thread; the rusty chain on the hook looked brittle enough to break at any moment. How it had hung on that long was beyond Sean. He reached in and grabbed the box, carefully lifting it so the hook would come free of the chain.

When it was loose, he pulled it out into the light and examined it closely.

He could see there was a thin, crumbling layer of wax coating the box that had worn down over time. As he handled the container, it broke away in chunks and flecks that fell to the ground at his feet.

Sean heard another noise. Or did he? His head snapped up, and he flashed a quick look around the woods. It had plunged back into the eerie, peaceful silence of a forest in winter.

Satisfied no one was there, he yanked out his hunting knife and began digging away at the wax along the seam between the lid and the main compartment. It didn't take much effort to pry the old sealant out of the grooves. In less than two minutes, he had removed all of the wax. He lifted the rusty metal clasp that was the final barrier to the contents and looked over the surface of the lid one more time. There were no designs carved into the metal, no emblem or logo that represented anyone's family or military designation. Just a plain metal box from two hundred years ago.

Sean swallowed and then raised the lid. He blinked against the freezing bite in the air, blinking to make sure he was seeing clearly. Inside the box was a piece of gold. It was flat and curved with grooves cut into either end, as if it fit together with other pieces like it.

"It's part of a ring," he said, the realization hitting him.

The section of the ring was about six inches from corner to corner. He took it between his forefinger and thumb and raised it to the light, inspecting every inch of the surface and edges. What was this thing?

He noted the bizarre symbols carved into the top and bottom. They looked like characters but were unlike any he'd ever seen before. They weren't Japanese or Chinese. For a moment, Sean wondered if they were Norse, but he quickly dispelled that, having seen those kinds of runes firsthand on several occasions.

Triangles, squares, straight lines, squiggly lines, circles, and other shapes covered the curved metal, all in what must have surely been some kind of sequence.

But what did that sequence say? What did it mean? Sean had no idea, but he knew this had to be one of the keys he was looking for. Did that mean the other two keys were the same as this, all fitting together to form a singular ring? And if so, why? What did it do? Or was it just some ancient treasure that Meriwether Lewis thought had better remain hidden?

Sean's instincts told him that it was the former, that this was part of something bigger and that the ring would lead him to a much grander find, something that the people who took President Dawkins wanted. But what was it?

He started to rise to head back to the SUV when he heard another sound. This time it was distinct. He'd passed off the previous few noises as paranoia, the result of an overactive imagination or simply being too alert, as he tended to be sometimes.

This was different. It was a clear snap of a twig. Sean quickly stuffed the gold into his pocket and shoved the empty box back into the tree's cavity. He raised his weapon and spun around, surveying the area.

"Sean?" a familiar voice shouted.

Sean lowered his weapon upon hearing his friend. He frowned, but that expression melted away as Tommy appeared on the edge of the forest behind him.

"Tommy? What are you doing here?"

Tommy's gloved hands went out wide. "Couldn't let you do this on your own. That's not how we work, buddy."

"I'm a fugitive."

"Yeah, I know. Which is why I sent the plane to Cambodia...with me on the manifest. If they're tracking my whereabouts, they'll think I'm on my way to get some street noodles in Phnom Penh."

Sean arched one eyebrow under his beanie. "Good thinking."

"I thought so."

"But I don't want you to get into trouble. You don't have to be here. You're innocent."

"So are you. Right? I mean, you didn't kidnap Dawkins, did you?"

Sean chuckled. "I was with you, idiot."

"Okay then. What did you find?" Tommy pointed at the flat curved piece of gold jutting out of Sean's coat pocket.

"Let's get back to the car, and I'll let you have a look. I've never seen anything like it." He twisted his head around in every direction, eyeing the forest around them.

"What?" Tommy asked. "What is it?"

"Nothing. I...I just get this weird feeling we're being watched."

Tommy took a quick survey of the land around them. "Then maybe we should get moving."

"Yeah," Sean nodded.

Tommy led the way out of the forest and back into the snowy hillside leading up to the two SUVs. Sean was in the clear when he paused and looked back into the woods. Something or someone was out there. He was sure of it.

24

ATLANTA

Emily had waited long enough.

She'd paced around her office for almost an hour, hands folded behind her back, head down, striding back and forth. The monotonous activity did little to calm the raging anxiety in her head, much less the twisting, rotting pain in her gut.

She'd given the Feds as much time as she thought they would need and then promptly drove over to the IAA building near Centennial Olympic Park. She sat in the parking garage for over an hour before she saw the last federal investigator leave the site.

The detectives and agents involved had taken their sweet time. Emily wasn't surprised. The government's investigators were always thorough, except when they were told not to be. There'd been many incidents throughout history that she knew had been swept under the rug or covered up in such a way to make things palatable for the American people.

She imagined this wouldn't be one of those cases.

John Dawkins, former president and currently the man she loved, had been abducted, which had sent both the justice and intelligence communities into a spin. Like dumping water on an ant hill, the two arms had activated immediately. Emily imagined their headquarters up in Washington would have been spilling out agents just like ants from the soil upon hearing the news.

Emily looked both ways and then trotted across the street and around the corner to the entrance.

The gray metal façade of the building shimmered in the waning sunlight. The surface reflected the faint oranges and pinks of the sky. Traffic was picking up as people poured out of the businesses and skyscrapers all around the city, anxious to get in their cars and sit in traffic for two hours before finally arriving home.

Emily stepped into the IAA headquarters and stalked through the lobby. Six or seven people were making their way to the doors, laughing, talking about something they'd read online. Another couple were talking about the implications of a discovery another archaeologist had made deep in the Baltic Sea.

Emily ignored most of the talk as she proceeded through the lobby, the hard soles of her shoes clicking with every step. The sound echoed off the marble tiles and the hard walls. She didn't care how much noise she made at this point. Emily wanted answers.

She made her way to the restricted entrance door and entered her personal key code that Tommy had given her when the new building was constructed. Emily was more than a friend to Sean and Tommy; she was family. That meant she was given an all-access pass to everything IAA. The door locks clicked, and she pushed through, stepping into a wide hallway on the other side. As she made her way toward the elevator, she considered how many artifacts had rolled through this corridor. Some of the world's most priceless treasures had graced this hall. Most of the extraordinary items IAA brought in were kept down in the basement, along with the laboratory where Tara and Alex worked. The layout of the building was similar to the original. It had been good foresight on Tommy's part for both structures, allowing for an underground section that would act as a kind of bunker or bomb shelter.

How fortuitous that had been when several years ago terrorists had blown up the original building. During the cleanup, the construction crews discovered that all of the artifacts and relics in the underground areas remained intact. A couple of things had shaken free of their cradles within display cases, but only relatively minor damage was sustained.

Emily stopped at the freight elevator and pressed the button with the down arrow on it. Thirty seconds later, the large lift door opened and she stepped on board, pressed the button for the lab floor, and crossed her arms to wait.

The door closed again, and the elevator descended into the bowels of the building. The metal walls inside the lift gave Emily a cold sensation, like being trapped in a steel coffin.

The thought fluttered away as the elevator dinged, announcing her arrival in the basement. The door opened and she stepped out into the hall. The wall opposite her was lined with huge windows, all the way from one end to the other. She could see Tara and Alex sitting at a table in the far corner, close to their computer stations.

Emily made her way down to the other end, foregoing the clean station that the workers and visitors would use to enter the lab, making sure they were free of contaminants. Emily figured the cops and Feds that had come to visit didn't use the thing, so why should she?

Tara and Alex were leaning back in their chairs as Emily entered the enormous room. They didn't move, save for Alex rubbing his temples with both hands. The young married couple looked exhausted. Emily had seen that look before after interrogations. Although what they'd endured this day wouldn't technically be called an interrogation, she knew that's exactly what it would have felt like for these two.

"Come to ask us some more questions?" Tara asked as Emily rounded the L-shaped computer station.

Emily eased into a seat at the table and crossed one leg over the other, then folded her arms. She looked like an irritated school teacher with a classroom of kids who wouldn't behave. Her dark brown hair was pulled back into the tightest ponytail ever made. Her forehead was free of wrinkles except the ones produced by her frown.

Her full lips seemed less so at the moment, stretched thin with a scowl that could have terrified a seventeenth-century pirate.

"Where is he?" Emily asked.

Alex leaned forward with a sigh and lowered his hands to the table. "We don't know."

"You know I'm Sean's friend. I have no intention of turning him over to the authorities, but I need you to work with me here."

Tara twisted the chair around. She scratched the back of her head. "Those dudes were here all day, Em. All day. They're convinced Sean took your boyfriend...I mean, President Dawkins."

"It's okay," Emily said. She disarmed her fierce expression and put on one that was a little more empathetic. "I know they must have worn you guys out." Emily leaned forward and put her forehead in her palm. "I'm just so worried about John. And Sean, too."

For all his flaws and for all the times Emily had been forced to bail Sean Wyatt out of difficult, often tenuous international situations, she loved him like a brother. The two of them had always had each other's backs no matter what. He'd helped her, too, along the way, made her a better agent, a better director. In no small part, her success at Axis was due to Sean Wyatt. That was something she'd never forget.

Her love of Sean was only trumped by John Dawkins. They were the two most important men in her life. Few had been allowed into her heart the way they were, and now they were both missing: one on the run, one taken. It was all she could do to fight back the tears, the burning emotions roaring inside her chest. Despite all the tight situations she'd been in, the challenges, the difficult spots, she'd rarely panicked and almost never reached the point of desperation, but she was there now.

She took a deep breath to wrest back control of her feelings and then exhaled. "You don't know where John is, do you." She said it more like a statement, purely based on logical assumptions.

"No, ma'am, we don't," Alex said. "But we do know which way Sean was headed."

"You do?"

Tara nodded to confirm what Alex had said. "Sean went to find the solution to a letter we received."

"Letter? Solution? What are you..." Then the epiphany hit her. "Another treasure hunt. Is that what this is about?"

Alex and Tara exchanged a wondering glance. They were in their late twenties now but still had some childish attributes, one of which that they both still looked very young. Another was that from time to time they could get a little deer-in-the-headlights look in their eyes. They had that look as Emily stared at them, probing for the truth. She knew Tara and Alex wouldn't lie to her. Whether or not they would spill all the beans on all this was something she needed to find out.

"Look," Emily said, sensing the hesitation on both their parts, "I need to find Sean. He might be in trouble. There are federal agents from one ocean to the next trying to find him. When they do, they will bring him in, and I don't know what I'll be able to do to get him free, even with my connections. I need to get to Sean before they do."

Tara swallowed hard, the pale skin on her neck folding in once as she did so. Her reddish hair shimmered in the sterile fluorescent light above. She bit her lip for a moment, then sighed. "We don't know where he is now. But we received a letter the other day."

"A copy, actually," Alex corrected. Then he noticed the irritated look on the two faces before him and retreated from the conversation with a surrendering wave of the hand.

"Right. A copy. Anyway, it was a letter from James Madison."

"The former president. Early nineteenth century. Go on."

"Yeah. So, this letter was apparently written in regard to something Capt. Meriwether Lewis found on the Corps of Discovery expedition."

"The Lewis and Clark expedition?"

"Correct. The same one. Anyway, the letter describes something important, something powerful that Lewis found. It seems that Lewis held back the information for years. When they left to venture west, Thomas Jefferson was the president. Lewis never gave Jefferson his full report. Which makes one wonder..."

"What was he hiding?" Emily's voice muttered the words.

"We also received a video," Alex cut in again, this time with helpful information. "It was slightly different than the ones the networks received. Ours had additional footage, footage that contained a threat from the people who kidnapped Dawkins. They told Sean that if he wanted the president to live, he had to leave town and follow the clues laid out in that letter. The first place he was heading was North Dakota, an historic location known as Fort Mandan. It was the sort of the staging point where the Corps of Discovery really started their journey west."

"I thought that was in Saint Louis," Emily countered, inadvertently showing off her historical knowledge.

"Initially, yes, but North Dakota was where they met up with a French fur trader and his infinitely more famous wife, Sacagawea."

"Ah," Emily said with a long nod.

Most Americans knew that name. She was one of the most famous of all Native Americans. Because of her, the expedition managed to survive through some extreme conditions, including brutally cold temperatures. And she managed to do it all with a newborn baby.

"They left Mandan," Tara continued, "and went due west, making their way toward Montana, Idaho, and Oregon, where they ended their journey at the mouth of the Columbia River."

Emily thought about the new information for a moment. It didn't take long for her to draw conclusions. "So, Sean went to Fort Mandan."

"Yes," Tara said definitively. "We've received updates from his burner phone on his progress, but only twice now."

"Twice?"

Tara nodded. "All he told us was that he found what he needed at the first location and that he was heading to the second."

"Where would that be?"

Alex slid a copy of the Madison letter across the table. He'd hidden it while the Feds went through everything: emails, computer files, paper files, trash, and everything they could get their hands on that wasn't bolted down or protected in a glass case.

He'd stashed the letter in his desk and had only just retrieved it mere minutes before Emily arrived. His plan was to look through it and try to figure out more of the riddle. He knew he couldn't necessarily reach out to Sean, but if there was a way to get him some help, that would make deducing the clues at least a little beneficial.

"This is the letter," he said, tapping the paper with one finger.

Emily reached out and drew it closer. She scanned the sentences in quick order and then looked up at Tara, then Alex, then back to the paper.

"He's trying to figure this out?"

Alex and Tara nodded simultaneously.

"And John's life depends on Sean figuring this out?"

"Looks that way," Tara confirmed.

A worried look fell over Emily like a veil.

"I...do have some ideas as to the solution to part two," Alex said, his timid voice cutting the silence like a dull knife, imprecise and clumsy, but his statement carried hope nonetheless.

"Tell me."

25

BARING

The phone rang twice before there was an answer on the other end.

"This is Winters. I hope you're calling from a secure line."

"I am, sir."

"Good. What's going on? I assume you're calling because you have an update for me?" His was a question, uncertain if that was truly the reason for the call.

"I do."

That was good news. So far, Admiral Winters had been in the dark on things. He'd partially wanted it that way. The less he knew, the more plausible deniability he'd possess, though he knew that would be of no concern once he had located the artifacts and brought them in for research.

Everything was riding on this gamble; his entire career, his home, his reputation, his life. If he was implicated—or worse, caught—he'd go to prison until the day he died. Winters had no intention of going to jail, which is why he was being exceedingly careful, making sure his contact didn't try calling from a cell phone. He also swept his home once a day to make sure no one had bugged it, not that there was any reason to. Not yet anyway.

Winters had been nothing but an exemplary sailor and citizen. He'd broken no laws, as far as anyone knew, but one could never be too careful.

"What do you have?" Winters asked.

Andrew Boyd paused for a second. Winters could hear sounds in the background—cars passing by, an 18-wheeler rumbling along with a loud grumble from the driver Jake braking. Winters knew that meant his man was on a pay phone somewhere. Where he was able to find one of those, Winters didn't know. Pay phones were a rarity these days, gone the way of the pager with the advent of advanced mobile devices.

"He found something."

Winters felt his heartbeat quicken. He'd hoped this wasn't some elaborate hoax by James Madison and Thomas Jefferson. He'd prayed that he was right about Meriwether Lewis, that the explorer *had* found something important, something powerful on his journey to the Pacific. Even with all the evidence, the letters, the things he'd seen, Winters wasn't sure. Now he knew. Now there was proof.

"What is it?" he asked with suppressed excitement.

"I'm not sure, sir. The guy I put on his tail couldn't get close enough to get a good view, but it looked like gold."

"Gold?" That was interesting. Why would Captain Lewis hide a piece of gold out in the middle of the wilderness of North Dakota? And what possible connection could it have to whatever the man had found out west?

"Yes, sir. That's what my operative said. Not like a chunk, though. It appeared to be honed, crafted into a shape. My guy only caught a short glimpse of it. Then Wyatt looked around. He said he had to stay hidden. Apparently, Wyatt was on edge."

"For good reason. The entire FBI is looking for him."

"True."

"How big was this piece of gold?" Winters pressed the issue, his curiosity spiking.

"Not big," Boyd answered. "He was able to fit it into his coat pocket."

This was good news. If Wyatt had found the first key, that meant they were a third of the way there. It was going to be close. The FBI was on Wyatt's trail, which was part of the plan but also presented another potential issue. If Wyatt were caught and arrested, that would slow things down. Sure, Winters could order his men not to do anything to Dawkins, but what would that accomplish? Winters needed Wyatt in the field.

"Your man with the FBI investigation," Winters said, diverting the conversation to another concern, "what is he saying?"

"They're close but not that close. Apparently, Wyatt stopped a robbery at a diner late last night, early this morning."

"Stopped a robbery?" That was interesting. Winters didn't see how that had anything to do with trying to find the key.

"Yeah. Seems he was there for a late-night bite to eat and ended up taking down three punks who were trying to knock off the till."

"Do the witnesses know anything?"

"Doesn't sound like it. The waitress didn't tell Petty anything helpful, so I doubt any of those people realize who he was."

"Quite the hero, Sean Wyatt." Winters let the words hang in his asset's ear for a moment. He knew very well how much Boyd hated Sean Wyatt.

"He's no hero," Boyd said, the venom dripping from his voice. Winters imagined the man clenching his jaw and gritting his teeth at the mere mention of the name. "He's a suck-up, and he's going to get what's coming to him."

"I know," Winters said. "Soon. I promise. But we need him alive right now, and we also need him not in jail, so make sure your guy in the agency keeps that hound Petty from getting too close."

"It's a tricky game you're trying to play, Admiral. Lot of moving parts, all dangling from one puppet master."

Winters didn't need to be told what he was doing. He knew the risks, knew the difficulty of an operation of this scale. Then again, the cliché claimed that the best things in life weren't free or easy. He didn't need stupid sayings to realize that. He'd fashioned himself into one of the most powerful men in the country, a personal adviser to the president and a revered commander in the United States Navy. Winters understood the risks, and he anticipated the rewards that would come from taking them.

"Keep on it," Winters said.

"Yes, sir."

Winters was about to end the conversation when another question popped into his mind. "How is the hostage?"

He didn't dare say the name over the phone. Even though there were no taps connected to his line; he'd checked again earlier that day as he knew that the NSA could always be listening. They had a file on every single citizen in the United States and all of the non-citizens—especially the non-citizens. There were bugs, video feeds, and endless streams of digital information going straight to NSA headquarters in Fort Meade, Maryland. Winters wasn't going to give them a layup just in case they happened to be listening to his conversation.

"He's doing fine," Boyd said. "Stubborn, wouldn't eat at first, but I knew the hunger would get him eventually. I tried to tell him this would all be over soon, but he won't say a word."

"Good," Winters said. "Better he keep his mouth shut. He ran it enough when he was in politics. The world could use a little silence out of him."

Winters harbored resentment toward the former president despite the fact he'd worked for the man for eight years. They'd disagreed on several issues, one being an attack plan Winters had suggested for a situation in Somalia.

The United States had avoided direct conflict with that coastal African nation since the 1990s, but a rise in terrorist activities and a potential cell forming in Mogadishu gave Winters cause for concern. He'd wanted to wipe half the city off the map, citing that most of the people who lived in those parts weren't innocent and the few that were could be written off as collateral damage. Dawkins had ignored the notion and come up with a more clandestine way to handle the situation.

The president, of course, had been proved correct, but that didn't stop Winters from believing his plan had been the best path to take.

That was one of several instances where he and the president clashed. Now, the retired politician would have to keep his mouth shut, locked away in the mountains of Washington State until his friend Sean Wyatt either came through and found a relic of immense power—or until he failed and Dawkins had to be executed.

Winters knew that the execution was a foregone conclusion, but Wyatt could prolong his friend's life for a while by tracking down the artifact.

"Anything else, sir?" Boyd asked, cutting the silence with a razor-sharp tone.

"No, that's all for now. Carry on and please let me know when you have another update. If Wyatt found the first key, that means he's on his way to the second, wherever that is."

"My guy said he's heading west, sir, which makes sense."

"He's taking the route Lewis and Clark took, going toward the Pacific."

"Looks that way."

"Excellent. Let me know when he finds the second key."

"Yes, sir."

Winters hung up the phone and leaned back in his leather chair. A lamp next to the end table to his right cast a yellowish glow over the room. He stared at the bookshelf across from him, volumes filling every shelf to the point of bursting. His eyes fell to one particular book, an older one with a dusty and worn black cover. It was the book that was responsible for this entire mission, the one that had caused him to believe in the powerful artifact he knew deep down Meriwether Lewis had discovered.

Soon, he thought, he would have the power to command the seas. Then no president or king or prime minister anywhere in the world would be able to stop the might of the United States military.

26

Emily's phone rang in her SUV. She glanced at the number on the console but didn't recognize it. That seemed to be the case now and then in her line of work. Her operatives used numerous phones and other mobile devices as a means of contacting her when they were in the field on assignment. Ignoring the call wasn't an option. It could have been one of her agents in need of help. Besides, no one had that number but people she trusted.

She rubbed her temples with her forefingers and stared at the phone. Next to it was a sheet of paper with a list of two dozen names. She'd marked through most of them, none of the leads coming up with anything useful in her desperate hunt to find the man she loved, John Dawkins.

Emily sighed and picked up the receiver. "Hello. This is Director Starks."

"Em, don't say my name."

She instantly recognized Sean's voice. She also knew exactly why he'd responded that way. It was unlikely someone was listening on her end, but nothing was certain.

"You okay?" she asked.

"Yeah, I'm fine. And...I'm not alone now."

"In a good way?"

"With a friend."

She understood. "Don't tell me where you are."

"I wasn't going to." She could almost see the wry grin on his face and the twinkle in his eye as he said the words with just enough sass to make her arch an eyebrow. "We're on the right track, though. What about you? You okay? Any leads?"

"I'm..." Her voice cracked for a moment. Emily Starks was one of the strongest women Sean had ever met. They'd been friends ever since he'd joined Axis, and in the years since he'd left. He trusted her implicitly. And she trusted him. Sean had never really heard her break down, and it made him feel awkward for a moment. She was a rock, and now that rock was crumbling a little.

"Sorry," she said. "It's just...it's hard."

"I know," Sean said. The smart-aleck nature he clung to nearly all the time was let go, replaced by a deep sincerity few knew he possessed. "But we're going to find him. You know that, right? He's fine. I'm sure of it."

"Have you heard from the people who did this?"

"Not since the other day," he admitted. "But we...we found something."

A spear of hope shot up through her chest. "What? What did you find?"

"These guys, they have us searching for something, something they thought Lewis and Clark discovered on their expedition over two hundred years ago. I don't know what it is or what they're planning to do with it, but there are three keys according to a letter from James Madison."

"Madison?" She played along, not letting on that she already knew about the letter. Sean didn't need to know that she was, as they spoke, on her way to find him.

She was well aware of what his reaction would be. He'd tell her to stay in Atlanta, to do her job, that he and Tommy were on the case, and that they'd figure out where John was and bring him back safely.

She was fine letting him think that. Sean was good, but even he needed help now and then, often when he didn't realize it.

"Yeah. It's a long story. My point is we're on the trail. Okay? And when we find this thing, whatever it is, I'm going to use it to get our friend back. Okay?" He was careful not to mention names in their conversation.

Tears blurred her vision, and she fought hard not to let them out. Her right foot slipped off the gas pedal, and she allowed the SUV to slow for a moment. There was no one behind her on the lonely road, no other irritated drivers to honk at her and flash angry gestures her way. One tear managed to slip past her defenses and roll down her cheek. Emily knew Sean was doing his best. He'd been put in a difficult situation with this mess. That reminded her of something she'd been wanting to tell him, but without a way to reach him there was no means.

"Still there?"

"Yeah. I'm still here." She stepped on the gas again and accelerated, getting the vehicle back up to a couple of miles per hour over the speed limit.

Emily had to give Sean the heads-up about what she'd learned. She always had her ear to the rails, constantly listening for what was going on in her often-corrupt world of government work. Now, instead of corruption, she was doing her best to stay ahead of the storm, a storm by the name of Matthew Petty. She'd heard of Petty, met him once during a briefing. She knew about his slow climb to prominence in the bureau and actually had a great deal of respect for him. He'd done things the right way and, as far as she knew, was a good person. The problem was he was also a bloodhound and would do whatever it took to bring Sean in, whether he was innocent or not. For the time being, Petty didn't know that Sean was innocent, he—like everyone else—believed Sean Wyatt was the one who'd taken Dawkins and was holding him for an as-yet unrequested ransom.

"There's a group, an agency. You know who they are. They're the ones looking for you."

He knew she was talking about the FBI, though it was possible more organizations had joined what was definitely a nationwide manhunt now.

"They went to the diner."

The phone went silent for a moment. Emily had no way of knowing where Sean was now, but she took his silence to mean that the Feds were close, maybe closer than he expected.

"Did you take down three kids there?"

"They weren't kids," Sean defended. "They were in their twenties, early twenties, I guess. They knew what they were doing."

"It was a robbery. I know."

"I couldn't just let them knock the place off. Not to mention I had a bad feeling about one of them, like he was going to shoot someone just for the fun of it."

"I understand, I do, but you have to be careful. If you are recognized...you'll be arrested. Once that happens, especially if it's the Feds, I don't know if I can help you."

"What about..." He hesitated to say it.

"What?"

"What about Gwen? Do you think she could help out?"

Emily had considered calling the current president for help, but she was out of contact at the moment attending a world leadership summit in Belgium. Not that it mattered. Even with all the strings she could pull, Gwen McCarthy was smart enough not to get involved with an ongoing investigation, no matter how much she may have trusted Sean.

Then there was the fact that Emily couldn't use her position to tamper with a manhunt of this magnitude. She had to play this one very carefully, deploying her talents as best she could while walking a tightrope with the other agencies and the politicians in Washington.

"No," she admitted. "Not yet. She's out of the country. Besides, I don't know what she could do. If she issued some kind of pardon or whatever it would be, that might only make her look suspicious. I'm sorry, but for now it looks like you're on your own."

"It's okay," Sean said. "I understand." He did and she knew it. He'd been around long enough to know how things worked, especially in

Washington. The way that town operated was one of the reasons she'd requested to move her agency to Atlanta.

"I'll keep my eyes and ears open. And if there's a chance to...leak a little information here and there, I'll see what I can do."

Sean appreciated the offer. A little misinformation could help them out, but he didn't want her to risk it. "No. Lie low on this one. I don't want you to get involved, not to the point where you could get into trouble. I'll call you again when I have more information. Hopefully, we'll be at our next destination by tomorrow."

"Where are you going?" She shifted the phone on her ear. Her face scrunched with a questioning expression.

"We don't know yet. But we will soon."

The call went dead, and Emily glanced at the console, wondering if she'd lost connection or if Sean had ended the call on purpose. She figured it was the latter. There were snow flurries fluttering around in the icy air beyond the windshield. Visibility was still decent, but it could get worse at any moment. She glanced down at the speedometer and increased her speed by a few more miles per hour. If the roads ahead got frozen over, she could slow down, but right now it seemed like everything was fine. She'd have to be careful, watchful, but she was making good time and quickly closing the gap.

She stared at the phone sitting in the passenger seat for another couple of seconds before setting her gaze on the road ahead. The dams holding back the tears broke, and Emily wept. She pulled the car over for a moment and lowered her face into her hands, saying a silent prayer that Sean would succeed and that John Dawkins would be okay.

27

MONTANA

S ean's eyes remained locked on the road ahead. There was nothing to either side, behind, or in front of them.

Tommy looked over at him for the hundredth time since leaving Bismarck and asked if his friend was okay.

Sean said that he was. "I'll let you know when I need a break or when we should stop for the night. I'd like to see how far we can get."

They'd left Tommy's vehicle at the University of Mary, a small Catholic college on the outskirts of the city. It was obscure enough that no one would think to look there, but also populated enough that one more car would go unnoticed by any of the student body or campus cops.

The two friends had crossed over the border into Montana earlier that evening. Sean and Tommy both figured that was the correct route, though the destination was still in question, as was the final location they'd have to visit to learn the truth about the Madison letter and what the deceased president, and Meriwether Lewis, were hiding.

They'd analyzed the clue for the last couple of hours but still hadn't come up with a solution. Cell service was spotty, even with the most reliable carrier in the nation. Tommy had conducted a few internet searches during the fleeting moments when he had service, but nothing had come up. There was one possibility, however, that had continued to linger in his mind.

It was getting close to 9:00 p.m. local time when the two rolled into the city of Billings. Sean rubbed his eyes and refocused.

"Let's stop here and get something to eat," Tommy said. "I'm hungry."

Sean nodded. "Good call."

He kept driving until he saw an exit with several eatery options on the blue highway sign to the right. Figuring one of those would do, Sean exited the interstate and took a right off-ramp, turning into a burger joint on the side of the road.

He parked the car and the two got out. As they made their way inside, Sean kept a close eye on their surroundings. There were a few other cars getting off the interstate. One went left, and two went right and passed the fast food place, disappearing down the road a few seconds later.

He held the door open for Tommy and, satisfied there was no one watching, followed him in.

They ordered their food, collected it a couple of minutes later, and found a seat in the back of the building, around the side where the restrooms were located. There, the employees wouldn't be able to stare at them, and that particular part of the restaurant didn't have any cameras mounted in the corners near the ceiling. One thing Sean had learned long ago was that while it was okay to be seen, it wasn't okay to be memorable, especially when you were trying to keep a low profile.

He was a fugitive. The longer someone stared at him, the better chance they'd recognize him. Then it would only be a matter of time before they were surrounded by blue lights and sirens, cops with guns, and a slew of federal authorities.

Sean unwrapped his burger halfway and took a bite. He was surprised at how good it was. The place wasn't part of a national chain. Rather, it appeared to be a local or regional franchise, which might have explained the quality. He took another bite of the salty, chargrilled burger and then washed it down with a sip of his drink. He greedily stuffed a handful of French fries into his mouth, suddenly realizing how long it had been since he'd eaten.

The two pulled out their phones as they ate and checked the connection.

"Might as well try to figure this out here while we have service," Tommy said.

Sean nodded and began typing in different search terms on his phone. "I still can't figure out what it means," he confessed. "Disappointment dwelling in the hearts of men? I mean, I know that we talked about Lewis and Clark being disappointed that they didn't find a water route all the way to the Pacific, but a specific location?"

Tommy took another bite of his sandwich while his phone performed the search. The screen went blank for a second, and then it populated with a series of results. Sean's did the same, though with different search results than his friend's.

Tommy chewed his food while he scrolled down through the list with his free hand. He flicked the screen slowly until he came to the bottom, then quickly rolled it back up to the top and tapped the first result.

"Got anything?"

"Maybe." Tommy scanned the page and then spun the phone around. He slid it across the table to Sean. "Take a look at that."

Sean read the headline at the top of the page and realized immediately that his friend was onto something. He swallowed the big chunk of food in his mouth, probably a little too soon, and it caught in his throat. To avoid choking, he took a drink and felt better.

"Camp Disappointment?" His eyes lifted as he looked questioningly at his friend, peeking under his eyelids.

"I can't believe I didn't think of it. I mean, to be fair, it's kind of an obscure location for most. Not the locals and not aficionados of the Lewis and Clark expedition, but for the rest of us..." His voice trailed off.

"I don't recall ever hearing about this place, either in school or working for you."

"It's not mentioned much in contemporary history, but if you're a historian specializing in that era, and in regard to the Corps of Discovery, then you'd know about it. I've read about it, but it was a long time ago. I'm certain I have several friends who know a ton more about it than I do."

"But you *have* heard of it."

Tommy nodded. "Yeah. So, and keep in mind I haven't read up on it in a long time, but Camp Disappointment was the farthest place they went to the west in hopes of discovering a river to the Pacific. It's where one of the primary objectives for their mission proved to be a failure. There is no river connecting east to west, thus their disappointment and the moniker that followed."

"Understandable. But what about the serpent's head? That's a tad strange, right? Any clue what that might be about and why the references to snakes two times in the clues? Not to mention why there isn't one referred to in the third part of the riddle."

"Let's try to stay focused on the task at hand. We'll worry about part three when we get to it." Tommy took a big bite of his burger and chewed while he kept talking, throwing traditional social convention to the wind. "I'm not sure why it keeps referencing a serpent unless it has something to do with a double meaning."

"Double meaning?"

Tommy's head bobbed up and down. "Yeah. So, think about it. Back in those days, the whole timber rattlesnake thing was still a big deal. In the American Revolution, the timber rattler was more of a national icon than the bald eagle. Snakes were everywhere. Eagles, not so much."

"Hence the Gadsden Flag with 'Don't Tread on Me' written on it."

"Right," Tommy jabbed a finger at his friend. "So, it could be talking about that in some vague way, but I have another theory."

"Can't wait to hear it." Sean shoved another clutch of fries into his mouth.

"The river." Tommy swallowed his food and waited a second, Sean guessed to build dramatic effect. "The river is like a snake. Rivers are referred to as serpents or snakes throughout history. If you look at them on maps, that's exactly what they look like. So, it might be that the head of the serpent we're trying to find is actually the head of a river."

"And at the head there's a stone that doesn't belong, hence why it says a stone misplaced long ago."

"Precisely." Tommy pointed a fry at his friend and then stuffed it into his mouth.

Sean thought about the solution and then looked back down at Tommy's phone. He tapped the screen, scrolled up until he found a small square representing a map, and then tapped on it. The screen blipped again, and then the map of Montana appeared, focused tightly on the area surrounding Camp Disappointment.

There was a monument there as a tribute to the Lewis and Clark expedition. Sean zoomed out of the close-up and looked at the distance between Billings and that spot.

"Gonna take a while to get there," Sean said. "Might need to hole up here for the night and then get after it early tomorrow morning."

"Yeah, I don't know if there are many places to stay in that area. It's kind of out there."

"Not to mention this weather is getting worse." Sean glanced out the window at the snow flurries beginning to fall through the glow of the street lights. "I don't mind driving on snowy roads, but at night it's too hard to tell where the danger is, especially if there's black ice. Most of these roads are taken care of, from what I can tell, but once we get out there off the main highways, I don't know if we'll be able to get through."

Tommy shook his head. "I doubt we can. I know it's slower, but we may have to take the interstate as far as we can before cutting off onto any of the side roads."

Sean had been afraid of that. He'd made the trip out this way once before and recalled that many of the roads that weren't considered main thoroughfares to travelers were actually some of the best and fastest ways to get through the vast state.

His eyes shifted as he noted the headlights of a car pulling into the restaurant parking lot. The sedan came to a stop near their SUV and switched off the engine. A large man with a big beer belly hanging over his belt got out of the car and waddled inside. He lumbered up to the counter to place his order, and Sean immediately forgot about him, figuring the man was not a credible threat.

There was another glimmer of light out beyond the parking lot. It was the residual corona of headlamps from another vehicle. The car was stopped, Sean assumed, behind another building across the lot. It appeared to be an appliance repair shop. Was it the owner closing up for the night? Or was it something more sinister?

Sean had been watching for someone following them during the entire drive from Atlanta. He'd not seen anything yet, but that didn't mean there wasn't someone out there.

The good news was they hadn't attacked yet. But if President Dawkins's kidnappers were following Sean, that meant he might have a chance at capturing them and getting information that could lead to the president's location.

"What?" Tommy asked, noting his friend's sudden distraction. He turned and looked at the large customer at the counter who was now waiting on his food and holding a massive cup of soda in his hand. "What's the matter?"

Sean had switched his gaze back to the big man in the restaurant, but he'd done it so Tommy wouldn't immediately look outside where the headlights of the mystery car had now disappeared. The vehicle didn't drive off; he would have seen it. The beams would have veered and turned, pointing in a different direction if the driver had backed out and spun around. Whoever was in the vehicle had simply shut them off, as if aware that their quarry had been alerted to their presence.

"Don't look right away," Sean said. "There's a car on the other side of that repair shop across the lot. It's hidden. You won't see it."

"How do you know it's there, then?" Tommy masked his look of concern with a veil of curiosity.

"Just saw the lights turn off."

"You think they're following us?"

"Maybe. But I'm going to find out."

Tommy frowned and looked down at his half-eaten meal. Then he lifted his eyes to meet his friend's. "What are you going to do?"

"I'm going to see if I can get anything out of them."

Tommy sighed. "I had a feeling you were going to say that. And what do you want me to do?"

Sean's eyes flashed to the window once more and then back to his friend. "You feel like working off some of those calories you just inhaled?"

Tommy's eyebrows lowered as he frowned. "Hey, you ate the same thing. And by the way, I've been staying in great shape. It's hard to get a healthy meal when you're on the road. I mean, come on, man."

"You done?" Sean's eyebrows shot up. "I wasn't making fun of you."

"Oh."

"I have a plan. But it's going to require a little running."

Tommy pursed his lips and then nodded. "Okay, lay it on me."

28

Tommy took one more bite of his burger for good measure. He knew that it could be a while before their next meal, if they even got one, and he wanted to make sure he had enough energy.

Sean laid out the plan, and while Tommy wasn't sure it would work, purely from the sheer simplicity of it, he agreed that it had a shot.

He stood up and walked to the bathroom, disappeared inside for a few minutes, and then returned. He glanced out the window and then down at his friend, gave a nod that he was ready, and then walked around the corner to the front of the restaurant.

The workers were busily cleaning up, mopping the floor, wiping down tables, and putting food away that would be served first thing when they opened the following morning.

Sean watched as his friend vanished around the corner. He knew what was going to happen next and didn't want to alert the driver should the person be watching. Truth was; Sean knew they were. If they had a tail, that asset wouldn't take their eyes off the two.

He often wondered how someone like that got any sleep, how they functioned. He'd done the job only a couple of times while working for Axis. He'd once been assigned to follow a high-level Swiss banker who was purportedly funneling money to a Russian hacking operation.

He'd followed the banker for a full thirty-six hours, only getting about four hours of sleep during the entire mission. He'd eaten twice and found that one of the biggest difficulties was finding a way to use the bathroom without being noticed. It was the little things, Sean thought, that could make or break a clandestine operation. Stuff that people took for granted or never even thought of became extremely challenging when a person had to do their best not to be spotted. Not to mention that the simple act of going to the restroom could lead to the target being lost for good.

He'd acclimated, adjusted, found a way to get the job done, but Sean never wanted to go on a hunt like that again.

A big part of him had considered sitting there in the restaurant until it closed and then going out to the SUV and catching some shuteye, forcing the tail in the other vehicle to wait it out.

There were, after all, two of them and only one of the enemy. On the other side of the coin, however, was the chance that the person in the car behind the repair shop was simply the owner, there to check on their inventory or do some routine task that Sean couldn't imagine.

Sean hoped that was the case. There was, though, a part of him that prayed the person in the car *was* following them. Chasing down a two-hundred-year-old riddle in hopes of finding some crazy person's archaeological dream had a ton of room for failure. Getting intel out of someone who knew the location of President Dawkins and shortcutting to the source of the problem was a better option in many ways.

It was worth a try.

Sean watched as Tommy walked over to the SUV and stood there for a moment. He opened the door and looked inside, then closed the door and walked around to the back of the vehicle. He glanced over at the road and waited until a car appeared, going toward the inter- state. It was a random vehicle, just a minivan whose driver was probably going home after a long day of work. It didn't matter. Tommy just needed a car to come by, any car. The minivan worked fine.

He abruptly spun around and jolted toward the back of the parking lot and a chain-link fence that ran along the perimeter. There were tall trees surrounding it, planted just on the other side. Tommy sprinted as hard as he could, his legs pumping hard and his feet pounding the pavement.

Sean crouched down and made his way hurriedly to the rear exit and slipped out the door. If someone was watching, they'd have their eyes locked on the man running across the lot.

Sean reached the corner of the building and stayed low for a second, watching the place where he was sure the car still remained. It took less than five seconds for the driver to switch on the beams and pull out of his spot.

Tommy's head swiveled toward the sudden bright lights. They blared at him like twin suns, momentarily blinding his vision. When he looked away, back to the fence ahead, he could still see the residual glowing circles in the darkness, the image of the headlamps temporarily burned into his eyes. He kept running, dipping in and out of the light, doing his best to dive back into the evening darkness as he pushed harder toward the fence a hundred yards away.

The car bore down on Tommy, racing at him as the engine whined and groaned, the gears shifting as the vehicle gained speed.

Tommy reached the fence and slammed into it, his weight causing the barrier to give a little. It rippled and waved for a couple of seconds as he clutched at the links and started to climb. His feet slipped, and for a moment he hung by his fingers, though only a couple of feet off the ground.

The fence was taller, around eight feet high, and its sharp spokes on the top rose menacingly as a warning to any who were foolhardy enough to try to climb over.

A squeal behind him, accompanied by the brightness of the lights and the sound of the motor, brought Tommy's head around once more. The driver had caught him.

The door opened and a man got out. Tommy couldn't tell how old he was, just that it was a man based on the outline against the back-drop of the headlights.

"Down. Now," the guy ordered. Tommy could make out the shape of a pistol in his hand.

Tommy looked at him, forlorn. "Take it easy," Tommy said. "I don't want any trouble."

"Off the fence." The guy wasn't much of a conversationalist. "Now!"

Tommy hesitated for a moment and then let himself slide down. He turned slowly toward the gunman, raising both hands in the process.

"I don't know what you want, but I don't have much." He wasn't lying. He'd left his money, weapons, pretty much everything in the car except for one firearm strapped to his right ankle. It was a 9mm subcompact. Tommy had no intention of making a play for the gun. He'd be cut down in an instant if he were to try something stupid like that. Besides, that wasn't the plan.

"What are you doing?" The man emerged from the shadows and into the light enough that it caught his face. He had a strong, sharp jawline that ended at the point of his chin. His lips were thin and firm, clamped shut like a bear trap. "Why are you running?"

The guy's accent was Northeastern. Not New York or Boston, defi-nitely not Jersey. If Tommy was correct, his initial thought was the attacker was from Philadelphia. He'd met his fair share of guys from that part of the country. One of his good friends in college was from there. He'd run a couple of bars and nightclubs, always shifting from one building to another once a joint had run its course.

This gunman sounded exactly like Tommy's friend from Philly.

"I...I don't know," Tommy said. He actually wasn't lying. He'd run because Sean told him to. Now that he thought about it, maybe Sean should have been the one to take off toward the fence. Tommy was in the best shape of his life, but he was no match for Sean's fitness level. Sean had been through intense training, both for fitness and for combat. He'd experienced things Tommy could only imagine. Through the years, Sean had maintained that exercise-and-nutrition regimen—well, except for the occasional burger like the one they just ate. As he thought of the meal, a swelling burn climbed up through Tommy's esophagus. Where was Sean?

The answer came within seconds.

"You don't know why you're running?" the gunman asked. "Well, that's fine. I don't need you anyway."

"Because you only need me?" Sean said from a few feet behind the gunman.

The younger man with the gun made the only mistake Sean needed him to. He turned his body slightly, which took the gun's sights off Tommy for the briefest of moments. The second he did, Tommy lunged out of the way.

The gunman started to switch back to his captive, but it was too late.

Sean clicked his tongue as a warning. "Uh-uh," he said, adding another layer to the implied danger. "Don't move now. I'm going to need you to toss that weapon."

The man swore at Sean, calling him an unsavory nickname. Then he told Sean where he could go.

"That's not very nice," Sean said. "Here I am extending an olive basket to you, and you're spitting in my face."

"Olive branch," Tommy corrected, now standing parallel to Sean about ten feet away.

"What?" Sean's head twitched to the side so he could see his friend better.

"Olive branch. You said olive basket. The saying is extending an olive branch."

Sean's head snapped back and forth. "Whatever. The point is: I'm trying to be civil, and you're not being very accommodating." Sean jabbed the pistol into the man's middle back so that the muzzle came to rest on his spine. It pressed hard into the bone. "A bullet right here will render you paralyzed at best. In fact, I'm guessing it wouldn't kill you. So, if you want to live the rest of your life without the use of your extremities, keep resisting, but I'm not going to kill you. I'm going to do everything I can to make sure you stay alive."

The man said nothing.

"Again, please, drop the gun. Okay, pumpkin?"

Sean could see the man's jaw clench, release, then clench again. He was fuming, nostrils flaring open and shut with every furious breath. Maybe he didn't understand how Sean and Tommy had gotten the better of him. Perhaps he was angry at himself for getting caught. Sean didn't care. He just wanted the weapon on the ground.

The man finally relented and tossed the gun several feet away. Tommy hurried to it and picked up the weapon, then raised it, keeping it level at his waist, aiming at the man's chest.

"That's better," Sean said. "So, now we're going to play a little game."

"One where you ask me who I work for, where your friend is, who I am, that sort of thing?" The guy's comment was sharp, a barb aimed directly at Sean so that all three men knew that this guy was no fool and that he'd been in a situation like this before. He was unafraid. Determination overflowed in the sound of his voice.

"Oh, you know this game?" Sean wagged the gun in his hand, still standing behind his prisoner. He shifted his feet and circled around to face the guy. He quickly realized his initial assessment was correct. The man was indeed young, early to mid-twenties. Was he former military? Special Forces? Sean knew he wouldn't get those answers. He could already tell this guy was stubborn, and getting any information out of him was going to be painfully difficult.

The good news was that the captive was going to experience most of the painful part.

"Since you know the game so well," Sean went on, "why don't you start with the first one you mentioned? Who do you work for?"

The guy shook his head. "You idiots. You don't understand. You're working for them, too, only you're not being paid for it. Not in cash, anyway."

Sean and Tommy both knew what he meant, especially Sean. They were working for whoever this guy worked for, only they were doing it pro bono, hunting down answers to riddles left long ago by former presidents and early explorers.

"So, if we're all in this together, maybe you should enlighten us as to who we're helping out." Tommy took a wary step closer to the man, still holding his weapon firmly in front of him in case the guy got any wise ideas.

The prisoner shook his head. "You don't understand. They'll kill me. They'll kill both of you." He raised a threatening finger. "They will kill everyone you love and hold dear. They're everywhere; don't you see?"

"You sure do talk a lot without saying much. Isn't that right, Schultzie?" Sean snorted derisively at the man. "If you're with us, no one is going to hurt you. Understand? Now, since you seem stuck on not telling us who you work for, why are you following us?"

The guy shook his head once more. "They want progress updates. You'd do well to go back to looking for the artifact." His voice was cool and calm, even-toned like he was reading the business section of the paper. He didn't seem afraid despite the warning he'd just been issued and the knowledge that came with it, knowledge that he would be offed just as easily as these two. "It's not too late. If you continue doing what you were doing, back on the trail, they will be none the wiser."

"And I suppose you'll just go back to following us and not hurt us in any way."

"That was the plan. Although if I needed to hurt you I would have done it already."

Sean wasn't sure if the guy was making a good point or just trying to overcompensate for the fact he was now at a significant disadvantage, unarmed and held hostage. Sean was leaning toward the second.

He jabbed the gun deeper into the man's back, pressing the cold metal hard into his spine.

The guy winced, but he didn't say anything.

"Look, man. It's cold out here. Just tell us what we want to know so we can get back on the road and figure out what it is we're looking for."

A puzzled look came over the man's face. It draped over him like a curtain, masking something deep within, an unspoken truth. "You... you don't know what you're looking for?"

Sean and Tommy exchanged a curious glance.

"What? You know what we're looking for?" Tommy pressed.

The prisoner started laughing. At first, it was a sinister chuckle, barely audible over the sound of the wind blowing across the lot and into the men's ears. Then the laughter grew until he was going all out, his white teeth brandished in the light of the streetlamps.

"Something funny?" Sean asked. "Why is it you know what we're trying to find? Maybe you should be the one leading this little expedition."

The laughter started to die, and within twenty seconds the serious expression was back on the younger man's face. "You don't get it. We know what we're looking for. We just don't know where it is. Understand? That's why we need you two idiots. You're going to hunt it down for us, and when you do we'll let your friend go."

So, they knew what Sean and Tommy were looking for. That certainly changed things. Sean wondered how they could know what he and Tommy were searching for if they themselves had never found it before. If they hadn't laid eyes on it, how did they know the thing even existed?

"What is it?" Tommy asked, bluntly.

The captive shook his head. "I can't believe you don't know. Then again, maybe they didn't relay that information on the video you received."

More confirmation this guy was legitimately working for whoever took Dawkins.

The prisoner said nothing.

"Look," Sean said, pulling the weapon away from the guy's back, "we don't want anything to happen to Dawkins, obviously. But I know for a fact there are FBI agents on my trail. They've been looking for me ever since your boss pulled that little gem of a stunt and leaked that I was the one who abducted the former president."

"We needed to light a fire under you," the man explained.

"Fair enough. Being accused of one of the highest crimes in the nation is certainly one way of doing that. Or your boss could have just called us and asked what we charge."

Tommy nodded.

The prisoner sighed, doing it in an overdramatic way that neither Tommy nor Sean would miss.

"It won't help you," he said. "Even if I did tell you what it was they wanted, the only thing that will get you there is solving the riddles. My employer couldn't figure it out, so he went after the two people who were world famous for that sort of thing." He bowed his head to the two of them.

Sean didn't let on, but their prisoner had just given a clue, albeit a small one, as to the identity of his employer. The guy said *he,* so it was a man calling the shots. While that didn't exactly narrow things down much, there was one other hint that got left out there in the open. He'd insinuated that all of the shots, the entire plan, everything was being called by one person. It wasn't an organization or secret society behind all this. It was one man.

"This person running the show," Tommy said, "who is it?"

"See, if I tell you that then you'll try to go run and tell your friends at Axis or in the government. Why are you worrying your mind with the inconsequential? It doesn't matter who you're working for. Just know that they're extremely powerful, have access to pretty much everything, including the government, and that if you don't get this done he's going to kill you and everyone you love."

Sean's first thought went to Adriana. He'd called her, but she didn't answer. In a way, he was happier about that, although it caused him to wonder if these goons had done something. Then again, he should be more worried about the goons if they'd messed with her.

"Tell you what," Sean said. "You've been nice enough. Maybe we just load you into the back of our SUV, and you ride with us. Will be easier than driving yourself all over the country. Not to mention you could sleep. Looks like you haven't slept in days, right, Tommy?"

"Definitely."

"You don't understand. I'm already dead."

"Already dead? Why? You haven't betrayed anyone. You're just helping out. I'd say your employer should be happy about that."

The prisoner shook his head. "No. Once he knows, he'll—"

The guy's head twitched. His neck stiffened, veins suddenly rising through the skin. His eyes fixed on some distant point, and then he dropped to his knees and fell over on his side. The legs and arms shook momentarily before the entire body went still.

Sean took a knee next to him within a second. He pressed the gun to the man's head and two fingers to his neck where he'd normally check for a pulse. Then Sean stuck a finger under the guy's nose. No breath came from the nostrils. Sean looked at his chest. There was no rise and fall of the lungs. He double-checked the pulse on the man's wrist this time, but he already knew what the result would be.

His suspicions were correct as he felt the still flesh. It was warm, but that would soon change in the freezing temperatures, especially at night.

Sean looked up at his friend. "He's gone."

Tommy's face contorted into a frown. "What happened?"

Sirens whined in the distance. They weren't close, but that would change in a hurry.

"I don't know," Sean admitted, "but we need to get out of here."

29

BISMARCK, NORTH DAKOTA

P etty got the call while he was in a hotel room in Bismarck, North Dakota. It was too late in the evening to leave right away. He was exhausted and needed to rest, so he took a twenty-minute power nap before loading up his gear, the small suitcase of clothes, and the few toiletries he'd brought along on the trip.

He drove through the latest hour of the night and into the wee hours of the morning. The moon and stars occasionally poked through the dark gray haze overhead. By the time Petty reached the Montana border, though, there was no sign of the heavenly bodies and their comforting light.

So long as the snow held off, he didn't care.

Petty didn't do snow. He detested it. When he was a child growing up in New England, he'd seen his share of the white stuff. Early on, he loved having a white Christmas every year. He enjoyed playing in it, throwing snowballs, going sledding, but as he grew older he realized how much of an inconvenience snow really was.

At the moment, there was only a thin layer of it on the ground, but that could change in the blink of an eye out here. He knew plenty about the weather in this part of the world and one thing was certain;

they were going to get snow. It was just a matter of when and how much.

There'd been warnings about a blizzard coming soon, but he didn't have time to worry about that. He had a mission, and that was all that mattered. Sean Wyatt had taken the president and had, apparently, tried to stop a robbery at a diner in North Dakota.

Now there was this.

The call had come from one of his people back in Washington. They'd gotten the alert about a murder in a parking lot in Billings, Montana. Normally, Petty wouldn't think anything of it. It was probably a meth head overdosing, or something along those lines. He didn't care and didn't see why the call was important until his contact laid the next set of details on him.

Two men had entered the same fast food chain parking lot about thirty minutes before the body was found. They'd gone in, ordered burgers, and eaten half of them before leaving.

The men hadn't cleaned up their tables, which was strange since everyone knew to clean up their food at pretty much any fast food place in the world. When the men left, they did so one at a time, which was another thing that struck the workers as odd.

Still, not much to go on or even warrant thinking about, that is until the guy in Washington told Petty the piece of information he'd been saving for last. One of the men who entered the restaurant had a very similar description to the man from the diner in North Dakota. It was a spot-on match. As far as he was concerned, Petty didn't need to even cross-reference it. He knew it was the same person. He believed it was Sean Wyatt.

Petty's exhaustion vanished, and it hadn't returned in the hours since leaving the hotel. By the time he reached Billings, the sun was starting to peek over the hills and prairies to the east, and Petty was feeling just fine.

The scene in the parking lot was a familiar one, at least for a murder investigation. There were half a dozen police cars sitting around a single area near the back of the parking lot. Most of the lights were off except for two cars that were clearly trying to keep people away from the scene. There was an ambulance, and the coroner's vehicle was also parked close by. Several of the cops were hovering around near the fence where another car, this one a civilian sedan, was sitting in the midst of the investigative work.

Forensics analysts were taking samples. Petty could also see the coroner zipping up the body in a dark bag, preparing to load it into their van. Every person in the motley crew was dressed for the weather, each wearing heavy coats or parkas, heads covered in thick hats, hands gloved, and boots on every foot. The temperature on the dashboard said it was twenty degrees outside, which was probably mild compared to what these people experienced once the full brunt of weather hit. This was just the appetizer.

Petty felt a wave of gratitude overwhelm him as he shifted the car into park and killed the engine. Where he lived in Virginia, it got cold in the winter. They even received their share of snow, but it wasn't like this, and it never lasted. There were good summers there, mild springs and falls, and the winters were only bad for a short time. This, this was next level.

He stepped into the freezing morning air, donned his FBI badge on a lanyard around his neck, and started toward the police line that was being passively guarded by two cops in precinct-issue coats.

Petty pulled back his own coat—still unzipped—and nodded at the two men in uniform.

The cops glanced at each other with bewilderment in their eyes and then pulled up the tape so Petty could pass through.

One of them said something about Feds. The comment came with an explicit adjective. Petty didn't even acknowledge it. He'd heard it all and knew exactly the kind of reception he was about to get.

A detective in a trademark trench coat and what looked to be Isotoner gloves stood over the crime scene. The coroner raised the rolling gurney and started pushing it toward his vehicle.

Petty glanced at the bag for a second but continued walking toward the detective.

The man in the trench coat was a shade over six feet tall, had thinning hair with a smattering of brown, long lines stretching out from loose skin around his eyes, which were dark hazel in color. He was probably in his early sixties, possibly late fifties.

Petty stepped up to him, flashed his badge again, and then went about fastening his coat to keep out the cold.

"Agent Matthew Petty," he said as the cop stared at the badge and then watched with disdain as Petty did up his jacket.

"You the detective in charge here?"

"Why in the world would the Feds be here? Are we really going to do this whole song and dance? It's my investigation, Agent Petty. I can't imagine why you'd poke your nose in."

"I don't want to get in your way, Detective..."

"Krantz. Robert Krantz. And I don't want you to get in my way, either. We have a handle on this, so you can run on back to whatever hole you crawled out of."

Petty ignored the barb. He'd been through this enough times to know what to expect and how to handle it.

"I'm not trying to solve your case, Detective. And I'm not going to step on any toes. I just need to ask a couple of questions, and I'm hoping you can help me. We think that your killer here might be involved with a case I'm working on."

The detective raised one eyebrow and planted his palms against his hips, letting the thumbs hang from his belt.

"Is that so?" He looked doubtful. It was clear this cop had either come across some thorn of a federal agent or he'd watched too much television.

"Yeah." Petty produced a picture of Sean Wyatt from his coat pocket and handed it to the detective. "This guy's name is Sean Wyatt."

The detective's face was red from the cold, but it flushed white within seconds. "Wait a minute," he said, his voice gravelly. He looked at the image another couple of seconds and then raised his head to meet Petty's gaze. "This is the guy they think kidnapped President Dawkins."

Petty glanced around to make sure no one heard the detective's booming voice. "Try to keep it down, Detective. I don't want to cause a ruckus. But yes, that's the guy. We believe he is headed out this way, probably has the former president with him, maybe in the back of a van, an SUV, we're not really sure."

"Not sure?" The guy guffawed. "You don't sound like you know much about it at all, Agent Petty."

The last barb got under Petty's skin. He stepped close enough that he could smell the cheap coffee and cheaper cigarettes on the detective's breath. The coat the man wore gave off an odor such as Petty had smelled in some of the poorer areas he'd visited where he grew up, shelters mostly, when he went to work at soup kitchens on Saturday mornings.

"I know it was Wyatt, Detective. No, we don't know the vehicle because he's likely changed three or four times since leaving Atlanta."

The detective backed off, sensing he'd hit a nerve. He just wanted to get back to the office and his little space heater under the desk.

"Look, I'm just trying to do my job same as you," Petty said, putting on his best sympathetic look. He softened his voice to appeal to the man's desire that was written all over his face, the desire to get somewhere warm. "We have reliable intel that Wyatt is the one responsible for kidnapping the president. We believe he's making his way across the country, cutting through North Dakota and now Montana. Witnesses said they saw him in a diner near Bismarck late last night."

"Bismarck?"

"That's right."

"Why is he going this way? Sounds awfully risky to travel across the country with a former president in tow. Doesn't really make sense."

"I agree. It doesn't. Yet here I am, chasing a ghost."

The detective eyed him suspiciously, but his stern gaze melted slightly. "What would you like to know, Agent?"

Finally. "How did he kill that guy in the body bag?" Petty jerked his thumb toward the coroner's vehicle where they were loading the corpse into the back.

The detective flashed a look in that direction and then returned his gaze to Petty. "He didn't."

"What do you mean?" The detective's comment caught Petty off guard.

"I mean, Wyatt, whoever...no one killed that man. He died from natural causes."

Petty's eyebrows lowered, his face drawn long with confusion. "Natural causes?"

"Yep." The detective crossed his arms. "No witnesses saw what happened, but the experts over there say he died from an aneurysm. Must have been out here to meet someone. We found a wad of cash in one of his pockets along with a driver's license. We ran the ID, but it came back as false. Will take some time to figure out who the JD really is."

Petty knew what he was talking about. JD was short for John Doe, which meant it could take days to get a positive identification, maybe less in one of the bigger cities, but from his experience, out here it was a crapshoot.

"So, we have a John Doe standing out here in a parking lot, no one around, middle of the night, and he just keels over and dies from a stroke?"

"Aneurism," Krantz corrected, "and yeah, that seems to be the case."

"Do you have an explanation as to why he was out here and why there are people in that restaurant over there who claimed Wyatt and his friend left in such a strange manner? Surely, the time those two left the burger place and the time of death are pretty close."

Detective Krantz nodded in a slow, backcountry manner. "Yep. They are close. No doubt about it, but we don't have any evidence that there was foul play involved or that your suspect—suspects, whatever—had anything to do with it. As far as we're concerned, this is just a drug deal that either never happened or went bad."

"Drug deal?"

"Yep. See this sort of thing all the time, not with a buyer dying of natural causes like this, but sure. Drug deals go down in dark parking lots like this all the time. I don't know if you've heard, but there's this thing called meth that's causing quite a crisis in this country. Not to mention the opioid stuff. Odds are, this guy was buying something from someone, and he happened to drop dead."

Petty listened patiently to the cop's story, though with every second he wanted to smack the guy in the face and call him a dumb hick.

When Krantz was finished, Petty drew a deep breath. "There are a few problems, of course, with your theory about the drug deal gone bad."

"Oh, really?" The detective's eyes widened, eyebrows lifted. There was a hint of irritation in his voice.

"Yeah, nothing major. Except that if this were a drug deal and, say, he was the dealer, you'd have found drugs in his car. Unless, of course, the person he was meeting took them. But don't you find that odd? I mean, if someone was going to go to the trouble of stealing this dead guy's drugs, wouldn't they take his money, too? And then there's the problem of the money. How much was it?"

"Ten."

Petty nodded. His eyes were huge orbs as he acted impressed, pouting his lips in the process. "Yeah, ten grand. Sounds like a buyer, not a seller. But if he was the seller, your dogs would have sensed something in his car, right? Did they indicate drugs anywhere in that vehicle?"

"No," Krantz said sheepishly.

"Right. So, he wasn't the seller, and if he was the buyer, any respectable drug dealer would have shown up and searched his pockets, taken the money, and disappeared. I know I would if I was a drug dealer with nothing to lose."

The detective bit his bottom lip against the blatant chastisement.

"So, what we have here is a known fugitive, seen by several witnesses, leaving that restaurant over there"—he pointed once more at the burger joint—"and coming out here to the parking lot where a body was discovered sometime later."

"It was death from natural causes, Agent Petty. It wasn't a

murder."

"I guess we'll have to let the autopsy decide that, won't we?"

"I suppose so."

Detective Krantz let out a long sigh. One of the forensics team members walked up and tapped him on the shoulder. It was a young woman, hair pulled back tight and tucked into a hat. She let the detective know they'd be finished in five minutes so the scene could get cleared up and everyone could be on their way.

He thanked her and watched for a moment as she walked away before turning his attention back to Petty.

"Look, leave me your card, and I'll give you a call if anything turns up. Okay?"

"How soon are you going to conduct the autopsy?"

"We'll do it right away. There won't be any red tape with a Doe like this one, so no holdups. Should have something back to you soon."

"Thank you."

"I don't know how that's going to help you, Agent Petty." Krantz's voice rose to make sure Petty heard him clearly. "It's a dead nobody. No signs of a struggle, no blunt force trauma, no wounds. He just expired."

Petty nodded. "Just let me know what the autopsy finds." He held out his business card. Krantz took it with an air of reluctance then stuffed it in his pocket.

"Will do."

Petty pivoted and walked away, crossing underneath the police line. He headed toward his car, still thinking about the conversation and the circumstances surrounding this bizarre murder.

It *was* a murder. He knew it. How Wyatt had done it, he wasn't sure. And then there was the other big question. *Why* had he done it? This stranger with a fake ID, what did he have to do with kidnapping the president? Was he involved somehow? He had to be, but what was the connection? What was his role in all of this?

Petty knew there had to be a connection. Now he just had to draw the line between the dots.

30

BROWNING, MONTANA

S ean's knuckles were as white as the snowbanks on either side of the interstate. He gripped the steering wheel tight, mirroring the fear gripping his senses. Most of the snow had been cleared off the asphalt, but there were still patches where it had accumulated overnight, spots either salt trucks had missed or where the plows had skimmed over, essentially hardening the snow to packed ice.

Tommy held onto the grip over the passenger-side window with a similar intensity, fully aware that at any second they could hit a patch of black ice and skid off the road. Sean wasn't going fast, a mere fifty miles per hour, but that felt like light speed in such dangerous driving conditions.

Going slower would have been the safe move, but they were running out of time. The weather was already going to slow things down considerably. They hoped to be at Camp Disappointment before noon, but at this rate it was going to be an hour or two later.

The two friends had risen early that morning, before the sun came up. They'd checked out of their modest hotel on the outskirts of Bozeman and loaded up the SUV.

Despite their fatigue the night before, the altercation with the guy in the parking lot had been harrowing and had served to energize them for another few hours. While Bozeman certainly didn't present them with the safest place to be, it was better than sticking around in Billings where cops and, most likely, federal agents were now combing the town to find Wyatt. If they had any clue that Tommy was with him, that would only make things worse. It would confirm any suspicions a federal pursuer might have as to whether it was Wyatt or not who was popping up both in the diner and now in a fast food place in Billings.

They found a small hotel on the north side of the city and holed up for the night. The two hadn't needed anything fancy; just a room with two beds and a shower. That was, essentially, what they got.

The room had been sparse, to put it mildly. While hotels across the country were constantly going through updates and renovations to keep up with the current trends in interior design, this one still looked like something out of a 1960s Elvis Presley movie. By the time the two friends collapsed in their beds, however, they didn't care what the room looked like as long as the door had locks and the pillows and sheets were clean.

Montana is a vast state. From end to end, corner to corner, it is the fourth largest state in the union and possessed seemingly unlimited acreage for farming, agriculture, and cattle or bison ranching. Dozens of reindeer farms also line the long roads that cut through the state.

Along the way, Sean and Tommy saw elk and deer roaming through some of the ranches as if they owned the land. It was a wild and untamed place for the most part, where nature still made most of the rules. Sean worried how long that would be the case. While the hills, endless forests, and mountains weren't necessarily to his taste, there was something pristine and spiritual about the highlands, the rolling prairies, and the occasional rock outcropping. He'd seen the big mountains in the western part of the state, though, and always thought it might be a nice place to retire someday, although he wasn't sure about how he'd cope with the cold winters.

Sean had made the mistake of checking the weather back home in Atlanta before heading out of Bozeman that morning. It was still in the upper sixties down there. He glanced at the temperature on the dashboard and saw it was in the mid-thirties. At least at that temperature the snow shouldn't stick as well to the pavement, which would make driving a tad easier, though he wasn't about to take any chances and hammer down on the gas pedal just yet.

The gray sky overhead offered little respite in terms of hoping there would be a break in the weather, a sunny day that would warm both their bodies and their spirits, but they were prepared as well as they could be.

On a normal day in the summer, the drive from Bozeman to Browning would only take around four hours, give or take. As Sean and Tommy pulled into the outer part of the city limits, they both glanced at the clock and saw it had taken closer to six.

The city of Browning, Montana, was small with a centrally located grocery store, a tiny post office, a school, and a sparse collection of homes. In many ways, it looked like the city that time forgot. Sure, there were modern amenities, some of the buildings had been updated to more current designs, but as far as the size was concerned Sean imagined it might have looked this way a hundred years ago.

Off in the distance, the snow-covered peaks of Glacier National Park spiked into the sky and disappeared into the gray haze. Sean had visited there once before and enjoyed the breathtaking vistas and spectacular natural beauty. He'd been keen on taking the Going to the Sun Road on a previous trip through this area, but about three quarters of the way up, he had to turn back. With nothing but a one-foot wall between his vehicle's tires and thousand-foot drops, he couldn't take it. He'd white-knuckled it most of the way, his breathing quickening with every harrowing turn. The views, while incredible, were also the stuff of his nightmares, framing both beauty and Sean's greatest fear in one picturesque setting.

He'd turned back with sweaty palms and a heart rate thumping like a jackrabbit. Adriana had been with him and had offered to drive, though he could tell she was unnerved as well, which had worried him because she never got thrown off by heights.

He vowed that the next time they came back they'd take one of the refurbished shuttles up to the top. Letting someone else drive somehow felt safer, and Sean could always close his eyes if he needed to.

Sean kept driving through Browning, following the directions he'd looked up earlier. They'd traveled through Helena, Great Falls, and now Browning. Another twelve miles wouldn't kill him—he hoped.

Getting to the other side of the city didn't take long, and within minutes the two left the little town behind and were once more exposed, out on the open range and surrounded by the snow covered rolling hills.

"Sure isn't much out here," Tommy said.

Sean shook his head. "No, there's not. Lots of places to hide a body, though."

Tommy let off an uneasy chuckle. "Yeah, I mean...not that we need that."

Sean said nothing for a bit, too long for Tommy. Sean kept his eyes on the road ahead and then slowly turned his head toward his friend, casting a creepy gaze his way.

Tommy let out a full-blown laugh. "Okay, buddy," he said amid the laughter.

Sean cracked a smile.

"Seriously, though, wouldn't want to get caught with our pants down out here. No one would find us."

"Yeah, no kidding."

They continued driving another fifteen minutes and then came to a spot on the road where it went slightly downhill.

Tommy looked at his map. "Slow down a little. It's coming up on the right."

Sean nodded and let off the accelerator. He tapped the brakes gently, still not fully trusting the plowed, salted road beneath them. The tires stayed true on the asphalt, and Sean guided the SUV off and onto the snow-covered gravel road to the right. He stopped for a moment, turned a knob in the center console to put the vehicle in four-wheel drive, and then stepped on the gas again.

The SUV's wheels all moved in unison, and it lurched forward, kicking up chunks of white snow in its wake.

Sean and Tommy both noted the huge sign that declared the site as the location of Camp Disappointment, where Lewis and Clark stood some two-hundred-plus years before.

The path wound its way down into a gulch, then back up a hill to an overlook where a monument stood at a rock outcropping. Tommy wondered if the SUV would be able to make the climb and whether the two of them should get out and hoof it, but Sean seemed determined to give it a go.

He'd done dumber things with vehicles in the snow before. His parents lived on a small mountain in North Georgia, just a few minutes from the Tennessee border. They'd moved there during Sean's freshman year in high school, which hadn't really affected his life much, except when—on the rare occasion—it snowed. The locally fabled "Blizzard of '93" had stuck Sean and his parents on the mountain for nearly a week. They'd been able to get by since the power was only out for a few hours, but people down in the valley weren't as fortunate. Some of them didn't have power for days.

Sean had reached a point of cabin fever where he was over being stuck at home with his parents and, being an immortal high school boy, decided to take his two-door coupe down the hill and see if he could get around on the roads.

The driveway was around a 10 percent gradient.

Fortunately, none of the neighbors had dared to venture out in the snow and the powder was still deep. It allowed him—somehow—to get down to the bottom of the nearly quarter-mile driveway. Getting back up, he discovered, was much trickier.

He made it nearly three-quarters of the way up to the top when his front-wheel drive started slipping. Then the terror set in as the car began sliding backward down the steep driveway.

Sean reacted quickly, doing the only thing he could do. If he'd pressed on the brakes, he'd have lost control altogether. If he'd let off the brakes, he'd have picked up speed and either careened off one side and hit a tree, or rolled up the embankment on the left.

He chose the latter, letting off on the brake pedal and quickly guiding the car to the left. The back-left tire rolled up onto the bank, and the vehicle came to a stop without so much as a scratch.

The experience had been harrowing for Sean, and he had never again tried to drive up a steep hill in the snow. This one, however, was different. It wasn't nearly as dangerous of an angle and he had four-wheel drive, unlike before.

He grinned as he recalled the memory and kept pushing forward.

The wheels churned under the cabin, grinding their way through the deep powder and up the hill toward the lookout. When they reached the top, Sean turned the SUV to the left, pointing the front of it out over the plains. He shifted the transmission to park, turned off the ignition, and pocketed the keys.

"You okay?" he asked, glancing over at Tommy, who was still gripping the handle over the door.

"Yeah. Just...you know, wasn't sure if that was a good idea or not."

Sean's head turned back and forth. "You don't trust me?"

"I remember the story you told me about your experience driving in the snow."

Sean laughed. "I was just thinking about that. Come on. We need to move."

They slammed the doors shut and trudged through the snow. The white powder came up just over their ankles. It was deeper than most snows they got back home but not as bad as it would be later in the winter.

Sean had heard from plenty of locals who told them about how deep the snow could get. One guy in a tiny outpost village called Pole-bridge said that he had twelve-foot plow drifts on either side of his driveway. Sean was glad that wasn't the case at the moment, but the dark clouds on the horizon served as a warning that more could be on the way any minute.

The two friends made their way, carefully, down a narrow path that led toward the mouth of the river. It wasn't completely frozen yet, but it was on its way. Thin sheets of ice floated on top of the water, colliding as they began to form a solid bridge across the cold liquid.

The snow got a little shallower as they descended the hill but then deepened again at the bottom where wind had blown great drifts up to the base of the climb. The two kept going, pushing ahead against a bitter easterly wind. Sean pulled his hat down over his ears more than once to make sure the appendages kept warm. The breeze stung at his skin, though he didn't dare complain. Tommy wasn't complaining, and so neither would Sean.

The path that led down the hill vanished in the white covering, and so the two were forced to make their own way, marching carefully across a meadow toward the wide confluence.

When they reached the edge of the water, the two turned left and headed west toward the mouth of the river. The river narrowed rapidly as the two progressed, walking underneath another rock outcropping that jutted up from the earth.

"That has to be it," Sean said through the polyester mask. He pointed straight ahead.

"Yeah," Tommy said with a nod. "Looks like it."

They pressed on, but it was slow going as the two men waded through the accumulation of snow.

When they were about fifty yards from their destination, Tommy's right foot sank deeper than he expected, and he let out a yelp.

Sean spun toward his friend, reacting instantly. He saw Tommy drop almost knee deep in the drifts. Sean stabbed out his right hand and wrapped his gloved fingers around his friend's forearm.

Tommy did the same, wrapping his fingers around Sean's wrist.

Sean tugged. "Come on, Schultzie," Sean gasped.

Tommy tried to walk his way up out of the hole, planting his left foot on what he hoped was solid ground, and then pushed hard with his quadricep while Sean continued to pull.

Tommy was a good twenty pounds heavier than Sean, but not too heavy that Sean couldn't use leverage along with his friend's effort to get him out. Schultzie's right foot came free, and he sprang out of the depression in the ground.

Sean went sprawling backward, landing in snow that went up above his face.

Tommy nearly landed on him but caught himself enough to take two clumsy steps before coming to a stop.

Sean popped up and looked at his friend, disregarding the powder on the back of his hat and jacket. "You okay?" he asked, glancing at Tommy's right foot. His first thought was that Schultzie had fallen into a puddle or an offshoot branch of the river. Something like that would soak his foot and lower leg in freezing cold water.

"Yeah," Tommy said, glancing down at his muddy boot. "I'm good. Just a soft spot in the ground, I guess. Probably from snowmelt or maybe a little runoff from the river."

Sean nodded and let out a relieved sigh. He didn't need to tell him to be more careful. Tommy was already being careful, and the last thing he would want was to be chastised. "Just lucky it wasn't worse," Sean commented.

"You got that right. I guess we need to watch it."

Just like Sean thought: no need to warn him.

"Let's take it a little slower," Sean said, "we're almost there."

The two moved ahead, this time at a more gradual pace, each planting their feet in the snow and then pushing down warily until they were certain it was solid underfoot.

The rock outcropping looped in front of them; less than thirty yards away now. The gray stone rose up from the ground and then bent outward slightly, like some ancient natural tower. The river seemed to spring up from under it, driven by an unseen force deep within the ground. Sean made his way over to the shore where timid ripples of the clear liquid lapped against the forming ice that abutted the dirt and rocks along the edge. He looked into it for a moment and then stole a sharp glance back toward the SUV. It was still there, alone in the lot, and from what he could tell, there was no one else around.

Part of him wasn't surprised. It was cold and miserable, though the locals were likely accustomed to this sort of weather. Then again, he doubted anyone following them were locals. Whoever was behind the presidential abduction could be from anywhere, even foreign. There was simply no way of knowing.

"So," Tommy said, cutting into the silence that only the wind dared interrupt, "we're looking for a rock that is out of place, right?"

Sean recalled the clue left by James Madison. "Yeah, that's what the letter said." Then he recited it. "Where disappointment dwelt in the hearts of the men, a second piece leads the way to what he feared. Find it near the serpent's head, beneath a stone misplaced long ago, and you will be one step from what took the fabled city of Plato."

Tommy nodded, unimpressed. He'd witnessed Sean's odd ability to remember things with remarkable accuracy. It was a trick he'd seen over and over again throughout their thirty-plus years of friendship.

"You hesitated," Tommy said.

Sean snorted a laugh. "For dramatic effect. But also because of what we're talking about here."

"What do you mean?"

"Don't you get it?"

"Get what?"

Sean couldn't believe Tommy wasn't making the connection. "Plato? This riddle; it's talking about Atlantis."

Tommy felt a rush shoot through his body. "How in the world did I not see that before? You're right! James Madison wrote a letter about Atlantis." He couldn't contain the excitement in his voice.

Tommy pointed at the rock outcropping and tried to collect himself, reeling in his fervor. "You think this is the stone misplaced long ago?"

Sean drew a long breath through his nostrils and wandered over to the base of the rock plinth. His head gradually tilted back as he looked up, scanning the tower of stone for a clue as to what they were supposed to find.

But it all looked the same, only broken up in a few places with cracks and sections that had fallen off long ago.

"I guess we're going to have to do a little work."

31

The FBI employs around thirty-five thousand people. Agent Matthew Petty had at least twenty of those working directly under him. He had his superiors to answer to—directors, subdirectors, and so on—but for the most part he could run his own game.

He'd been undercover a handful of times, most of them dangerous situations. Twice he'd infiltrated deadly cartels, one based in Juarez and the other in Guadalajara. He was accustomed to being on his own, not being tethered to a half-dozen other agents.

That he could move faster, get things done quicker in the field, on his own, and be less noticeable, was the main source of his irritation at the moment.

He was on the phone with his boss and didn't like what the man was saying.

Ted Hollis was more than just the big boss. The FBI had a leadership structure arranged much like a spider's web. It was intricate, stretching over a vast network of agents, support personnel, and specialists. The system was broken down into different, often complex categories, but the top of the food chain was simple enough for everyone in the agency to understand.

There was the director, the deputy director, the associate deputy director, and the chief of staff. Those final three positions composed the senior staff of the bureau.

Hollis was the director, which put him in charge of the entire agency. And he wasn't happy with Petty.

Petty sat in his car for a moment as the director ran through a series of political nightmares he was juggling. Each one of the problems he listed was directly related to the missing president.

"How is it that one of the most famous people in the world, with a face that almost everyone knows, somehow managed to up and disappear like a fart in the wind?"

Petty ignored his crass comment. He was wondering the same thing, though, and had—up to that point—only come up with fragments of an explanation. While Petty didn't necessarily like the director as a person, he respected the position and the authority the man wielded.

Hollis had been the one to invite Petty into a new subset of the bureau, a group known only to a few, called Group Z. While the FBI certainly had agents out in the field either working autonomously undercover or in the open in certain theaters, Group Z was designed to allow greater freedom for agents who'd shown tremendous promise during their careers. Only agents who exhibited a talent for getting results on their own were invited in.

Requirements were stringent. To even be considered, an agent was required to have performed a minimum of two assignments under deep cover. The training was difficult, too, even more so than the usual regimen general agents were put through. Intensive psychological testing was conducted on every subject to ensure they were both mentally prepared for the rigors of what was to come, as well as clever enough to improvise on the fly, especially in dire situations.

Petty had jumped at the chance when Hollis offered. Taking the job meant he'd have to be on the road more, almost all the time, but that's what Petty wanted. Getting out of DC wasn't a bad thing. He loved the town, but the traffic, the constant hustle and bustle, and wading through the knee-high manure of committees, meetings, and filing reports was something he couldn't escape fast enough.

Now, instead of reporting to a conference room full of peers and supervisors, he reported to Hollis—and only Hollis.

Not that this way of doing things didn't have its challenges. Petty recalled reading a quote from Aristotle about how the most efficient form of government was a monarchy with a good monarch. He still doubted that would work in practice, though he'd learned that the theory was very true. Committees were too much like big government, squabbling about mission statements and arguing over the best way to get things done, often without accomplishing anything.

There were, of course, drawbacks. Hollis was headstrong, and his ego was infamous in the law enforcement community. He'd been a federal agent his entire career, grinding his way up the ladder with hard work and fierce determination. He, like Petty, didn't appreciate reporting to others, playing by others' rules. Most of the people in the bureau knew that was why he'd pushed so hard to become the director.

No one could deny the man's pedigree, his résumé, and his intense ambition. John Dawkins had made him the twenty-first director of the FBI during his first stint in office and had kept him around during the second. From the sound of it, the new president had no intention of removing him from office. Hollis had done an impeccable job of doing the Washington dance, bobbing and weaving his way through the political maze and coming out clean on the other side. If Hollis kept it up, he'd soon take his place alongside the likes of J. Edgar Hoover and Robert Mueller, the two longest-serving directors in FBI history.

Petty respected that about him, along with the fact that no one had ever been able to dig up any dirt on the man. Petty had done his best to keep his record just as spotless, and he hoped Hollis appreciated that. Just as with Hollis, Petty's only vices were a good cigar now and then and a nightcap of bourbon.

All that was far behind Petty at the moment as he listened to his superior rage on the other end of the line.

"I'm working on it, sir," Petty said in response to the rhetorical question Hollis had asked. "I have a few good leads."

"Leads?" Hollis's voice thundered. "I don't care about the friggin' leads, Petty. We know who took the president. We know it was Sean Wyatt. We know where he lives. Where he eats. Where he works. We know everything about the man. We know he got married recently, though we don't know much about his wife." He paused at the tripping point in his rant. "That doesn't matter," he corrected quickly.

"My point is we know who we're looking for. Why in all of God's green goodness can we not find him?"

Petty swallowed hard. He understood the director's anger and frustration. He was feeling the same emotions, though not able to direct them at anyone in particular. He took out his irritations on the pillows of the hotels he stayed at or at the firing range, at the gym, or out running hill sprints. Petty's life was one of solitude. Both of his parents had died years ago. Cancer ripped his father away from him; his mother a victim of a heart attack. He'd made few friends at the bureau, which was another reason he made a perfect candidate for Group Z.

Unfortunately, Petty couldn't tell the director what he was thinking. He knew Sean Wyatt was a master of the disappearing act. He'd done it for years now, even after leaving government work to go into a private project with his friend Tommy Schultz. The truth was, Sean could go anywhere, be anyone. Petty was lucky he'd been able to put together a couple of weak leads. He knew it was better than what anyone else had come up with so far. Most of the available investigative manpower in the government was on the case. The NSA was doing their thing, listening, watching, and waiting for a mistake to pop up on their screen like a big red flag. The FBI and CIA were also doing everything they could to locate the missing former president.

Petty kept his finger on the pulse of all their efforts, as best as one man could anyway. So far, he hadn't heard anything except the sounds of the other branches—as well as his own—spinning their wheels.

"I'm on Wyatt's trail, sir," Petty said. "I'm closing in on him. I should have him within the next day or two."

"He's on the move?" Hollis skipped through any potential details about what was going on and went straight to the assumption. That was one thing Petty liked about the guy: he could connect dots rather quickly.

"Looks like it, sir."

There was a momentary pause on the line, and Petty imagined the man rubbing his chin with a thumb and index finger as he pondered what that could mean.

"Why?" Hollis asked, smashing the silence with his baseball bat of a voice. "Why would he be moving? That would make things extremely difficult."

"I don't know why, sir." The admission stung even though Petty knew it shouldn't. He'd done more, gotten further in this investigation than anyone else. "And I agree," he added quickly. "It doesn't make sense. Transporting a prisoner like that, across the country, would be difficult to say the least. Not to mention that prisoner happens to be a high-profile person."

"So, why? Why isn't Wyatt holed up somewhere in a cave or in the mountains or in an underwater laboratory in the ocean?"

Petty knew better than to snort at the last comment, even though every fiber of his being wanted to. It was a humorous comment by his boss but one that hadn't been made for entertainment. He was merely conveying the extensive capabilities of the man they were hunting.

"I've been working on that, sir. The only thing I can come up with is that Wyatt knows if he sits still too long, we'll zero in on him sooner or later. Not many people understand our processes, systems, and way of doing things in the field better than him. He'll try to stay a step ahead of us the whole time."

"He's doing it."

"I know…" He let the words hang for a moment.

"Is there something else, Agent Petty?" The gruff voice on the phone softened for a moment as the director picked up on something that was left unsaid.

He was good at making those kinds of reads on people—another reason he'd climbed the ladder to the top.

"Yes, sir. There is."

"Well? I don't have all day, Agent."

"First," he hesitated, "I'm not sure Wyatt took the president."

Another silence bomb hit the line, and for eleven seconds no one said anything. Petty waited for it.

"What in the Sam Hill do you mean, you don't know if Wyatt took the president? Of course he did. He said so on the video we received."

"I know, sir. And I'm still on his trail, but we never saw Wyatt on the video. He didn't show his face. Don't you think that's a tad odd?"

"Are you saying he was set up?"

"Maybe. I'm not sure."

"Why are you just now coming to this conclusion?"

"A man was seen in a diner out here last night. He stopped a robbery, might have even saved a few lives in the process. The man was different in appearance, for the most part, than Wyatt, but there were some things witnesses said that made me think it was him. He must have changed his look."

"Obviously. What's your point?"

"Sean Wyatt knows he's a fugitive," Petty said. "He knows we're after him, that every agency across the nation is tracking him down. He's a hunted man. Why would he risk going out of his way to stop a robbery at a diner when he knew that could also mean more people would potentially recognize him? I mean, he took the weapons from the thieves, gave them to a customer and one of the waitresses, then told them to call the cops. That doesn't sound like something a guilty person would do, especially someone who'd abducted a former president."

"No, it doesn't."

Petty could tell he had his boss on the same train now, both from the hesitation in the older man's voice and in the agreeable way he commented. Knowing that, Petty pushed in to his next point.

"There's something else, sir."

"What's next, you gonna tell me he's walking on water and raising the dead?"

Another gruff example of Hollis's humor. Petty cracked a smile but didn't laugh. "No, sir. This has to do with a homicide in Billings, Montana."

"Billings? A homicide?"

"I managed to piece together a trail after Wyatt left Atlanta. He's going west, as I mentioned in our conversation yesterday and in my reports."

"Hard to forget."

"Anyway, he came through here. I couldn't have been more than a few hours behind based on what witnesses said."

"More witnesses?"

"Wyatt and another man, probably Schultz, stopped in a fast food place here in Billings. Witnesses said they saw the other man leave first, then the one we think might be Wyatt. Shortly after, a man was found dead out in the parking lot."

"Wyatt killed him?"

Petty shook his head. "No. I doubt it. The coroner was initially calling it a result of natural causes, that the guy died from an aneurysm."

"And you don't buy that?"

"No, sir. And I don't think Wyatt killed him."

"Why not?"

"Because I went to the coroner's office. The examiner said that what they found inside the man's skull was unlike anything they'd ever seen. It looked as though a minuscule explosive had detonated in his brain. It mangled the brain tissue, sir. Killed the victim almost instantly."

Hollis took a long breath. "Who was he?"

"That's the messed-up part about all of this, sir. He was CIA."

32

BROWNING

Sean had never wanted a snow shovel in his life. He'd never needed one, either. Living in the South meant only facing a few inches of snow every year, and that was during a banner season. Usually, the snow melted within forty-eight hours and didn't require extensive shoveling, blowing, or plowing.

As he scraped away swaths of powder at the base of the rock column, he wished he had a snow shovel more than ever.

He and Tommy had been at the tedious task for nearly an hour, sweeping away the snow with their arms and boots, digging into the drifts in search of a rock that was, as the Madison letter suggested, out of place. After a grueling amount of work, however, they'd come up empty, and Sean was beginning to wonder if they were in the right place. Worse, he wondered, had the sign they were supposed to be looking for been removed long ago?

That was one of the biggest battles when it came to finding ancient artifacts. Everyone knew about grave robbers, crypt thieves, or treasure hunters that stumbled onto old ruins and started snooping around. The great pyramids in Egypt were one of the more famous instances where historians believed thieves broke in and stole the priceless treasures within before they could be examined, cataloged, and either studied or displayed in museums.

Sean doubted that's what happened here on the prairies of Montana, but it was certainly possible. The area was teeming with history. From military engagements to the famous expedition of the Corps of Discovery to the cultures that held this land sacred for so long, Montana was still a land of mystery.

"Maybe we need to go back to Browning and get some tools," Tommy said, breaking the silence the two had been working in for nearly the entire time.

"I thought about that," Sean said. He planted his hands on his hips and breathed heavily. He was thirsty, and the cold air scraped the lining of his throat as he breathed in through both his nose and mouth. The dry air seemed to suck the moisture out of them, much like the two had experienced in deserts around the world.

He reached down and took the water bottle from the mesh side pouch on his gear bag. The liquid was getting thick inside and was on the verge of turning to ice. Sean downed the remaining contents quickly. He flinched at the icy cold splashing down his throat, but he knew if he didn't drink it now it would be frozen in the next fifteen minutes. Maybe sooner.

Tommy saw his friend finish his water and decided that was a good idea. He grabbed his bottle out of his rucksack and drank it greedily. When he was done, he wiped a few droplets from his mouth with the back of his glove and stuffed the empty bottle back into his bag.

"It has to be here," Tommy said.

"It really doesn't," Sean retorted. "Someone might have moved it a long time ago. Or maybe we're in the wrong spot."

He shared his thoughts from before even though he knew his friend was probably thinking the same thing.

"Could be," Tommy agreed reluctantly.

They'd made good progress considering the circumstances. With nothing more than their arms and legs to clear away the snow, it might well have taken much longer had the snow been a little wet or packed down harder. Still, they had turned up nothing.

Sean took a few steps over to the base of the column and braced his hand against it, using the rock tower as both support and as a shield from the brutal wind. It was easily two degrees warmer in the shadow of the rock plinth. He looked up again at the outcropping shooting up twenty feet into the air with its odd overhang jutting out at the top. Standing underneath it, he realized he had a different perspective on the tower. He lowered his eyebrows, afraid his eyes were playing tricks on him after being out in the whitewashed prairie for so long.

His breathing slowed.

"What is that?" Sean asked, pointing up to the roof over his head.

Tommy looked at his friend and then followed his gaze up to the rock overhang. When he realized what it was that caught Sean's attention, his eyes drifted back to his friend.

"I hope that we're not supposed to try getting up there," Tommy said.

Sean nodded with a grave expression. Then he turned to his friend with a mischievous glint in his eyes. "Afraid of heights now, Schultzie?"

Tommy guffawed. "In this cold? On that rock? Yeah. Because I know we don't have the gear to do it."

"No free climbing?"

Sean had watched Tommy attempt a few free climbs back when they were in college. He'd never gone very high, but certainly higher than Sean was ever willing to go without a harness and rope.

Sean recalled what happened to one of his friends from high school when he was screwing around on a fairly tall climb on top of Lookout Mountain in Chattanooga. The guy had gone up about thirty feet on a ninety-foot rock wall when his fingers slipped on a ledge. Gravity pulled him back to the trail below where he landed on a boulder.

His pelvis was shattered, several vertebrae and other bones were broken, and he had a severe concussion. He lived, but Sean knew much of his life after that incident would be wrapped around pain and taking medications to ease that pain. Fortunately, Sean didn't believe they were going to have to attempt something so foolish in this biting winter cold.

Under the rock ceiling overhead was a section of stone that appeared to be black. Not dark enough to stand out at first glance, which was why he hadn't seen it before. The rock was faded, almost to more of a charcoal-gray color. The rest of the stone surrounding it was more of a light gray.

Sean traced a line back onto the tower and then ran down it to the base of the formation to a place where he and Tommy had missed. The snow there was piled up about two feet high, blown by the hard winds from the prairies.

Sean shuffled over to the spot where he'd drawn his imaginary line then got down on his hands and knees and started swiping away at the powder anew.

Tommy stepped over to him and hovered for a moment, looking down at his friend as he cleaned away another spot. "You think this is where it might be?"

Sean didn't answer at first as he frantically cleared sheets of snow, carving out a wide circle until the dirt, grass, and rocks underneath were exposed. He stood up and let out a series of gasps, trying to catch his breath. He wiped his nose with the back of his glove for what must have been the hundredth time and then nodded.

"Yeah, I do." He pointed down at the ground. "It's going to be too hard to dig through, though, so we're going to have to go back into town and get some tools."

"You thinking shovels, a couple of mattocks, that sort of thing?"

Sean nodded. "I wish we could use something more powerful, but if there's another artifact underground here, the last thing we need to do is risk damaging it."

Tommy gazed out onto the prairie. A dark surge of clouds was heading their way, filling the void between the pasture and the sky above. That meant more snow was coming, though he couldn't tell from which way.

"We better hurry, then," Tommy said. "Time's not on our side, and neither is the weather, so it would seem."

Sean agreed, and the two hiked cautiously back up to their vehicle and got inside. The warmth from the cabin had dissipated long ago, and the only immediate relief the interior offered was a break from the incessant wind.

Sean turned the key and the engine groaned to life. Cool air began to pour out of the vents at first, but would warm within a few minutes. He flipped on the heated seats by way of a little rolling switch in the center console. Then he put the vehicle into reverse, backed up using the rear camera display on the dashboard, and when he was lined up with the tracks from before, shifted into drive and plowed ahead through the snow.

Tommy used his phone to locate a hardware store in the middle of town while Sean drove. The trip back into town didn't take long, and they were able to find the little hardware place with ease.

It wasn't much, a small mom-and-pop place with a tin roof over-hang on the sidewalk out front and green beams supporting it. There was little to no organization inside. Tools were haphazardly thrown together along with every manner of parts, screws, nails, bolts, nuts, washers, and a wide assortment of electrical equipment.

Fortunately, Sean noticed the digging tools in the back of the building and beelined it to them. He selected a couple of their shovels with wooden handles and two mattocks to help break through the frozen tundra.

Sean had done his share of digging back when he was in high school and college. Nine years of working in lawn care and land-scaping taught him how to pick and use the best tools for the job, digging being one of those.

Southeastern Tennessee presented a variety of challenges when it came to digging a hole. The red clay made the task difficult, and it was always worsened with the many rocks and roots that could be expected within the soil. While he'd have preferred to grab one of the power tools that would quicken the job at hand, he knew it was too risky. He'd considered that before and knew that if they somehow damaged the next piece of the puzzle, it could throw off everything and leave President Dawkins dangling in the wind.

Manual tools were the only ones they could reliably control. It would just take a lot longer to penetrate the frozen earth. It was still late fall, technically, so the worst winter months were yet to come. That's what Sean told himself as he walked to the front of the store where the checkout counter was located. The reality was it very well could be frozen through a good section of soil. He shook off the thought.

The shop clerk was an older man. He had narrow eyes pinched together by thick skin above and below them. His ruddy complexion was framed by a gray beard speckled with patches of snow white that matched his hair. He wore a red-and-black flannel coat and a pair of khaki work pants. The man was shorter than Sean but of a stouter build, probably twenty pounds heavier.

"Doin' some diggin' out there today?" the clerk asked in a friendly voice. His tone was heavy, and it bellowed throughout the store with a hint of what linguists called the Rocky Mountain dialect.

"Yes, sir. Just doing a little work for a friend." Sean tried to pass off their awaiting chore, though he wasn't lying. Every step they took was a step closer to helping free John Dawkins.

The man's brow wrinkled with three deep lines cutting through the skin. "Doesn't sound like a very good friend, making you dig holes in this kind of weather. Most people around these parts get that kind of work done before the snow returns."

"Yes, well, he's not always thinking ahead." Sean tried to play along, but he could sense this guy was a talker. He imagined few people came into this hardware store, maybe a dozen in an entire day. Since arriving ten minutes ago, Sean hadn't seen anyone else. He placed four twenty-dollar bills on the counter as the guy lifted the tag on one of the tools and began entering the dollar amount.

"Yeah, it's been a cold one, though this is just the beginning. I guess you boys don't get winters like this back where you're from." He eyed Sean suspiciously.

Tommy joined him at the counter and felt a flutter cut through his chest. "Where we're from?"

The man chuckled. "There it is." He jabbed a finger at Tommy. "You two are from the South, aren't ya?"

"Yes, sir," Sean said. There was no point in fighting it. He doubted this guy would make them for the fugitives they were. Then again, Sean might as well throw him off the scent. "Mississippi. Starkville." He hated lying, but there was no sense letting this guy accidentally connect the dots if he happened to see their faces on the news.

"Oh, way down there. Yeah, I doubt you two get much of the white stuff down that way." The guy finished ringing up the total.

Sean noted the amount on the display and then pushed the four bills across the counter to the clerk. He'd estimated correctly.

The clerk looked at the twenty-dollar bills, scooped them up, and hit another button on the old register. It dinged, and the till slid open with a thud and a jingle of coins. He put the money inside, counted their change, and deposited it in Sean's palm.

"Thank you," Sean said, suddenly eager to get out of the store before the older guy could start up further conversation.

Sean and Tommy both just wanted to get out of the building and, ironically, back to the frigid seclusion of the prairie. The last thing they needed to do was linger long enough for this guy to recognize them. Even with their altered appearances, it wouldn't be a stretch for someone to connect the dots.

Something caught Sean's eye behind the clerk's right shoulder. His eyes narrowed. The skin on his brow crinkled. His heart beat faster in his chest.

Unconsciously, he reached out and tugged on Tommy's coat sleeve. His friend's head snapped toward him.

"What?" Tommy asked.

"Hey, I forgot. There's one more tool we need." He turned back to the clerk. The old man's head tilted up as he took his eyes off the register.

"Oh?"

"Yes, sir. You don't happen to have a manually operated auger, do you?"

"An auger?" The man scratched his beard and then nodded. "Yeah, I think we have a few of those in the back. I'll go check."

Tommy's eyebrows clenched together as he looked at his friend.

Sean fired a quick *trust me* glance his way.

"Tommy, you know which one we need. Would you mind going back there with him? I need to check my list real quick." Sean fumbled for his phone as if that was where this mythical list existed.

"Sure," Tommy said. His voice betrayed the fact that he had no idea what Sean was up to or even which auger he was talking about. Tommy had never used a tool like that before, and it was evident in the confusion on his face, but he trusted Sean. He knew that when Sean gave him that look, it meant just shut up and play along.

The cashier waddled around the counter. He motioned for Tommy to follow him while Sean stood at the counter and watched until they were out of sight.

Once they were gone, Sean rechecked every corner, every seam in the ceiling where it met the wall. There were no cameras, as he'd confirmed upon walking into the place, but he prided himself on being extremely careful. He hurried around the other side of the counter, worked his way around the stool behind the register, and stared at the items on the wall that had caught his attention.

He looked back down the empty aisle directly behind him. No sign of the others. He could hear the old man telling Tommy about the small selection of augers they had and the benefits of each one.

Sean returned his gaze to the wall and the things hanging to the left of the window at shoulder level.

There, on the wall, hung a section of the golden ring. It was hanging from two nails driven into the drywall. Next to it, an aged newspaper clipping displayed a picture of a younger version of the cashier. Sean's eyes read the paragraph quickly. He learned that the humble hardware store owner had hit a stroke of luck one day while using his metal detector out at Camp Disappointment. Historians were baffled at the strangely shaped piece of gold. None seemed to know its origin, why it was there, or why it had been cut into that particular form.

The man in the image was holding up the piece for the camera, a proud grin on his face and a metal detector propped up with his other hand.

Sean glanced back down the aisle again. It sounded like the old man's sales pitch was coming to an end. They'd be back up front in seconds.

Inside Sean's mind, a battle raged. He couldn't steal the gold. It was something this old man was proud of, something he'd kept for years as what was probably his greatest find in what must have been hundreds of fruitless metal-detecting ventures.

But this was the piece Sean and Tommy needed. Without it, Dawkins would die. He doubted the old man would understand their predicament. Even if Sean laid it all out on the table, he doubted the guy would be sympathetic.

Then again, Sean couldn't be a thief. Not to a good person like this store owner. For all Sean knew, the guy might be hanging onto it to pass down to his kids or grandkids. It might even be part of some retirement plan where he wanted to sell it.

Sean sighed. He couldn't do it. Not even with Dawkins's life on the line. He'd have to go the only way he knew. He'd tell the shop owner the truth.

33

BILLINGS

Petty pictured the director shifting in his leather chair, sitting up straighter and maybe even leaning forward a bit to make sure he'd just heard correctly.

"Did you just say you think this man was CIA?" Hollis asked.

"No, sir. I didn't say I think that. I know he was. I ran a check on him. He was definitely CIA."

"Well, what in the blue blazes was he doing out there in Billings? And why on earth was he talking to Wyatt?"

"That's assuming they did bump into each other."

"I'd say that's a fair assumption, Agent Petty. Wyatt and Schultz walk out of a restaurant; a guy ends up dead in the parking lot a few minutes later. Seems like their MO to me. And by the way, I thought we checked on Schultz. Isn't he supposed to be out of the country or something?"

Petty's lips creased. "He faked the passenger manifest on that flight, sir. Easy enough to do when you have the resources. Schultz is here. I know it. And those witnesses confirm it."

"Fine. Let's say you're right. What is the CIA doing working with Wyatt?" His voice grew quiet, concerned, and just above a whisper.

Petty imagined his boss looking out the windows on either side of the wooden door to his office, making sure no one was watching or listening.

They'd both been in this game long enough to know that someone was usually listening in on everything. From text messages to emails, phone calls to internet searches, Big Brother was always there, even for people who were primary cogs in the machine of the American empire.

"I don't think the CIA is working with Wyatt, sir." He let his words sink in.

The director didn't respond immediately, instead letting out a long sigh and then a couple of clicks of the tongue as he processed the information.

"Let me get this straight," he said, finally, "you're suggesting that maybe it wasn't Wyatt who abducted Dawkins and that whoever did it could be hooked in with the CIA?"

"I'm not saying that's what's going on, sir, but I'm saying as things sit right now it's the only explanation that makes sense. Look at the facts. Wyatt has had an impeccable record with no prior incidents regarding his mental well-being. No hint whatsoever of disloyalty to the United States. Financial data indicates he's got more money than he's ever had in his life and certainly more than he needs. Every month, he keeps piling up more without spending much of it. So, he's not doing it for the ransom."

"A ransom that wasn't requested."

"Precisely. So, that leaves the question of motivation falling squarely on a couple of options. The biggest of those is revenge."

"But Dawkins and Wyatt are friends. They have been for years."

"My point again, sir. Why would Wyatt do this unless he had been crafting a plan like this for years to get back at Dawkins for something that may have happened prior to his presidency?"

There was another pause. "But you've already ruled that out, haven't you?"

"Yes, sir. I think I have. I think someone framed Sean Wyatt. I don't think he's the one behind this at all. Someone wants him out of the way."

There was a chuckle from the other end of the line. "That won't be a short list. Do you have any idea how many missions that man has completed? That's not including the ones he's done for the IAA since leaving Emily Starks's side."

Petty sensed the hint of disdain in his boss's voice. He and the other directors in the intelligence community weren't exactly fond of Starks. She operated outside the bounds of their jurisdictional protocols, their binding rules, and their limitations. The last part was the most frustrating to many, including Hollis. He'd hoped that his brainchild, Group Z, could eventually morph into what Axis was: a nearly autonomous organization that answered only to one or two people. Alas, Group Z was still beholden to dozens of others, including himself.

"I am aware, sir," Petty said. "And while most of the people who crossed Wyatt's path are either dead or in a prison somewhere, there are other possibilities that come to mind."

"Such as?"

"Maybe we're looking in the wrong place for his enemies, sir. What if whoever is behind this is someone that had a bone to pick with him or, worse, wanted to get some payback for a wrong they believed Wyatt had done to them long ago?"

"Such as?"

"I don't...know yet." He stumbled through his response, knowing the reaction it would get from Hollis. He quickly recovered before his boss could rebuke him. "However, I have some ideas."

"Go on."

"What if Wyatt wronged someone, someone on his side? During his time with Axis, he had to step on some toes here and there, right?"

Hollis thought about it. The nature of Axis was to step on the toes of those in other branches of government agencies. It was what they did. They crossed lines, worked in the shadows, and often barged into cases and wrenched them from the hands of people in the bureau and other organizations.

It had happened to Hollis on two particular occasions that had led him to dislike Emily Starks and everything she stood for. It stood to reason that Wyatt could have done the same thing, and while he was just doing his job or following orders it wasn't out of the realm of possibility that Wyatt might have pissed off the wrong person.

"Where would you like to start looking?" Hollis asked. "I'll get a team right on it."

This was something Petty had been considering since before he found the dead man in the parking lot. He'd wondered what the chances were that Wyatt wasn't the one behind the presidential abduction, and it was this path his mind chose to take.

"Wyatt didn't work for Axis that long. And you know what he did before that. If he made any domestic enemies, it would have happened during the time he worked with Starks, before she was the director of Axis."

"You're not suggesting she has something to do with this, are you?" Hollis sounded incredulous for a moment.

"No, sir. Of course not. She may be a lot of things, but she's not capable of doing something like this—no matter how good a friend she is to Wyatt."

"What then? Go back and look over his records from that time?"

"Good luck getting those, sir."

Hollis knew that despite the candid nature of the comment, Petty was right. Even the director of the FBI didn't have the clearance to see what Axis had been up to during Wyatt's stint there. Whatever happened there was kept there and only shared with one person in the world—the person sitting in the Oval Office.

"What then?" Hollis asked; no more satisfied than he was a moment before.

"Wyatt was in the Middle East for a short time. It was one of the only assignments during his career with Axis where he was involved with a few joint operations with other agencies and branches of the military."

"What are you saying, exactly?"

"I'm saying that most of his career was working exclusively with Emily Starks or on his own. At least, that's what I've gathered from studying the man's history."

Hollis knew Petty was thorough; it was yet another reason why he'd been chosen for Group Z.

"And you think in that small period of time he was in the Middle East he may have encountered someone who now wants him dead... or maybe blamed for something like this? Sounds to me like someone is jumping to some pretty big conclusions."

The director wasn't wrong. Petty knew it. The man was a walking, talking, fine-toothed comb. He was calculating, precise, and he almost never went on hunches. Now, Petty was essentially asking the man to go on a gut instinct, which was little more than a guess.

"I'm saying it's not out of the realm of possibility, sir. Just have someone do a quick check. See if there were ever any instances where Wyatt was involved in an altercation. Maybe he was arrested in some Podunk town for getting into a bar brawl or something."

"I think someone like that would have been brought to my attention."

"Probably, sure, but what if it wasn't? Something happened. I know it. We need to find out who is really behind this, sir."

"Who is really behind this," Hollis snapped, "is Sean Wyatt, at least for now." He sighed, a signal he was going to relent, at least partially, to Petty's request. "But I'll put someone on it. Larson isn't doing much right now. I've seen him walk by my office four times already."

Petty knew who Larson was, a desk jockey who was a darn good analyst but hardly a good worker. The guy took every chance he could to skip out of the office, though no one could really figure out where he was going. Some joked that he was a superhero in disguise. Larson certainly had the look for it; even the black-framed glasses that always seemed to be perched on the edge of his nose, as if deciding to jump or hang on for dear life. Larson would do, though he might not have been Petty's first choice. In this matter, he didn't have many options.

"Thank you, sir," he said.

"You're welcome. But this hardly takes Wyatt out of your sights. Find him. Bring him in. If, and I do mean if, he didn't abduct the president, maybe he'll have an idea of who did."

Hollis ended the call, and Petty slid the phone across the surface of the hotel room desk. He leaned back, raised his hands over his head, and stretched his arms until his spine cracked once. Then he twisted his neck back and forth to get a little extra stretch before running his hands through his hair and letting out a long exhale.

He was tired. The game of chasing down criminals was beyond exhausting, and he'd grown tired of it, at least in part. Another part of him still loved the chase, loved the thrill of solving crimes. It was like a puzzle to him, a game that he got to play in real life.

Petty glanced around the shabby hotel room and sighed. He was close and he knew it. Sooner or later, a break would come. It always did.

The phone on the edge of the desk started ringing again, and he felt a sense of dread course through him. He didn't recognize the number, but it was from a Montana area code.

He choked back the irritation mounting in his mind and picked up the device. "This is Petty. Go ahead."

"Agent Petty?"

He rolled his eyes. "Yes?" He let the word elongate so that the person on the other line would have no doubts as to his irritation.

"This is Officer Underwood out of Browning, Montana. We got a call about something I think you might be interested in."

Petty doubted that would be the case, but he humored the man anyway. "What would that be?"

"I was directed to you by your office, sir. They said you were the one to talk to if someone had information about Sean Wyatt, the guy who kidnapped President Dawkins?"

Petty knew he had filters in place to protect against false positives. There were any number of hoops callers would have to jump through to get to him. On a given day, the FBI and affiliate agencies received hundreds, even thousands of calls from witnesses claiming they'd spotted someone on the Most Wanted List. Truth was most of them were grasping at straws, hoping to cash in on the rewards attached to some of the higher-profile criminals.

Most of the time, he never even fielded a call. His office did a good job of making sure the only calls that came through to his phone had a significant heft of legitimacy to them. Now and then, however, one slipped through.

He doubted that was the case since the man on the other end of the line was a cop. Still, Petty was skeptical.

"Yeah, I'm working the Dawkins case."

"Good. Because we have a couple here who claim they had Sean Wyatt and his buddy in their hardware store a few hours ago. I thought you might want to know about it."

Petty's spine stiffened. "You're sure?"

"They only have one video surveillance camera in the store. It's an old one. Not very clear. Resolution sucks, but it definitely looks like Schultz. We ran some image matches and are pretty sure it's him. The other guy fits most of the bill for Wyatt, too, though he's done some changes to his appearance. We figured it was to keep a low profile."

Petty's heart quickened. Could he really be that lucky, that a couple of country folks from western Montana actually spotted Wyatt and Schultz? He didn't dare get his hopes up, at least not consciously.

"Can you send me the images?"

"Sure."

Petty relayed his email information to the cop and waited in silence. He heard the pecking of keys in the background and then a swooshing sound as the email was sent.

"There you go," Underwood said. "Should be in your inbox shortly."

Petty rubbed his finger across the mouse trackpad, and the screen bloomed to life. Within seconds, an alert button appeared in the top-right corner. It was the email from Dale Underwood.

Petty clicked on it and scrolled down to a set of four images. They were in black and white. As the officer had said, the pictures were kind of grainy. The resolution wasn't great, but there was no mistaking the men in the picture, at least not to Petty. He'd stared at the pictures of the two men enough times over the last few days that he'd recognize them even if they had paper bags over their heads.

"That's them," Petty said into the phone. "Where are they now?"

"Not sure, but the couple from the shop said it looked like they were heading north."

"What's to the north, other than Canada?"

Underwood chuckled. "Well, there's mostly farmland. Lot of ranches up that way, but we have plenty of ranches out here. You already knew that, though, I'm sure."

He did, but Petty didn't say it.

"Anything else?"

Officer Underwood paused a moment to think. "I guess there's the monument to the Lewis and Clark expedition out that way. Lot of snow right now, though. Not much to see. And it's cold out. Can't imagine why anyone would want to go see that in this weather. Besides, I doubt those guys are there. Wyatt is a fugitive, and that makes his buddy an accomplice."

"True, but why would they be at a hardware store?" Petty scanned the images again and noted what the men were buying at the checkout counter. From the looks of it, they were going to do some digging. "Why the tools, Officer?"

"Not sure about that, either. Ground froze a little early out here this year. Been a cold early winter. Normally, it takes a few months for the frost to get down into the soil, but it's already pretty deep now. If they're planning on digging somewhere in these parts, they're in for a tough day."

Why would they be digging? Petty let the question rattle around in his head for a moment. Then a sudden and horrific conclusion reared its ugly head like a rabid meerkat popping out of a hole in the ground.

Were Wyatt and Schultz going to bury a body? If so, whose?

"What were they driving?" Petty asked with frantic intensity.

"Um...says here they were driving an SUV. Toyota 4Runner."

"Did the owners of the shop say they saw anything suspicious in the car?"

"You mean like a former president tied up in the back? No. They didn't mention anything like that." Apparently, it was Underwood's turn to be a tad sarcastic.

Petty closed his laptop and slid it into his bag. He hadn't even unpacked all his things yet, though he rarely did much unpacking on the road. He preferred to be mobile, able to move at a moment's notice. And this moment was giving plenty of notice.

"Send every available officer you have to that...monument or whatever you said it was."

"Camp Disappointment?"

"Sure."

"But I thought I told you: No one in their right mind is going out there right now, especially to dig. And if you think they're hiding a body, there are a ton of better places than that."

"Just do it, Officer. That's where they went."

"How do you know?"

Petty didn't want to confess that it was a gut instinct. He also didn't feel like relaying his reasoning. It was a historic location. Wyatt and Schultz worked with historical stuff all the time. It was their job. Sending a bunch of Montana cops out to the monument might have been a big leap of faith, but it was one Agent Petty was willing to take. After all, there were no big rewards without taking big risks. The only thing he was risking right now was probably pulling a few county cops away from their coffee. That was a risk he was fine taking.

"Do it," Petty said. "I'll fill you in later."

"What are you going to do?"

"I'm heading that way. If you find Wyatt and Schultz, exercise extreme caution. They're armed, dangerous, and very clever. I'd hate for you or any of your men to end up dead."

He ended the call before Underwood could reply. Petty tapped on the map application on his phone and entered the town of Browning. He sighed at the sight of how long it was going to take him to get there. He'd just put his faith in a bunch of cops he didn't know, who likely hadn't ever been on a manhunt like this before. There was nothing else he could do. He had to trust they'd do their jobs.

He was close now, and Petty finally had the break he'd been waiting for.

34

Tommy and the shop owner appeared around the corner of one of the aisles. The old man was holding the manual auger that Sean requested. Tommy glanced at his friend, wondering if he'd done what he needed to do.

Sean shook his head. Tommy rolled his shoulders as if to ask, "Why not?"

"This be all, then?" the clerk said as he rounded the corner and set the tool down on the hard glass counter.

"Actually," Sean said, "while you two were in the back, I couldn't help but notice the newspaper article behind you along with that piece of gold."

The old man's forehead wrinkled as he frowned. He turned and looked over his shoulder at the gold piece and the newspaper clipping. "Oh, that?" He chuckled. "Yeah, found that about twenty years ago out at Camp Disappointment. Was just dumb luck, really. I was out there in the middle of the day one summer. It was a Sunday. I know because I caught flak from the wife about skipping church." He chuckled again. "I told her I went to the morning service and that was probably enough for the Good Lord. Then I found that. She had to eat crow for a month." He looked over his shoulder at the thing hanging on the wall. There was a fond pride in his eyes as he recounted the story.

"That's amazing. Did you find anything else with it?" Tommy asked. He did his best not to press too much.

"No," the man said with a shake of the head. "Just that piece of gold. To be honest, I don't know what it is or what it was for. There were lots of natives in this area hundreds of years ago. We figure it might have belonged to some tribe or something, but we've asked around, done a ton of research, and we can't figure it out. Truth be told, I'd love to know what it is. You can tell it was shaped by someone a long time ago. The curve, the cut, and those odd jagged teeth on each end sure do look like they were carved on purpose. I wish I knew what it was."

Tommy and Sean exchanged a knowing glance before returning their attention to the shop owner.

"Mister..."

"Owensby," the old man said. "Cliff Owensby."

"Mister Owensby, we have something you might be interested in."

Tommy reached into his inner coat pocket and pulled out the section of ring they'd found earlier. He gently set it on the table and watched Owensby's reaction.

The old man's eyes widened with disbelief. "Where did you get that?"

"There's a lot more you need to know first, Mister Owensby."

The clerk looked up from the gold. "Who are you two?"

Sean nodded at the gold on the wall. "Fit that with this, and I'll tell you everything."

It took a moment for Owensby to understand what was being asked of him. He was in a daze, stunned by the appearance of something that looked just like his gold piece. Then he nodded. "Yeah. Yeah, let's have a look."

He turned around and took the gold off the wall, spun back to the counter, and carefully pressed one end into the end of the piece on the surface. It was a perfect fit.

"It looks like a ring," Owensby said, his voice reverent.

"That's what we believe," Tommy said. "We're investigating an ancient mystery, one that we believe could rewrite the history books."

Owensby was still shocked. "Mystery? What kind of mystery?"

"That's not all, sir," Sean cut in. "You need to know something."

The man's eyes lifted once more from the ring and bounced back and forth between the two customers.

"I'm the guy that's being blamed for kidnapping the president. I'm Sean Wyatt."

The enamored look on the old man's face changed to one of fear. "What did you just say?"

"Sir, we didn't take the president. But the people who did are after this ring and whatever it is connected to. We don't have much time. The people who took President Dawkins gave us one week to figure out this mystery. If we don't, they're going to kill him. John Dawkins is a personal friend of mine. I don't think I have to tell you that if I did take him, I wouldn't be standing here right now, telling you the truth about who I am."

Owensby listened quietly. His eyes darted from Sean to Tommy and back again. When Sean was done talking, he blinked rapidly and slowed his breathing.

Sean noticed him take a quick look at the shotgun that was hanging under the counter. Sean had seen it a few minutes before when he'd stepped behind the register to look at the ring.

"You're a wanted man."

"I know," Sean said. "And that makes my friend Tommy here a wanted man, too. But I promise you, sir, I didn't abduct the president. And if we can't figure out what this ring does or what it's linked to, whoever took him is going to murder him."

The room seemed to pause in time. No cars went by outside. The men stood, unmoving. Even the motes of dust illuminated by a stray beam of sunshine appeared to freeze in midair.

"Look," Tommy said. "We understand if you want to call the cops."

"Or if you want to use that shotgun behind the counter to hold us," Sean added.

Owensby's eyes twitched, wondering how Wyatt knew about the gun.

"But if you want the president to live, the best way to do that is to let us borrow that piece of gold. You can look us up. Do it on your computer right now. You'll see that we're legitimate historians, not some treasure hunters out to make a buck or steal something from an honest, hardworking man like you. And we certainly didn't take the president."

Tommy nodded his head in agreement.

"I could have taken that thing while you two were in the back, but I didn't. I can't do that. It's not right. That piece of gold clearly means a lot to you. I would never strip something so important from someone else. I'm no thief. And I'm not a kidnapper."

Owensby held up his right hand and sighed. "Just...stop talking. Okay? Please?"

Sean and Tommy were both thrown off by the man's abrupt command of the situation, as well as by the way he issued the order.

"There's a lot of people looking for you out there, Wyatt. You know that."

"I do," Sean confirmed with a nod.

"You'd be stupid to come in here and tell me who you are."

"That, too."

Owensby crossed his arms and took on a gruff expression. His eyes were slits as he sized up the two men standing across from him. "Takes a lot of guts to do something as stupid as what you two just did. I should call the cops right now."

"We understand," Sean said.

"But...seems to me I can't recall the number."

Sean allowed a glimmer of hope to shine into his heart. He caught his breath.

"Anyway," Owensby went on, "I'll just finish ringing you boys up here." He laughed. "No pun intended."

"Thank you, sir." Tommy blurted the words.

"Yes, thank you," Sean added.

"For what? Selling you boys some tools? Not that you'll need them. I suspect you were going to go digging for that thing anyway, right?"

"Yes, sir," Sean said, humbled.

Owensby grinned. "Well, you might want to take these tools with you. Never know when you could need them down the road."

"Mister Owensby, we will bring this piece back to you when all this is over. You have my word."

The old man raised one hand again to stop Sean from saying anything else. "If you bring it back, great. And if you don't, no big deal. Finding this thing was one of the only fascinating parts of my life. Just because it's gone doesn't mean it didn't happen. Besides," he turned to the newspaper clipping, "I still have this to remind me. Don't sweat it. You two just go do your thing. Find the former president, and bring him home safely. I was always a fan of his. I hope you can work it out."

Sean nodded. "Yes, sir."

Owensby finished loading the tools into a canvas sack and then slid them across the counter. He pushed the two ring pieces closer to Tommy, who took them with a nod and put them into his coat pocket.

"You two be careful out there. Like I said, lot of people looking for you."

Sean handed him another five twenties. "Keep the change."

"Oh, now, you don't have to do that."

"I know. And you didn't have to give us this, either. Please, it's literally the least we can do."

Owensby bit his bottom lip. "Okay, fine. But only because I have to keep the lights on."

They said their goodbyes and walked out the door into the freezing cold. Sean slung the bag over his shoulder and turned toward their SUV that was parked just around the corner. He pulled his scarf up over his lips and nose to keep his face warm. Tommy followed close behind, doing the same as he looked up and down the street to make sure they weren't being followed.

The two friends turned the corner and made their way down the block. The SUV was parked several spots down.

Sean stepped off the sidewalk and onto the snow-covered street just behind the vehicle. He set the heavy bag on the ground and reached into his pocket to remove the keys. His thumb pressed down on the button, and the security system beeped. The doors unlocked. Sean reached out to open the back door when two SUVs appeared out of nowhere, engines revving and tires sliding on the slick road.

Coming to a scrunching stop, they blocked in the two friends and their ride..

Even before the vehicles had come to a stop, the doors on the passenger sides flew open, and two masked men got out, both holding pistols.

Sean couldn't get to the weapon inside his coat fast enough.

"Get in the car," one of the men ordered. His accent was strange, muted by the ski mask covering his face and lips.

Sean raised his hands and looked over at Tommy. His friend wore a forlorn expression, like they'd been on the cusp of winning a major championship only to watch it slip away in the final minutes of the game.

Another masked gunman got out of the second SUV and rushed around behind Sean and Tommy. He carried two black pillow cases, one in each hand. The man slipped one of the makeshift hoods over Sean's head first, then Tommy's. The gunmen dragged the two over to the open SUV and shoved them into the back seat, where another gunman was waiting on the other side, holding his weapon.

The last thing Sean thought before the door slammed was that it was odd the gunmen didn't bind their hands or wrists.

Once the door closed, the driver stepped on the gas and drove away, leaving the second SUV in the street as the team of gunmen checked to make sure no one had seen what had happened.

Sean's nostrils filled with the scent of fine leather and that oddly comforting smell of a heater running. The cabin interior was certainly a welcome change to the frigid cold outside, even if they were suddenly prisoners.

"You're making a big mistake," Sean said. "We were close to figuring this whole thing out."

"I know."

The driver's voice was female and eerily familiar.

"We're clear," she said. "They can take off their hoods now."

The gunman to Sean's left yanked the pillow case off his head. Tommy was left to fend for himself.

"What in the world is going on here—" Sean's angry voice melted, the words hanging on his lips. He looked into the front seat at the driver, then into her eyes in the rearview mirror.

"Emily?"

35

"That was reckless, Boyd," Admiral Winters said. His voice seethed through the earpiece in Andrew Boyd's phone and wormed its way into his ear. "Leaving a dead body like that in a parking lot?"

"He'd been compromised, sir," Boyd explained. "He got stupid. I had to put him down."

"Yes, well, perhaps he did get a little stupid. I can only go on what you're telling me, but the fact remains we have a corpse in a county freezer right now, and the second they realize your man was killed by something implanted in his brain they're going to start asking questions, questions that we cannot...will not answer."

Boyd understood the man's tone. He also understood the admiral's concern. "There's no way this could ever be connected to you, sir. And don't worry, I've taken care of the body as well as the coroner's report."

Winters didn't want to know. The less he knew about that side of things, the better. He knew, at least he hoped he knew, that Boyd wouldn't be so stupid as to say anything else about it over the phone. No matter how careful, no matter how tight security was, certain things should never be said over the phone lines, especially when it had to do with murder.

"Nothing can be connected to me," Winters said. There was a storm raging under the deliberate, quiet tone.

"I'm well aware, sir."

"Good."

"He had to be eliminated. He was a loose end. Wyatt got to him. Like I said, he'd been compromised. If I hadn't pulled the trigger on that, no telling what he might have said."

"I thought," Winters said, "your team knew what was at stake. In fact, I know they are aware of what is at stake because I helped vet them for you. You have some of the best in the world at your disposal."

Boyd knew that was true. This mission had no room for error. Mistakes would be punished quickly and ruthlessly, like cutting out a rotting tooth.

"Yes, sir. I'm aware."

"Then don't do this again without my say. Understood?"

"Yes, sir." There was no point in offering excuses or explanations. Boyd wanted to tell his superior that he'd tried to avoid getting orders from the man because keeping the admiral's involvement to a minimum was a high priority and one that Winters himself had mandated. Yet here the man was, telling him that he wanted to be the one to issue orders for things going on in the field. It was a contradiction but one Boyd had no choice but to accept—for the time being.

"Good. Now, tell me where Wyatt is. How are they proceeding?"

Boyd swallowed. That was the next part he'd wanted to avoid. So, he lied. "We're tracking them through the Northwest, sir. It appears they're headed directly along the path Lewis and Clark took."

"As I predicted."

"Correct."

Winters sighed. "Very well. Continue as planned. Keep close watch on them. The last thing we need is Wyatt getting loose and tracking one of us down."

"That's not going to happen, sir. He has no clue we're the ones behind this. And he won't—until it's too late. When that happens, I'm going to put a bullet in his skull."

"Fine. Just make sure there are no more sloppy loose ends like the one in Billings. Understood?"

"Yes, sir."

Winters ended the call and stared at his phone for a moment to make sure that the line was disconnected. Then he set the device down on his opulent desk and looked out the window, his eyes growing pensive as memories rolled through his mind like a flash flood.

For as much as Winters professed to know about this mysterious missing artifact and how to find it, there was still one critical fact he couldn't attain, not without the forced assistance of the experts.

The admiral had told Boyd about it when the plans for this operation had initially been discussed. Winters had approached Boyd. He'd hunted him down, finding the perfect candidate to run the entire mission. Boyd fit the profile perfectly. He was former special ops, a warrior in every sense of the word, loyal to the military until it was no longer loyal to him. Winters knew that wasn't the military's fault. It was Sean Wyatt's. Playing off that bitter resentment and a thirst for revenge, Winters made an offer that Boyd could never refuse in a million years.

It was a chance to get back at the man who'd stripped him of everything he'd worked for, everything he ever had, and everything his family had built over the last century.

The pitch had been an easy one to make, and the plan was set in motion.

For Boyd, it was a chance at payback. For Winters, it was a twofer. And he could get revenge on the president that had handcuffed him with budget cuts and talk of downsizing the military.

It had been frustrating. No, infuriating was more the word. Luckily, Winters had come up with a plan that would reinvent American military power.

As a navy man and a lover of history, he'd always enjoyed stories about Atlantis. The myths and legends surrounding the ancient lost city were fascinating, especially to a young man sailing the seas. For the longest time, he'd considered them nothing more than fantasy, epic tales woven by a Greek philosopher, perhaps out of desire to live in such a place. Atlantis had long been a sort of utopia in the minds of many. Surely, such a place didn't exist. Or did it?

Winters's hobby had led him down any number of rabbit holes, chasing ghosts wherever he could find them in his spare time. He'd gotten married when he turned twenty-nine, and with marriage had come the loss of his passion for Atlantis. It was a silly project, one that his wife had suggested was along the same lines as reading comic books or being passionate about sports. He didn't dare bring up the amount of time and money she spent on her own hobbies.

So, he'd walked away from his search for more than twenty years. When his wife died suddenly from a stroke, he'd been plunged into despair. He put everything he had into his work with the navy. Winters had already been climbing the ladder for some time, but with nothing left in his life except work, he pushed harder than ever. And he returned to his studies of Atlantis.

There were new angles, television shows depicting possibilities he'd never considered, and then one day he came across something unexpected. It was an obscure book he found while sifting through a local bookstore. The shop was small, but Winters enjoyed going in there. The place had several first editions for sale, rare ones that went for a premium. He and the shop's owner had developed a bond over the years, and it was only when Winters was taken into the man's circle of trust that the shopkeeper shared with him his private collection.

There was a backroom, locked by three different deadbolts and sealed with a fireproof door. Winters had stepped into the place with eyes wide. The owner knew about his love of the Atlantis story and took him into the secret room to show him something he claimed he'd only ever shown one other person in his life.

It was a small book. The hard green cover had faded through the years. It was worn down on the corners, and the pages had turned a dim yellow.

The book was based on a theory about what had happened to Atlantis, and it was steeped in a great deal of both historical and scientific research. The author claimed the disappearance of Atlantis was the direct result of implementing a defensive weapon of cataclysmic power known as the Omega Ring.

According to the book, this doomsday weapon was meant to keep enemies at bay and was capable of wiping out entire navies, even destroying islands within a certain radius. The author suggested that the creators of the weapon had miscalculated its capabilities and, when testing it, accidentally destroyed their entire city along with everyone in it.

The Omega Ring was, supposedly, lost to the annals of history and had faded into obscurity, never to be seen again. The author, however, believed that the weapon had somehow survived the incident and been transported to a land far away where it would no longer be a threat to Greece or the rest of the world.

Then came the story about Meriwether Lewis, the young military captain who ventured across the country at the behest of Thomas Jefferson. The author talked about how Jefferson used the Corps of Discovery expedition as a cover. The public was told that the expedition was to map the newly purchased land west of the Mississippi. Lewis and his friend Clark would travel to the Northwest in search of a water passage to the Pacific Ocean and, along the way, detail as much as they could about the land.

The truth behind the venture was much more covert. Some would say sinister. Admiral Winters couldn't believe his eyes as he read the story the author portrayed. He claimed that Lewis found something when he was in Oregon, something that both terrified and fascinated him.

When the expedition was over and everyone returned home, Lewis kept his reports, afraid to share them with the president for fear that the man would want to return to the West Coast, dig up what he'd found, and use it.

At first, it had seemed like a wild tale, something of pure fiction, but the more Winters read, the more plausible it seemed.

He'd taken vacations to the Oregon coast, made his way over the border into Washington, and even gone into Canada to investigate. Every time, however, he came back empty. He had made the journey down the Lewis and Clark Trail, traveling across country and stopping in every famous place, and even a few that weren't, along the way. Still, he found nothing. Until he discovered the Madison letter.

Just when he'd considered giving up hope and abandoning his obsession, a new idea popped into his head. He'd seen Sean Wyatt and Tommy Schultz on numerous news reports detailing their exploits and their knack for uncovering ancient secrets. They were the perfect puppets for his scheme. All he had to do was find the proper leverage.

He knew from Wyatt's reputation that he and his friend Schultz could be trouble, but if properly handled with great care Winters was confident that he could manipulate the two into doing what he needed. Other than the hiccup with Boyd killing one of his own men in Billings, it seemed things were going according to plan.

Winters was well aware that he was far from out of the woods yet, but he was closer now than he ever imagined. Soon, the power of the seas would be his to command. Not only would the United States be forever the unquestioned power on water, but he would become the most feared man in the entire world.

36

BROWNING

"What are you doing out here?" Sean asked over the whine of the car's engine.

Emily shook her head. "We don't have time for that right now. We need to get out of here." Her voice boomed over the noise in their ears. Her eyelids were slits to protect against the icy gales.

The road stretched out for miles in front of them without another vehicle in sight. The peaks of Glacier National Park towered into the sky in the distance.

"What do you mean?" Tommy asked.

"You're being watched," Emily said. She pushed the sunglasses up higher on the bridge of her nose. "Someone's following you."

"Again?"

"Yes." She didn't ask for clarification on what that meant. Plus, she had a feeling he knew. "And that's not all. We need to move quickly."

The two men looked around, twisting their heads in every direction.

"You won't see them," Emily said. "But they're out there. Sean, you of all people know better than to expect a tail to be so obvious."

"Sorry."

"One of my operatives is driving your SUV. Other than that, I don't think there will be any witnesses."

"Except for the shop owner back there."

"Did he recognize you?"

"No, but he won't be a problem. He's a good guy."

Emily wasn't so sure, but she didn't press the issue.

Sean knew not to ask any more questions at the moment. Emily was in full director mode even if Sean didn't work with or for her anymore. Tommy, however, wasn't accustomed to being ordered around. He was about to fire a flurry of questions toward Emily when Sean caught his gaze and shook his head.

"Let it go," Sean whispered.

Tommy caught his meaning and nodded.

He cradled the second segment of the golden ring in his palms as he leaned back into the rear seat of the Sequoia. The ring segment fit perfectly with the other, connecting via a perfectly cut set of teeth on each end. Now there was only one left, one piece that would complete the ring.

But then what? What happened after that?

Neither man had an idea, but they hoped that once the ring was completed they would be able to parlay that into getting President Dawkins back safely.

Emily kept her eyes fixed on the road ahead. Gripping the wheel tightly as she guided the SUV down the road.

"What's going on, Em?" Sean asked.

"We think the people who are following you are the same ones who are really behind the Dawkins abduction."

"Figured that much."

"That's not all."

"Figured that, too." He winked.

She shook her head. "Always the smart aleck. Local law enforcement will be on their way shortly."

"To Camp Disappointment?" Tommy asked. The information suddenly reeled him into the conversation.

"That's right. I got word that they're sending out a bunch of county and state cops to surround the area and bring you in."

Sean processed what she was saying. "But if they did that, they'd figure out we don't have Dawkins." He knew he was reaching.

"Yeah, okay. You realize that whoever is behind this is not going to give up that easily. What I need to know is what are you doing way out here in the middle of nowhere digging around in the frozen soil?"

Tommy leaned forward and showed off the two segments of the golden ring in his hands. "We're looking for this," he said.

"What is that?" Emily asked.

"We're not sure yet," Sean confessed, "but it has one more piece to it. I guess we'll know what it does or what it is when we find the last section."

"And why is that so important?"

"Because the people who took Dawkins are forcing us to figure out an ancient riddle that apparently revolves around this thing," Tommy answered in a long breath.

"I can't believe you brought him into this," Emily said, motioning with a flick of the head toward Tommy.

"I didn't," Sean admitted. "He found me, too, just like you did. Guess I'm not as good at disappearing as I used to be."

"You were never that good," Emily quipped. She let the dig linger in the cabin like a belch. Then she cracked a smile at her old friend.

"That hurts," he said, pretending to be devastated.

Her grin broadened into a full, sarcastic smirk. "Just saying. If he can find you…"

"Hey." Now it was Tommy's turn to be insulted.

The SUV began to climb a long, straight hill. At the top, the three occupants saw another vehicle appear, rolling toward them quickly. From the looks of the headlights and the rack on top, they were certain it was a squad car.

"Looks like I got to the two of you just in time," Emily said. "Do me a favor and duck down, please."

Sean didn't have to be told twice. He leaned forward, unclipping his seatbelt so he could get almost entirely onto the floor. Tommy, too, ducked down, lying across the back seat to stay out of view through the windshield.

"If they pull me over, we're going to have a tough time getting out of it," Emily said through barely parted lips.

Sean knew what that meant. They couldn't fight or shoot their way out of it with the cops. That would never fly. He didn't have an issue taking the life of a bad person who was trying to hurt him, a friend, or someone innocent. Cops, on the other hand, were just doing their jobs. He couldn't use lethal force against someone who had a family, a wife, kids, or friends that loved them.

So, he said a silent prayer that the car heading toward them wouldn't stop.

It took less than thirty seconds for Emily to realize it wasn't a police car. It was the right model and make, a Dodge Charger with a roll cage on the front and a rack on top. It wasn't, however, a police cruiser. She glanced down at the two men attempting to stay out of view and decided to let them linger a few seconds longer. It wasn't often she got those kinds of kicks.

"Is it gone?" Sean asked. He sounded like a child.

"Almost," Emily said, her tone full of sincere urgency. "Just lay low another few seconds."

The Charger passed the SUV with a whoosh. "Just hold on," she said, her tone still full of concern as she looked into the rearview mirror, making sure the "threat" was gone before telling Sean and Tommy they could get back up.

The two men sat up in their seats and reengaged their seatbelts.

"That was too close," Sean said, twisting his head slightly to look back through the rear window.

"No kidding," Tommy said. "How in the world did they find us?"

"And where are the other people you mentioned?" Sean added.

"Oh, they're here," Emily said, still holding onto her little prank, "but we might be able to lose them now that your car is back there. That little ruse may buy us some time but not much. The Feds are on your tail, too, Sean."

"I figured."

"That little stunt you pulled back in Billings caught the full attention of the FBI. The director has put one of his top men on the case. He's here in Montana now. He's the one who called in the cavalry back there. Name is Matthew Petty. He's a good agent, too good sometimes. It's a sure bet he'll know something went down here, though I doubt he'll trace it to me."

"That's a big risk you're taking, Emily, coming out here to help us."

She shook her head. "The bigger risk was doing nothing. I love John, and if I have to break a few rules to find out what really happened to him, then I'll do it."

She drove the SUV back into Browning. When they came to a four-way stop, Emily turned the car to the west and kept the speed at the town's low limit until they were beyond the city boundaries and the speed limit increased to a more reasonable level.

Ahead, the massive Rocky Mountains of Glacier National Park rose from the prairies high into the sky. The clouds parted and revealed one of the snowy peaks for a moment, only to cover it once more in the soupy gray that permeated most of the atmosphere.

"So," Emily said, breaking the temporary silence, "tell me all about what it is you two are doing out here and what you're hoping to find."

Sean relayed the tale to her, telling her all about the video they'd received at the lab, his narrow escape from Atlanta, and how he'd pieced together a few of the clues—enough to figure out that Fort Mandan was the first place he needed to go. Then he told her about how Tommy found him. Sean also threw in the side story about the diner and how he'd stopped a robbery.

"That one probably cost you," Emily said.

"Maybe," Sean admitted, "but what was I supposed to do, let them rob the place?"

"Perhaps."

"You know me better than that."

"I do. Always the Boy Scout."

He snorted a laugh.

"Where are you going next?" she asked. "You said you need one more piece to complete that ring. And you think the people behind this will be satisfied with that and give John back?"

"I doubt it," Sean said. "I was hoping that would be the case, but I have a feeling these aren't the types of people that will keep their word."

A sudden sense of dread washed over Emily. "Do you know if he's still alive?"

Sean shook his head. "I have no way of knowing that, but I think he is."

"Why do you think that?" She used the voice he'd heard many times before. It was the tone that demanded answers even if they weren't accurate or well founded.

Sean couldn't explain, and he didn't want to say it was just a hunch. Luckily, he didn't have to.

"We have a letter from President James Madison," Tommy explained. "It was included with the video of John. We've figured out the first two sections of the riddle. Now, there's only one remaining. Once we have it, we'll make the trade with these goons."

Emily nodded. "Fine. We're going to Columbia Falls. We'll stay there with my friend for the night. Maybe while we're there you two can figure out the last part of this riddle, and we can get to John in time."

Sean didn't say anything, intentionally leaving out the part about how they were on a tight timeline.

If they were being followed, then the people reporting back to whoever was in charge would know that Sean and Tommy were getting closer with each step.

He turned around and looked out the back window again. No one was within sight. For a moment, he wondered if the people behind this entire game were in an aircraft, watching them from above, but he quickly dismissed the thought as irrational.

"Was there a tracking device on the 4Runner?" Sean blurted. The epiphany came to him abruptly.

"Probably," Emily said, "but there's something bigger going on. I don't know who is behind this, but they probably have strings attached in all kinds of places. I'm talking the bureau, the CIA, NSA, even the military. It seems like most of the heat is still on the East Coast right now, but we still have to be careful. And I know that one particular FBI agent is on your tail."

"Oh yeah? How do you know that?"

"Because his superior told me."

Sean and Tommy both arched their eyebrows. They were rarely caught off guard by Emily's connections. She answered only to the president, which meant many people had to answer to her. That fact just sort of hung there in the minds of her friends, but now and then when she said it out loud it seemed heavier.

"Director Hollis briefed you about this?" Sean asked. He knew who the FBI director was. Didn't particularly care for the guy, but he didn't hate him, either. Hollis came across as just another ladder climber, someone with a thirst for power and a cushy government pension at the end of a long career. That didn't make him a bad person and, as far as Sean knew, the guy wasn't as corrupt as some of the others in DC. Maybe he wasn't corrupt at all. Sean always hoped that was the case.

"Yes, he did," Emily said. "He has one of his best on the case, like I told you a minute ago. You may or may not realize that the FBI has a special operations unit under Hollis's direct control. It's newer; most people—even in my line of work—are unaware it exists. It's called Group Z. No clue where the name came from, but they are composed of some of the best agents the bureau has to offer."

"Sounds like someone might be invading your turf a little there, Em."

"Hardly." She blew off the comment, though there was a tone in her voice that alluded to the possibility he was right.

In Emily's world, there weren't many jobs like hers and certainly no agencies that operated the way Axis did. If the FBI had put together something similar, it could have been perceived as a play to hedge some of her operations, though only on a domestic scale. Then again, once someone had a taste of that kind of power, it was hard to pull them back.

Still, Emily didn't feel like her job was in jeopardy. She felt more secure in her career than most. She'd proved herself over the years and was a trustworthy asset in the president's arsenal. Emily Starks wasn't going anywhere anytime soon unless it was on her own terms.

"Petty is on the trail," Emily said. "He won't stop until he finds you two, which means the clock is ticking."

"The clock was already ticking," Tommy said from the back, trying to joke a little.

"Well, now it's ticking faster. Whatever you two need to do to clear your names, do it and do it soon. The noose is closing in, and I don't know how long I can hold off the executioner."

"You make it sound like so much fun," Sean joked.

"It's not supposed to be."

"I know. Tommy and I end up in these situations more than we'd like, and it's never fun, but this is worse." His tone grew contemplative, sincere. "I love John, too, Em. And there's nothing that will stop us from finding out who took him. When we do, they'll pay. I can promise you that."

Emily wasn't much for bravado or talk about revenge. It wasn't her thing. Justice, that was what she fought for, and while punishing those who were responsible for John's disappearance had a certain level of appeal to it, she also didn't want to become the monster she was hunting.

"Right now, let's just worry about getting to Columbia Falls. Once we're there, we can get cleaned up, get some rest, and try to figure out where you two knuckleheads need to go next."

"Already working on it," Tommy said.

He was scanning a copy of the letter in the back seat, reading over the last passage that he hoped would lead them to the third clue and, subsequently, the third piece of the ring.

Up ahead, the road rose and fell, climbing over the hills and then rolling back down again onto the plains. The mountains of Glacier

National Park loomed like stone giants shrouded in frigid shadows and cradled by gray clouds above.

The scene was ominous, and Sean hoped that the visual wasn't a sign of things to come. They'd been somewhat lucky so far, and Emily showing up when she had was beyond fortuitous. But Sean also knew that luck could turn as fast as the weather in Big Sky Country. The sooner they figured out the last part of this riddle, the better.

37

BROWNING

Agent Petty winced against the raging wind. The air seemed full of darts, each stinging his face and eyes with every passing gust. The wind, though, wasn't bothering him as much as it might have had the circumstances been different.

Instead, the focus of his ire wasn't the weather. It was the blatant incompetence of local law enforcement.

Petty had called in the cavalry, ordered the sheriff and as many cops as he could muster to head out to Camp Disappointment to arrest Sean Wyatt and Tommy Schultz. The fugitives were to be detained until Petty arrived and could question them.

None of that had happened. And it stoked the already burning fire in Petty's gut.

"How? How did you let them get away, Sheriff?" His voice echoed through the valley and bounced off the rock outcroppings. Petty made no attempt to hide his fury and the absolute disappointment he felt.

The sheriff shook his head. His cowboy hat carried a thin layer of snow on the brim. The man's face was red from the biting cold, and he narrowed his eyes behind his sunglasses to keep from tearing up.

"Now, hold on just a dang second," the cop said. "There was no one here when we arrived, Agent. Maybe you got some bad information. I pulled half a dozen cops in on this little operation. You have effectively wasted my time and the time of all these other guys, too." He motioned to the other six cops standing around. All of their coats were zipped up tight, hands covered in leather gloves. A few had scarves pulled up over their mouths to keep their faces warm.

Petty shook his head and looked out over the area. They were standing on the overlook, the parking area where Sean's vehicle still sat.

"Seems like my information was good," Petty said, pointing at the vehicle. The doors to the SUV were still open. The cops had checked it out upon arriving but found nothing of use inside other than the registration. The vehicle belonged to Tommy Schultz but had been purchased as a company vehicle for the International Archaeological Agency. A quick check of the tags reiterated that fact. "He was here," Petty reinforced. "That car belongs to his best friend. I suppose that's just a coincidence."

The sheriff bit his bottom lip and adjusted his belt. His gut was hanging over the waistline, and the maneuver did little to prevent that from happening again.

"Look, I don't know what you want, Agent Petty. We did what you asked. No one was here."

"You did what I asked?" Petty leaned sideways, letting how truly incensed he was be expressed by his posture. "Are you serious right now? Because what I asked you to do was arrest Sean Wyatt and hold on to him until I got here. But you didn't do that, did you? I mean, I don't see Sean Wyatt anywhere!" He spun around, making a full-blown mockery of the sheriff and his team. "Is he...is he in one of your squad cars over there?"

"No." Petty answered his own question. "Well then, where is he? He was right here! How did he get away?"

The cop swallowed back his anger and answered the question. "There were...other tracks when we got here. Someone must have picked them up. Maybe they knew we were coming." There was more than a hint of disdain in the cop's tone—and a healthy dose of suspicion, as well. "Maybe you told someone we were coming. You trying to cover up your own investigation, Agent?"

The man was grasping at straws, and they both knew it. Petty had seen that trick a million times. When someone felt like they were being blamed and knew they were in the wrong, deflecting some of that blame was a useful tool. But it wouldn't work on Petty. He'd used it before and he was too smart to fall for it himself.

"Where. Did. Sean. Wyatt. Go?" Petty's voice remained steady, full of righteous indignation.

"We don't know. I already told you that."

"The tracks. Do they go back into town?"

"The road was already cleared when we got here. Has been all day. Only place we saw tracks were here, on this gravel patch of trail leading up here to the overlook."

"And could you tell which way they turned out of here before you and your men drove all over the snow and crushed the evidence?"

The cop shook his head in shame. "No."

"Of course not!" Petty threw his hands up high in the air and then let them fall, slapping against the outside of his legs with a pronounced *whap*.

"I don't think they went back into town, though. If they had, someone would have seen them. We would have passed them. On our way out here, we didn't see any other vehicles on the road."

"They could have left before you even left your donut-covered desk."

The sheriff snorted a derisive laugh. "I wish we could get donuts out here. Good ones, anyway." He clearly didn't care that the federal agent before him had passed a snide comment his way. That or he simply didn't understand the insult.

Petty had to admit: He was raking this guy over the coals pretty hard and the man hadn't winced, had even thrown back a little smart-aleck jab of his own. The cop had moxie; Petty would give him that, but the problem still remained. Sean Wyatt was on the loose.

Based on what the sheriff said, Wyatt was probably heading west, toward Glacier National Park, but why? Did he hope to find sanctuary there, perhaps hide out in the dense forests until things died down?

Surely not.

It was much too cold to try and make a go of it in the great outdoors, at least without the proper equipment and training. Petty was certain Sean had picked up some wilderness survival training along the way, but the man was no expert, and on top of that he was in a part of the world he didn't know that well. Petty figured Sean had visited this area before, but it was hardly the woods out behind his childhood home.

Sean was out of his element out here in the wide-open West.

Petty had his team back in DC running checks for any known associates Wyatt might have out here, but so far nothing promising turned up. *What was he up to? Heading to Canada?*

That wouldn't work, either. The northern border was already on lockdown, the Canadian authorities watching for him to pop up in some desperate attempt to flee the country. Even with extradition in place, finding Wyatt in the vast wilderness of Canada could prove tricky were he able to make it there.

Still, that didn't seem like what was going on here. Petty didn't know for sure, but it seemed like Wyatt was following a very specific path.

"What is this place again?" Petty asked.

The sheriff had fallen away to his thoughts and barely heard the question.

"I'm sorry; what was that?"

"This place," Petty said, waving a hand around. "Camp Disappointment. Why is this important?"

The sheriff looked at him like he'd fallen out of a turnip truck and landed on his head. "Why is it important? I guess they didn't teach you about the Corps of Discovery expedition in your fancy schools back east."

Petty kept his face like stone, giving no quarter. "Why don't you educate me?"

"Lewis and Clark expedition? Ever heard of that?"

"Of course. Everyone knows about that."

"Well, its official name was the Corps of Discovery expedition. It was put together by Thomas Jefferson to learn about the land they acquired in the Louisiana Purchase. They were also looking for a water passage from the east to the Pacific Ocean. It was in this spot they finally realized that there would be no river cutting all the way through the nation to the west. They had to go the rest of the way on foot."

"Thus their disappointment."

"Correct."

"Not a very flattering title for a historical landmark."

The cop shrugged. "If we're done here, Agent Petty, my men and I would like to get back in our cars and head into town. No point in standing around out here freezing to death."

Petty nodded absently and stood there looking out over the land while the cops filed into their vehicles, each one grateful to be out of the frigid air. One by one, the police drove away, their tires flipping chunks of mushy snow into the bumpers as they left.

Petty remained for a few minutes, still gazing out at the landscape. Why were Sean Wyatt and Tommy Schultz following the Lewis and Clark Trail? Is that what they were doing? Petty returned to his car and slid into the seat. He took off his gloves and set them on the passenger seat, then held his hands in front of one of the vents for a minute to warm his still-cold fingers.

When he had enough feeling in his digits, he took the phone out of his coat pocket and pulled up the search app.

The connection was weak, only showing a single bar of cell coverage in the top-right corner of his phone, but it was enough to allow at least a slow connection to his LTE network.

After several seconds, the screen changed and populated with a list of search results. Petty tapped on the images tab at the top and then waited as the device repopulated the screen with new results, this time all pictures.

One of the first ones he noted was a multicolored map of the

United States. It was divided into sections, territory owned by the USA, land owned by the Spanish, and then Canada to the north.

He zoomed in on one area and noted it was Saint Louis. A white line shot up from there and went north through South Dakota and into the lower part of North Dakota. The line stopped at the words *Fort Mandan*. Then the trail went west, crossing into Montana and cutting across the entire state until it reached Idaho. Eventually, it ended on the coast in Oregon, at the mouth of the Columbia River.

Petty sighed and looked up through the windshield into the stark sky. He returned his gaze to the screen and traced the line back to this spot, the very place he was sitting. It was labeled on the map, too: Camp Disappointment. Based on the previous path Wyatt and his friend had taken, it was right along the same line as the Lewis and Clark expedition.

But why? Why in the world would those two be following that famous path that was taken over two hundred years ago?

Petty's mind raced.

"Think, Matt. Think."

He remembered his mother teaching him when he was little. Matthew had grown up with a learning disability that kept him out of the first and second grades, not attending school with other children until his third-grade year.

He had trouble with abstract challenges, and they often resulted in fits of anger and tantrums over his inability to figure something out. His mother—a saint in his eyes—never faltered, always encouraging him to push through the difficulties both in his studies, and in life, and to think his way into a solution.

"Think, Matty, think" was a line she'd used countless times during his youth. She always forced him to figure things out, even when it seemed like no answer was feasible.

Now, here he was, trying to understand something that was out of his realm of expertise. He was accustomed to certain kinds of investigation, but this—this was more like code breaking in a way.

"What's the connection?" he said to himself. "What do Wyatt and Schultz want with Lewis and Clark?"

That question led him to another, a more powerful one: "What do Wyatt and Schultz do?" He paused. "They're historians, archaeologists."

He'd learned a good amount of information regarding Wyatt and Schultz's activities around the world, how they were able to solve problems and figure out ancient mysteries with uncanny success. It had made the duo famous in some circles, and they were developing a reputation as two of the greatest treasure hunters of all time.

He recalled reading that neither of them wanted to be known as treasure hunters, that those who went by that moniker were people uninterested in preserving history and only focused on increasing personal wealth.

Those weren't the kinds of things a criminal would say. That thought brought Petty back to a distracting one from earlier. Did Wyatt really kidnap the president?

He shook his head and made himself come back to the issue at hand. Why? Why were these two on the same trail the Lewis and Clark expedition took over two hundred years ago?

The answer seemed obvious now.

Wyatt and Schultz were looking for something. They were on a hunt, trying to find something left behind by Lewis and Clark, or maybe a series of items related to that expedition. There were dozens of possibilities that tried to pop into Petty's skull, but he pushed them back. Whatever Wyatt was trying to find was irrelevant at the moment.

Perhaps Wyatt had abducted Dawkins because the former president was privy to knowledge about whatever Wyatt was trying to find. Rumors ran wild in that regard. There were fascinating theories as to what the presidents really knew about aliens, ancient technology, and where some of the nation's greatest treasures were hidden. Was that why Wyatt had taken Dawkins? It was certainly plausible.

Petty looked across the map and noted the endpoint at the edge of the Pacific Ocean.

"Well," Petty said, "I may not know where you're going today, but I know where you'll end up."

38

COLUMBIA FALLS, MONTANA

Emily pulled into the driveway. The gravel was covered in a thick layer of snow, and it crunched under the tires as she drove ahead. The four wheels turned, slipping now and then on the slick, unstable surface beneath.

The drive from Browning to Columbia Falls had taken nearly ninety minutes, when it typically took much less than that. Snow fell the entire time, limiting visibility and causing the roads to be far more treacherous. Four-wheel drive helped as long as it was mostly snow on the roads and the road crews had salted the pavement prior to the storm coming, which caused the dry powder to melt into slush.

Still, it could have been dangerous, and Emily did everything in her power to be cautious, keeping a firm grip on the wheel at all times.

They'd arrived safely at their destination, and as Emily steered the SUV up a slight hill, the cabin appeared around the bend in the trail. There was a huge garage to the left with two big bay doors and a carport built into the right-side end. An old tractor sat there hooked up to a long belt. From the looks of it, the owner of the place had rigged the tractor as a sort of mill.

Sean stared at the cabin with wide eyes. "This. Place. Is. Awesome," he said.

He opened the door as Emily shifted the vehicle into park and killed the engine. Tommy stepped out, too, his boots crunching as they sank deep into the fresh powder. A heavy layer of snow coated the cabin's roof, along with the shorter roof that hung out over the entrance atop the stairs.

The second SUV pulled up next to them, and two men dressed in black peacoats got out. Their weapons were holstered within the folds of their outerwear, but Sean knew just how fast those guns could be produced if needed.

Emily made a circular motion with one finger. "Check the perimeter," she said. "When you're certain it's clear, you guys can set up camp in the downstairs apartment. Should be beds for all of you, plenty of food in the fridge, and water, too. You know the routine. Two-hour shifts." The men nodded and drew their weapons, then they spread out to check the area. Two went around behind the cabin. Another one trotted through the snow to the back of the garage and adjacent outdoor shop. The last of her operatives moved quickly back down the driveway, scanning both sides of it to make sure no threat was hiding out in the forest.

The cabin was three stories tall, including the basement. The windows of the lower floor were only seven or eight inches above ground level. A large porch jutted out from the front of the cabin. It stood over the entrance to the basement, which appeared to be another apartment, the one Emily assigned to her agents.

"Who did you say owns this place?" Tommy asked.

"Not sure I did." Emily shut the driver-side door and walked around to the back. "You guys wanna help me with your gear, or am I also the bellhop?"

Sean snapped back to the moment. It was like being in a winter wonderland, surrounded by dense forests of coniferous trees, all coated in pure, fresh snow. There was an eerie silence to winter settings like this. Sean had always sensed it. He didn't know how to describe it, but whenever he felt it, he was never afraid. It was a serene sensation, a kind of odd peace that permeated everything: the mountains, the trees, the rocks, the animals, the snow, and even him.

Sean remembered some of the bigger snowstorms he'd endured in his younger days. The last one was when he'd been living in Chattanooga. That night, around six to eight inches of snow had fallen, covering the city in a pristine white blanket. Sean had awoken early and gone outside before anyone else was up. That was the last time he'd felt this kind of serenity. There were no sounds of cars, people, or pets. Just a heavy quiet. Feeling it again, he wished it was a sensation he could get more often.

Back in Southern Tennessee and North Georgia, snow was a rarity, only coming around once or twice a year, and when it did, the accumulation was almost nothing, a few inches here, half a foot there. When it snowed more than a couple of inches, cities shut down, schools closed, offices worked on delays. In the South, unlike up here, there was no real need to invest money in machinery and resources that could keep the roads clear.

Sean sighed and walked around to the back of the vehicle. Emily stepped aside so he and Tommy could grab their things. Then Sean shut the back gate and followed Emily and Tommy toward the cabin.

They ascended the stairs with caution. The last thing any of them needed was a foolish injury due to carelessness. A hospital visit wouldn't be possible. Once they set foot there, federal agents and local law enforcement alike would pounce.

Emily stopped at the door and entered a passcode on a little panel to the right of the doorframe. She pressed the enter button, and the front flap on the panel flipped open on a hinge. Inside was a single brass key. Emily took the key, inserted it into the door, and twisted. The door opened easily and swung wide.

The three stepped into the cabin and closed the door behind them. Tommy half expected it to be warmer than outside, but he quickly realized that it was almost as cold inside the cabin.

"Does this place have heat?" Tommy asked, rubbing his hands together to warm them.

"Over there," Emily motioned to a black woodstove in the corner of the room. There was a short stack of wood next to it, as well as kindling and some stacks of newspaper.

"There's more wood outside," Sean said. "By the garage." He'd noted the pile on their way in and had already counted on this place being heated solely by fire.

"We do have electricity, though," Tommy said. He flipped on a light in a side hallway. There was a washer and dryer and a large sink. To the right of those, at the end of the corridor, was a bathroom with a sink, toilet, and shower-tub.

Sean noted the thermostat on the wall near the entrance. The screen was blank, the little box disconnected from any source of power. He understood why. Running heat in there would consume a decent amount of energy, energy they could use on lights.

Sean walked through the foyer, under a set of stairs going up to the second floor, and took in the cabin's interior. The kitchen and dining area were to the left. There was a back door between the kitchen island and a small dining table. To the right were a couple of upholstered chairs that looked like leftovers from a 1970s garage sale, a brown faux leather couch, and a dark brown coffee table.

"I'll get the fire going," Sean said. "You guys figure out where you want to sleep."

He noted the little bed in a corner near the stove. It was a double, barely large enough for one adult.

"I'll sleep upstairs," Emily said. "There's one bed and a futon. Either one of you can have the futon. Unless you wanted to share this double down here."

Sean bellowed. "That's one way to get warm."

Emily cracked a smile.

Tommy chuckled. "True."

Sean set to work stuffing newspaper, kindling, and a couple of smaller logs into the stove while Tommy wandered over to the back door and unlocked it. He stepped out onto the little porch and looked down the stairs. To the right, situated just beyond the boundary of the yard, a section of the forest had been cut back to provide a narrow trail. The path was unkempt, nearly allowed to be overcome by plant life. Tommy followed the trail about thirty feet into the woods where there was another, smaller building.

"Is that a smokehouse back there?" Tommy asked when he returned, jerking his thumb outside. He pulled the door closed again and locked the deadbolt.

Emily shook her head. "Sauna. My friend built this cabin with his own hands, his own money. Didn't want to use banks. Doesn't trust them. So, a few decades ago, he started saving up from month to month, putting some money aside to build this place. He wanted to be debt free and have his own home to live in. That's exactly what he did."

"And he built a sauna."

Emily nodded. "He said in Scandinavia, particularly Finland, when they're building a house the first thing they build is the sauna. So, that's what he did. He has a funny story about bringing his wife here for the first time. The sauna was finished and operational, but the house still had a ways to go. If you meet him, get him to tell you about it some time."

"This friend," Sean interrupted, "where is he now?"

"He lives down in Big Fork, about forty...maybe forty-five minutes from here. Moved several years ago but kept this place. Probably sentimental reasons, but he claims it's because he rents it out in the summer to tourists coming to visit the park. He used to be a park ranger out here. Did that job for thirty years before he retired. He's been all over these mountains, the forests, knows every nook and cranny out in this wilderness. If you're ever lost in Montana, my friend is the guy you need to be with."

"Sounds like this dude is some kind of survival rock star. What's his name?"

Emily flashed a wry grin.

"Oh, come on. Why don't you want us to know his name? You know I can find information like that pretty easily."

She shrugged and walked up the stairs. "Do it, then," she said as she entered the bedroom and disappeared from view.

Sean shook his head and looked back into the stove. The newspaper was burning brightly. The kindling, too, was flickering, licking the logs with hot yellow and orange flames. He watched it for a few more minutes, and once the wood was burning on its own he closed the door to the stove.

"This thing will have the cabin warm and toasty in no time," Sean said. There was more hope than fact in the statement.

He held out his hands over the flat surface and let the new warmth seep into his skin. It wasn't much. The temperature inside the cabin was at least in the mid-forties, though it could have been lower. From the looks of it, the place hadn't been used in a while, probably not since the end of summer. A thin layer of dust coated some of the shelves, an old television that had rabbit-ear antennas sticking out of the top, and even the coffee table.

Sean walked over to the kitchen and found a couple of candles, one on top of the counter and the other on the table. He took out two more matches, lit the one on the table first, then the one on the counter. Within seconds, the smell of balsam fir filled the room from the scented green wax.

Emily came back down the stairs, her overcoat gone. She was now wearing a gray hoodie with an Atlanta Falcons logo on the front.

"What's your plan?" she asked. The question was as direct as she so often was.

Sean appreciated that about her. No bull; just straightforward and upfront.

Tommy held the letter in his hand and set it gently on the table. "Still not sure where we go next. The last part of this riddle is confusing. I mean, if I had to guess, I'd say we're heading to the area around where Lewis and Clark stopped at the Pacific. Station Camp."

"That's at the mouth of the Columbia River?" Sean figured he knew the answer but asked anyway.

Tommy nodded. "Correct. And if we look at the last clue, it sure seems like the reference is congruent."

He pulled out his phone and set it on the table. Then he typed in a single word and tapped the search button.

The internet connection was slow, and it took several seconds before the screen flickered and changed to a new one, a page full of results written in blue text. Tommy clicked the top one and then narrowed it to maps. When the map appeared, he used his thumb and forefinger to zoom out.

Sean and Emily leaned over his shoulders, hovering low to see what he was looking at.

"Astoria?" Sean asked. There was a splash of humor in his voice.

The map on the display was of the area around the mouth of the Columbia River and the border between the states of Oregon and Washington.

"Don't worry," Tommy said with a chuckle, "we're not going looking for One-Eyed Willy's treasure."

"You sure? Because that's the place, you know."

"What are you two talking about?" Emily asked.

Sean's eyebrows pinched together. He almost looked insulted. "Seriously? *Goonies*? You never saw *The Goonies*?"

"Oh. It's...been a while. Like, I don't know, thirty years?"

"Goonies never say die, Em," Tommy said. "Anyway, no. We're not looking for pirate treasure. Not that I know of. Whatever Lewis found will be in this area here." Tommy pointed at the map and used his finger to draw an imaginary circle.

"You assume," Sean said.

Tommy's head shook back and forth. "No. Take a look at the clue again. It talks about the last place they camped, the final camp. The secret is buried in a dark chamber—probably in a cave, knowing our luck—across the river to the southwest." Tommy moved his finger across the inlet to a peninsula that jutted out into the water where the river met the ocean.

Sean narrowed his eyes and peered at the name of the place on the map. "Fort Stevens?"

Tommy nodded.

"What is it?" Emily asked.

"From the looks of it, I'd say it's an old military installation," Tommy said. "Doesn't appear to still be in use."

"It isn't," Sean said. "It's a state park now. No soldiers anymore."

Tommy and Emily both shared a glance. They knew better than to question Sean's knowledge about things like that. Somehow, he had a penchant for obscure, arcane information. The history and current state of Fort Stevens fit that bill.

"So...I guess this is where we go next?" Tommy asked.

Sean nodded. "If this is the right place, we'll have a long drive ahead of us tomorrow. We'll need to get some sleep, but I suggest we get out of here as early as possible. I doubt we'll get to the coast before sunset."

"Agreed," Tommy said. "So, Fort Stevens. That'll be a new one for me."

Sean nodded and walked over to the futon. He plopped down on it and fluffed a pillow that was lying on one end.

"I'm not going with you," Emily said, looking over at Sean as he propped up his legs on the couch. "If the Feds find me with you, they'll charge me with aiding and abetting. I'll be an accomplice. And while I want to get John back more than anything—"

"You can't risk it," Sean finished her thought. "I know, Em. I know. Besides, you can't do much good from behind prison bars, can you?"

She looked crestfallen, her eyes dropping to the floor for a moment in dejection. "No. I can't." She shook her head. "I'll do all I can remotely, but this is as far as I can go on this little mission. We had to get you out of Montana."

"I know," Sean said with a wave of his right hand. "Petty is on our tail. I'll take care of him when the time comes."

Emily didn't like the sound of that, but Sean eased her mind by adding, "Not *take care of*, take care of." He put a finger to his head, shaping his hand like a pistol and pulling the trigger to let his thumb fall like a hammer. "I mean as in I'll make sure he understands everything that's going on."

Somehow, that didn't make her feel a ton better, but it would have to do for now.

"Good night, you two," she said. "See you in the morning." Emily turned and started toward the stairs again.

Sean closed his eyes and folded his arms across his chest. "No, Em, you won't."

39

ANNAPOLIS

Adriana watched closely as the night's guards changed out with the morning shift. She'd been observing them for nearly two full days, watching their every move. She paid special attention to Admiral Winters. The man kept strange habits, though the systematic approach to his daily routine was to be expected for some of the things he did.

He was a lifelong military man, which meant he'd settled into the rut of going to bed at a decent hour and waking up early. She'd observed his bedroom light going off at almost the same time the last two evenings, and as she'd anticipated, he'd woken up at the exact minute and hour both mornings. There was no need to wait around any longer to learn about his sleeping habits. That much was easy to figure.

What she needed to know was whether or not Winters had a weakness she could exploit, a way to get inside his home without alerting the PSU guards that were constantly keeping watch.

The sky overhead was clear, and the sun shone brightly. Snow covered the sidewalks, about two inches deep, while the streets were wet with mushy salt and remnants of the accumulation from the day before.

Adriana's car was at the corner of the street about a half block from the admiral's home. Based on the last two days of observation, she knew he would be leaving to go to his office in the next few minutes.

There was, of course, a chance he could break routine and do something different, but that was unlikely. Men like him were creatures of habit, and they rarely did anything to change what was working. That systemic discipline had been ingrained in him. Going off script in the military could cost not only one life but many. That was the importance of following orders. Commanders usually made decisions based on the best data available, and ignoring that could have catastrophic results. It was easy to see why that mindset filtered into everyday military life.

The morning guards took their places along the outside of the brick townhouse and assumed their stoic poses while the night patrol left for the day.

By her count, Adriana noted two guards at the front of the home, one on either side of the steps leading up to the house. There were also two in the backyard, one at the gate and another at the top of the stairs going into the rear entrance. She'd seen two more enter and leave every time there was a changeover, which meant there was a total of six on patrol at any given moment.

Not odds she liked but hardly insurmountable. The issue with these guards was that they were the best of the best of the best, the elite of a combination of military units that could do anything, take down anyone, and wouldn't hesitate to kill if provoked.

There were two more stationed in a townhouse across the street. She'd seen them come and go twice now; each time, the men gave a look toward Winters's home that she easily identified as a check, a subtle way for them to make sure nothing was going on. So, there were eight total security guys on his detail. How many reinforcements were there? Double was a safe guess. And if any one of them called for backup, there would be a lot more than that on their way.

Adriana knew she was running out of time. She had to get to Winters now. She sighed and looked in the rearview mirror. A postal

Jeep was driving down the street. She'd noticed it the last couple of days. The vehicle would finish its route on this street, going straight through the intersection and all the way to the end. Then the postman would turn right, work his way down the next road, and then come back through this area on the perpendicular street, hitting the side Winters's house was on before going back down the opposite direction.

Adriana watched the Jeep approach, stopping, starting, and doing it all over again with every mailbox it reached. There were cars along the street in front of and behind her, which forced the postal worker to get out at every address, take the mail up to the entrance of the home, and deposit it in their mailbox or through the delivery slot.

It was a thankless job. Adriana didn't envy it in the slightest, though it did give her an idea. Today, the postman wasn't a man at all. It was a postwoman. The lady was white with red hair and a pale, freckled complexion. Adriana picked up every last detail of the woman as she drew nearer. As luck would have it, she was about Adriana's size and height.

The idea wasn't one Adriana liked. Then again, she didn't have much choice. It was her only in, the only one she could think of. This was her chance, possibly the last one, to get into Winters's home and have a nice little chat with the man.

The problem with that would be the men across the street would know what was going on. They'd see her approach the house, whether in disguise or not. That meant she'd have to take them out first.

She looked back in the mirror at the postal worker as the woman climbed out of her Jeep and trudged through the slippery snow, and up a short flight of stairs. She rang the doorbell and set a box, along with a stack of envelopes and magazines, on the welcome mat before turning around and walking back down.

Adriana moved her car a little farther down the street, parked along the curb, and resumed watching the postal worker as she continued her stop-and-go deliveries.

The woman parked again, got out, and went up another flight of stairs to a home with a bright red brick façade. Adriana decided to move. She was running out of time and didn't have the luxury of waiting forever. She'd have to make her play now.

She looked in the back of her vehicle for something she could use to gently knock the woman out, but all she had with her was a few changes of clothes and a bag full of weapons. Most of the weapons in the rucksack were nonlethal, guns she'd picked up from Helen that packed a heavy electrical charge but wouldn't kill a human being.

There were, of course, a few standard firearms—just in case. Adriana didn't want to use any of those on this innocent postal worker. This woman checked in to her job to deliver the mail and drive a little white Jeep around the city in all manner of weather. The last thing she thought about when she woke up this morning was that some stranger was going to render her unconscious, take her uniform, and run off with her vehicle.

One of those thoughts brought an idea.

She slipped out of the car and eased the door shut, then took off at a brisk walk down the side of the street, skipping between a couple of cars parked behind hers so she could use the sidewalk.

Just ahead, the mailwoman climbed into her Jeep and stepped on the gas. The engine groaned a gravelly tenor sound until she stepped on the brakes again another twenty feet ahead. There were multiple mailboxes at the next home. Adriana watched as the lady gathered two stacks of mail and a couple of cardboard shipping boxes.

Right when the postal worker stepped out of her Jeep and onto the sidewalk, Adriana deftly cut to the right and back onto the street. She watched carefully as the mailwoman took the letters to the steps and started her ascent. Now Adriana hurried, running quickly to the back of the Jeep. She peered through the rear window and saw what she hoped would be there.

Hanging on a bar that stuck out from the driver-side cabin was another postal uniform.

Adriana swallowed and grabbed the latch. She hoped it was unlocked but didn't expect it to be. She took another look at the woman delivering the mail. She was nearly at the top of the steps and completely focused on the task at hand. She was being careful not to drop the boxes or any of the letters, but the battle was quickly being lost as one of the smaller boxes teetered on the edge of another.

Adriana tugged down on the latch and was relieved to find the door swung open. She reached in and took the uniform off the hanger, then started to close the door. She froze when she heard a slapping sound. Wincing, she peeked around the corner of the Jeep and saw the postal worker picking up some of the envelopes and one of the boxes she'd dropped on the top step.

The woman turned her backside toward Adriana. The Spaniard quickly reached into the mail truck and grabbed a few envelopes. No sense in worrying about a federal crime now.

With another nervous swallow, Adriana shut the door silently and turned the latch back up to secure it. She skirted around the edge of the Jeep and crouched low, pretending to tie her shoe. A red SUV drove by on the other side of the street. Once the vehicle was a safe distance away, she drew a knife from her belt and stabbed the front-left tire in the sidewall. She jerked the knife out of the rubber, shoved it back in its sheath, and stood again as air spewed from the fresh wound.

The damage would set back the mailwoman's progress by at least an hour, possibly even ruin her day, but it was an acceptable form of collateral damage and far better than knocking the woman out to steal her Jeep. This way, no one got hurt.

Adriana took off at a steady walk, rolling up the uniform as she moved. By the time she was at the vehicle in front of the Jeep, the new clothes were tightly rolled and tucked under her armpit so the mail-woman couldn't see them.

Now all Adriana had to do was change before the deliverywoman made it back to the admiral's street.

Her Trojan horse was a risky play, but it was the only one she had. With time running out, she didn't have the luxury of coming up with something more elegant. It would have to work. John Dawkins's life depended on it, and maybe so did Sean's.

40

ASTORIA, OREGON

Fort Stevens was a little over eleven hours away from Columbia Falls by car—if the weather cooperated. Until that morning, Sean and Tommy had been lucky.

Their luck changed overnight.

When they woke up, their new SUV was covered in a fresh blanket of snow, as was the rest of the area. Most of the storm had moved on, leaving behind several inches of fresh powder and a few gray clouds overhead to sprinkle flurries on spots the rest of the blizzard might have missed.

Sean woke up around 3:30 a.m. local time. He showered, dressed, and made a pot of coffee, choosing to let Tommy sleep for a few more minutes before they left. Tommy had showered the night before, so when four o'clock hit, he was ready to go when Sean woke him.

Emily and her team stayed behind in the cabin, and while Sean intended to not wake her, he was pretty sure the smell of coffee and the sounds of the and the door opening and closing would have roused her. She didn't make an appearance, but Sean knew she was a light sleeper. There were too many missions where the two of them had had no choice but to share a bed, or at least a room. Nothing ever happened between them as far as romance was concerned. She wasn't his type, and Sean got the vibe he was definitely not hers. They were great friends, but any sort of intimate relationship was never on the table. He was glad for that. It could have made things awkward later on down the road.

When they left earlier that morning under the cover of darkness, he didn't feel the need to thank her or say goodbye. He'd convey his gratitude later. Right now, they had to hurry. With the uncooperative weather, it would be a challenge to get to the coast by nightfall. Even though they still had another day or so, Sean didn't want to risk it. The sooner they could figure out this whole thing, the better.

The drive took nearly thirteen hours, which was better than either Sean or Tommy would have believed possible given the conditions.

They first cut through Astoria, a place Sean and Tommy both knew from their childhood as the location where one of their favorite movies was based. Then they proceeded out of town and across a bridge that took them to the peninsula where Fort Stevens State Park was located.

Fortunately, there were still a few hours of daylight left despite the churning gray soup overhead.

Tommy was the last one to drive and found a place to park in one of the public areas. There weren't many other vehicles in the lot. While the weather was considerably warmer than where their journey had begun thirteen hours prior, there was still a chill in the damp air. Rain spat on them in annoying little droplets that seemed more like the heavens were sweating.

Sean looked around the area and pulled his raincoat hood up over his head. Tommy did the same as he got out of the truck and walked around to the back. The rear gate lifted, and they each grabbed their rucksacks, slung them over their shoulders, and then looked around again, surveying the area for both trouble and a clue as to where they should go next.

Tommy closed the rear hatch after a few seconds and then turned to his friend. "Where to now?"

Sean took a deep breath and sighed. "Visitor center?"

Tommy closed his eyes slowly, grimacing at the answer. "Seriously?"

Sean chuckled. "No, moron. Of course not. Let's have a look around."

Tommy bit his bottom lip while Sean took off down the path leading into the park.

As the two proceeded deeper into the state preserve, sounds of the ocean crashing against the shore mingled with the occasional howls of wind. There were stands of evergreen trees on either side of the trail, spaced apart now and then by large rocks and patches of undergrowth. Up ahead, they could see where the trees thinned and eventually gave way to flat, open spaces. It reminded Sean of the coast of Maryland, or perhaps South Carolina where the lowlands met the water.

As they left the cover of the forests behind and walked out into the open near the tip of the peninsula, they saw one of the bunkers off to the right and a long, concrete structure straight ahead facing out toward the Pacific. The building was several hundred feet across. There were multiple openings where windows used to be, and wide doors dotted a curved area in the center of the structure. There were two other openings on either side of the semicircle. Sean figured them to be loading bays, but they could have been anything. Just off to the right of the half-circle wall, a tower stood two stories high, propped up by two concrete pilings. The entire structure appeared to be cut out of the hill and, as such, wet green grass ran up the sides of parts of it. The grass ran across the expanse of the peninsula, giving the place an Irish or Scottish sort of feeling.

This last iteration of Fort Stevens had been built prior to World War II. It bore a resemblance to so many similar defense projects Sean and Tommy had seen over the years as they toured the country and researched various historical military installations.

When it was in operation, Fort Stevens had been part of a fortification known as the Harbor Defense System. Along with forts Canby and Columbia just across the border between states, the three forts were designed to protect the mouth of the Columbia River and that portion of the Pacific Coast from enemies. Fort Stevens was occupied and fully operational from the time of the Civil War until the end of World War II, when it was shut down and eventually turned into a state park. The property boasted over four thousand acres of natural beauty combined with a rich military history, making it one of the more fascinating and exceptional parks in the nation. During the warmer months, visitors could walk the beaches, do some camping or hiking, and take the opportunity to view the incredibly diverse wildlife in this part of the lush Pacific Northwest.

One of the interesting, and somber, facts that Tommy noted during his research of the facility was that Fort Stevens was located near the middle of what is known as the Graveyard of the Pacific. This swath of death and destruction stretched from Tillamook Bay in Oregon all the way up to Vancouver Island and Cape Scott Provincial Park.

The waters off the coast were the home of more than two thousand known shipwrecks. Strange and unpredictable weather patterns along with treacherous underwater terrain made for difficult sailing through that stretch of the sea. Estimates said more than seven hundred people had lost their lives in shipwrecks along the graveyard. Still more perished with each new year despite increases in technology, sailing knowledge, and the warnings residing in the minds of every sailor within a hundred miles.

Tommy had heard of the fort and the surrounding area several times, but never took a moment to check it out online or in books. It seemed, he was always too busy.

"This place feels like it's haunted," Sean said as they trudged down the damp path. The gravel under their feet crunched with every step. The trail curled around to the other side of the hill and continued around to the point of the peninsula. There were outcroppings of trees over their shoulders in the other direction, where the land rose slightly to a plateau.

"Yeah," Tommy agreed. His head twisted around several times, making sure there was no one else about.

Off in the distance, near the shore, there were a few people hanging around looking out at the water. An older couple held hands as they walked along the beach, their heads bowed.

Sean led the way around the entrances, the windows, and the curved wall in the center and kept walking until he reached the end of the structure. "You think we should go inside and check it out?" There was trepidation in his tone.

Tommy pulled out the piece of paper from his coat pocket and held it in both hands. The top corners flapped in the breeze as he read the passage again.

"I don't think so," Tommy said. "This thing tells us that whatever we're looking for is going to be hidden a thousand paces from the innermost corner."

"That's assuming the fort, or an earlier iteration of it, was here back in Madison's time."

"There was a small fort built here when the explorers came through, though it was simple, not like some of the other forts of the time. From what I read, they built it more as a way to stake their claim on the land and let it be known that the United States military had been there and would be coming back."

Sean looked back toward the direction they'd just come from and fixed his gaze on the corner. "I guess that would be it, then?" He pointed at the end of the building nearest the path.

"I suppose so," Tommy said.

The two marched back down the trail and stopped at the corner where the concrete building came to an end. Tommy held up the paper again, almost as if he was looking at a map, then lowered the page and stared out away from the corner toward the plateau he'd noticed before.

"Up there?" Sean asked, noting his friend's gaze.

"Looks that way."

"Okay, then."

The two left the fortification behind and hiked off the path, through the marshy grass toward the hillside. Some of the ground was soft under their boots, and they had to move carefully, watching their every step.

Once they reached the gently rising slope, the ground became firmer and more consistent, allowing them to move faster. As they reached the top of the hill, Sean looked back out at the plain below, just to be certain they were alone.

They kept walking, and soon the trees blocked their view of the fort and the coast just beyond. There was also less wind here, which neither of the two minded. The breeze coming off the ocean and the Columbia River had made the chilly air feel colder than it was. It was still way warmer than where they'd been the last few days, traipsing across North Dakota, Montana, and part of Idaho.

The small forest opened up again into a meadow. The clearing was full of tall grass like they'd seen down by the fort and along the pathway from the parking area. Tommy stepped out into the middle of it and spun around in 360 degrees.

"Did you forget to count your steps?" Sean asked.

Tommy bit his lower lip. He looked like a kid. "Um, no?"

"How many do you have right now?"

"Three—"

"Nope," Sean cut him off.

"Fine. I forgot to count. The letter said a thousand paces."

"Yeah, I know what it said," Sean quipped. He fired a disdainful look at his friend and then laughed. "You're such an idiot."

Tommy chuckled and shook his head in shame. "I know. I know."

"Seriously, you had one job."

"Okay, first of all, I had two jobs. Getting us in the right direction was the first. So, would you mind sharing with me how many steps we've taken so far?"

"Eight." Sean still had the expression on his face that told Tommy to have another slice of humble pie.

"Okay, so eight hundred steps. That means we have—"

"Two hundred to go?"

"You know, you're hilarious. Just keep it up, and you'll be walking home."

"Sure I will. Can we please keep moving? I'm thinking just over that ridge." He pointed in the direction of a mound in the middle of the meadow.

Tommy sighed and then started trudging through the grass again. When they'd walked over the top of the mound, a new structure came into view.

"What is that? Looks like some kind of bunker."

Sean slowed his pace and stared at the concrete building. "That's exactly what it is," he said.

"I didn't see anything about this on the maps I studied."

"And it probably wasn't in any of the brochures you read or on the park's website. Right?"

Tommy nodded. "Right."

"Well, we've come all this way. Might as well have a look."

"Yeah."

The two skidded down the mound and walked the last one hundred steps to the little military building. Compared to the main fort, this building looked like nothing more than a storage shed. Sean figured it was about fifty feet long, though that was difficult to assess from his angle. It was only one level, and the windows were small. The rusted metal door on the end hung slightly ajar.

"Why's the door open?" Tommy asked. "You think someone's in there?"

Sean's eyes narrowed as he peered at the building. "No. Probably just some local teenagers using it as a place to get drunk on weekends. Still..." Sean drew the pistol from his inner holster and held it down at his side. "Better—"

"Safe than sorry? You really need a new line. You know that, right?"

"Solid burn, Schultzie." He walked ahead toward the open door, keeping a close watch on the woods surrounding the bunker.

He reached the door and stopped, stuck his gun in first to check the immediate area on the other side, and then nudged the door farther. Inside, the place was completely abandoned. There was no furniture, no equipment, just a few empty beer cans scattered around. As Sean suspected, it was a weekend drinking place for local kids wanting to avoid being caught by parents or police.

Tommy joined his friend inside the small space and looked around to the left. The corridor ended abruptly at a blank wall.

Sean moved ahead and rounded the corner immediately opposite of the doorway. Another corridor presented itself, but there were no rooms to be found and no other doors.

The two stalked forward, weapons drawn and at their sides, gripped with both hands. Sean reached the end of the narrow hallway and turned left. More light came into the space from windows along the top of the concrete walls. He came to another corner and poked his head around it. There was nothing except another door, the back way in and out of the old building.

A deep frown crossed his face, and he let his right arm sag to his side, still holding the pistol in that hand.

"What in the world?" Tommy asked. "This has to be the place."

Sean drew in a long breath through his nostrils and let it out slowly. He looked back down the hall again and scratched his head with his free hand. "Unless that mound out there was where the thing is hidden."

"Could be," Tommy said, "though based on what you told me, this would be closer to the right distance."

"That's if there really was an older fort where the current one is standing."

The two spun around again, checking the walls with a closer eye, inspecting every inch of the bunker. The wooden floorboards were old and worn down. They creaked with every subtle move. The breeze whistled through the opening where a window used to be.

"What are we missing here?" Tommy asked. He put his hands out wide and let them fall, clapping against his hips. "This building couldn't have been anything more than a munitions store or a place to stow equipment."

Sean nodded. "Yeah, unless..."

His eyes fixed on the floor about fifteen feet away, midway down the hall.

"Unless what?"

Sean tiptoed over to the spot in the floor that had caught his attention. There was a chunk missing on one of the wooden boards closest to the wall. Most of it was flush against the bottom edge where the concrete met the top of the flooring. Sean got down on one knee and waved his free hand over the little opening. It wasn't big, maybe the size of a watch face, but he felt cool air flowing out of it.

"This isn't the bunker," Sean said. He could see Tommy was about to ask an obvious question, so he kept talking. "Bunkers are usually underground. This place is just the entrance to it. It's not big enough to be an armory, and there aren't any additional rooms. The bunker must have been covered up. I bet if we pull up these floorboards, we'll find a way down into the real bunker, and that is where we—hopefully—will find whatever it is we're looking for."

"Okay," Tommy said. "So, we need to get something to pry up these boards."

"Now, that," a new voice said, "is a good idea."

Tommy started to raise his weapon. Sean's reaction, too, was quick but immediately threatened by the newcomer.

"Don't," the voice said. "Keep your hands right where they are."

They couldn't see the man. He was keeping his face just behind the corner, only revealing one eye so he could aim the Glock at his targets while maintaining safe cover.

Sean froze.

Tommy lowered his gun back to his side.

"Now, put those on the floor, please. I don't want to shoot you."

"Then why are you pointing a gun at us?" Tommy asked.

"Because I'm a federal agent. And you're under arrest for the kidnapping of former president John Dawkins."

41

Adriana stared out the windshield from her vantage point at the end of the street. She could see one of the guards standing out in front of the steps of Winters's home. She knew the other one was there, probably on the porch, but he was out of sight at the moment.

She looked at her watch. Noting the time, she opened the door and stepped out of her car. The postal uniform was loose on her, and she immediately realized that her assessment of the mailwoman's size had been a tad off. It didn't matter. She could still wear the outfit, and the fact that it was loose allowed her movement to be less restricted.

Adriana shut her car door and trotted around behind the row of buildings on the opposite side of the road from Winters's house.

The long row of townhouses was connected at the back with a side street that allowed residents access to the rear of their homes where the garages and a few carriage homes lined up from one end to the other.

She'd made a mental note of which building housed the security observation team, and the second she was out of street view she sprinted down the alley until she came to the correct house.

There were no guards in the back and no signs of life inside, either. She knew that was part of the plan and gave no credence to it.

She opened the back gate and walked across a segmented pathway made from concrete hexagons, climbed the short staircase to the back porch, and stopped at the rear door.

Adriana didn't bother to look up at the camera hanging from the exterior wall. She'd already seen it before opening the back gate. The men inside would know she was there. That was fine. They were going to know the second she knocked on the door.

She looked in both directions with a sidelong glance, then rapped on the door with her right hand, holding the envelopes in the other. The letters rested on her fist, a delicate balancing act that covered up the small pulse pistol in her hand.

The deadbolt inside the door slid from the receiver, and then the knob lock clicked. A second later, a man in a black windbreaker with a shaved head and dark eyebrows appeared. He had a stern look on his face, almost crotchety.

"What's going on?" he asked.

"Mail," Adriana said with a smile. She tried to keep it professional —but sort of flirty without overdoing it.

"We don't get mail here," the guard said. His tone was overwhelmingly suspicious.

"Oh?" Adriana twisted her head and looked down at the envelopes. "I'm so sorry. I have the wrong address. My mistake. You wouldn't believe how often that happens to me in a given day."

The guard didn't say anything. Instead, he started to close the door on her, but a thump from the gun in her hand sent a pellet straight to his neck. Instantly, the man started gyrating and convulsing. His eyes fixed on some far-off point in the sky as he collapsed to the deck with a thud.

Adriana dropped the letters on his chest and stepped over the man's body as he continued to shake. He'd be unconscious in a moment. The barbs in the pellet would deliver a chemical into his body that would keep him down for a couple of hours. When he woke, he'd be fine, although sore and probably with a headache.

She aimed the weapon into the hallway and swept it to the left. There was a small bedroom in the back. The bed was neatly made and looked like it hadn't been slept in. Either that or these military guys were fully entrenched into their systematic way of doing things, which included making the bed every morning.

Adriana eased the door shut, leaving it cracked open in case she had to make a fast getaway.

She kept her knees bent and crept down the hall on the edges of her boots. She heard movement upstairs. The ceiling creaked where someone was walking around or, as she suspected, shifting their position. It was the second guard. He wouldn't take his eyes off the house across the street, not if he was as well trained as she believed, but he would certainly be curious as to who might have been knocking at the back door.

Within ten seconds, he would probably start hailing his partner on their radios. After another ten seconds without a response, he would assume something was wrong, come out of the room with gun drawn, and find the source of the problem.

That gave her less than twenty seconds to get up the stairs and neutralize the threat.

She rounded the bottom of the banister and ascended quietly, using the edge of the steps to make sure the wood didn't squeak or bend.

Two steps from the top, the other guard called out. "Ricky? What's going on down there?"

Crap.

She'd thought there was more time, at least another five seconds. This guy was apparently impatient. She knew he'd step out of the bedroom door in a moment, and she was exposed on the staircase, looking up to the open hallway that ran to the front of the house.

There was a bathroom directly across from where she was standing. It was her only chance. She couldn't make it back down the stairs fast enough to take cover on the main floor. The bathroom was closer, both to her current position and to the target.

She hurriedly scaled the last couple of steps and then ducked into the bathroom just as the cracked bedroom door opened wide. Adriana pressed her right shoulder into the near wall between the sink and the doorframe. She was just out of sight from the guard's vantage point, though anyone on the steps would have easily seen her. Lucky for her there weren't any more security guards in the building.

Footsteps clicked beyond the doorway. They were slow, methodical, laced with suspicion that she knew the man carried in his mind.

"Ricky?" the voice called out again. "What's going on down there? You on the toilet again?"

Adriana pushed a little harder against the wall, doing her best to minimize her frame so the man would pass by without seeing her. Unfortunately, the drywall wasn't nailed down as tightly as it should have been and produced a faint squeak from the pressure of her shoulder.

She winced and clutched the pistol in both hands, ready to fire.

The sound of movement ceased outside the bathroom door. There was only one conclusion. The guard had heard the wall squeak.

She ducked down, crouching low to the floor just as a series of clicks erupted from the hallway outside. The wall over her head exploded in dust and debris as the guard fired five rounds. The suppressor attached to his weapon muted the sound of the weapon to be almost silent.

Adriana leaned back against the wall, digging her shoulders in. As always, she didn't panic. She'd lost that instinct long ago. It was trained out of her in the crucible of the school where she learned the deadly arts of the ninja.

The guard outside the room stopped firing. She knew what was coming next. He'd poke his head in, leading with the gun. Adriana didn't give him the chance.

She swung around and kicked out her legs, driving her body backward across the floor as she raised the pulse pistol. The man in the black coat appeared and aimed his weapon at her.

Adriana's movement threw him off just enough to enable her to fire first. The first round missed his head by an inch, sticking to the wall just behind him. The second pellet, however, struck home right above his nose. Electricity coursed through his body. He managed to raise his gun and fire two more shots, but they were clumsy and poorly aimed. One bullet thumped harmlessly into the floor. The other shattered the bathroom tiles above the tub.

She squeezed the trigger one more time, and a second pellet struck the guard in the collarbone. This one dropped him to his knees, and a moment later his face hit the floor with a smack near her feet. She kicked her legs two more times to push away from the man and then crawled up to a standing position, keeping her weapon aimed at him until all movement stopped.

When he was still, she let out a few breaths of relief and then stepped over the body and back into the hall. She turned right and walked to the front of the house and went into the bedroom where she'd seen the men watching over the admiral's home across the street. It was a risk to look out the window, but a quick glance told her what she had suspected. There were still two guards in front, one on the porch and one down on the sidewalk just beyond the gate. She afforded herself one more look in the cars surrounding the immediate area, just in case there were more agents waiting in vehicles, hiding out in case of an emergency. From what she could tell, there were none.

That meant there were six guards to go, maybe two more inside, and two in the back.

"Okay," she said, "time to go."

Adriana hurried back down the stairs and out the back door. As she walked over the body of the guard on the deck, she bent down and scooped the earpiece out of his ear. Wouldn't hurt to be in on the conversation.

She cleaned off the tip with the cuff of her shirt and then planted the device in her ear. Then she picked up the envelopes and scurried down the steps, back down the street, and around the corner, slowing to a steady walk once more as she rounded the corner of the Main Street at the crosswalk.

When the light turned red for the crossing traffic, the walk sign illuminated, and she strode deliberately across the street. She walked up the steps of the neighbor's home two doors down, just to keep up appearances, then kept going until she arrived at the corner of the small fence surrounding the tiny front yard of Winters's home.

The guard standing on the path noticed her right away. She attempted to diffuse his alertness with a kind smile. He simply nodded and looked back out at the street, checking for signs of trouble.

He touched his ear and heard the man's voice as she watched his lips move.

"Derek, how's it looking over there?"

Derek must have been the man she'd left upstairs in the bathroom. She didn't respond, didn't let on that she could hear anything he was saying.

When she reached the front gate, she pulled up on the latch and started to go through, but the guard held up one hand, still pressing a finger to his ear.

"Stay right there, ma'am."

She frowned. "I'm sorry. Do you live here?"

He stumbled for the answer. "No, but it's my job to protect the person who does. You can give that mail to me."

"I'm sorry," she said in a sympathetic tone. "This is certified mail. I'm going to need a"—she stopped and held up the envelope, pretending to read it—"Mr. Winters to sign for this."

"Can't allow that, ma'am. He's given us permission to handle any incoming packages. Security reasons."

"What's the issue, Rodgers?" The guard on the porch was approaching the top of the steps, looking curiously down at the situation unfolding on the lawn.

"Mailman says Winters has to sign for something."

"First of all, I'm not a man," Adriana said in the most indignant tone she could muster. It wasn't hard. His comment actually did piss her off a little.

The guy turned back to her, an uncomfortable look suddenly

written all over his face. He was the type who wasn't accustomed to being put into spots like this. Throw him into a ditch in Afghanistan and he'd do just fine, but with a humble postal worker he'd just insulted, not so much.

"I'm sorry. That's not what I meant, ma'am. You have to understand, though, we can't allow you to hand-deliver that."

"Fine," she said. "I'll have to take it back to the main office. If he wants to come pick it up himself, he can. But I'm not permitted to give this to anyone other than the recipient named on this envelope."

"Now hold on just a second," the second guard said. He was descending the steps now and had a brash scowl on his face. He was clearly the one in charge for this shift, and the fact she was willing to walk away and inconvenience his employer didn't sit well.

"We have permission to collect all incoming parcels. It's our job to inspect everything before Winters gets it."

She stared at the man as he hit the pathway with his right foot and continued his approach. His right hand was extended, hoping to take the envelopes from her.

"Now, if you need him to sign for it, I can take your pad in or whatever it is you use and have him sign it, but I can't let you see him."

"This guy sounds important," Adriana commented.

"You could say that." The guy in charge sounded cocky, as if guarding the admiral somehow made him more of a man.

Adriana pretended to consider the guy's offer. "I'm really not supposed to."

"It'll be fine. Look, we're all on the same team here. We all work for the government. I won't tell anyone if you don't. We'll just take it in to him, let him sign off, and be done."

She swallowed as if her entire career in the postal service hinged on the decision. Then she relented, extending the envelopes out to the man in charge. He offered a consoling yet disdainful grin and then nodded. He turned around and started to walk back into the house.

The other guard turned his head. "I'll stay out here with her," he said.

Taking his eyes off her was his mistake, and she made him pay for it. In a flash, Adriana took the pistol out of her coat and fired a round into the side of the guard's neck. He grimaced and grunted before falling to the ground. The other guy was too slow in reacting. By the time he turned to see what had happened, Adriana had already taken two big steps, closing the gap to mere feet. At point-blank range she had no problem hitting the side of his skull with one of the pellets.

He, too, dropped to the ground, letters fluttering through the air like rectangular snowflakes.

Adriana let the men lie there in the yard, shaking uncontrollably as she ascended the steps and kicked in the door.

She swept her weapon to the right and drew the firearm from within the folds of her coat, just in case things got nastier.

To her surprise, she found an older man sitting in a high-back leather chair near a fireplace to the right. He was sipping a glass of bourbon and had the newspaper folded across his lap. Her abrupt entrance clearly caught him off guard, and he nearly spilled his drink.

"Who are you?" he asked.

She slammed the door shut, locked the deadbolt, and stepped into the great room.

"Admiral Winters?" She asked as she continued deeper into the home, keeping both weapons trained on the man's chest.

"What is this?" he asked, incensed at the intrusion. "What did you do to my guards?"

"Shut up. I'll ask the questions. Your guards are going to take a little nap. If you tell me the truth, you'll be lucky to get off the way they did." She wagged the pulse pistol in her right hand. "This one gives you a nap. This one...the nap is permanent. Got it?"

His eyes were wide, full of confusion, but he nodded. The one thing he understood was the woman's threat.

"What do you want?" The admiral muttered as if holding the words back like wild horses, unwilling to let them go.

"Where is John Dawkins?"

The man's brow furrowed. Deep wrinkles cut into his forehead just above his nose. Similar lines stretched across his cheekbones below the eyes. He offered a scoffing snort.

"Dawkins? Haven't you heard? John Dawkins was taken by Sean Wyatt. It's all over the news."

Adriana raised the Springfield 9mm in her left hand. "I thought we had an understanding, Admiral. I guess I was incorrect. Now, I'm going to ask you one more time. If you try to lie to me again, I'm going to shoot you in the shoulder. The collarbone is a bad place to get shot. The rounds in this mag will shatter it and put you in more pain than you've ever imagined...until I shoot you in the knees. First, the right one, then the left."

"My guards in the back will be coming in any moment," he sneered. "And if you fire that thing, they will charge in here and cut you down like an animal."

"I know about your guards in the back. They're taking a little nap, too."

"Oh," he said. "Well, then. I guess you got me." He raised his free hand as well as the one holding the drink. A sly grin crossed his lips.

Something was wrong. Why the expression like he'd just gotten the drop on her?

A split second later, she realized the fatal mistake she'd made.

In her rush to steal the postal uniform and take out the guards, including the ones across the street, she'd made the untypical mistake of forgetting there were two more in the house.

She spun to her left as the butt of a pistol whipped across the side of her head. A dull pain accompanied the hard thud against her temple. She fought the overwhelming urge to vomit, pass out, and collapse, but the fight was one she couldn't win.

Adriana dropped to the floor on her side and closed her eyes. The last thing she saw spinning in her field of vision was Admiral Winters standing from his chair and taking another sip of whiskey as he looked down at her.

42

ASTORIA

Sean stared into the man's eyes as he slowly lowered his weapon to the floor. Sean knew the gunman was a federal agent. The government-issue jacket, the pistol, even the way the guy was standing there all reeked of US Department of Justice. There was no fear in the man's eyes. And there was likewise an absence of doubt as to what he would do if Sean tried anything brash.

Tommy lowered his weapon as well, though he couldn't take his eyes off the gun. It was aimed at Sean, but he got the distinct impression that the second he attempted to disarm the newcomer or take a shot, his friend would die and Tommy would immediately follow.

Sean felt the weight of his gun leave his fingers, and he pulled his hand away, ever so carefully.

"We don't have the president," Sean offered.

"Shut up and step away from the weapon," the agent ordered.

"It's the truth."

"I said shut up and step away from the weapon, or I will shoot you right here and now. Understood?" His voice thundered in the confined space, echoing off the hard concrete walls and reverberating back through the corridor seemingly three or four times.

Sean tipped his head forward with a subtle nod and then shuffled backward.

"You," the agent said, nodding at Tommy, "kick yours over here."

Tommy didn't hesitate. He pressed the tip of his boot against the gun and flicked it forward. The weapon slid across the floorboards, stopping with a clack against the wall near where the agent stood using the corner as cover.

Once he was satisfied the two were disarmed, he stepped out from the corner and fully into view.

"I'm agent Matthew Petty," the stranger said. He pulled his jacket aside to show off a federal ID. "Where is the president?"

Sean cast a questioning glance at Tommy, as if his friend might better know how to answer the query.

Tommy had the same confusion in his eyes.

"We don't know," Sean answered, turning back to Petty. "We're trying to find him, too."

Petty tensed his grip on the weapon, doing it visibly so his two prisoners could see he wasn't buying what they were selling.

"I don't have time for this," said Petty. "Tell me where he is. Is he alive?"

"He's telling the truth," Tommy said. "We're trying to—"

"Shut up." Petty's weapon shook in his hands. The man was clearly tired and frustrated. "I'm going to give you three seconds."

"You're not listening, Agent," Sean said, taking his chance to cut the gunman off. "Someone took Dawkins, but it wasn't me. Someone was posing as me in that video. I was framed."

"I've heard that before."

"I know. Believe me, I know. But if you are who you say you are, then you know that I am friends with Dawkins. And you also know I served our country with honor. I've never committed a crime in my life. Think about it, Agent Petty. None of this makes sense. You have to see that."

Petty searched Sean's eyes for the truth. He was an expert in being able to tell when someone was lying simply from their body language and in the way their eyes moved, twitched, or darted nervously. Even the subtlest, almost unnoticeable flinch could be detected by Petty's honed expertise. He saw no lie in Sean's eyes, though he wasn't fully convinced yet.

Petty had his doubts. He'd been unconvinced that Sean was the one behind the president's abduction. Now, here Wyatt was with his friend Tommy Schultz. Were they working together in this whole scheme? Or was there something else at play? Petty kept his weapon trained on Sean's chest, though his finger relaxed on the trigger, just slightly.

"Why are you here?" Petty asked. "Why did you run? If you didn't do anything wrong, it sure seems strange that you're trying to get away."

"You wouldn't do the same thing if you were falsely accused?" Sean's question carried weight with it. He'd worked for the government before, been trained in many ways just like Petty. Sean knew how he would have viewed things if the situation was reversed. "Look, if I was in your shoes, I'd have the same doubts," Sean said in his calmest tone. "But if we took Dawkins, what would we be doing out here? And ask yourself this: Was there a ransom demand? Whoever took Dawkins wants something, but they didn't tell the public what that was. Has the FBI or anyone else been alerted to some kind of demands?"

"No," Petty said. He couldn't hide the reservations in his voice. It cracked—and showed his hand.

"That's why we're here," Tommy said. "Whoever took Dawkins is looking for something, something very old."

"He's telling the truth," Sean said. "Look in our eyes, Matthew." Sean risked using the man's first name. "If we had the president, we'd be hidden in a bunker somewhere or in a cave in the mountains. But we're not. We're here, in Oregon, at an old military installation, trying to solve a mystery."

"Why? Why would you be doing that when you're the most wanted man in the country right now? Why risk that?" Petty's face was grave, determined to root out the answer to the question he'd been asking himself the last few days.

"Because the people who took Dawkins demanded it."

Petty's expression softened. He listened as Sean explained what had happened with the video, the message from the mysterious kidnappers, and the letter from former president James Madison. Sean told the short tale of how they'd come to figure out the first location that was mentioned in the letter, why he ventured to North Dakota, Montana, and now the Oregon coast. He also was sure to let Petty know that Tommy had nothing to do with this, that he was innocent and had found Sean after he'd left Atlanta. That didn't matter to Petty, Sean knew. Schultzie was an accomplice now, at least in most lawmen's eyes. He was just as guilty as Sean as far as they were concerned.

Petty listened intently until Sean was finished with his tale that had served to land them all here at this mysterious bunker in Fort Stevens State Park. When Sean was done, the room fell silent once more, and the three men stood there in a stalemate of words.

Petty drew a long breath and exhaled through his nose. He abruptly lowered his weapon and gave a nod. "I believe you," he said. "But that doesn't mean much."

"You do?" Tommy sounded hopeful.

"You're right," Petty admitted. "None of it makes any sense. The motive for any kidnapping is usually pretty clear. It's usually for money, but sometimes for revenge. Either way, it's always to satisfy some personal desire. Yet here you are, in a bunker in Oregon, looking for something, just like you seem to always be doing with your jobs, whatever those might be."

Tommy allowed a little chuckle to rise from his chest. "We get that a lot."

"Anyway, I knew something was fishy. The diner in North Dakota, the dead man in the parking lot in Billings; nothing added up. The diner, though, really gave it away for me. No way would a guilty person, trying to avoid being recognized, have helped out in that situation. That's not what a criminal does."

Sean said nothing, but his head dipped slightly, acknowledging the comment.

"So," Petty said after a moment of consideration, "what are you two doing out here? And where is Dawkins?"

"We don't know the answer to the second one, Agent Petty," Sean confessed.

"Call me Matt."

"I was told I had one week to figure out the riddle in a letter from James Madison. If we could decipher it and find whatever it's alluding to, the kidnappers said they would let Dawkins go." Sean said the last few words with a dense layer of regret. "Of course, we know the second we deliver whatever it is we find they'll kill us, and President Dawkins, too."

Petty nodded. "That's how it usually goes. What is it you two are looking for?"

Sean sighed, a little embarrassed. "Actually, we don't know for sure." He held up one hand. "Mind if I reach in my pocket? Not armed."

"Sure," Petty said.

Sean pulled out a section of the golden ring. Tommy produced a similar piece. The shiny yellow metal glimmered in the sunshine that filtered through the windows, causing the gold to glint and flash.

"Wait," Petty said. "You two don't know what it is you're looking for here?"

Tommy and Sean cast a sidelong glance at each other. "No, sir," Tommy said. "The letter isn't clear about it, only that it's dangerous. President Madison seemed pretty spooked by it."

Petty looked around, taking in their surroundings for the first time since arriving. "And...you think it's here, on an old military site?"

"I've been considering that," Sean said. "Based on what we learned from the letter, whatever is here...the thing that Meriwether Lewis found...spooked him enough that he didn't relay his report to the president for a couple of years. In fact, he waited until after Jefferson was out of office to give his full report to the new president, James Madison."

"Hold on a second," Petty said, putting up a hand. "Meriwether Lewis? As in, the Lewis and Clark expedition?"

"The very same," Tommy confirmed.

Petty sighed and scratched his head. "So, what is it exactly that you're saying, guys? That someone kidnapped the former president, and they did it to make you run some errand across the country, figuring out a two-hundred-year-old riddle from one of the Founding Fathers? All so this mystery person can have whatever it is that Meriwether Lewis discovered?"

"Yeah," Sean said.

"Pretty much," Tommy voiced the words almost at the same time.

"So...it must be pretty valuable, then."

"Or powerful," Tommy corrected. "Meriwether Lewis was a strong guy, young and healthy when he died. The circumstances surrounding his death were vague, pretty sketchy actually. Historians don't agree on how he died—whether it was suicide or murder. I believe that someone was after what was in his reports. They must have known or heard about what he found and wanted it for themselves."

"But what could be so powerful, so terrifying? I mean, if it was just a huge gold stash, that would be something you'd want to keep secret. But afraid of it?"

"A weapon," Sean said.

The other two focused on him. He looked back into their eyes, his icy gaze unrelenting.

"It would have to be a weapon," he reiterated. "Or something that could be made into one."

"That's why the military built Fort Stevens," Tommy said. "I mean sure, there were other strategic reasons, but why not get two for one?"

"Exactly," Sean agreed. "And whatever that reason is, we think it's right below us."

Each man's head dipped, and they all stared at the wooden floorboards.

43

ANNAPOLIS

Adriana woke to a pounding in the side of her head. Her skull felt heavy, and she sensed gravity pulling on it harder than usual. She engaged her neck muscles and tried to raise her head, but she was like a bobble head doll, her skull seemingly moving on its own, wherever the spinning Earth carried it.

Her eyes cracked open, but she quickly shut them again as a blinding light pierced her pupils. She squinted to keep the light out until her vision could adjust. She felt something hard against her back, the primary source of the pressure pushing against her shoulder blades. She couldn't move her hands and arms, and soon realized they were tied behind her back. Her feet, too, were bound to a chair. The duct tape cut into her skin just above the ankles.

She attempted to open her eyes again. Slowly, they lifted, dragging across her eyeballs like sandpaper. She blinked at the pain, which only enhanced it until the orbs were well lubricated. Even then, the bright light hurt, cutting into her vision for another ten seconds until they adjusted.

"She's awake."

A man's voice. Who was it? Was it familiar? She couldn't tell at first. The room was still hazy and still tilted to the left, dragging everything in her field of vision with it. She saw the outline of a figure straight ahead, standing near a window. Yes, a window. Her surroundings were becoming clearer and every second brought a bit more clarity.

Adriana was in a house, but where? She glanced to the right, not daring to move her head too quickly for fear she'd aggravate the dizziness all over again.

Another figure appeared by the window. He'd come through a door just to the left. She turned away again, quickly taking inventory of the room.

It was the first thing she'd been trained to do as a child on her initial visit to the ninja school. She noted the wooden writing desk to her right. There was no chair, but she figured the one that belonged to the workstation was the one she was strapped to. There were pictures on the wall. Seeing the faces was still difficult, but she recognized some of those nearest her position. There were diplomats, politicians, military leaders. Then it all came back to her.

Admiral Winters.

She saw him standing next to the former president. It was at some highly official Washington gathering, probably a fund-raiser or perhaps some kind of gala that was simply put on to entertain the nation's elites.

He was smiling broadly in the photo, arms around the president and some other military adviser. The grin on the admiral's face appeared to be fake, or maybe that was just her suspicion overriding her usually sound judgment.

"So, you're back. Wonderful." A new voice cut into her thoughts, and she snapped her head around.

The room spun again but only for a moment. That was good. Whatever they'd done to her was wearing off—although the pain thumping from just above her left ear made her think the only thing they'd done was hit her on the head. Then she remembered what happened. She'd been struck with something hard. A pistol? That seemed right.

She looked straight ahead into the eyes of Admiral Winters. The man was wearing a United States Navy windbreaker and a pair of khakis. His hands were behind his back, and he rose up onto his tiptoes, then lowered himself back down.

"I have to say," Winters began, "I'm a little surprised you were able to take down four of my guards so easily." Winters turned and glanced at the door. One of the other guards, probably from the back of the house or maybe one of the ones stationed inside. Didn't matter to her. If they knew about the admiral's plans, they were going to die. She'd make sure of that. No more pulse pistols or electrocutions. The plan began to formulate in her mind even as the haze continued to clear.

"Obviously, they'll be relieved of their duties immediately. Can't have amateurs around. I'd end up dead." He bellowed a laugh and slapped both hands against the sides of his legs. Then he raised them and folded them across his chest. A stern look plastered itself onto his face. His eyes burned with anger.

"What did you think you were going to do here?" he asked, indignant. "Were you going to come in here and kill me? Did you think you could get information out of me? Is that it?" He leaned forward. She could smell the liquor on his breath mingled with the ashy scent of cigars.

She looked away as if in disgust, but it was to continue doing recon on the room. The floor was hardwood. She'd already noted that. The walls were painted with stripes; cream and hunter green. It was a tad ostentatious for her, but she didn't hate it. The drywall stopped about three feet from the floor where white shiplap paneling took over and ran to the skirtings below.

There were two guards at the door now. She recounted how many there were before. Two across the street, two in front of the house, two in back, two inside. Eight. Where were the other six? That didn't matter at the moment. She'd find them soon enough. She also figured no cops had been called. She would be in the back of a squad car or in a cell if that was the case. No, Winters had no intention of sending her to prison or letting her face charges. He was going to handle this the old-fashioned way, the way dirty Washington had discreetly taken care of problems for so long.

"Don't feel like saying much?" Winters asked. He stepped forward and grabbed Adriana by the chin, tilting her head back. "You're foreign, aren't you? Not from America. If I had to guess, I'd say you're Bosnian? Serbian, maybe?"

She jerked her head away and immediately wished she hadn't, though the spinning only lasted a couple of seconds.

"Where is John Dawkins?" Adriana snarled. She looked like a caged lion, ready to pounce on its prey and rip the unwitting victim from limb to limb.

She didn't strain against her bonds, though, for fear she'd give away her next move. Adriana had already formulated a plan. Now she just had to keep this moron talking.

He shook his head again. "Oh, that." He stiffened and let go of her chin with one last pinch. "Did you think he was here? I assure you, sweetheart, he's not. You must have thought I would be stupid enough to bring the former president into my home against his will. John Dawkins is far away from here, and once you're out of the picture there will be no one else who can tie me to his abduction. You're the last loose end, sugar." He said the word with obvious pleasure, fully aware that it annoyed her as much as when he called her sweetheart.

"Well, me and Sean."

Another derisive snort from the admiral. "Sean? That's cute. Right about now he's being corralled by my team." He read the look on her face. "Oh, not to worry. Sean and his friend will take my guys right to the Omega Stone, and when they do Sean will die. Maybe you two can meet up somewhere else—if you believe in that kind of thing."

Adriana did believe in an afterlife. She also had no intention of going there just yet. Her eyes narrowed, and she leaned forward. "You don't get it, do you?"

The admiral's eyebrows tightened. "What's that?"

"Your men, the ones with Sean? They're already dead." She paused, letting him lean in a few more inches. "Just like you."

Before he could say anything else, Adriana planted her feet on the floor, pushed hard through her toes, and drove her body up. Her forehead was aimed perfectly. She dipped her head slightly and struck the target with devastating force, all within a fraction of a second.

The admiral's nose crunched, the bone snapping and shattering beneath the soft tissue. He screamed and grabbed his face as the momentum from the blow sent him stumbling backward.

Adriana flew nearly two feet into the air, remarkable considering she was tied to a chair. Then she let gravity work for her. She dropped like a bomb—right toward Winters.

The admiral's backside hit the floor, and his head whipped back, smacking against the hard surface. The blow dazed him and a dull pain in the back of his skull mingled with that already pulsing in his nose.

His face and hands were covered in blood a nanosecond before the legs of the chair struck both sides of his torso. The wooden edges that had seemed so benign before now tore through the fatty flesh on his sides, ripping through skin and tissue on their way to the surface below.

When the chair's feet hit the floor, the bolts holding the legs in place strained. They didn't give way, but the wood around them did. The chair snapped and splintered. Adriana's hands were still tied behind her back and her legs were still bound, but they'd been loosed when the chair broke. She noted a tear in the duct tape and stepped on it, lifting the other leg free to rip the remaining strip.

In the same motion, she dropped back down to the ground, twisting and snatching a splintered piece of wood from the debris surrounding the admiral. She stopped, the sharp point of the fractured chair a mere inch over the groaning man's Adam's apple.

The entire maneuver had taken less than three seconds.

The guards had made the mistake of facing each other, perhaps to engage in some silent conversation or speculation as to what they were going to do with this prisoner before, or maybe after, she was dead.

That had been Adriana's cue, her momentary opening of which she took full advantage.

The guards' reaction had been quick, but by the time they'd realized what happened and drawn their weapons, it was already too late.

"Shoot me, he dies. Understand?" she asked in a clear, concise, and pointed voice.

Underneath the stake in her hands, the admiral writhed, still clutching his bloody nose. Thick crimson liquid continued to seep through the cracks in his fingers. It pooled on the dark wooden floor under his back as well, the wounds on his sides also oozing.

The guards didn't know what to do. This woman was threatening to kill the admiral, the man in charge of the entire United States Navy. If they shot her, though, he would die. At the very best, he'd survive and never be able to speak again, but that was a long shot.

She bent her legs a little more, and the tip of the spike brushed against the admiral's throat.

He froze stiff, afraid to swipe at the makeshift weapon lest she drive it through his neck and into the floor beneath.

"Do what she says, you idiots. She'll kill me." His voice was whiny, muffled by the involuntary tears that came instinctively with a broken nose.

The guards hesitated another second.

She encouraged them by tilting her head to the side.

Then the two gradually let their weapons down. They set them on the floor and then stood slowly.

"Hands in the air, please. I'm sure you two know the drill. Kick those over here for me." She gave a nod indicating where she wanted the weapons.

The men did as told, lifting their hands above their shoulders. They kicked the guns, and the weapons slid across the floor, one hitting the admiral on the top of the head, the other skidding to a stop next to her right foot.

"Good. Now, step over there to the corner."

The men shuffled to their left and stopped beside a black wooden bookcase.

"You, on the floor. Facedown." She issued the order to the man nearest the bookshelf. "Then you lie down flat on top of him."

The two men scowled. "Do it."

They hesitated, and then obeyed. The first got down on his hands and knees. The other looked less sure about whether or not he should do it. Then he relented, climbing on top of his partner's back. He lay down flat with his chest against the bottom guy's shoulder blades.

Adriana deftly curled the wooden shard around and began working the edge of it up and down. It took nearly twenty seconds, but she felt a section of the tape split. Once that happened, she pushed harder with the broken chair piece while pulling with her wrists. The tape gave way, and her hands shot free.

She immediately reached down and picked up the nearest weapon with her right hand, careful to keep it trained on the two men in the precarious position in the corner.

She stopped next to the other gun and crouched down to remove the tape still clinging loosely to her ankles. Once she'd ripped it out of the way, she picked up the second pistol and stood.

Winters was wriggling around now, his hands still cradling his nose as he stared furiously at the woman holding the guns.

"Now," Adriana said, "it's question-and-answer time. If you don't tell me what I want to know, I will kill your two men here, and then I will go to work on you. I realize that these two aren't worth much to you. Sure, they're loyal, but you'd sacrifice them to save your own cowardly tail."

The guards' eyes filled with questions, worry streaking across their faces.

Winters said nothing.

"Where is John Dawkins, Admiral? What did you do with him?"

"I don't know what you're talking about."

Adriana nodded, her lips sticking out slightly. She stepped backward and stopped next to the desk. The admiral's cell phone was sitting on it. She touched the screen and found the device was still unlocked. Then she tapped on the camera app and cracked a smile.

"Not smart, Admiral, leaving your phone unlocked like that. Would be a shame if someone gained access to it."

Winters forced an agonized laugh and called Adriana a filthy name in the process. "You think I'm stupid enough to use my personal phone for anything that could implicate me? You got nothing! You hear me? Nothing! And pretty soon the other guards and every cop in this town are going to be here, knocking down my door. You won't get out of this alive; I can promise you that." His voice trailed off.

Adriana snickered. "You're right. I don't think you'd be stupid enough to use your own phone for anything that could get you into trouble. That's not what I was suggesting."

His face twisted in confusion as she propped up the phone on the desk and then walked over to where a roll of duct tape sat on the counter.

44

D ust plumed up from the opening as Sean ripped up the last of the boards from the floor. The tiny motes were accompanied by a musty odor as they spewed out into the room.

They each removed flashlights from their gear bags, hoisted them back onto their shoulders, and then shone the lights down into the dark abyss.

Beyond the fog of dust, they could make out concrete steps descending into the darkness. The steps were lined with more concrete to the right and a painted, metal railing on the left. Chips of black paint had peeled off years ago, exposing the steel underneath to the elements.

As the three pointed their lights into the cavity, they saw the stairs descending at least two levels. Sean stayed close to the wall, while the other two looked down between the staircases.

"Hard to tell," Tommy said, "but it looks like it goes down at least a couple of levels."

Sean remained near the wall, unwilling to look over the edge of the railing for fear it was a much farther descent than his friend suggested.

"Shall we, gentlemen?" Petty asked, motioning down the stairs with his light.

The other two nodded, and Tommy took the lead, keeping one hand on the rail while he kept the flashlight's round beam trained on the damp stairs below.

"Careful, guys," Tommy said as he took the first couple of steps. "It's a little slick."

Gradually, the three made their way down the first flight, rounded the turn, and continued their descent. Their movements were slow, hindered by the wet stairs. The concrete surface had worn smooth over time, and more than once Sean nearly lost his footing. He was relieved when, after only climbing down three flights, they arrived at the bottom.

That relief was short-lived as they stepped off the stairs and onto the ground.

The high shaft of the stairwell ended abruptly over an entryway. It was surrounded by poured concrete on three sides: left, right, and overhead. Plus, directly in front of the three men—opposite the stairs—was a sealed metal door. An old keypad hung from the wall next to it containing all the letters of the alphabet. It almost looked like whoever put it there had taken all the keys from an antique typewriter and glued them into the rectangular metal box. A tiny red light beeped on the top edge of the device that faced the visitors.

"This thing has power to it?" Tommy asked. "That's strange."

Petty stepped close to the keypad and peered at it. He frowned and pushed on the door since there was no handle, another strange detail he hadn't really noticed on his initial inspection of the entrance.

"What is this?" he asked.

Sean flicked his eyebrows. "Government black site?" he joked.

"You never know," Petty admitted.

He'd heard all about those places, the locations around the world where the CIA interrogated prisoners using less-than-legal methods. This wasn't one of those and every man in the room knew it, but that didn't answer Petty's question.

What was this place?

"So, we have to enter a password to get in," Sean said. "Any clue as to what that might be?"

Tommy stared blankly at the keypad. His eyes blinked over and over again as he tried to consider what the passcode could be. He doubted there were any traps set, any security measures in place, though that could end up being a dangerous assumption.

He and Sean eyeballed the concrete box surrounding them and looked back at the staircase, assessing every potential crevice.

"What about the letter?" Sean asked. "Maybe the clue to the passcode is in that letter."

Tommy arched a suspicious eyebrow. "Sean, the letter was written like, I don't know, 130 years before this place was built. I doubt there's anything in it that would have been used as some kind of password."

Sean rolled his shoulders. "Humor me."

Petty watched the exchange as if at a tennis match.

Tommy pulled the letter out of his jacket and looked over the lines, scanning them quickly for any clue that might lead them to a solution for the passcode.

He shook his head. "Nothing, man. I really don't see anything on here that would work."

Sean was looking closely at the paper, leaning over it and craning his neck to get a better view. "What about that?" he asked, pointing at one of the last words in the letter. "Why is it all capitalized?"

Petty shifted to get a closer look. "Yeah, that's odd. And why would he say it like that?"

Tommy read the final paragraph out loud. "This is the reason for our precaution, our vigilance against such mystical and relentless threats. The ring of three has been spread across the land, and only one with wits, courage, and a humble heart should take the challenge. For if you complete this journey, death must surely await, and the OMEGA will come."

"What does that mean?" Petty asked.

"Omega is the end. You've heard that verse from the Bible, right, about the alpha and the omega?"

Petty shrugged and tilted his head to the side. "I don't go to church."

"But you've heard it."

"Yeah, it rings a bell."

"Well, the alpha is the beginning, and the omega is the end."

"It's all Greek to me," Petty said with a laugh.

Sean and Tommy looked at him with disdain.

Petty settled down again.

"Don't do that," Tommy said.

"What?"

"Go for the obvious joke. Don't do it. You're better than that."

Petty cracked his neck to the right and bit his bottom lip. "Fair enough."

Sean got back to the problem at hand. "That still doesn't explain why James Madison capitalized it." He paused for a second. "Unless..."

"Unless what?" Tommy asked, unable to wait any longer to hear what his friend was going to say.

"What if what's on the other side of this door is some kind of ancient superweapon? Maybe that's why Madison emphasized it with all caps, as one last warning to anyone foolish enough to set foot here."

"Could be," Tommy said. "But we can't just leave. John Dawkins's life depends on us getting through this door and finding whatever is inside."

Sean knew his friend was right. That still didn't make it any easier. "There could be a failsafe on this keypad, Schultzie. We enter the wrong letter or number; it might go into some kind of permanent lockdown."

"You think they had that kind of tech back then?" Petty asked, skeptical.

"They were way ahead of where most of the public thinks they were back then. Our government has had a remarkable way of staying ahead of everyone, especially its own citizens, for the last few hundred years."

"So, only enter the code if you really think that's it," Tommy advised.

Sean stepped close to the panel and stared at it, hesitating. "It's the only thing we have to go on. Unless you think there's another word or sequence in that letter we haven't picked up on yet."

Tommy shook his head. "If I had to guess, I'd say it was that. Whoever built this place might have had access to the letter or at least some kind of similar warning from Madison, passed down through history to each leader that followed."

Sean gave a determined nod. "Omega it is, then."

He raised his hand and pointed his index finger at the O on the keypad. He pressed it. A click came from within the wall. He pressed the letter M and got the same result. Sean realized he wasn't breathing as he continued pushing on the keys, one letter at a time. When he typed the A, he stepped back and let out a long exhale.

Several clicks echoed from the other side of the door. The little red light on the top of the keypad turned green. A gust of stale air burst out from between the crack of the door and its frame as the door swung open.

Sean stepped back, as did his companions, and they stared straight ahead as the thick metal door continued to swing open, driven by a hydraulic piston at the top.

Their eyes fixed dead ahead into the next area. No one said a word.

Beyond the door's threshold was a space that looked like something out of a science fiction movie from the middle of the twentieth century.

There were weird glass display cases set atop metal stands. The floor and walls were made from the same concrete as the alcove where the men were standing. The ceiling was rock, jagged and naturally formed by time and pressure. Whoever had made this place kept the ceiling the way they'd found it. Perhaps they figured all those thousands of tons of rock were enough protection. From what, though? Nuclear war? Invasion? Worse?

Sean stepped bravely into the next room.

It was expansive, stretching a good hundred feet to the far wall. There were no windows, and no portals to allow light to flow into the area. As the others followed Sean into the strange space, lightbulbs flickered on along the walls. They cast a dim yellow glow, barely doing more than the flashlights the men carried.

A low hum filled the chamber; a constant drone. It sounded—no, felt like it came from within the floor.

Sean walked slowly, moving with caution as he approached one of the display cases. There were three in the room, all lined up in a single row. Each case contained a stone tablet about one foot in length, maybe ten inches wide. Sean stopped at the first tablet and gazed through the glass, shining his light into the case to get a better look.

"It's Greek," Sean said.

Tommy was standing close by, just to Sean's right. He nodded as he looked at the stone. "It sure is." He frowned. "Very old Greek."

"What do you mean?"

Tommy pointed at the piece of stone. "It's a little different than the Greek I learned. Still, it's similar enough that I can read it."

"What about this over here?" Petty asked. He was standing next to the wall, just to the left of the entrance. He faced the wall where a metal placard was bolted into the concrete at all four corners.

Tommy and Sean strode over to him and stared at the characters etched into the metal plaque.

"Japanese," Sean said.

"Yeah," Petty agreed. "It says that the three tablets were discovered by Japanese sailors before the war and that they brought it as well as the weapon to this place, voyaging across the sea and enduring great trials before they left it here—in what they hoped would be its final resting place."

Sean and Tommy stared blankly at the man.

"What?" he asked with a laugh.

"You speak Japanese?"

"Oh. Yeah, came with the territory. I was assigned to a pretty big case involving one of the Japanese crime syndicates. Went undercover for six months. Turns out, I picked up quite a bit of the language, though honestly I thought I'd forgotten it. That was years ago."

"Sounds like you still got it," Sean said.

"I guess so." Petty beamed.

"So, it is a weapon." Tommy reinforced what Petty had deciphered.

"Now it's starting to make sense," Sean said. "The Japanese puzzle box I received; that was why. The Japanese brought whatever these things are to this place. They were the ones who found them first."

"And were apparently scared enough to sail across the Pacific to get these things as far away from their country as possible."

Sean nodded his agreement.

"Okay," Petty said, "so what's with all the Greek you guys were talking about a minute ago?"

"Let's have a look," Tommy said and turned back toward the first display case.

He and the others walked over and stood around it on three sides.

Tommy bent his knees slightly so he could see through the glass without any glare from the lights. His eyes flitted left to right and back again as he pored over the lines of the ancient language.

When he was done, he stood up straight. The color in his face drained to a pale white.

Sean looked at his friend with concern. "What's wrong, Schultzie?"

Tommy took a long breath through his nose and blew it through his lips. "See that?" He pointed at a section of the tablet that had been carved out of the stone in the shape of a small curve.

"Yeah." Then it hit Sean. "The ring. These tablets were the containers, so to speak, for the gold pieces."

Tommy nodded.

"What does it say?" Sean pressed.

"And what is that thing over there?" Petty asked, pointing to something at the end of the row of cases.

The other two leaned to the right so they could look beyond the other two tablets and see what had caught Petty's interest. There was a white plinth jutting up from the floor. The concrete surface ended, and where the pillar stood, it was surrounded by metal grates.

The shape of the pillar was cubical, rising about four feet above the floor. It was cut like a cube, not entirely dissimilar to the tablets in the display boxes, though it was made from pure quartz.

Tommy felt his heartbeat quicken, and he rushed to the next tablet. More Greek filled the surface of the stone, ending as the previous one had, with the same strange symbol.

He hurried to the third tablet and quickly read through the engraved message. It, too, had a curved slot for a piece of the golden ring just as the others had. And it also contained the same odd symbol.

Tommy's forehead wrinkled. Crow's feet stretched out from the corners of his eyes. He finished reading the message carved into the tablet and then looked over at the stone column once more.

He caught a glimpse of something shiny, metallic, on the top of the pedestal. He stepped over to it, followed by the other two, and stared down at the flat top. There was a circle cut into it. Two metal prongs were raised slightly from within the quartz. And there, fit perfectly into the ring, was the third section of the golden hoop.

Tommy swallowed hard as he stared at the anomaly.

"Schultzie?" Sean's voice cut the silence like a freight train in a funeral parlor. "What do those tablets say?"

Sean stepped close and looked down at the piece of gold.

Tommy answered in an absent tone, as if he was now on another planet. "The tablets speak of a great weapon. It was designed to defend against the Athenians as well as foreign threats from the sea."

"Okay," Petty said. "Where is this weapon?"

Tommy stared at the white crystal. "This is it," he said.

Petty looked with dismay at the quartz pillar. "What do you mean, this is it?"

"You can see here the other two sections of the ring fit into this hoop that was dug out of the crystal."

"What does it do?"

"There's only one way to find out," Sean said. He took the section of ring he'd kept in his jacket pocket and held it up in the light. The gold shimmered in the dull glow.

"Where did you guys find those?" Petty asked. There was a curious look on his face, like a child searching for the hiding place of his Christmas presents.

"Along the way here," Sean answered, leaving it vague for now.

He started to put the piece of gold down into what he suspected was its place when Tommy stopped him.

"No, wait." Tommy put out his hand and grabbed Sean's wrist. "Remember what Madison's letter said; the warning."

"Death, destruction, all that. Yeah, I remember."

"Well, there's something else you need to know."

"What's that?" Sean asked, looking at his friend with patient eyes while inside his patience was wearing thin. They were running out of time to help Dawkins, and every second that passed only put them further behind.

"The messages on the tablet," Tommy started. "They all contain warnings."

"What kind of warnings?"

"From what I could discern, this weapon is a land killer. It could wipe out an entire island in one go."

"I'd have to see that," Petty quipped.

"There's one more thing," Tommy added quickly. "The symbol at the bottom of those tablets, it's the symbol for one of the greatest mythical cities ever known to man."

"New York?" Sean joked.

"No." Tommy remained serious. "It's the symbol for Atlantis."

Sean's eyebrows pinched together at that statement. "What did you just say?'

"I think we might be standing over the machine or weapon that destroyed the fabled city of Atlantis. Those tablets contain warnings with direct references to the lost city."

Sean took his hand away from the pillar and stared at his friend while Tommy continued to explain.

"Based on what those tablets say and what Agent Petty here was able to discern, my guess is that the Japanese stumbled upon this artifact some time long ago, realized how dangerous it was, and shipped it across the Pacific to a new land where there were few inhabitants and where it was a safe enough distance away from the empire." He looked at his friend, then at Petty, then back to Sean. "How am I doing so far?"

"That actually makes a ton of sense, Schultzie."

"Thank you." Tommy took a dramatic bow.

"The problem now is, how do we get this thing out of here to get it to the guys who took Dawkins? Or do we just close up the door, seal it, and get out of here?"

"That, Sean, would be a bad idea." The new voice echoed from the entrance to the room.

Sean spun around first, instinctively reaching for his gun.

Tommy and Petty likewise twisted around, stuffing their hands into their coats to draw their weapons. Every one of them was too late.

The men standing in the doorway were holding pistols and submachine guns, and one held a smaller version of an AR-15, pistol length with a gray brace in place of the stock.

At first, Sean didn't recognize the men. He scanned their faces but kept coming up with nothing. That is, until he locked in on the one standing at the center of the group. There was something familiar about him, something that caught Sean off guard and also filled him with dread.

The man stepped forward, a SIG Sauer sidearm in his right hand. He offered a smug grin and then took his own bow.

"Hello, Sean. Remember me?"

Tommy and Petty looked over at Sean, who was still piecing together details from long ago.

Then something clicked, and his eyes widened. "Boyd? Andrew Boyd?"

45

ANNAPOLIS

"We're here live with a very special guest on today's show," Adriana said with the exuberance that could have only come from a well-experienced Hollywood actress.

The camera was pointed at Admiral Winters, hogtied to the floor, his bloody face squarely in the middle of the screen. Behind him his guards were lying one on top of the other, their hands and wrists also bound.

She held the pistols in her hands. The muzzles had empty water bottles fixed to them as makeshift silencers, a trick she'd only used once up to that point in her adventurous life.

"That's right," Adriana went on, "it's Fleet Admiral Forrest Winters!"

She kept her face away from the camera, but the guns were pointed at the three men, one for Winters and the other for the guards.

"Admiral Winters, as you may or may not know, is one of the Joint Chiefs of Staff and the head of the United States Navy." She made a sound like a teenager finding out they were going to see their favorite boy band, adding "ooooh" at the end of it.

"We're here today to get a confession from Admiral Winters

regarding the disappearance of former president John Dawkins. As you can see, the admiral hasn't been very forthcoming about the truth behind the abduction, which is why we're here today."

Winters swore into his mouth gag and kicked around, but he couldn't get free.

"Sorry, folks. I had to put that rag in his mouth. Apparently, the admiral cusses like a sailor." Adriana let out a fake laugh at her dumb joke. "Anyway, we're here to find out if Admiral Winters will confess the truth. Or will he let two of his loyal guards be killed to protect himself?"

Adriana walked around to the front of the phone. She'd made a mental note of where it was aimed and knew where she could stand without showing her face. She stopped short of the admiral and took out his gag, keeping her back to the phone's camera. No one watching the video would know who she was.

The admiral shouted. He screamed for help. Then he went into full empty-threat mode. "Congratulations, lady! You're going to spend the rest of your life in jail. Smart move! Every cop, every federal agent in two states—they're all on their way right now."

She shrugged and nodded. "Yeah, that's probably true. Still, this is going to be a fun show. And you need to be nicer. After all, we're live on social media."

He looked back over at the phone. She'd told him what she was doing, that she was going to live-stream everything.

"I wonder how many likes and shares we have so far, Admiral." Adriana chuckled. "Oh, well. I guess we'll find out later. Like I was saying, I wonder if you will let your two guards over there die or if you'll confess the truth to save them."

"You already know the truth. You're crazy!"

"Okay, then. The question of the hour is: Did you orchestrate the abduction of former president John Dawkins? And if so, where is he now? And remember, if you lie to me I kill your guards."

"You're out of your mind. You hear me? You are going away for a very long time unless you let us go."

"Three seconds, Admiral. Did you do it? And where is Dawkins now?" Adriana's tone changed to one laced with evil. There was no compassion there, no mercy—only pure, unadulterated menace.

The man shook his head.

She raised the gun in her right hand and pointed it at the guard on top.

"One."

"I already told you, nut job, I didn't take the president!"

"Two."

"What is wrong with you? I didn't have anything to do with his disappearance."

"Three."

The gun popped twice. Plastic erupted on the bottom of the water bottle fixed to the barrel. It wasn't as good as a real suppressor, but it did the job, keeping most of the gun's report contained within the room.

She looked down at the admiral, who was struggling to twist around so he could see if she'd really killed the two guards. Adriana shook her head and walked back to the phone and laid it on its face for a moment.

The live feed was black for a moment, and then the room reappeared when she tilted the device back on its edge.

The scene was now of the admiral, still where he was before, and the two guards. Now, however, those guards were motionless. Their eyes were closed, and dark blood oozed out of their foreheads.

Adriana walked back around into the shot and stopped next to the admiral once more. She nudged his chest with her boot, spinning him around enough so that he could see the two dead guards.

He screamed obscenities, some she'd never heard before. The swearing came between empty threats and promises. "They'll hang you for this!" was but one particular example.

Adriana kept the second pistol loose at her side. "Now, everyone, are you ready to see if the admiral will tell the truth to save his own skin? Keep in mind, Admiral, we are live on the air right now. So, with that in mind, I'm not going to go through the process of torturing you, as much as I'd like to. I'm going to give you two shots. Ha ha! The first one will hit your crotch. And the second will go right through your head. Yeah! And believe me, folks, I'm going to wait as long as I can between the two."

Adriana hovered over him and aimed the pistol down at the man's groin.

"No! Please, don't!"

She let her finger visibly tense on the trigger. "Sorry, Admiral. Say goodbye to...whatever's down there." She raised the weapon another few inches to add effect.

"No! Wait! Wait! Stop! Please!"

She lowered her head, glaring at him. "Talk."

"Andrew Boyd has him. Okay? Andrew Boyd is the guy who took him. He and his men...they...they threatened me, okay? I didn't have a choice. I had to give Dawkins up."

Adriana nodded and then stiffened her spine. "Well, there you have it, everyone! Admiral Winters was behind the abduction of President Dawkins." She chuckled for a moment, her voice sultry and sinister.

"No, please. You have to believe me. I didn't have a choice! Please!"

"I'm giving you a choice now, Admiral," Adriana said. She walked back over to the phone and stopped the recording. "Now everyone in the world knows what happened, well, at least your version of it. Personally, I think you were the one pulling all the strings. This Boyd character might have the president, but I have a feeling it was you calling the shots. Either way, it doesn't matter anymore."

She tapped one of the apps on the phone, opened the man's profile, and began to upload the video to YouTube. Once it was there, he'd be finished.

"What are you doing?" His voice was panicked.

"Well, I might have lied earlier when I said we were live. We weren't, but don't worry, that confession is on its way to the internet as we speak." His eyes were wide with fear.

Adriana watched the phone until the video was done uploading to YouTube. Then she typed in the words "Admiral Winters: I Kidnapped President Dawkins."

She hit save and then watched to make sure the video was live-streamed, uploaded, and public. Then she took the phone over to a bucket of ice, she assumed for the liquor the admiral had been drinking. A thin pool of water had collected at the bottom. She looked into the bucket, over at the admiral, and then dropped the phone.

"What are you doing?" he shouted. "You're insane! I'll have your head for this!"

She shook her head and looked over at him. "No, Admiral, you won't. I just uploaded the video to YouTube. It will go viral within minutes. And your life will be over. Of course, there are...other options."

His eyebrows lowered. "What do you mean?"

She picked up one of the pistols and detached the makeshift silencer from the end. Then she took the second gun and did the same, taking the taped-on suppressor from the muzzle. The second weapon, she stuffed into her belt. The first, she took over to the admiral and stood for a moment, looming like an executioner from a thousand years ago. She looked down at him, not with pity or with anger. Her gaze was one of curiosity, bordering amusement.

She bent down and ripped the tape off his wrists. Then she walked back over to the counter and pulled the slide several times, counting down the rounds as they clinked on the surface of the desk. When she was sure there was only one left in the chamber, she scooped up the remaining cartridges and stuffed them in a pocket.

"What I mean is," she set the pistol on the desk; "you don't have to go to prison if you don't want to. In fact, a guy like you would probably be pretty popular there. So, maybe you do want to go. Either way, you're done. Your career, your name, your life—it's all over, Admiral. Everything you've worked for is gone."

She left the pistol on the desk and walked out the door.

She'd picked up one of the radios from the guards she knocked out earlier. The show was to make it look like she'd killed the men. What she'd done was much more humane. She'd turned the camera and then walked over, thumped each one on the back of the head to knock them out, and then went back to the phone to finish the show.

To the world and even to Winters, it would appear she'd killed them. A little blood she'd scooped from the floor around Winters made for good special effects on both guards' heads. To the phone's camera and to Winters, it looked just like they'd been shot.

She pressed on the radio button and spoke. "We have trouble. Upstairs. Hurry."

Adriana tucked into the back corner of the laundry room as the two guards in the back of the house burst through the door and sprinted upstairs. The sounds of their footsteps mingled with sirens in the distance. As she stepped out of the back door, she could hear the screams of the guards coming from the house.

They were begging the admiral not to do it. They shouted at him, telling him to put the gun down.

As Adriana hit the street in the back and turned away, she heard a single gunshot and the sound of broken glass.

She rubbed down the pistol in her hand with the underside of her shirt and tossed it in a garbage bin, then picked up her pace to a trot.

46

ASTORIA

"Ding ding ding!" Boyd yelled in a mocking tone. "We have a winner!"

He sauntered across the floor, followed closely by his men as they fanned out, essentially blocking any way out. Aside from Boyd, there were four other gunmen, all similarly dressed in their skullcaps, black jackets and matching pants, and black boots.

"You know, Sean, I wasn't sure you'd remember me. It's been a minute, right?" His voice climbed to a new pitch at the end. Boyd stopped ten feet from Sean. The pistol in his hand was still at his waist, casually pointed in Sean's direction.

Sean noted the way that Boyd and his men were dressed and went with it. "You five just come from a rave or do you just all coincidentally shop at the same Hot Topic?"

Boyd snorted a laugh and shook his head. "Still think you're so funny, Sean. I heard that about you. Always cracking jokes, trying to make light of a bad situation."

Boyd turned and fired his pistol. The suppressor on the barrel toned down the decibels, even in the confined space. The end of the weapon puffed, and Sean shuddered as the round hit Agent Petty in the chest.

Petty staggered back, a confused and terrified look filling his face. His eyes were wide with fear, mingled with pain. He touched the hole in his chest as he kept stumbling backward until he tripped over his right heel and fell onto his back. His head hit the floor with a thud, and his eyes rolled up behind the eyelids.

Sean and Tommy watched, sickened by what had occurred.

They turned back to face the killer. "Good one, Boyd," Sean said. "You just killed a federal agent. Add that to the long list of charges you're already piling up, including kidnapping the former president."

"I'm sorry if I gave you the impression I cared, Sean. You act as if I'm going to get caught in all of this. I assure you, I've planned everything perfectly, and there's nothing you can do to stop us."

"Where is Dawkins?" Sean sneered. He looked like a rabid animal, ready to pounce any second.

"Oh, he's safe," Boyd answered. "Undisclosed location. I'm sure you understand. Bringing him here would have been dramatic, sure, but it also would have been a logistical nightmare. That old guy is a real pain, as I'm certain you can understand having been friends with him for the last eight years or so."

"If you've hurt him..."

"You'll do what?" Boyd arched both eyebrows. "You're in no position to do anything, Sean." He stepped closer and motioned to Sean's jacket. "Take off the coat, nice and slow. You too, Schultz." He waved a hand at Tommy. "Do anything stupid, and I kill Sean."

"You're going to do that anyway."

Boyd puffed his lips and nodded. "You know what? That's true, but don't you want him to have just a few more seconds of life? I mean, if it was me staring down the barrel of a gun, I'd do everything I could to savor every moment I could."

"I'll remember you said that," Sean growled.

Sean and Tommy unzipped their jackets and dropped them to the floor, exposing the weapons holstered at their side and under their armpits.

"Only two guns, Sean? Traveling light?" Boyd laughed and motioned for his men to disarm the two captives.

Two of the men trotted over and started methodically removing the weapons. Sean kept his hands out to his side as his frisker made sure he didn't have anything else on him, checking his ankles and thighs. At one point, the gunman was a little too thorough in the nether regions.

"Hey, take it easy down there," Sean said. "I'm a married man."

The two guards also sifted through the jackets, and each pulled out a section of the golden ring. They presented the two metallic fragments to their boss, depositing them into Boyd's palm before resuming their previous positions.

"Married?" Boyd's voice boomed. "Sean, I had no idea you were married. Congratulations. I can't believe I didn't get you anything."

The gun fired again. This time, the barrel was pointed at Tommy. It fired a second time, planting another round into Tommy's chest.

Sean watched in horror as his friend fell backward and rolled onto his side. Within a couple of seconds, Tommy lay motionless on the floor. Sean turned back to Boyd and snarled.

"I will rip your heart from your chest! He has a wife, too."

Sean lunged forward, but Boyd stopped that right away, squeezing the trigger two more times, grouping the bullets tightly in the center of Sean's chest.

Sean's eyes widened at the sudden pain. He looked down at the holes in his hoodie and then back up into the eyes of the man who'd just killed him and his best friend. He wobbled, teetering on the edge of blacking out and tumbling into the depths of the void. He looked over at Tommy's still body on the floor, then to Agent Petty. He, too, was still motionless, dead at the hands of this punk.

The room swirled in Sean's eyes. He looked back to Boyd, who was wearing the same smug grin. *I've won*, Sean thought. *And I've failed.*

Sean tripped over his shoes and stumbled backward, passing the quartz tower as he lost his balance and fell to the ground. His eyelids grew heavy. The deep pain in his chest began to fade. Then, Sean closed his eyes and surrendered to the encroaching darkness.

Boyd chuckled. "What a moron," he said. Then he motioned to

his men. "Pull their bodies over there to the corner. I don't want to trip over them while I give this little baby a test run."

The men immediately snapped to it, each grabbing one of the bodies by the ankles and dragging them out of the way.

Boyd held the ring fragments in his palm. He stared down at them for the first time, a boyish wonder in his eyes. He ran one thumb across the smooth golden surface of one piece of the ring, taking a second to admire its odd beauty.

Then he turned and faced the quartz plinth. He gazed at the beautifully carved cube rising from the metal grates around it. There was the hint of a draft coming up from below, a tantalizing glimpse that there was more to discover down in the depths of this hillside. Did the shaft go below sea level? It must, he thought, since they'd already descended three stories. What else was down there?

His four men joined him by the pillar, the second-in-command standing closest. He was a fairly young guy, mid-thirties with short dark hair cropped to the side in a sort of wind-swept spike.

"What's next, sir? We taking these back to the admiral?"

His name was Marcus Scott. He was one of the men who'd been with Boyd the longest. They'd worked several theaters together and even more missions. He was a stone-cold killer; a true soldier.

Boyd had heard someone say once that a good soldier is one who sees the enemy as not human. That made the killing easier. Scott was a very good soldier.

"Yes, we are going to take these back to the Admiral. I got what I wanted. We all got paid. There's just one more thing I want to do."

"What's that, sir?"

Boyd rubbed his thumb on the golden fragments in his palm. He stared at them in a trance, as if the shiny objects were speaking to him, calling to him.

"I want to see what this thing does."

"Sir, the Admiral—"

"Isn't here, Marcus. What's the difference? We'll give him the coordinates, and these...whatever these golden pieces are after we take it for a test drive."

He looked down at the curved bed cut into the top of the quartz pillar. One of the pieces was already in place. It didn't take a genius to figure out how the other two fit.

Boyd placed one of the fragments into the depression. It connected with the first piece and the metal prong sticking out of the quartz. A new sound, higher pitched like a jet plane on the other side of the runway, joined the low hum that had been in the background since their arrival. Boyd turned his head in all directions, looking around the room. He was a little surprised by the new sound but not deterred. He held out the final piece of gold over the hoop and paused for a moment, as if reconsidering.

"Don't do it!" a familiar voice shouted over the drone in the room.

Boyd was tempted to spin around, raise his weapon, and open fire. But he knew better. It took less than a second for him to realize what had happened.

He twisted his head around to the right and saw Sean Wyatt standing there with a black pistol in his hand. The barrel was aimed straight at Boyd's right eye. From that range, Sean would never miss. The other two men were also standing by his side, each holding two weapons pointed at Boyd's four mercenaries. Despite being outnumbered, there was nothing Boyd's men could do.

"Drop the guns, and put the gold down, Andrew," Sean said.

Boyd snickered at the way Sean used his first name. Sean was trying to get under his skin. Boyd felt the smooth surface of the gold against his fingertips still hovering over the final slot in the quartz.

Boyd kept chuckling, his head bobbing as he did so. "You know, I should have seen that coming, Sean. Kevlar?"

Sean didn't have to pull up his hoodie to show the man. He simply nodded. "Courtesy of our friend the federal agent you shot."

"Not smart," Tommy added.

"How did you know I wouldn't shoot you in the head?" Boyd asked.

"I didn't," Sean admitted. "But you never were the most thorough. Before you were court-martialed, I studied everything about you, knew your every move, everything you'd ever done in the military—

and out. You were sloppy, which is why it's important for you to have some cronies around to do what you want, to handle things you can't. Truth is, you were never a great soldier, Andrew."

The words cut deep, but Boyd didn't care what Sean Wyatt said, even if it was true. "I always got the job done, Sean. You know that. I was willing to do whatever it took. That's patriotism. Something you wouldn't know anything about."

"Okay, we're done here," Sean said, cutting off the conversation. "Put down the weapon and the gold. Time for you to tell us where John Dawkins is."

"Dawkins?" Boyd gave a dramatic nod. "Yeah, he's already dead, Sean."

Sean's eyes narrowed. He didn't see Tommy flinch behind him.

"You're bluffing," Sean said.

"Well, I guess it doesn't really matter."

"What's that supposed to mean?"

"You know, Sean. You're right. I'll do what you said and put down my things."

He slowly bent forward, lowering his pistol toward the ground. At the same time, he subtly dropped his other hand toward the top of the pillar. When he felt it graze the crystal, he let the gold fall from his hand.

Boyd had taken care to position the gold directly over the last slot in the column's surface.

Sean watched with uncertain fear as the fragment clicked into place.

The second the gold touched the other two pieces and the third prong, a harsh rumble resonated from the earth, shaking the room, the ceiling, the entire structure. A thumping noise also accompanied the humming. It came from deep within the floor. Its steady pulsing was in perfect time, like a giant metronome with steel pounding steel. It reminded Sean of the sounds of a blacksmith shop where they used the world's biggest anvil.

A sudden jolt shifted the floor, and Sean lost his balance. He reached out his free hand to steady himself as he fell. He didn't lose his grip on the gun, though, and as Boyd lunged back toward the entrance Sean managed to squeeze the trigger once.

The gun popped loudly, though the sound was absorbed by all the other noise in the room. The round clipped Boyd's shoulder as he dove clear and took cover behind the nearest pillar.

Sean crashed to the floor. His right hand took more of the brunt than he intended, and he felt his thumb crunch under his body weight, smashed between the weapon's grip and the floor.

He howled in pain and let go of the weapon as the nerves in his hand screamed out in agony.

Behind him, Tommy and Agent Petty were keeping an eye on the four guards when things started going awry. The floor lurched again, and the two men stumbled backward against the wall. As they were thrown off balance, the four mercenaries reacted. Two of them went for their weapons, while the other two charged Tommy and Agent Petty.

Tommy whipped his gun around to try to get off a shot, but he was too slow. The mercenary was on him in a flash. The man's boot shot forward and struck Tommy in the gut.

He doubled over, his abdomen pulsing with pain as he dropped to his knees. The mercenary moved fast, seizing the chance to end the fight in less than five seconds. He raised his fist, ready to strike Tommy in the temple, a blow that would render him unconscious at best.

Tommy managed to gather his wits enough to raise his left hand as the fist came down hard. It smacked against his palm. It hurt, but it wasn't the knockout blow the villain was looking for. Tommy raised his weapon and aimed it at the man's groin. He squeezed the trigger, but the guard saw Tommy's plan and swiped his free hand in front of his waist. He smacked the gun as the muzzle erupted.

It was a lucky move by the mercenary, but not so lucky for one of his team members. The bullet had sailed behind him and struck one of the other guards in the face.

The man wavered for a moment, reaching up to touch the wound below his eye with his free hand. Then he collapsed to the floor with a thud.

The mercenary attacking Tommy didn't look back. He grabbed the gun by the barrel and twisted it hard to one side. The move twisted Tommy's wrist into an awkward position and he had no choice but to let go.

As the mercenary switched the weapon from one hand to the other, Tommy mirrored the man's move, grasping the barrel and yanking it to one side. A pop came from the man's wrist, and Tommy used that moment of pain to press the attack. He pushed hard off the floor and launched the top of his head into the man's nose.

The appendage crunched. The guard shrieked, and the gun fell to the floor with a clack.

Tommy rose from the floor, ready to finish the fight by any means necessary.

Petty fired one shot into the abdomen of another gunmen mere seconds before the guy could get off a shot of his own. The wounded man stumbled backward, his gut burning with a searing pain. He tried to raise his weapon, but Petty squeezed the trigger two more times. One of the rounds missed, but the other struck home just below the man's neck. He wobbled and then fell onto his face as blood spurted from the wound and trickled from the corner of his mouth.

The guard closest to Petty launched himself forward, lowering his shoulder and head as he drove into Petty's ribcage. The tackle drove Petty back into the wall where his head hit the surface with a sickening smack. The room instantly blurred, and Petty felt his knees go weak. Everything swirled as he surrendered to the calling of sleep.

The mercenary stood up, taking the weapon from Petty's unmoving hand. He raised the gun and aimed it at the agent's head. He was about to pull the trigger when a new sound boomed through the chamber.

The wall beyond the quartz pillar began to crumble. At first, it was just a few loose chunks of stone, but as the shaking continued more pieces broke free and fell.

Damp, rain-soaked air blew into the room from outside. Dark clouds roiled overhead dumping sheets of rain to the earth.

The mercenary paused, distracted for a second by the collapse of the wall. He looked out into the sea as it churned. Whitecaps on the dark water foamed at the top of every wave. Out away from the coast, the crests of the waves grew higher, pushing toward the coast with devastating speed.

47

ASTORIA

The distraction was enough.

Sean saw the mercenary about to end Petty's life and for the moment forgot about Boyd. Sean charged toward the man and jumped through the air, extending his right boot.

The gunman never saw the blow coming.

Sean's heel struck the mercenary in the kidneys and plowed him forward into the wall. The man's head hit the wall and though dazed he was able to turn around and fire a wild shot in Sean's direction.

The gun wasn't well aimed, and the bullet sailed away to splash down in the angry sea. Sean kicked the gun from the man's hand with a snap. The toe of his boot struck the weapon and launched it through the air. It landed on the rain-slicked floor near the collapsed wall and slid over the edge, down into the ocean below.

Sean punched the guy in the jaw once, twice, and started to hit him a third time, but the mercenary raised his forearm and absorbed the blow. He countered with a jab into Sean's gut. Sean tensed, ready for the strike, but it didn't take away from the pain that shot through his abs as the fist drove deep.

The mercenary shoved Sean's fist back and kicked hard with his right foot, sending Sean sprawling a dozen feet away.

The mercenary stood, regaining his balance, and was about to attack when he heard another voice.

"Don't move!" Tommy shouted.

The guy looked over to see Tommy standing there with a pistol extended. The weapon was aimed at the side of the mercenary's head. The guy was beaten, and he knew it. He slowly raised his hands and put them on top of his head.

Sean turned to his friend. "You got him?"

Tommy nodded. "Yeah. Go get Boyd."

Sean didn't have to be told twice. He took off at a sprint, running toward the door.

He burst through the doorway and instantly took inventory of the alcove leading into the chamber. It was empty. He looked up and saw the shadow of a man ascending the stairs.

He wanted to yell at Boyd, to let him know he was coming for him, but Sean wanted the element of surprise. The chase was on, and there was no way Sean was going to let Andrew Boyd get away.

Sean pumped his legs, careful not to slip on the damp steps as he climbed. His hand slid along the railing, more of a guide than anything else. He kept his eyes upward, watching as Boyd's hand did the same, running along the surface of the railing as he made his escape. Sean could feel his thighs burning with every step, but he didn't slow as he reached the second floor, then halfway up the third.

As he neared the top, he could see a faint light seeping in through the hole they'd created when ripping up the floor earlier. A howling sound blew through it, as if a banshee had been awakened from a long slumber to haunt this very ground.

Sean reached the surface and slowed his pace, though only for a moment. He popped his head out of the cavity and looked around. There was no sign of Boyd. Sean climbed out of the stairwell and jumped out the nearest door—the one in the back. He looked both ways and then ran around the bunker to the front. There, nearing the trees in the clearing, was Andrew Boyd. He was running as fast as he could, kicking his legs up like an Olympic sprinter, minus several miles per hour.

The sky overhead had turned a shade of black unlike any Sean had ever seen. It wasn't just dark. It was a shade of onyx. The clouds turned over and kneaded within themselves like thick black dough. Lightning flashed, streaking through the darkened heavens. The wind whipped through Sean's hair and pelted him with raindrops the size of dimes. Each droplet pounded him hard, reminding him of getting caught in a storm on his motorcycle. The trees bent sideways, their branches flapping like wings. Any leaves that had stuck around for the winter were torn away, and the evergreens that lined the forest clearing did all they could to hold onto their green tips.

Sean took off again to give chase. He could see which direction Boyd was going and realized that his quarry was attempting to head back to the parking area. But Boyd's path was slightly off course. Sean saw instantly that he could cut Boyd off if he circled around. It would be close, but Sean knew he was faster.

He darted across the meadow, back toward the hill leading down to the parking area. He kept an eye on Boyd as he made his way closer to the edge of the clearing. Boyd looked back and saw no one, luckily for Sean. Had he run straight at the man, Boyd would have seen him.

Sean watched as Boyd reached a short slope leading back into the trees. The man slipped in the mud, falling facedown into the hillside. He scrambled to get up, kicking his feet and clawing at the earth like a wild animal trying to rut.

As Sean reached the edge of the clearing, a crack of thunder exploded overhead and he winced at the deafening sound. This was no ordinary storm. Had it been generated by the Omega device? How was that possible? He recalled what he'd heard Tommy say about Atlantis and that this was the machine responsible for its destruction. He wanted to think about it, to ponder what it all meant, but he was on the hunt and couldn't afford distractions. He pushed the thoughts to the side and kept running.

He leaped into the cover of the tree line and pushed on, now bending his run to cut off Boyd. Any second now, the other man would realize his mistake and correct it, making a right turn to get back down the hill and, Sean assumed, make his escape.

Sean kept up the pace, though he moved stealthily, running on the balls of his feet to ensure as little ground contact as possible. Less chance of stepping on a twig, kicking some leaves, and alerting his prey. That was more out of habit than necessity at this point. The storm's frenzy blocked out most other sounds.

There. Sean caught a glimpse of Boyd skirting the edge of the forest toward the top of the hill. Sean quickened his pace, making a beeline for where he anticipated Boyd would be at just the right moment.

Sean's arms swung hard at his sides. His breath came in quick gasps, lungs burning from the cold, damp air. His legs were like Jell-O now, but he didn't stop. A gust of wind changed course and smacked him across the face with a low-hanging fir branch. The stinging pain sent a momentary fury through Sean's mind and body, but he maintained his course, closing the gap with Boyd: forty yards, thirty, twenty, almost there.

Boyd turned his head to look back over his shoulder again, and that's when he caught his first glimpse of Sean. Had he looked five seconds before, even three, he might have avoided what happened next. Sean lowered his shoulder like a pro football linebacker and launched himself. His shoulder dug into the man's ribcage, arms wrapping around like a vice as Sean drove Boyd into the ground.

Boyd gasped for breath. The tackle had knocked the wind out of him, but he was alert enough to react when Sean rolled over him and tried to straddle his torso. Boyd slung his elbow around and struck Sean in the side of the head. The grip so tightly held by Sean's knees against Boyd's sides eased, and Boyd was able to rock back, push up with hands and feet, and send Sean sprawling head over heels into the muddy grass behind him.

Sean hit the ground with a splat. He grimaced against the throbbing pain on the side of his head, put his hands down into the mud, and tried to get up. Boyd had rolled over onto his stomach and was still heaving, trying to get air back into his lungs. As he rose from the wet earth, he suddenly felt the relief of oxygen flowing back down through his windpipe and into his chest.

Boyd stared at Sean as he struggled to get up.

Clumps of wet mud clung to Sean's face. His vision blurred for a moment, partially from the blow to the head, partially from the wind-whipped rain that continued to pelt him.

Boyd bellowed a sickly laugh over the howling wind, shaking his head back and forth. "Couldn't leave well enough alone, could you, Sean?"

The blurriness in Sean's eyes cleared, and he rose to face his enemy. "You talking about Dawkins or what you were up to in Iraq all those years ago?"

"Obviously, you had to get involved with Dawkins. That's why we're here, right? We needed you and your pal to lead us to this thing. And look." He waved his hands around. "Looks like the Admiral was right. This thing really is a nasty weapon."

The storm kept circling overhead.

"You have no idea what you've done, Sean," Boyd went on. "I mean, you made me a lot of money. The Admiral certainly pays well."

"So, that's it? Money? I guess I shouldn't expect more from a scumbag like you, Boyd."

"Oh, no, Sean. Of course, there's more to it than money. The Admiral delivered a prize better than any amount of cash I could hope for. He delivered you."

Sean peered into Boyd's eyes. They were cold, reckless, and afraid of nothing. He was a man with nothing to lose because he'd already lost everything once. The only thing he had left to hang every thought, every desire, on was revenge.

"Vengeance is a bit cliché for you, don't you think?"

Boyd shuffled to his left, and as he did Sean realized how close they were to the cliff. The rocky ledge dropped off into the raging sea below. Sean remained focused on his opponent and moved to the right to mirror his movement. It was also to get away from the precipice, which had sent a sudden shudder through Sean's gut the second he noticed it.

"Vengeance is never cliché, Sean. If you weren't so busy being all high and mighty, you'd know. My guess is you've got a long list of people you screwed over. In fact," he wagged a finger in the downpour, "I'd wager that's why you really left Axis. Isn't it? You left because you pissed off one too many people."

Sean ignored the barb. It was a reach, whether Boyd knew it or not, and Sean knew it wasn't true. Sure, there probably was a list of people who wanted to get back at him for something, but he'd never wronged anyone who was in the right. Boyd's mistakes had come back to haunt him and cost him almost everything he'd worked for. Was that Sean's fault? There was no point in trying to reason with someone like Boyd. It was as effective as talking to a barn. There was one question, though, that Sean kept coming back to in his mind.

"You keep talking about your friend, the Admiral," Sean said. "After I kill you, who do I have to go after next?"

Boyd's face creased with an evil grin, like he was holding the secret to the greatest treasure of all.

"Let's just say you're not the only one who screwed a bunch of people over, Sean. Your friend Dawkins made his own enemies, powerful ones. Not to worry, though, about him. When I'm done with you, I'm going to make sure Dawkins is the next to go. I'll make it quick...relatively."

He hadn't given a name, but Boyd had revealed enough for Sean to go on. Maybe it was a slip. Or maybe it was Boyd thinking he was clever. Sean hadn't expected the man to give him anything. He figured he was going to have to track down this mysterious admiral through a series of channels and connections he hadn't used in a long time. He still would, but having a few key pieces of information would cut out a lot of wasted time and effort.

None of that mattered for the moment. Sean had to finish this fight first.

Boyd reached down to his side and drew a combat knife from its sheath. He held out the long, intimidating blade, letting it dance from left to right in an almost hypnotic sway. The sharp metal was coated in black Cerakote, only revealing a hint at the edge's silvery steel where the weapon was honed to a razor finish.

Sean immediately realized just how naked he felt without a weapon. He'd run out of the building to pursue Boyd and didn't take a second to grab a gun, or something he could use in a fight. He didn't regret the move. It was out of necessity. Another two seconds, and Boyd might have escaped, disappearing into the grove surrounding the clearing without any chance of being caught.

He was here now. No sense in pining about what he should have done.

Boyd tossed the weapon from one hand to the other, taunting Sean into making a move.

"You just gonna keep playing with that thing, or are you gonna use it?"

"I thought I'd let you go first," Boyd said. "But if you insist..."

He took a step forward, the blade clutched in his right hand.

Right-handed, Sean thought.

Always get as much information in as little time as possible. That was one of his first rules of combat. In the field, there was no time for dossiers, no way that you could research an enemy before you took him on. You had seconds, especially in a one-on-one scenario like this.

Boyd being right-handed might not have seemed like much to most people, but it was a key factor for Sean to consider. It meant that if he took out his opponent's favored hand, the fight would be all but finished. That wasn't to say Boyd couldn't use his left hand, he could be ambidextrous. But it was something, and Sean always looked for the tiniest edge. He'd beaten better fighters than him over the years simply because of those tiny details.

Sean shifted his right foot away from the cliff, feeling the mud squish against the side of his shoe. The rain came down harder now, sheets of it dumping out of the sky. It wasn't the typical spitting rain that the Oregon coast was accustomed to. This was a Southern kind of storm, angry and violent. Off to Sean's left, the sea continued to rage, the water appearing as black as the sky above.

"When I'm done with the president," Boyd said, "I'm going to gut that pretty little wife of yours."

Sean felt a splinter of flame shoot through his gut. It burned up through his chest and stuck in his throat. *He's just trying to get a rise out of me, take me off my plan, my game. This is my game.*

"You'd be wise not to mess with her, Boyd," Sean said. "I don't think you can handle that one."

Boyd's eyes flashed angrily but with a twinge of being humored. "I'll take my chances."

His right eye twitched ever so slightly, and Sean knew what would follow.

The enemy stepped forward, a long purposeful stride followed by a second as he closed the gap between them.

Sean maintained his stance. He ran through every possible move, every potential attack that Boyd would have learned in training and might use in the field. Sean read the man's body language, the way his shoulders tilted slightly one way, the positioning of his legs.

Look at the body first, the knife second, he reminded himself. It wasn't something he'd been taught by the government. That was a little checklist he'd thought of on his own.

Boyd's speed quickened with his third step. He was only two steps away now, two long strides. Sean knew what was coming; the almost unnoticeable shift in Boyd's arm position was a glaring tell.

Sean twisted his body to the side, minimizing the targets he knew Boyd would attack. Another step and Boyd was nearly on him. The enemy's eyes narrowed. His jaw set firm. The blade dipped back, only inches, but enough for Sean to know the lunge was coming.

The final step—Boyd surged forward. He held the blade's edge out toward Sean, a common tactic for most who knew what they were doing. It allowed the attacker to slash a big chunk of the torso—ribs, abdomen, possibly a shoulder—before drawing the weapon back into the side of the victim's neck for what would be a double-killing blow.

Time slowed down. Sean blinked once, clearing the rain from his eyes. He let go of the throbbing from where he'd been struck by Boyd a moment before. The sounds of the storm, the sea churning beyond the cliff, and even the wind all melted into a low drone.

Boyd swung his weapon. It was a quick move and executed with the utmost precision. Sean had anticipated it, though, and as the razor's edge swiped at Sean's stomach, he arched his back and sucked in a gulp of air. The tip of the blade sliced through his shirt and ripped into his flesh.

Sean winced at the sting coming from the left side of his gut, but he didn't lose focus. Boyd's movement was too fast. He'd been too aggressive on the attack.

Sean dropped his right hand hard, slamming it down onto Boyd's wrist. The blow didn't knock the knife free, but that wasn't Sean's intention. His fingers wrapped around Boyd's wrist just above the hand and pulled as hard as he could. Boyd felt his momentum shift. Sean braced the back of his opponent's right arm with a palm to the back of his shoulder and then leaned back.

He spun 180 degrees, digging his heels into the mud to keep from losing his balance. Boyd was now at the mercy of physics. Centrifugal force pulled him away from Sean, who held his arm with a death grip.

Then, Sean abruptly let him go. With Boyd's speed of attack, he'd sealed his own fate, and made it all too easy for Sean to end the fight in one clever move.

As Sean released the man, he stumbled back and onto his butt, splattering mud around him. He watched as Boyd flew out of control toward the cliff's edge. The man couldn't stop himself. His legs flailed wildly, one step, two, and then he was gone. He tumbled over the side of the cliff and disappeared.

Sean sat in the mud for a moment, catching his breath. Then the stinging came back. He glanced down at his bloodstained hoodie where the knife had torn through the fabric and opened a cut in his side.

He grimaced and pushed himself up out of the mud.

He staggered over to the precipice. He pressed his hoodie into the wound to stem the bleeding. Sean's fear of heights disappeared for a moment as he stopped at the edge and looked down.

To his surprise, Boyd was there, hanging onto a rocky crag with his fingertips. His knife was gone, and his knuckles were as white as two-week-old snow. Boyd turned his head and looked down at the foamy sea smashing against the rocks below. The storm was getting worse. The tide had risen quicker than normal, much quicker.

Sean stared at the man for a couple of seconds. A million witty comments popped into his head. It was a blessing and a curse, being a smart aleck. In this case, he didn't use any of them, though the thought of telling Boyd to "hang in there" had surfaced more than once.

He knelt down, careful to keep his weight back from the edge.

Boyd stared into Sean's eyes with terror in his own. "That was clever, Sean." He struggled to pull himself up, but his fingers slipped and he had to readjust his grip.

Sean nodded. "No one threatens my people," Sean said. "Dawkins. My wife. Tommy." He leaned forward a few inches. "No one."

Sean raised a fist and brought it down hard toward Boyd's right hand. Instinct kicked in, and Boyd let go of the ledge. Sean held his fist over the rock where his opponent's fingers had been a nanosecond before.

The reaction was all Sean had intended.

Boyd's left hand slipped from the wet rock as all his body weight suddenly shifted to those four strained fingers. His wide eyes fixed on Sean as gravity finally won the battle and pulled him down toward the rocky shore.

Sean watched as the man plummeted, tumbling head over heels until his back slammed into a jagged rock that jutted up from the roaring waters seventy feet below. The blow was jarring, sudden, and instantly mortal.

Boyd's body lay there unmoving for several seconds, the eyes still staring lifelessly up into the tormented sky. Then a giant wave crashed over the rocks, and the body was gone, ripped into the furious sea.

48

ASTORIA

Sean hurried down the stairs, gripping the rail with one hand and his wounded abdomen with the other. Once he was back at the bottom, he discovered the lowest level was flooded in a foot of water.

Through the door, he saw Petty aiming a pistol at Boyd's lone remaining mercenary. Tommy was furiously digging through the water. It looked like he was trying to find something.

Sean waded into the room and stopped next to his friend. "What are you doing?"

Tommy looked up. For a moment, relief filled his face. Then he saw the blood seeping through Sean's shirt. "You're hurt. You need to get out of here." His voice was nearly a shout, competing with the sound of the storm and the constant drumming from deep within the chamber.

Sean shook his head. "Not before we shut this thing down." He turned to Petty. "Get him out of here, Agent."

"I'm not leaving you two here." Petty yelled over the noise.

Sean leaned closer. "He knows where Dawkins is. If you two die down here, Dawkins dies, too. Get him out of here. Get somewhere safe. Understand?"

Petty hesitated.

Sean could see he was mulling over the order. He could also see that Petty knew he was right.

"Okay," Petty relented. "But you two hurry. If you can't shut it down, then get out of here."

"Sure," Sean said.

He turned back to Tommy as Petty glanced at the two friends.

Petty shoved the mercenary toward the door and followed him out.

"How do we turn this off?" Sean asked. "The tide," he pointed at the gap in the wall. Water was splashing in with every surge of the sea. "It's rising too fast."

"It's a self-destruct weapon," Tommy said, his voice booming. "The Atlanteans designed it as the final solution in case of an attack. If they couldn't defeat an enemy, then they'd take out everyone, including themselves."

"That's great. How does that help us turn it off?"

"I don't know if we can."

A wave crashed into the outer wall and sent a huge blast of seawater into the chamber. The level visibly rose nearly a foot in the room.

"We have to get the ring off the pillar," Sean said. He was already searching the flooded floor for the white column, but there was no sign of it.

"It sank into the floor," Tommy said. "Once it was activated, it dropped down. Maybe that's some kind of failsafe."

Sean nodded. The water was up to his thighs now and climbing every second. They'd be waist deep soon.

Then he remembered the layout of the room. He turned back to the three display cases that contained the ancient tablets. He recalled that they were all in line with the quartz plinth. Sean followed the line from the cases and estimated the area he figured the pillar would have gone down into the floor.

He waded over to that spot and stuck his head into the water. A second later, he pulled out again and took a breath. "Too dark and murky," he said. "Can't see a thing."

On cue, the lights along the wall began to flicker. Soon, they would be plunged into utter darkness with nothing but the dim gloom outside to give them light.

Tommy sloshed over to where his friend was doubled over and stopped next to him, staring down into the black water. He submerged into the cold liquid and stayed down for three or four seconds before coming back up.

He coughed and wiped the water from his eyes. "You're right. Can't see anything."

Sean dove in again; he kept his eyes closed and let his fingers do the searching. He felt the metal grate below and worked through each square in the frame. Another surge of water blasted into the chamber, and the current ripped him away from the spot.

He rolled under the water and felt something hard hit his back. He struggled for a second as the current pinned him against whatever was behind him. Then the force eased, and he kicked up. When he reached the surface, Sean realized that the last surge had knocked him back against one of the display cases. Not only that; it had filled the room up to shoulder level. And the ocean kept coming.

Tommy was floating now, doing his best to dog paddle and hover in position, but he wasn't anywhere close to the center of the room now.

"We have to get out of here," Tommy shouted.

The lights flickered again; then they went dark.

The room fell into black shadow. The water rocked Sean back and forth, but the wall was at least holding off some of the motion of the waves. He fixed his eyes on the spot where he'd been before. He could see through the outer wall and out to the sea. Almost no light penetrated the dense clouds overhead, but there was enough that Sean could gauge where he'd been and where he needed to go.

"Get out of here!" Sean shouted to his friend.

"I'm not leaving you here. We go together, Sean."

"Not this time, Schultzie. Just go! I'll catch up." Sean paddled three times and then dove into the water headfirst.

He kicked his feet as hard as he could, pulling himself down toward the floor with his hands. He nearly bumped his chin on the bottom but struck the concrete with the heel of his right hand first. His feet kicked harder now. Sean shoved his hands forward, fingers steepled and pressed together in a prayer before each breast stroke.

When he'd gone another three seconds, he stuck one hand down to feel the floor. There it was, the metal grate. His senses were almost useless now. The frigid waters had numbed his fingers. He could only hear sloshing and churning in his ears. And in the darkness he was nearly blind.

Sean worked his way forward, gripping the grate as hard as he could for fear another surge would knock him back again. He felt around with his right hand, patting the surface of the floor, then moving a few inches forward, then patting again. He'd only been under for twenty seconds, but his lungs already begged for air. Holding his breath was not something Sean had mastered, and now it was his sole regret in life.

He refocused, rubbing his hands around on the grate with more vigor now. He felt something different, something smooth. A pang of disappointment struck him. It was the concrete floor surrounding the grate. He thought about going up for air and diving back down, but he couldn't risk it. He might not get back to this spot again, and if he didn't there was no telling what could happen.

Sean forced himself to continue. He realized that if he'd found the concrete, while not what he was looking for, it could give him bearings on where he needed to go. He searched the floor again and found the corner of the grate. Perfect.

Sean turned his body, still kicking his feet and clutching the grate with one hand, and pulled himself straight forward toward the center of the metal floor. He ran his fingers along the surface until he felt a gap, then something else. It was the opening where the quartz pillar had been.

He stopped and held tight on the lip of the metal with both hands. Then he waved his fingers back and forth over the area where the top of the pillar should have been. It wasn't there. How was that possible? Had it been blown out by the waves? Sean doubted it. And if that was the case and the machine was still working, that meant there was no turning it off.

No. He had to believe it was still there, submerged somewhere.

He swallowed. Now his lungs were burning. His entire body was numb. His arms and legs felt like pudding, almost useless against the freezing waters. He gave no thought to hypothermia or dying. There was one thing in his mind: *Shut down this machine.*

Sean stuck his hand down into the opening and felt nothing but more liquid. He pulled himself closer to the floor until his chest was nearly touching the grate. His fingers grazed something hard down below, then something smooth. The ring.

He wedged his biceps against the opening to keep his body steady and tried to work a fingernail under the ring's bottom edge to pry it up, but he found it was stuck firm. Something was holding it in place. Was it magnetic?

It didn't matter what was holding it there. Sean had to get it out of its housing, and he only had another fifteen seconds of air left in his lungs, if that.

He dug at the gold, pulling with every ounce of strength he could muster into his fingers, but it wouldn't budge.

Sean grimaced. He could feel the force he was exerting starting to tear the fingernail free on his middle finger. His lungs screamed for air. It was all or nothing now. He wasn't going to go up for air. Too many people would die if he failed.

With a last desperate effort, Sean maneuvered to the right and shoved his left hand down into the hole. Both arms were wedged in tight, almost too tight to fit. He felt the ring with all his fingers now. He closed his eyes and pulled with every ounce of strength he had left, even as his mouth opened and sucked in a gulp of water.

The ring pulled free. Sean felt a surge of relief a split second before the saltwater hit his lungs. Then his body shuddered. His fingers let go of the golden ring. And he floated into unconsciousness.

TOMMY NEVER LEFT. Not even when the lights went out or when another surge of water rushed into the room. Sean had been under for too long. Was his friend okay?

Suddenly, the wind calmed. The water didn't drain from the room, but Tommy sensed that the worst of the storm was over. Had Sean found the ring?

There was no sign of his friend and panic set in. He started to swim toward the spot where he thought Sean might be. Something hit his right hand, and Tommy twisted his fingers to grab it. It was a wrist. Sean's wrist or one of the mercenaries?

He pulled at it and dragged the body above the surface. He felt the hair and in the dim twilight could make out the outline of Sean's face. His eyes were closed, and he wasn't moving.

"Sean?" Tommy shouted.

No response.

"Sean!"

He pulled his friend close, wrapping his forearm around Sean's chest like he'd seen lifeguards do on television. He kicked his legs, harder and harder, paddling with his free arm to add speed to his desperate rescue.

Tommy dragged his friend through the entrance to the chamber. He reached the stairwell with a last-ditch effort against his burning muscles and the numbness of his skin.

He propped Sean up on the steps a few feet above the water line and smacked his friend's cheeks. Tommy could barely see anything, but he knew Sean wasn't breathing.

"Sean! Wake up, buddy!"

Tommy tilted his friend's head back as best he could and then started chest compressions. He hit the thirtieth compression and then took a breath, pinched Sean's nose, and ducked his head. Tommy pressed his lips against Sean's and blew once, twice, three, four times.

No response.

"Come on, buddy!" Tommy yelled.

He started the compressions again. "Stay with me, Sean!"

He hit the thirtieth compression again and breathed into his best friend's lungs.

Still nothing.

Dear God, Tommy thought.

Tears formed in Tommy's eyes. It was the only sensation he could feel, a stinging, burning at the corner of his eyes.

He pressed on his friend's chest, once, twice, three times. "Don't you die on me Sean Wyatt. Not yet."

He pushed his lips to Sean's again and blew. After the fourth breath, Tommy rose up and started to do the compressions again when he felt Sean's body shudder.

Immediately, Tommy turned his friend's head to the side as Sean heaved, convulsed, and spit up a gush of water. He coughed, gagged, and vomited more liquid.

Tommy was huddled over Sean, cradling his head. Sean's coughing fit eased, and he began to shiver. He looked up into Tommy's eyes and searched him for answers.

The tears rolled down Tommy's cheeks, mingling with the salt-water and rain. He swallowed, choked, and bit back a wave of emotions.

"Did we stop it?" Sean asked.

Tommy looked around. The water level was no longer rising. In fact, it seemed to be receding, inch by inch. "Yeah. Yeah, I think you got it."

Sean exhaled and drew in a painful breath. He frowned, a dirty scowl like he'd just been given the most disgusting entrée imaginable. "Did...did you give me mouth to mouth?"

Tommy laughed and wiped the tears from his face out of instinct even though his entire face and body were soaked. "Yeah. And you know, you're a really good kisser. I see what Adriana sees in you now."

Sean closed his eyes and forced a laugh, though he stopped shortly after from the pain it bought his chest.

"Hilarious," Sean said, using a line his friend often used. "You're hilarious."

49

S ean watched the television from the comfort of his hospital bed. The news was going wild with the viral video of Adm. Forrest Winters confessing he was the one behind the abduction of former president Dawkins. The news anchors were talking about how no one could identify the woman in the video and that authorities were still looking for her. Sean allowed himself a smile. He knew who it was. She was on her way here, to Portland. Her flight would arrive in just over an hour.

The first thing he wanted to do was kiss her, partly due to the relief he felt at Adriana being okay and partly to get rid of the last kiss his lips had endured at the hands of Schultzie.

Special Agent Matthew Petty's name was all over the headlines, as well. He'd managed to find one of the men involved in the Dawkins kidnapping and forced him to give the president's exact location. A team was on site within thirty minutes, extracting Dawkins from a cabin about an hour outside of Seattle.

Petty was offered a promotion by Hollis, though he initially thought of turning it down. He was getting close to retirement and taking a new position with more responsibility wasn't what he had in mind. He eventually caved to the notion that the world still needed people with morals to guide the various agencies of the world. So, he took the position and would be moving into his new office in the coming weeks.

The former president watched the news report from a chair in the corner of the room. Going to check on his friend Sean had been an order no one was going to challenge, despite the president's doctors urging Dawkins to at least go through a quick physical evaluation.

The president told them he was fine and that he could be evaluated once he'd seen the men who'd saved the Oregon coastline, and perhaps the entire Pacific coast, from devastation.

Emily sat next to him, holding his hand in a vise-like grip. She'd immediately flown to Portland when she received word about Sean.

Tommy was there, too, standing by the window, looking out at the city in the hills, the bridges over the waterways, and the lush green trees that dotted the landscape.

Sean sighed and looked over at Dawkins. "Admiral Winters, huh?" Sean asked. His voice was still weak, and it cracked with each word.

"So it would seem," Dawkins answered. "I guess he wasn't too happy with some of my budget moves during the second term. He thought I was crippling our military." Dawkins shook his head. "I guess he ignored the fact that we had a military surplus during the second half of my stint in office. And that our military remains the most powerful fighting force in the history of humanity. Those types can never have enough."

Sean nodded absently. "So...he wanted to find this thing and weaponize it, turn it into something the military could use as a defensive force?"

"And offensive."

Sean rose up slightly and looked over at the president with a questioning glance. "Offensive?"

Dawkins nodded, put his hands on his knees, and stood. He walked over to the open door and eased it shut, then looked at Sean, then Tommy, then Emily with an expression that told everyone in the room he was about to share a deep secret.

He drew in a deep breath, exhaled, and began.

"It was called the Omega Project," Dawkins said. "Capt. Meriwether Lewis discovered it on his expedition in the early 1800s. He didn't have a clue what to do with it, but he feared it. He discovered the tablets, the golden ring fragments, and knew that this thing could be a scourge to a new nation. Of course, he had no clue what it could do, just that the warnings were emphatic. Being a superstitious sort, he heeded the caution given by the tablets and set out to hide the ring fragments until the day technology could harness what power was at work there."

"And didn't tell Jefferson what he found," Tommy added.

"Correct. He wasn't sure what the president would do, so he kept his reports secret until James Madison entered the office. Even then, Lewis didn't give away everything, instead warning Madison of the grave danger that existed at the mouth of the Columbia."

Dawkins took a step closer to Sean's bed.

"You knew all this?" Sean asked.

"No," Dawkins shook his head. "I knew some of it. Every president since Madison has known of the Omega Project. Madison built the fort there. Then it was improved, reinforced through the years. Then after World War II, we sealed it and closed the fort. The leaders of the time figured the best way to keep the Omega machine safe from the world was to let people forget about it, to ignore it, and to set up a state park there so that whatever power was there would be hidden in plain sight."

"Sounds like a big gamble," Tommy said.

"It was. And it likely would have paid off if not for the fact that Admiral Winters stumbled on the Madison letter. That letter was intended to be passed down from one president to the next, never seen by any eyes other than whoever held the Oval Office."

"How'd Winters manage that?" Sean creaked.

"That, my friend, is something I've put my best people on. We'll figure it out."

"Aren't we your best people?" Tommy asked with a wink.

Emily stood up. "You definitely are."

She looped her arm around Dawkins's waist and pulled him tight. "And I will never be able to thank you enough."

Sean grinned at her. "You helped, you know. You got us out of Montana."

Dawkins turned and looked at her with a suspicious stare. "You aided and abetted a fugitive?"

Her cheeks reddened. "Maybe."

Dawkins's lips curled into a broad smile. "I'm dating a criminal." Beaming with pride, he looked at the other two. "That's pretty cool."

"Well, you *are* a politician," Tommy quipped. "So, maybe you both are?"

The room burst with laughter. Sean's was quickly replaced with a fit of coughing. When the laughing died down again, a new silence filled the space. It was the quiet of contemplation, of satisfaction, and of wonder as to what would come next.

"The Omega Project," Sean said. "Fascinating." He knew that there was one more thing he needed to do as soon as he was out of the hospital. He glanced at the rucksack sitting on the floor in the far corner. Before the ambulance arrived, he'd asked Tommy to take one of the pieces of the golden ring and stuff it in a pouch. There was a hardware store owner in Montana who deserved to keep it. On top of that, the government would likely never find it. A few men in black suits had come by earlier and asked him about it, but Sean blew it off. He wasn't a dishonest person, in fact he always tried to tell the truth. He'd once heard a quote from Mark Twain about that, something along the lines of "if you always tell the truth, you never have to remember anything." He wasn't sure if that was the exact line, but it had guided him most of his adult life. In this instance, however, he definitely misled the guys in suits. "The ring broke apart," he'd said. "The third piece must have fallen into the ocean." All the while, the chunk of precious metal was in his gear bag, not ten feet away from them.

"Yes," Dawkins agreed with a nod. "Our research teams are unearthing the machine as we speak, though most of their work so far is in draining the site. Most of the sea water receded, but there are still some spots in the fort that are flooded, and that device is not limited to the room you found. It takes up nearly a full acre of underground coastline."

"Hard to believe that thing was brought over here on boats," Sean said.

"Indeed. And that is, in itself, a tribute to how desperate the Japanese were to get rid of it. They must have known its power, its capability. Why they set it up here, we may never know. I'd have thought they would have kept it disassembled. I suppose that part of the story will remain a mystery."

"Maybe we'll find the answers someday," Tommy said.

"Perhaps. For now, you two need to get some rest." He folded his arms and took on the look of a parent. "I'm sure there are plenty more mysteries out there and lots more trouble for the two of you to get into."

Sean and Tommy shared a brief chuckle.

"Yes, sir," Sean mumbled. "I'm sure you're right."

THANK YOU

AUTHOR'S NOTES

Come. Gather 'round the fire and I'll share with you the facts vs the fiction of this adventure.

Insert a little laughter here.

Seriously, though, I love this part of a story because I know I always enjoy reading this kind of thing from other authors. I've been told by many readers that they feel the same. So, I try to give some insight into the stories realities and the parts that are fiction.

Fiction-

The ring that was discovered in three fragments is something I concocted, though the science behind some of its properties is very real. As to it being a key to a cataclysm engine, who knows? Could a device like that exist and have been the downfall of an ancient civilization or was it just bad luck and Atlantis was wiped from the map via natural disaster? Of course, to consider that question in that specific context, you would have to assume Atlantis was real. That is something that we must leave to speculation.

However, during my studies I have discovered some interesting technology from the ancient world and I believe it is entirely possible that some of the kingdoms and empires of the past could have been working on a devastating weapon such as the one in this tale. Armies and naval powers have always sought to create such a weapon and control of the seas is another topic that was well-documented in the past, though much of it was based on superstition.

Obviously, the events of this story are a complete figment of my imagination, as are all the characters.

The letter from James Madison is also fiction, though it's possible something like that did exist. The subsequent clues were also made up on my part.

Locations-

All of the locations in this story are real and I was lucky enough to be able to visit most of them in the summer of 2018 when my wife, my daughter, and I drove out west for my wife's 40th birthday.

It was an amazing journey and I highly recommend much of it to those who love to travel. There was also a lot of vast nothingness, but the destinations were worth it.

Glacier National Park was breathtaking and terrifying. As someone who is deathly afraid of heights, I only made it up about three quarters of the Going to the Sun Road before I had to pull over and turn back. My knuckles were white, palms sweaty, and my breathing was in quick bursts. Honesty, I don't know how I made it that far. My wife was more than happy about turning around as well.

Hohenwold, Tennessee is a tiny town a few hours west of where I live in Chattanooga, Tennessee. I was out there a few years ago and while there isn't much in that area, the views of the mountain to the south and the rolling hills, plains, and farms are beautiful.

One of my favorite parts of this story was being able to write in the town of Astoria, Oregon. I'm sure the locals there get tired of it, but that's the price they pay for fame.

In case you didn't know or forgot, Astoria was where the movie The Goonies was filmed. That movie was one of my favorites as a child and I still watch it whenever I see it on television. It, along with the Indiana Jones movies, were the inspiration behind everything I write. Those films instilled in me a love of history, mystery, adventure, and the instincts of a suspicious treasure hunter who is always wary of taking things at face value.

Fort Stevens is a real place and is visited by many people every year, along with its sister forts near the mouth of the Columbia River.

You might also be surprised to know that the bunkers I detailed at the park are real, though somewhat tricky to find depending on the time of year and the growth of the grass and brush around those spots.

I did add in the secret passages, but don't think that's always the case. (I'm narrowing my eyes at you.)

Ha!

The Mysterious Death of Meriwether Lewis- This part of the story is very real and I did, to the best of my abilities, get everything as accurate as possible in regards to how Captain Lewis died and the cover up surrounding his passing.

It is truly one of the most bizarre tragedies in American History. This man was a hero. He would have been treated like a celebrity, much as the astronauts were in the 1960s and 70s.

While his mental health issues are documented, the fact that he did not give his reports of the Corps of Discovery Expedition to Thomas Jefferson and delayed on giving them to Madison certainly spark deep speculation, especially from minds like my own.

I mean, why would someone shoot themselves in the gut and then the head? Yet that is what was determined to be the cause of death.

Maybe their weapons weren't as effective back then and to do the deed required two shots. I doubt it.

Unfortunately, the only witnesses to the passing of Captain Lewis are also history's biggest suspects. Now that everyone from that period is gone, I suppose we may never know the truth. In my opinion, it is one of the most fascinating and sad cold cases in history.

As always, I leave you to concoct your own conclusions.

OTHER BOOKS BY ERNEST DEMPSEY

For my friend Stacy Reid.

ACKNOWLEDGMENTS

None of my stories would be possible without the great input I get from incredible readers all over the globe. My advance reader group is such an incredibly unselfish and supportive team. I couldn't do any of this without them.

My editors, Anne Storer and Jason Whited, must also be thanked for their amazing work and guidance in crafting these stories. They make everything so much better for the reader.

Last but not least, I need to give a big thank you to Elena at Li Graphics for the incredible cover art she always delivers, along with beautiful social media artwork.

I also need to give a shoutout and thank you to my friend Ernie Lommatsch. Before I met him, everyone called ME Big Ern, but he's a good five or six inches taller than me and a far tougher cat. He was a ranger at Glacier for a few decades, built his cabin with his own hands using money he saved up from week to week. He's an avid hunter, a knowledgeable outdoorsman, and I'm happy to call him my friend. We were lucky enough to book his cabin on airbnb.com and I have to say it was providential. We became quick friends and he's even writing a book about his adventures in the wild. So, a big thank you to Ernie for his hospitality and kindness to strangers from the south.

Last but not least, thanks to my stylist, Monica, for always being such a good sounding board while cutting my hair.

Printed in Great Britain
by Amazon